SON OF SECRETS

The Indigo Chronicles

Book One

THE PATH KEEPER

Book Two

SON OF SECRETS

Book Three

CHILDREN OF SHADOWS

Releasing 2021

N.J. SIMMONDS

SON OF SECRETS

The Indigo Chronicles, Book 2

Livonia, Michigan

Poem "The Keeper Can't Reach" by Robert George Dew. Used with permission. All rights reserved.

Quotations from *Alice in Wonderland* by Lewis Carroll, "Ephemera" by William Butler Yeats, *Romeo and Juliet* by William Shakespeare, and *Wuthering Heights* by Emily Bronte are all Public Domain.

Editor: Rebecca Rue
Proofreader: Jamie Rich

SON OF SECRETS

This book is a work of fiction. The characters, incidents, and dialogue are drawn from the author's imagination and are not to be construed as real. Any resemblance to actual events or persons, living or dead, is entirely coincidental.

Published by BHC Press

Library of Congress Control Number: 2019945394

ISBN: 978-1-64397-043-1 (Hardcover)
ISBN: 978-1-64397-044-8 (Softcover)
ISBN: 978-1-64397-045-5 (Ebook)

For information, write:
BHC Press
885 Penniman #5505
Plymouth, MI 48170

Visit the publisher:
www.bhcpress.com

For Pete, Isabelle and Olivia
Forever

THE KEEPER CAN'T REACH

Disappear and stay right here
Along all shores, withdraw from fear.
Erase the face—the low profile
Replenish the beauty, go rest for a while.

Go to the deep, where the Keeper can't reach
Where mystic lovers endeavour.
Play at the gate, where it's never too late
A child, once again. Forever.

Belong with the stars, visit Pluto and Mars
Chariots of golden hay.
Tenderly caress the womb of the nest,
The Keeper can't reach you today.

—Robert George Dew, 1977—

'Alice: How long is forever?
White Rabbit: Sometimes, just one second.'
– Lewis Carroll, *Alice in Wonderland*

PART ONE

ARABELLA
BEGINNING OF THE BEGINNING

I AM ARABELLA and this is the beginning. The very beginning.

My first life was one of shadows, filled with men that ruled and women who hid.

A land of forgotten children and spent lives. A waste.

But I returned. Over and over again, I returned. For him.

When you love for the first time, that love resides deep within your soul. It doesn't vanish or fade away; it grows in size and strength. Like the sun, it gets larger, brighter, warmer, and more powerful. It's bigger than the lives it touches. Like the sun, it can never be extinguished, even when you can no longer see it.

Our souls are nothing but light and love, but they have memories. Our minds may forget from lifetime to lifetime, but our souls do not. I carried a burning fire inside of me for over two thousand years, hoping that one day it would cast away the shadows and help me find the one I'd been searching for.

Then one day it did…

1

HE HAD COMPLETED her once, but now she was empty, staring down into a deep, dark chasm of her own making. Every night Ella fell asleep fearing the next day would be the day she would finally fall into the terrifying abyss and never see light again.

Why had she allowed it to go this far? A habit. A distraction. Like a quick stop in a fast food drive-through, she would slow down and take what she wanted. Devour it. Desperate to feel full and whole again. Then she'd be sick to her stomach. Sick with what, though? Guilt? Loss? Misery? Anger? Or maybe it was nothing. Just deep black nothing.

'You're beautiful,' he said, his lips brushing her earlobe. She didn't like it when he did that, but she let him. 'You're like a peach. So juicy.'

His dark hair reached his shoulders, and his eyes were black in the half-light of her room. Every guy was beginning to look the same. She turned away and let him caress her breasts, wincing at the roughness of his fingertips against her soft skin. He entered her from behind, quickly, like it didn't matter. She didn't care; she preferred it that way. It was better when she couldn't see their faces and she could replace them with the face of another.

Bringing them home always seemed like a good idea at the time. Then, just as quickly, it didn't. This one was nice enough, and if she closed her eyes and thought back to the big old bed in the tiny shepherd's hut, hidden deep within that rain-soaked Spanish mountain, she'd be fine. If she thought of blue eyes and white feathers and last words, she would climax. After all, that was the only reason she let it get this far—to remember him and to forget him.

'Are you OK, Ella?' the man asked, their bodies now nothing but a sweaty, tangled mess of limbs. He brushed her hair off her shoulder and planted a kiss in its place. 'We make love and you're happy,' he said, pronouncing his aitches like he was clearing his throat. 'But now you look sad, like you want to be somewhere not here.'

She didn't answer.

'Maybe I go, yes?'

Ella turned around and faced the man—more of a boy really. Too young to understand.

'Sorry, it's not you, Pablo.'

'My name is Paulo.'

She rolled away from him again and sighed. Sliding out of her bed, he put on his shirt and trousers, stuffing his underwear and tie into his pocket. It was still dark outside, but through the window she could just make out a thin sliver of gold on the horizon.

'I go. It's fine. You don't have to explain.'

Ella couldn't be bothered to walk him to her front door. She could already feel self-disgust drip drip dripping into her veins. Just like the last time with her last conquest. These boys helped for a small moment in time, but as soon as it was over, their presence multiplied her pain.

'Ella, one more thing,' Paulo called over his shoulder. 'Did I get the job?'

She must have looked confused because his cheeks coloured slightly.

'The interview the other day. You needed a chef? I got it, yes?'

With another sigh she got out of bed and walked naked to her front door, opening it for him wordlessly. The boy looked at the tiled floor, his eyes following his own footsteps out of her apartment and along the hotel corridor. Slamming the door behind him, she let out a low moan as she flung herself back on the bed, still warm from their bodies. Her pillow muffled her scream.

'Where are you, Zac? Look what I've become!'

2

ELLA'S PHONE WAS ringing, drilling a hole through her already pounding head. She considered ignoring it until she realised the sun was streaming through her bedroom curtains and it wasn't the weekend. *Shit!* She jumped up and then sat back down again. Too much wine last night and probably tequila. *Fucking tequila!* Why did it always seem like such a good idea in the moment?

She rubbed her hands over her face and groaned. Had she sung karaoke last night? Well, that was a given, of course she had; she always did when she went to Bar Fortuna. It was such a dive, but it was fun and the barman never let her pay for drinks. She glanced around the room and was relieved to see she was alone and Paulo or Pablo, whatever his name was, wasn't there this time. Their one-night stand last week had been more than enough. She'd promised herself no more meaningless sex after that encounter, and she'd lasted five days so far. Tarifa was a small town, and she was sick of bumping into past mistakes.

The phone was still ringing. She picked it up and saw the time on the clock by her bed.

'*Mierda!*'

'And good morning to you, too, Ella,' the girl's voice at the other end of the line said, laughing. 'Your ten o'clock appointment has arrived early. Don't worry, I told him you were in a very important conference call and would be down shortly.'

Ten o'clock. Ten o'clock. Who the hell was her ten o'clock?

'Location director from Planet Pictures. LA big shot,' the woman added, responding to her silence.

Paloma, her new assistant, had only started working for the hotel the previous month and already had the uncanny ability to read her mind. She was ridiculously beautiful too, and Ella would have been lost without her—even though the girl was completely averse to technology and insisted on doing all admin with pen and paper. Ella mumbled her thanks and went to hang up, but she could still hear Paloma's tinny voice talking at the other end.

'Sorry, what?'

'I said he's brought someone along with him. A *really* handsome man. *Muy guapo!* I recognise him. I think he's famous.'

Ella rolled her eyes. Like she cared about guys right now? She thanked her again, and then remembered something.

'Oh, Paloma, have we had any more applications for the chef position?'

'No, but a man named Paulo keeps calling. Said you interviewed him last week and...'

'No. Keep searching. I'll be down in ten minutes.'

Ella hung up quickly and sat on the side of the bed with a thump. Surely there was more than one chef in Tarifa? She felt bad about ignoring poor Paulo, but the last thing she needed at work was a constant reminder of how fucked up her life was and how low she had sunk.

Every man she'd met since she lost Zac had been a mere distraction to keep her busy until he returned again. She always chose the ones with long dark hair, blue eyes or that serious intensity Zac had. But who was she kidding? These men didn't even come close. Ella was fooling herself that she was getting on with life when she wasn't. In fact, she was doing a very bad job of waiting for someone who may never return. He'd promised that if he survived he'd come back for her, but when? It had been three years since she'd lost him, and in that time, she'd heard nothing—not from him or his kind.

At first, she'd waited. Pining like a dog that'd lost its master, confused and lost, Ella had visited every place they'd ever been together. She'd become dangerously thin until her father insisted she move in with him until she regained her strength, both physically and mentally. The memory of her first year without Zac was now nothing but a misty blur of life in a transparent husk of a body. She'd floated through each day barely breathing. She may as well have been dead. Then her mother had bought the hotel, a distraction while she sorted out her own marriage crisis, and Ella threw herself into their joint project. Getting back on her path had been her one aim, it was what Zac had begged her to do as he'd lain dying at her feet, but she was deluding herself. Whether moping about or shagging about, Ella wasn't dealing with anything. She wasn't admitting to herself what every day brought her closer to realising—Zac wasn't coming back. He either wouldn't make it back within her lifetime, or he was dead forever. Either way, she had to put thoughts of her soulmate aside and sort out her life. That meant no more men and no more tequila.

The bathroom mirror was not being kind this morning. There was just ten minutes until her meeting and she looked like shit. All she could think about was going for a swim, jumping straight into her own private pool and washing away the self-disgust like she always did when she woke up with a thumping head full of regret. But she was running late and didn't even have time to bathe. She brushed her teeth and then splashed her face with cold water. With no energy for a shower, she ran a flannel over herself quickly and sprayed her body with deodorant. The strong scent made her dizzy and more nauseous.

Last night's eye make-up still clung forlornly to her lashes. Yesterday, she'd been sporting a sexy smoky-eyed look; this morning her face simply screamed 'hangover.' She licked her finger and ran it under her eyes before applying a bit of blusher and a swipe of lip gloss. It was too late to wash her hair, so she ran her fingers through it instead, shaking them through the long chestnut curls and leaving it hanging loosely over her shoulders. That would have to do. She didn't care if she was meeting a hotshot Hollywood exec or the guy who delivered the bread on a Friday morning—she couldn't remember the last time she'd made any real effort with her appearance anyway.

Her assistant had sounded breathless with excitement on the phone, but Ella couldn't muster an ounce of excitement. When her mother had married Richard Fantz, with his dozens of hotels around the world and mansions in Marbella and London, Ella had been thrown into a dazzling world of riches and sycophantic hangers-on. She'd met directors and actors, pop stars and billionaires, and she'd hated them all. They were all the same—vacuous, vain, and insanely insecure; it was why the idea of taking over the running of a small hotel near the windswept town of Tarifa had appealed so much. She was back in Spain where she'd grown up—where she belonged. Nobody there knew who she was or where she had come from, and that was just how she liked it.

She ran up the stairs from her ground-floor apartment and slowed down as she neared the hotel foyer, catching her breath and scrolling through the emails on her phone to check the name of the person waiting for her. As she passed the large gilt mirror in the hallway, she noticed a small toothpaste stain on the collar of her shirt. *Bollocks!* Covering it with her hair she stepped into reception, a large smile plastered on her face. Head still throbbing, and cheek now twitching, she hoped whoever was waiting for her wouldn't notice just how hungover and tired she was.

'Good morning, Mr Patterson. I'm sorry to keep you waiting.'

A tall man wearing a light suit and shiny shoes raised his hand to her. His mobile phone was pressed against his ear, and he was deep in conversation. Ella stopped talking and picked at the corner of her thumbnail. What a surprise, another rude bastard. She didn't have time for this; she hadn't even gone through the emails from the day before or had her morning team meeting. God, she needed a coffee!

Paloma walked over to her with a small glass of espresso, which Ella drank in one go and handed back to her with a grateful smile.

'I'm going to promote you,' she whispered to her assistant with a wink.

Paloma elbowed her lightly and twitched her head to the side, raising her eyebrows at someone standing by the main entrance. Ella followed her gaze and her stomach lurched violently.

No way. What the hell was *he* doing in her hotel?

A man was leaning against the back wall reading an English newspaper, oblivious to the two women watching him. He hadn't changed much since she'd last seen him three years ago in London. He still had sandy-coloured hair, although now it was a little longer and swept back off his face. He'd grown broader over the years. His crisp white shirt clung to his arms and shoulders, nipping in at his small waist. The look was complete with perfectly fitted jeans and a pair of Ray-Bans firmly in place. Every inch of him screamed expensive.

Josh de Silva. Josh bloody de Silva. The hottest, yet the vainest guy she'd known at university and the last person she expected to see in her hotel. Well, she wasn't going to talk to him—not after the way he'd treated her the last time she'd seen him.

Ella tucked her hair behind her ear and straightened her shirt. Seeing him was like being hurled back in time, back before she knew what she knew and life had seemed straightforward. She'd thought about Josh quite a bit lately, about how strange it had been that every girl on campus had adored him, yet he'd instantly made a beeline for her—the only person not interested in him. Men like him liked the challenge,

pernatural James Bond. He has the daring of Indiana Jones combined with the charm of a young Hugh Grant—but with sexier eyes. The girls love him.'

Ella was pretty sure Billy loved him, too. So, Josh was big. Blockbuster movie big. This was too weird. What were the chances of one of his films being shot in her hotel?

Her stomach ached with a sickening twist as the realisation of what was happening hit her. Fate appeared to have finally caught up with her. If what Zac had told her all those years ago about Josh's part in her destiny was true, then the chances of the actor being at her hotel were high. Very high.

She shuddered and ran up behind Billy, who was heading for the centre of the old converted monastery which, thanks to Ella, was now the prettiest hotel in the area.

'Interesting architecture,' Billy said, soaking in the sight of the cobbled patio, small orange trees and carved fountain. He took photos on his phone of the galleried walkway that ran along the middle of the courtyard and made notes in a leather-bound notebook. 'I read that parts of the monastery were built in the fifteenth century. Great details. Are they original Moorish tiles? We could definitely use this space for some of the scenes. We'll have to talk dates soon, as we need to clear at least three weeks. Ah, the chapel. I've been looking forward to this part. Come on, chop-chop, I haven't got all day.'

The chapel was in the heart of the building, accessible from the patio by a side door. You could also enter it from outside via two wooden double doors set in the base of the turret.

As they stepped inside, she heard Billy's intake of breath. Even after having lived at the hotel for two years, the ornate little church still took Ella's breath away. Stained glass windows depicting scenes from Jesus's crucifixion ran along one wall, sending colourful shadows across the wooden pews. Walking down the aisle was like stepping into a rainbow. Different decorative touches had been added over the centuries, from Moorish to rococo, but it was the enormous cross above the altar which took centre stage. It had been gifted to the monastery by French monks during the Renaissance period, its tips sporting sharp, pointed fleurs-de-lis, giving it the appearance of two crossed spears. Although magnificent, it was far too large and Gothic for the pretty little chapel. It gave Ella the creeps.

'I love that cross,' Billy said, staring up at the altar. 'So vampirical. This place is perfect for the movie.'

Ella nodded silently as Billy pointed out historical features, asked about lighting, and discussed the possibility of moving furniture around. His droning voice became a distant buzz. All she could think about was the fact Josh was just a few rooms away. She never thought she'd see him again. If they spoke, would he apologise for the way he'd treated her before Zac had hit him? She sighed. What did it matter? He probably didn't even remember her.

'Is this the base of the tower?' Billy asked. 'I saw it from the car as we pulled up to the hotel. Is the rest of the tower still in use? Could we film up there? I bet the views are great.'

Ella hadn't had a chance to renovate the entire hotel yet—perhaps allowing the turret to be used in the movie would be a way to finance its upkeep? Ella nodded, thinking that she'd have to get the main door to the turret fixed if they were to film up there. It had originally been built as a watchtower. Over the years, the monks had used the room at the top as a library, and it was still full of dusty books and dark mahogany bookshelves blackened with age. When she'd first moved into the hotel with her mother, the locals had talked of the legend of 'the monks and the wanton woman.' They said there was a secret passageway from the chapel to the tower where randy monks would secretly meet a mysterious, evil woman who had them under a spell. Pretending to pray for the evening, they would sneak up to the top of the tower in turns via a hidden entrance. Ella had thought it was all nonsense until one day, while polishing the gold on the altar, she'd pushed a panel and a door had opened against her leg that led up a rickety old stairway to the top of the turret.

There was an official entrance from the street, too, but there was no key for that door, so until the discovery of the secret entrance Ella hadn't investigated the library. She never mentioned to anyone what she'd found and would often visit the top of the tower, in secret, via the chapel. It was her sanctuary once her mother had walked away from running the hotel and left her floundering. She'd take a duvet and pillow up there, and some nights, when sleep refused to settle—Zac and his bright blue eyes the only things she could see—she would go to the chapel, pray to a god she didn't believe in, and then clamber up the old stairs to the tower where the moon seemed larger and within reach. The windows were arched and crafted of stone, like that of an old castle, looking out over a sandy bay and restless ocean. The window ledges were wide, and upon them she would lay among the ancient words and dusty tomes of the past, the sound of the waves lulling her into a restless slumber.

'…I'll ask my assistant to email you and we'll take it from there,' the location manager said, handing her a business card and walking back to the reception desk. Ella trotted behind him, wondering if she should say something about needing to talk to Josh.

They reached the foyer, but the actor was no longer there.

'I'd definitely like to shoot a few scenes here in the autumn,' Billy said, grabbing his bag and walking toward the hotel entrance. 'I have your details. I will get the office to email you about timings and we can discuss fees.'

Ella held the door open for him and spotted Josh outside in the sunshine talking to someone in a smart cap. Their chauffeur, probably. The actor was leaning against a shiny black car, his shirt sleeves rolled up and his eyes squinting against the sun as he laughed at something the driver said. There were his dimples again. Her traitorous stomach gave an almighty flip.

'Billy, would it be possible to have a quick word with...?'

The location manager's phone started ringing, and he held up his hand at her, stepping back into the hotel. Ella shut the door again and waited for Billy to get off the phone. This was ridiculous and embarrassing. Did she really have to say anything to Josh? Her boyfriend had hit him three years ago. If he did remember her, he probably still hated her. She walked back to the reception desk and ducked back into the office. Paloma was waiting for her with a frown on her face.

'Did you speak to Mister de Silva?' she whispered.

'No. Why would I want to talk to him?'

'You're the hotel manager. You should go and greet him. That Billy man just told you they'll be filming here in six months. Introduce yourself to the actor. Say hello.'

Why was Paloma making such a big deal about speaking to Josh?

When Ella had first moved to London, the new it-girl stepdaughter of a hotel mogul, the newspapers had delighted in linking her and Josh together even though she'd never met him. Then, by the time she'd started uni and discovered that he too attended, her friends had also tried to set them up. Even Zac, before they'd got together, had told her that Josh was her destiny. And now Paloma? Was Ella the only one who didn't think she and Josh were a match made in heaven?

Anyway, she was certain the whole 'destiny' thing didn't apply anymore. Josh was a famous actor now, and she was just a girl with a complicated past and the mother of all hangovers. Why couldn't this be happening on a day when she didn't look like shit?

Billy was now pacing the empty foyer, his hands making jabbing motions, and the odd expletive floated over to the front desk as his gesticulations got wilder and wilder. Ella was standing behind the front desk, shuffling papers and making herself look busy, when the hotel door opened and Josh stepped in. She ducked out of sight.

'Everything all right?' he asked Billy.

The location manager, now red in the face, replaced his phone in his pocket.

'No, far from it. That was our hotel. Your suite has flooded—a burst water pipe. They are fully booked and are trying to arrange an alternative accommodation, but the only other five-star hotel is miles away. Bloody peasant country!'

'It's not a problem. I'll stay here. Looks nice enough.'

Shit! If he stayed at her hotel, then she'd definitely have to talk to him. Her heart began to hammer against her ribcage.

'No, no, you can share my hotel room,' said Billy, heading for the exit. 'This place isn't good enough for you. Come on, I can't wait to tell that so-called five-star hotel manager what I think of him.'

'Our penthouse suite is available all week, Mister de Silva,' Paloma called out from the check-in desk. Ella, still hiding, widened her eyes at her assistant who winked back at her.

'Perfect,' Josh said. 'I'll get my bags out of the car. Billy, I'm going to skip this afternoon's meeting. I'll see you back at the hotel in the morning. I need to chill for a bit. No need to look at me like that, I'm sure I'll be well catered for here.'

Perhaps Ella couldn't fight fate after all. Her stomach performed another Olympian flip. Josh was staying in her hotel, and her hangover had just cranked up a notch. It would be a miracle if she made it to the end of the day without being sick.

3

'I'M NOT TAKING him to his room!' Ella hissed.

Paloma uncrossed her arms. '*Sí, sí,* you are. Here.' She handed her the key card for the penthouse suite. 'His bags are up there already. He's having a drink in the bar, and I told him the manager would take him up when his room was ready. Go!'

What the hell was going on with Paloma? Why wasn't she clambering to show the sexy actor to his room herself? Ella rummaged through her bag and took out her lip gloss and make-up mirror. Her pale face was tired and peaky. Popping a mint into her mouth, she sprayed some perfume at her neck in a feeble attempt to mask the smell of last night's alcohol seeping out of her pores.

'Good idea, Ella.' Paloma smiled. 'Look pretty.'

'I'd settle for looking human.'

• • • • •

Josh was sitting up at the hotel bar with a bottle of beer and a small bowl of olives in front of him. The room was empty except for the barman, who kept glancing over at the actor. When he saw Ella, the barman jerked his head excitedly in Josh's direction and grinned. She smiled and gestured for the barman to leave, much to his disappointment. There was no way she wanted an audience for this.

'Josh?'

Her voice came out as a quiet squeak. He hadn't heard her. She wasn't sure if she wanted him to remember her. After all, obscurity was why she'd moved away from London to the middle of nowhere in Spain, to be forgotten and start afresh. She took a step closer and called his name again. This time he looked up. She'd forgotten how beautiful his almond-shaped eyes were.

'Sorry, err, Mister de Silva. I'm not sure if you remember me. We…'

Jumping off the bar stool, he shook his head from side to side and gave her a slow smile.

'Ella? Ella Fantz?'

She screwed up her nose at the mention of her old name. Ella had changed her surname back to her father's name, Santiago de los Rios, two years previously—it had been the only way to move on and leave the troubles of her time in London behind. Fantz was her stepfather's surname. Not only had it made her a laughingstock, but it had also come fully loaded with all the associations of the Fantz hotel dynasty and the horrific things her stepbrother Sebastian had done. She took a deep breath and forced herself to look at Josh properly. Here he was, a part of her old London life, in quiet Tarifa, infiltrating the privacy she'd created for herself.

'Ella! Wow!' He gave her a quick squeeze.

Still holding onto the tops of her arms, he stepped back and took her in. His eyes travelled over her face and her plain blouse and skirt, her attempt at looking like a hotel manager. They settled on her eyes, holding her gaze for a second too long.

'I thought you'd disappeared off the face of the earth,' he exclaimed. 'You look incredible. What are you doing out here?'

His accent was still London-with-money, but the ends of his words were now sprinkled with a slight American lilt. He remembered her but clearly his eyesight was failing—she looked far from incredible. Taking another deep breath, she attempted to still the butterflies in her stomach which were competing with the rising nausea from her hangover. She could feel beads of sweat collecting on her brow.

'This is my hotel,' she said, shrugging. 'I've just been having a meeting with your colleague, Billy. Apparently, he's chosen it as the location for your next film. Bit weird, eh?'

Josh raised his eyebrows.

'Yeah. Huge coincidence.'

His eyes hadn't yet left hers and she could feel her neck going red. It must be all the alcohol she'd drunk the night before—a boozy flush. Why on earth would Josh be getting her flustered? OK, so he was attractive and looking at her in a really intense way, but she'd never reacted this way to him before. Actually, that was a lie. She'd kissed him once, an ill-advised lingering kiss at a fancydress party after the first time Zac had left her. She'd only kissed Josh to deter the advances of another guy, thinking she'd never see Zac again. But she *did* see Zac again; he'd come back for her and then hit Josh as they'd all stepped off a bus together. The entire thing seemed so ridiculous now; they'd been teenagers when they'd last met. She'd forgotten all about their kiss—until now. His pretty face was staring straight at hers, making her chest turn red and blotchy with the memory. She fanned herself with Josh's key card.

'Let's go to your bedroom,' she said. 'Shit. Crap. I mean, I need to show you to...to your hotel room. Suite. Penthouse suite. Follow me.'

He grinned. This was painful.

• • • • •

'And here's the minibar. The TV is pretty easy to work; this is the remote control, and you can get CNN and Sky News and a few BBC channels, including some sports. This is the lovely roof garden that covers the entire top floor. It has lovely sea views, and over there you can just about make out the rooftops of Tarifa. It's the nearest town to here; it's lovely.'

Lovely, lovely, lovely. Shut up, Ella! How many times are you going to say the word 'lovely'?

'There are tea and coffee facilities near the desk, and if you want room service you simply have to dial…'

'Ella,' Josh said, laying his hand on her arm. 'I know how a hotel works. Why don't you sit down? We haven't had a chance to catch up yet.'

She followed him outside to the large roof terrace and perched on the edge of a raffia armchair. She'd overseen the restoration of the hotel two years ago, and the penthouse had been her favourite room to style. It was decorated in white with sea-inspired touches such as driftwood sculptures by the bed and blue-and-white striped cushions on the outdoor furniture. The view really was incredible. From this height, they could see Tarifa's ubiquitous kite surfers and the white triangles of sailing boats on the horizon. It was hot for April, but a steady breeze was blowing, carrying with it herby smells from the kitchen gardens.

'I'm so happy my hotel room flooded and I'm here instead. Billy's driving me mad. He's great at his job, but he can be a bit…possessive. It's like Planet Pictures owns me or something. Well, I guess they do.'

Josh stretched his arms, making his shirt travel up over his taut middle before falling back in place. *Christ!* Had he seen her looking?

'I only came along with him to Spain because I needed a break. Instead, I've had to listen to him go on and on about "the industry," and he never lets me out of his bloody sight. I feel like I'm being babysat by a pervy uncle or something.'

Ella nibbled on her thumbnail and then, realising how ugly her fingernails were, sat on her hands.

'I must sound like a spoiled brat,' he continued. 'Problem is, everyone thinks being famous is glamorous, but it's not. I mainly sit around all day waiting. Waiting to be sent scripts, waiting to be offered a casting, waiting on set, waiting for make-up. It's boring. I'm a go-getter; I'm not good at just hanging around.' He moved his chair closer to Ella's and sat back, gazing up at the blue sky. 'I mean, don't get me wrong, I obviously work out in the gym. A lot,' he said, laughing, rolling up his shirt sleeves to reveal strong bronzed forearms. Ella dragged her eyes away and focused on the sea behind him. 'I do the odd TV and magazine interview and get to go to great clubs with some of the world's hottest women. Fame has its perks, but it's not all that fulfilling. To be honest, it's nice to get a chance to go back to basics sometimes, like sitting here in a simple hotel having a conversation with someone normal.' He leant forward and tapped her on the knee. 'Actually, I remember you being be a bit of a celeb yourself, what with Richard Fantz being your stepdad…'

Ella gave him a tight smile. She'd hated every part of her old life.

'…but now you're out here in the middle of nowhere, and you're just Ella. No one cares what you're doing anymore, which must be nice.' He sat back and placed his hands behind his head, smiling at the sky. 'And hey, now you get to be part of one of my films, too. How awesome is that? Bet that's the most action this old place has had in a while.'

Yep, he was still a complete and utter idiot. So what if he was more handsome than she remembered? He still thought the world revolved around him. Arsehole.

He closed his eyes and tilted his face up to the sun. He was clearly used to bathing in a golden glow. In Josh's world, everybody's gaze must be warmer and brighter than the sun's. How could anyone be so sure of themselves and look so at peace? His eyelashes cast long shadows over his cheekbones, and his full lips were frozen in a self-satisfied half smile. His shirt had risen over his stomach again, revealing a thin line of golden hair leading down from his navel to beneath his waistband. Ella gave an impatient sigh through her nose, making Josh's eyes snap open.

'You're very quiet, Ella. You never used to be this shy. You OK?'

She nodded.

'My bad, my bad. You're probably really busy with beds to make and paperwork to do, and I've been here wasting your time prattling on about Hollywood. By the way, if you speak to Billy again, could you not mention that we know each other? It's just that he'll be straight on the blower to my agent and then she'll get hysterical, scared we'll be photographed together and the media will have a field day. Especially after everything that was written about you a few years ago. No offence, but my PR team is really careful about what girls I'm seen with. You get it, right?'

'Yes. Of course,' she said, standing up, grateful to be getting away from him. 'Wouldn't want to put you in an awkward position. I better go. I'm ever so busy with…stuff. Lots of stuff to do. Beds to make and stuff. Enjoy your stay.'

'Great seeing you again, Ella,' he called after her, his feet now resting on the edge of the armchair, his dusty shoes making the new cushions brown. 'Oh, and be a doll and send up a few crates of beer when you can. Thanks.'

He grinned and stretched again, putting his hands behind his head and closing his eyes before looking back up at the sun.

And there it was, exactly why she hadn't liked him the first time they'd met as teenagers. Charming? Yes. Attractive? Very. Completely full of himself? Abso-fucking-lutely.

• • • • •

The day had dragged. Ella had written a few emails, returned a few calls, and had a meeting with her staff about guest privacy. She'd had to tell them that Josh was staying at the hotel, and the ripple of excitement that travelled among the girls in her team irritated her. How did they know who he was? Had his movies even reached southern Spain? No matter how busy she made herself, all she kept thinking about was that Josh de Silva was upstairs in her hotel. And that he was an idiot—an arrogant, handsome, and really sexy idiot. The worst kind.

All day she'd fought the temptation to find out more about what he'd been up to in the three years since she'd last seen him. By early afternoon, she finally succumbed and searched online for Josh, regretting it instantly. There he was, smouldering eyes and biceps, looming out of every glossy magazine cover she could think of.

'Josh Talks about Sex and Leading Ladies'

'Sexy de Silva Nominated for Golden Globe'

'Naked Josh on the Beach'

'My Three-In-A-Bed Romp with Josh de Silva'

The fluorescent magazine headlines screamed at her from the computer screen. How on earth had she not seen any of this? He'd dated all of her favourite actresses and singers and had even modelled in *Vogue*. It bordered on surreal and a little bit ridiculous. No wonder he was so full of himself. Well, he didn't impress her. Last time she'd seen him, he'd been running after a London bus in the rain with a bleeding face. Not so sexy or glamorous.

She rushed her lunch and was about to start planning next year's brochure design when the Skype symbol flashed up on her laptop screen. *Shit!* She'd forgotten about the call she'd planned with Kerry and Mai Li. Her late start that day, her crappy hangover, and of course Josh's arrival had completely fried her brain.

Considering how useless she'd been since Zac's disappearance, it was a miracle her friends had kept in touch at all. Ella had hardly spoken to a soul the year following his presumed death, even during the times she'd returned to London. Then she'd thrown herself into the hotel project, trying to keep it afloat. She'd never told either of them the truth about Zac, and neither of them had ever visited her in Spain. But that was about to change.

She clicked on the Skype symbol, and her laptop screen divided in two. Mai Li on the left, with her petite porcelain face and glossy black hair in its sharp bob, and Kerry the human Barbie on the right. Ella smiled at her friends, looking like little dolls in their translucent boxes.

'Hey, girls!'

'Ella! We were just talking about our trip over,' Mai Li said. She gave her the thumbs up and bobbed up and down on the spot.

These girls were her only real friends and she'd missed them. With her birthday coming up soon, Ella had vowed to stop moping about Zac, and everything that had happened, and celebrate in style.

'So, you're both coming out to see me at last?' she asked.

'Of course! BA all the way, baby! Mai Li and I are going to crack open a big bottle of bubbly and be totally sloshing drunk by the time you pick us up. It's going to be so, like, *amazing* to be in Spain for your birthday. I know twenty-three isn't a biggy, but it's not like you did anything on your twenty-first. We're going to make this one *epic!*' Kerry sung out the last word, waving her hands above her head.

Ella thought back to her twenty-first birthday when she'd done nothing but cry. Every birthday, Christmas, New Year, and anniversary of the date Zac had vanished, she'd waited for him. Sometimes she'd visit her father in the Andalucian mountains or wander London's Hampstead Heath or Waterlow Park in Highgate, all the places that had meant something to her and Zac in their short time together. And there she'd wait and wait in the vain hope he would miraculously appear as quickly as he'd disappeared.

But he hadn't.

'Good. I've decided twenty-three is going to be my happy number,' Ella said. 'I just want to celebrate it with everyone I care about. Which is basically you two and my parents.'

Kerry shook her head to indicate what a sad, sad world Ella lived in, but Mai Li squealed and clapped her hands.

'I'm so excited! I've never been to Tarifa. Apparently, this April is going to be hotter than ever. Is there a beach nearby? Shall I bring a bikini? I promise we'll make this your best birthday ever.'

Ella smiled at the image on her computer screen of her friend's dark bobbed hair swaying with every word she said; her enthusiasm always cheered her up. On the other side of the screen, Kerry had started painting her nails a lurid bright green.

'Mai Li, Tarifa isn't the Maldives. Chill. And, Ella, I've been waiting *years* for you to finally cheer up. You know what we need on this girl's trip? A big awesome drinking sesh and a bloody good lay.' That was her answer to everything. 'Seriously, Ella—like, when was the last time you had a man?'

Ella thought back to Paulo, the young and sexy chef she'd been ignoring, and then thought about Josh again. Oh God, should she mention him? Kerry had always had a thing for him. Ella wouldn't have met Josh at Indigo had it not been for Kerry. If she knew she'd missed seeing him by a few weeks, she'd go crazy. Although, knowing her friend, if Ella said he was at that moment half naked on the roof terrace of her hotel, Kerry would jump on a plane straightaway just to get a glimpse of him. No, there was no point. He'd be gone by the morning.

'I'm fine without a man, thank you very much,' Ella replied. 'The only man I've ever really loved…'

'Stop! Stop, stop, *stop*. Please don't mention that frigging Zac again or I'm going to drink this nail varnish and put myself out of my misery!' Kerry shouted. 'It's been, like, *forever* since he left you. We want you to get a boyfriend. A *real* one. One that lasts more than a few weeks.'

As far as they were concerned, Ella'd had a falling out with her mother about her stepbrother Sebastian and she'd run off to Spain with Zac. Then he'd left her. They had no idea who he'd really been, *what* he'd been. Or that there was a strong chance he was dead and never coming back.

'Kerry, be nice. Ella had her heart broken and it takes…'

Kerry cut Mai Li off.

'I know, but move on, girlfriend. I'm serious. Please, Ella, please tell me you are at least having sex again.'

'Yes, I've had a few…encounters. It's just that it's too painful because I always choose ones that remind me of Zac.'

'Blah blah blah. This is boring, and I have to go.' Kerry waved her freshly painted nails in front of her face, reducing the screen to a blur. 'I've got an event in town about the extinct Andamanese language of Bo that I need to get to. Honey, I'll see you at the airport on the twenty-seventh, OK? And OMG get some decent guys lined up because I want me a matador. Mai Li, I'll call you about our flight plans.' She blew a kiss and her side of the screen went blank.

Ella laughed. Her friend was writing her PhD paper on something-or-other-linguistics-related but still spoke like a dumb extra from an American teen show.

'Thank God Kerry's gone,' Mai Li said. 'She's been driving me mad lately. She's been so grumpy because that Brazilian lecturer she liked never called her back. You know how much she likes smart older guys. Actually, she likes thick young ones, too! She's going to be a handful when we meet up; you better warn the town that a man-eater is coming. So, have you had a nice day?'

'Kinda.' Ella shrugged. 'A Hollywood type was here today looking at the hotel as a location for some film.'

Mai Li grinned and gave her the thumbs up again. 'Ooooh, that's so glamorous. You might meet someone famous.' Then she stopped, remembering who she was talking to, and shook her head like she was trying to erase what she'd just said. 'Whatever, I know you hate all that. Actually, I'm glad we're chatting alone now because I wanted to ask you something weird and Kerry always gets all matter-of-fact about stuff. I can't ask her anything emotional. It's about that job I've been offered.'

'What about it?'

'It doesn't feel right. I know I'm being ungrateful because it pays well, and I beat loads of other graduates to the position but… it sounds weird…but this strange thing happened where I randomly met a guy at a party the other night. By some strange coincidence, he works at this firm I've always been interested in working at, and he said he may be able to get me an interview there. Kerry says I'm mad taking risks and to accept the original job, but it doesn't feel right. Am I being stupid?'

Ella thought back to all the conversations she'd had with Zac about fate, destiny, and life paths. He'd told her that coincidences didn't exist, that life events unfolding in a convenient way were actually signs you were following your preordained life plan. Likewise, when things were a battle or felt wrong, it was a warning you were going in the wrong direction.

'Listen to your gut, Mai Li. Go with what feels right. Sounds to me like you already know what you are meant to do.'

Ella thought about Josh. Did *she* know what the right thing to do was? There had to be a greater meaning behind why fate had sent him to her hotel. Her stomach clenched, and she gave a long sigh.

'Mai Li, sorry, but I have to go. I'll be in touch before you come over.'

Fate. Destiny. Did they really exist? How many times had she asked herself *What if?* and imagined every other possible scenario that could have played out had Zac not killed himself?

He'd said he had to do it so he could return to her. But how? When? None of it made sense at the time, and it still didn't. With his last breath, he'd promised he'd be back for her; all she had to do was follow her path and get on with her life. She was trying to but failing. Zac didn't make mistakes. Fate never made mistakes, either. She thought about Josh turning up out of nowhere and the flood in his hotel room forcing him to stay at her hotel.

Zac had specifically told her that when the universe dropped an opportunity in your lap, you mustn't shake it off; you had to notice and act on it, or it would keep presenting itself until you had no other options. Was her destiny at that very moment on the top floor of her hotel acting like an arrogant dick? And what would happen now that Zac was no longer there to distract her from what was meant to be?

There was only one way to find out.

She checked her hair in the mirror, swallowed down her nerves and made her way up to the penthouse suite.

4

ELLA KNOCKED ON the door and cleared her throat. She really should have changed or at least had a shower first. Oh well, she wasn't going to stay long anyway. It wasn't as if she even liked Josh; he was still a bit of a creep—during their last chat all he'd done was talk about himself and pose a lot. *But oh God, that body.* No! She'd promised herself no more men, and she'd meant it. She was about to turn around and go home when the door opened.

Josh was silhouetted in the doorway, wearing nothing but tight swimming shorts. A puddle was forming at his feet, and his chest sparkled with tiny drops of water. Ella swallowed and cleared her throat again.

'Ella! Come in!' He grabbed her hand and pulled her into his room. 'I was just having a beer in the hot tub. You *have* to check out this view. It's amazing.'

She was yanked from the doorway and past his bed, onto the terrace where the coffee table was littered with bags of crisps, bottles of beer, and piles of paperwork. Josh stepped back into the hot tub, stretched out his arms, and gave an exaggerated sigh.

'I fucking love this place. Cool hotel, Ella. Cool hotel.'

He took a swig of beer and closed his eyes while she stood there, once again motionless and wondering what the hell she was doing. He opened one eye, then the other, and turned his head in her direction.

'Get into the tub. Have a beer.'

He nodded at the three unopened bottles in the ice bucket beside her. A boozy Jacuzzi with Mr Hot Stuff was something dreams were made of. Well, it was the fantasy of every girl in the world that read glossy magazines and watched cheesy films. But it wasn't hers. Among her friends, Ella was the reckless one, the one with few morals and very little shame, but she wasn't one of his pathetic groupies. She was the manager of the hotel in which Josh's movie was going to be filmed, and it was going to make her a lot of money. Not only that, she did not want to give the jumped-up idiot the satisfaction of falling at his feet.

'No thanks. I was just here to ask what you're doing for dinner.'

It was out of her mouth before she'd had a chance to figure out why she was *really* there and what she wanted. Josh looked at her with an expression she couldn't quite fathom. Counting silently, she waited for an answer. One…two…three…four…five seconds was a long time to be stared at.

'You're here to take my food order?' he asked.

'Well, no. Not exactly. Unless you want me to?'

'I was thinking room service and the sports channel tonight.'

'Oh. Well we have a chef issue right now, as in we don't have one, but I may be able to rustle up a sandwich for you.'

'Or maybe you could order me a pizza?'

'I could do that.'

Ella ran her jagged thumbnail across her teeth and gazed at the sun glittering over the ocean like someone had scattered tiny diamonds over the waves. Tarifa was where the Atlantic and the Mediterranean met—two seas colliding, merging, fighting to become one. She thought back to Zac's last words about following her life path. Fate. Coincidence.

What was she doing in Josh's room? Was today going to be the day she finally took control of her destiny? She had to test it.

'Or I could cook you dinner at mine?' she said.

Josh hauled himself backwards out of the hot tub with just his arms and sat on the edge. There wasn't an inch of fat on him; his rippling stomach folded over in thin tanned strips, and his shorts were so low Ella could make out the top of his hip bones. He ran his hands over his wet hair, took a swig from the bottle of beer beside him, and gave Ella a lopsided smile.

'I'd like that. I'd like that a lot.'

She explained how to find her apartment and said she'd see him at eight o'clock. Then she asked herself what the fucking fuckety fuck *fuck* she was doing!

• • • • •

Why the hell had she offered to cook for Josh? Her stomach had been aching and twisting all day, but she couldn't decide if it was from excitement, nerves, complete dread, or her hangover. She opened her front door and any good feelings she'd had about testing fate quickly evaporated.

Her drunken antics the night before, and her rush to get to work that morning, meant her apartment looked like a cross between a bar and a brothel. Her bed was unmade, her clothes and underwear were scattered all over the floor, and her lamp was hanging off the bedside table.

'No more nights out and no more thinking about men,' she mumbled to herself as she picked up an empty bottle of tequila from the rug. Scenes of Paulo the chef in her bed the previous week and Josh sitting on the side of the hot tub flashed through her mind. No, she had to get her act together!

Ella started cleaning her mind and apartment by opening all the windows to get rid of the stench of stale alcohol and sweat, and then she ran around picking up the debris from the night before. She changed her bed sheets, straightened the furniture, washed up, swept the floors, and glanced at the contents of her fridge.

Double shit! All she had in there was half a lemon, three bottles of wine, some sweet chilli sauce, and a piece of hard cheese. Classy. Why on earth had she thought cooking for Josh would be a good idea? She phoned for a pizza and then ran to the bathroom.

Her intention was to have a quick shower and then think about what to wear, but once she was under the hot water, her mind brimming over with a thousand 'what if' questions, she completely lost track of time. She'd just started towelling herself dry when there was a knock on the door.

'I'm coming!' she shouted. Surely the pizza wasn't here already? She wrestled into underwear that rolled and clung to her damp body, threw on a strappy cotton dress and roughly dried her hair with a towel before running to the door and yanking it open. But it wasn't the pizza guy.

'Hey,' Josh drawled, a half smile twitching at the corner of his mouth. 'Nice outfit.'

She looked down to where his gaze was resting on her body, realising that her damp dress was clinging to all the wrong places. Her hair was also soaking through the back of her dress. She gathered it up and twisted it into a knot at the base of her neck, her skin prickling with embarrassment. The online magazines had shown her what kind of girls Josh was friends with—their tiny pampered dogs were better dressed than she was.

'Sorry. I haven't had a chance to do my hair or make-up. My apartment was a mess, so by the time…'

'Ella, you look great.'

He'd changed into a loose black shirt and jeans and held a bottle of red wine in each hand, which he handed over to her. She beckoned him in and accepted a kiss on the cheek. He smelled of expensive cologne, and her stomach began its usual acrobatics act. Why was she nervous? She knew him; he was just the kid she went to uni with, for God's sake. Plus, she'd only invited him for dinner out of curiosity and to test her fate theory. Curiosity, that was all. Nothing more.

'I thought we'd eat outside,' she said.

They crossed the apartment to the French windows that ran the length of her back wall. Josh stopped to stare at something hanging on the wall.

'This is cool,' he said, pointing to a large white feather suspended between two panes of glass in a frame. 'What bird is it from?'

'Nothing, it's nothing. Leave it. Let's just go into the garden.'

She didn't want to think about Zac right now. She waited for Josh to step outside, and then she placed the framed feather under her bed, using the opportunity to take a few deep breaths and steady her nerves. If she didn't eat something soon, she was going to be sick.

'Wow, your view is nearly as amazing as mine.'

The dining area overlooked the ocean, and Ella had laid the table with fresh linen and flowers. The apartment was on the ground floor and the inside consisted of an open-plan room and bathroom. It wasn't that spectacular, but it was the outside she loved the most. The cobbled terrace featured two wicker sofas, a shaded dining corner and a long, narrow swimming pool inlaid with tiny turquoise-and-gold tiles with a large stone Buddha at one end. She was no gardener, but bright pink and purple bougainvillea spilled over the back wall where there were steps that led to the beach; she had her own private bay that was cut off from the hotel's beach by large rocks on either side.

Josh peered over the edge of the wall and let out a low whistle.

'You have your own beach?'

Ella joined him looking out over the sand dunes.

'It's tiny, just a bit of sand and some rocks. I hardly go down there. I prefer swimming in the pool.'

He ran his hand over the Buddha and turned in a full circle, taking in the little lanterns dotted around the garden and the bright flowers that shouted for attention against their backdrop of deep blue sea and sky.

'Your place is amazing. Thanks for the dinner date.'

'It's not a date.'

What the hell was the matter with her? Were they always going to play this game—Mr Arrogant and Little Miss Rude? Thankfully, she was saved by the doorbell.

Josh was grinning when she returned laden with pizza boxes.

'Ah, my kinda girl. Wine, pizza, and a sea view. What are you doing to me, Ella?'

Doing to *him?* She had absolutely no idea what she was doing full stop.

She'd ordered too much food; her gluttony was the worst thing about having a hangover, but Josh seemed delighted with every box and bag he opened. He was laughing in disbelief as if he'd never seen a pizza before.

'Are we expecting company?' he asked, peering inside the pizza boxes.

'No. Why?'

'I live in LA; women don't eat in LA. You don't know how refreshing it is for me to be sitting with a woman who actually likes to eat. Wow, that's a lot of olives on there.'

'Oh, I didn't think. You don't like olives?'

'No, no, I love them but I always pick them off my pizza. I like their flavour but not the texture.'

Now it was Ella's turn to laugh.

'Same here.'

'No way! Seriously? Do you know how weird that makes us?'

She nodded and tried to stop grinning. It didn't mean anything. Just because they had one strange thing in common didn't mean Zac was right and Josh was her true love.

'How are your parents?' he asked.

'Fine.'

'How do they feel about you living out here on your own?'

'If by "they" you mean my mum and Richard, they aren't together anymore. She's decided to spend all her money travelling the world so she can find herself, while he hangs around wondering what he did wrong. It's pretty fucked up to be honest. This hotel was one of her whims, until she got bored and left me to run it alone.' *And I found out that my real father was a priest*, she wanted to add, *and I think my mum still loves him but is fooling herself that he's not the reason for her crazy midlife crisis.*

'I did read something about them splitting up. Sorry about that. So, what's it like living out here in Tarifa?'

He spent the rest of the evening asking Ella question after question, and when she answered he listened, really listened, as if he was going to be quizzed about her life after dinner. She wasn't expecting such genuine attention from him.

'So, did you complete your degree at RCU?' she asked him.

He took a bite of pizza and nodded.

'Yep, a first in American History and Politics. Comes in very handy when memorising film scripts and smiling at a camera.'

So, he could be witty, too.

'Well, you never know, stardom may not last forever,' she said. 'You've always had fans, even back in uni. Do you remember Mai Li and Kerry?' She added another black olive ring to the ever-increasing pile on the side of her plate. 'You sat with us at that bar in Camden, Indigo. It was the first time you and I met.'

'I remember meeting you, but... Oh wait, was Kerry that blonde that kept shaking her cleavage at me? She was scary!'

'We're still really good friends.'

'Oh, sorry,' he said with an apologetic face, making Ella laugh.

'They're coming out at the end of the month for my birthday.'

'Cheers. Happy birthday-to-be,' he said, clinking his glass against hers. 'What are you doing to celebrate?'

'Nothing much. Just going out with my friends and some family, maybe out to dinner somewhere. Not a big deal.'

Josh opened the second bottle of wine and topped up her glass.

'Shame I'm off in the morning. It would've been nice to have joined you all.'

'Really? Who said you were invited?'

She had meant it as a joke, but now he was blushing. Josh was blushing! She had no idea he had the ability to get embarrassed...or look that cute.

'I was kidding!' she said. 'My friends would have loved to see you again.'

'No. You're right; you hardly know me. I was being presumptuous.'

She stared at her plate because looking at his almond-shaped eyes and that dimpled smile was making her giddy. Had to be all the wine they were drinking. Was he as cocky and self-important as she'd first thought? Or was all that bullshit an act? Maybe she was being too hard on him. Then she thought back to the last time she'd seen him in London, what he'd said to her, and how Zac had practically beaten him up for being a spiteful little shit who thought he was God's gift to women. Men like him didn't change—did they?

'I'm sorry,' he said, cutting into her thoughts.

'What for?'

'For what happened on the bus the last time I saw you.' *So he did remember.* 'I deserved that thump your boyfriend gave me for chatting you up. I've felt bad about it for a long time.'

'*Chatting me up?*' Ella shouted, her voice louder than she'd intended it to be. 'Josh, you wouldn't let me off the bus unless I kissed you. What the fuck was that about? That was sexual harassment and you deserved everything you got!' She hadn't meant to get so angry, but now he was sitting opposite her it was all flooding back. His jeering friends, the stiflingly hot bus, the way he'd called her names for not kissing him. She dropped her voice to barely above a whisper. 'You scared me, Josh.'

He looked down at his plate, his mouth set in a hard line as he ran his finger along the edge of the napkin. He didn't say anything for a long time. When he finally looked up, she wasn't expecting to see so much pain in his eyes.

'I'm sorry. I was a total mess back then. It's no excuse, but I had some stuff going on and…'

He stopped. Perhaps he was expecting her to roll her eyes or keep shouting at him, but he'd listened to her all evening, so it was only fair that she give him the opportunity to explain.

'Go on,' she said.

He rubbed a hand over his face and took a deep breath. 'I've never said this to anyone before, but do you remember that fancy dress party? When you came as Helen of Troy and asked me to pretend to be your boyfriend to scare off that pervy guy?'

Of course she did. That was the night of their one and only kiss—a stage kiss, just to keep up the pretence. Although all that had happened before he'd been a creep to her.

'I had a massive crush on you,' he said. 'When I kissed you that night, it wasn't an act. I just never had the guts to tell you how I felt. To be honest, I used to get really nervous around you.' He looked down at his plate and let out a light laugh while rubbing the back of his neck. Ella looked down at her plate too. It was the last thing she was expecting him to say. 'Anyway, it was the night of the party that I found out my dad was cheating on my mum. The bastard wasn't even hiding it—I caught him making out with a woman dressed as Marilyn Monroe. You'd left the party by then. I confronted him in the men's bathroom, so as not to embarrass him in front of his work colleagues, and he punched me in the stomach.'

Josh looked up, his eyes locking on hers. She had to strain to hear what he said next. 'My own father punched me. After that, all I kept thinking about was you. I'd given you my number that night and I thought we'd meet up. I kept telling myself that life was about to get better—but you didn't call. So, when I saw you get on that bus two weeks later, I followed you. I'd been drinking, I was with my mates and I was angry at my dad and, well, you know what happened. As I said, there's no excuse and I was totally out of order, but I want you to know that I've felt bad about it ever since.'

Ella had been quite happy thinking she knew everything about Josh—spoiled brat and sexist idiot. Simple. But the man before her was far from the strutting peacock he'd appeared to be a few hours earlier. He was either an amazing actor or he'd just lain himself totally bare before her.

'I had no idea,' she said.

He reached over the small table and lifted her chin. She tried to look away but he tightened his grip just a little, so she had nowhere else to look but in his eyes. They were shimmering, as if the sun that an hour earlier had been warming her bare shoulders was now lighting him up from the inside.

'Ella, I've wanted to say sorry to you for years. You were the last person I wanted to hurt. Back then you were the only one who ever treated me like a normal guy.' His thumb made tiny stroking motions on her cheek, making her shiver. She could hear her own heartbeat mixing with the rhythm of the waves crashing behind them. What was he doing? If he didn't take his hand off her face soon, she was going to forget how to breathe altogether.

'You always did that,' he said. 'You still do.'

'Did what?'

'Make me feel normal and, well, you remind me what a self-inflated idiot I can be. I could do with more people like you in my life.' His fingers were burning her skin. 'My parents treated me like their golden boy. I was their only child for a long time, mummy's little dolly and dad's trophy. Now I'm surrounded by people that are paid to suck up to me all day. But you, you're refreshing. I reckon you're good for me.' He finally let go of her face and stared over her shoulder at the beach behind her. She didn't have to turn around to know the waves were getting bigger and darker—she could hear them building themselves up to a stormy night. He shifted his gaze back to her, his face as troubled as the waters. 'I wish I didn't have to leave tomorrow. I'm really glad I bumped into you.'

Ella took a long gulp of her wine and nodded. This was the last thing she expected to happen over a slice of pizza. She felt like a fish on a hook, yet she was surprised to find herself enjoying the sensation. Was Josh flirting with her? Or had he been in LA for so long that he spoke to everyone with such emotional drama and fake sincerity?

'So, what happened to your boyfriend then? The mysterious kickboxer?' he asked, tucking into another slice of pizza as if they hadn't just had a moment.

She didn't want to talk about Zac, which shocked her because she always wanted to talk about him. Zac never left her. Even though she hadn't seen him for three years, it was as if the ghost of him was forever beside her. She hadn't felt his shadow the entire evening, but at the very mention of his name his memory was next to her again. Watching. Making her wonder what the larger plan was and whether she was playing the game correctly.

'Zac and I became a couple the night that he hit you, and we went on to have an amazing Christmas together.'

Josh raised one eyebrow and gave her that wonky smile again. 'Glad to know my swollen face helped facilitate your love life. What happened between you guys? I'm guessing he's not about anymore. I didn't notice any photos of him in your apartment.'

Why had Josh been looking for boyfriend proof in her room?

'It didn't last. I haven't had a serious relationship since him actually. We were only together for a few weeks and then…' She picked at the pink skin around her thumbnail. At first it had been a comfort telling herself that Zac would return, keeping him near, but perhaps her misguided hope was holding her back. Was she ready to banish Zac's shadow forever? She took a deep breath.

'He died. On the second of January, three years ago.' Ella bit down on her lip. *Don't cry, don't cry.* 'Everything was perfect; we were happy but…'

Josh was already out of his seat and crouching down beside her, pulling her head into his shoulder.

'I had no idea he passed away. I'm so sorry.'

Ella had never been one for hugging, but she let herself fall into him. His shirt smelled of cologne and the ocean. Josh comforting her about Zac was totally weird, and even stranger, for the first time it wasn't her late boyfriend she was thinking about. It was Josh.

This was the last thing she'd expected from him. She closed her eyes and rested her head against his chest. They stayed like that for a few moments, his hand stroking her hair, until her eyes snapped open and she sat up with a start. Something was vibrating in his shirt pocket. The moment was over.

'Your phone is ringing.'

Mouthing an apology, Josh answered it. He walked to the wall behind her and leant against it as he talked in hushed tones. She could feel the warmth of his stare like a ray of sunlight running along the back of her neck. It radiated through her, the heat travelling down her spine and spilling into her chest, finally reaching the pit of her stomach and turning into a scorching ball of flames. She turned around and their eyes met for a split second before he looked away. *Fuck!* What the hell was going on? Was this fate working, or was her recent 'no more meaningless sex' vow making her hornier than normal? *It still doesn't mean anything,* she repeated to herself.

'You won't believe this,' he said, returning to the table and sitting in front of her again. 'That was Billy, the location guy. He has severe food poisoning and said there's no point meeting him tomorrow.' He poured them both more wine and flashed her a huge smile. 'I don't fly out to LAX until Saturday, so it looks like I'm staying here a few more days. How awesome is that? Best coincidence ever.'

Coincidence? Like hell it was! She put both her hands around her wine glass, holding onto it like it was the mast of a ship in a storm. She tried to match her breathing to the rhythm of the waves behind her, but her stomach was churning as much as the sea. Coincidences didn't exist. This was good old-fashioned fate at work pushing her and Josh together. Again.

Zac's shadow over her life was slowly beginning to fade. He had been right all those years ago—mistakes didn't happen; only miracles did. She and Josh were meant to be together. Fact. And Zac was dead. Another fact.

She turned to Josh but he was already looking at her, a questioning expression on his face. He gave her a half smile, a dimple forming on his cheek. Was he really her future? There was only one way to find out—at least this time Zac wouldn't be coming between them.

5

ZAC RUBBED HIS eyes and blinked until darkness gave way to grey shadows. Wherever he was, this wasn't where he'd died. Running his fingers along the cold stone walls, he felt his way along the edge of the room, sticky cobwebs gathering on his fingertips. He counted his steps from one end of the space to the other—seven by five—and then stumbled, tripping over something. In the semi-darkness, he reached down to the sandy ground and ran his hand along the object. It was a long wooden box. There were three of them side by side in the centre of the room. The air smelled stale and dusty, like the basement of an old house mixed with the scent of rotting wood, earth, and death.

His first thought was of escape; his second was of Ella. He had to get to her. She had to know he'd survived.

A small chink of light shone from the farthest wall. The gap was no bigger than a coin, but it was large enough for Zac to peer through and look outside. All he could see was green, a faint scent of grass confirming there was a park or field nearby. He pressed his ear against the hole but there was no sound, just the chatter of birdsong. The wall was old, and as he picked at the crack it began to crumble, his nails filling with gritty sediment, but it wasn't enough to make the hole any bigger. He pushed and hit it before punching the wall as hard as he could. His knuckles cried out in pain, but his urgency to get out of his stone prison was greater than his discomfort. In fact, pain felt good. Any sensation was a sweet relief and a reminder that he was alive. *Alive again!*

He kept pounding harder and harder and, although it was still too dark to see if he was making any progress, he could feel the wall slowly giving way. For over an hour he continued to punch, kick, and push the wall until the hole widened and pieces broke off. He pulled at it as if he were clawing his way up through the depths of the ocean to the surface, and as he sent chunks of concrete smashing at his feet, he was finally able to take a deep breath and taste his newfound freedom. The light breeze on his skin felt so good.

The hole wasn't yet big enough to fit through, but it allowed sunlight to pour into the room. He glanced behind him where the long wooden boxes were now illuminated. Coffins, all in various stages of decay. One had a lid missing, and out of another a skeletal hand hung through its rotten side. Zac shuddered and continued to kick at the hole in the wall until he was finally able to squeeze himself through the gap and crawl his way out into the sunshine. Scrambling to his feet he coughed as the fresh air reached his lungs.

He was at the back of a tomb, a small stone mausoleum with pillars whose carvings had long been eroded by time and weather. Ivy grew over the greying stone walls. A chain-link fence was directly in front of him, and beyond that stood tall oak and elm trees. Leaning against the fence, he winced as a sharp pain shot through his bruised and bloody hands. His middle finger was bent at a strange angle, and three of his nails had been ripped out of their beds by his frantic clawing. It was the first time he'd seen his own blood. He stared at his hands, his eyes slowly adapting to the bright sunlight, and watched as the grazes and cuts on his knuckles disappeared and his hands and nails returned to normal. He smiled. So, he hadn't lost everything after all. He licked his index finger and rubbed the blood off his other hand. There was no longer anything beneath the blood, and neither was he in pain anymore.

He'd returned and, it seemed, so had his power to heal.

With one long stretch his body clicked and popped as his spine realigned itself. How long had he been trapped in that tomb? A thin film of grime, dust, and sweat was caked in streaks on his arms and embedded into the folds of his elbows and wrists. When he'd died, he'd been bare-chested, yet now he was wearing a T-shirt that had once been white but was now various shades of grey, green, and black. He also had on the same pair of jeans he'd worn on his last day. He brushed himself down, clouds of dust filling the air like warm breath on a cold day, and rubbed at the cobwebs and mud on his trousers.

As he patted his legs, he noticed a lump in each pocket. Strange. He pulled out a bundle of banknotes from his left pocket, a mix of euros and sterling still neatly folded into different denominations as if he'd placed them there only yesterday. He hoped that was the case and that he wasn't far from where he'd left Ella. With any luck, time and distance had been kind, and it wouldn't be too much of a hardship to reach her. At least he had money on him; if it was still in date. How many years had passed? Feeling newly hopeful, he reached into his other pocket, retrieving a long gold necklace with an unusual amethyst pendant hanging from it, and searching deeper he found two matching rings. He smiled. Everything was exactly where he'd left it.

But how long ago was that?

He closed his eyes as images of his last day flashed before him—the swipe of the blade and the darkness that followed his last memory of Ella's anguished cries as they'd taken him away.

Instinctively, he twisted his arm up under his top and felt his back. There were two hard lumps below his shoulder blades but nothing more. No hole or gnarled scar. A heavy sadness blossomed in his chest, but he reminded himself that those small raised mounds beneath his skin represented something greater than what had once been in their place. He was free and, most importantly, nobody knew he'd survived. Not yet.

He stepped out from behind the tomb and found himself face-to-face with an elderly lady. Dressed in black and standing beside a gravestone, she was clutching a bunch of daffodils wrapped in cellophane. She yelped at the sight of a bedraggled man exiting the tomb and crossed herself. Zac mumbled an apology, walking quickly past her to the gravel path. He must look like a creature from the living dead. He was.

Making his way slowly along the cemetery path, he inspected each tombstone and read their inscriptions. They were written in English and dated back hundreds of years, but that didn't help determine what year it was now. A few minutes later he spotted a large stone statue of a lion peeking out from the undergrowth, followed by a crying angel and another crumbling tomb. He knew exactly where he was. Highgate Cemetery. There was no place like it in the world. Not only was Zac in one of the leafiest and most affluent areas of north London, Ella's house was just a few minutes' walk away. Had he been placed in that tomb out of respect for the love they'd shared? Or was it to mock and spite him? It didn't matter anymore; his plan had worked. He was free.

Zac broke into a run, his body leading him through the myriad pathways and gaining strength with every step. Pushing through the undergrowth, he zigzagged over and around headstones and statues, no longer noticing the brambles catching on his clothes or the wild rose thorns scratching his arms. His mind was focused on three easy steps: get out of the graveyard, find Ella, and be with her for the rest of her life. It was that simple.

6

ARRIVING AT THE cemetery gates, Zac was relieved to see the streets beyond were empty. The combination of weak daylight and lack of traffic told him it was early morning—probably the weekend. Ella's house was just up the road, but he had no idea how long had passed since they'd both been in Highgate. Did she still live there?

He closed his eyes again and attempted to feel her. She'd always been with him—since he'd first met her two thousand years ago, he'd had the ability to sense her in every part of his being. Where she was and what she was feeling had never been a mystery. He was able to find anyone that way, but right now all he felt inside was an empty echo of his former self. Ella was no longer there, and it scared him.

His skin prickled and every hair on his body stood on end as the realisation suddenly hit him—he'd come back to life, which meant he'd been right all along. His mother had to be alive too! Was this how she'd felt, awakening from her own fate all those years ago when his father Mikhael had torn Zac away from her, leaving him a defenceless orphan? Had his mother roamed the streets like he was now, desperately trying to find him, to feel him, her very soul yearning and reaching out for her little boy?

Zac had once been a powerful being, but his skills had somewhat diminished upon his return. He could still heal himself, his smooth unblemished hands were testament to that, but he could no longer feel people and as much as he tried, he couldn't disappear and reappear at will as he'd once done. Zac had returned part human. But which part?

He trudged up the hill to Highgate Village, passing the café where he'd once sat watching Ella take her morning jog, waiting for her to forget him. The café was closed, but as he peered inside he caught a glimpse of his reflection.

He ran a hand over his face; it was not a pretty sight. His hair, which had always hung to his shoulders in dark waves, was now a matted clump, dusty and full of debris. He picked a leaf out of it and tried to run his fingers through it, to no avail. Strangely, it hadn't grown any longer than it had always been and neither had the hair on his face. His eyes stared back at him as dark and haunted as the memories of his last day, their usual bright blue now reduced to a lifeless grey. His tanned arms were pale and his cheeks were sunken. Considering he'd been shut up in a tomb without food or water for who knew how long, he could have looked a lot worse.

Heading toward the crest of the hill, he smiled at the sight of the newspaper stall where he and Ella had once met, comforted to see it was still in the same spot near the bus stop. He jogged up to it, recognising the man organising the magazines on the racks. The vendor's appearance hadn't changed either—another good sign that Zac's dramatic demise had happened fairly recently.

The newspaper headlines screamed their usual sensationalist cries of blame, fear, and celebrity news, but Zac wasn't interested in their contents. He ran his hand over the date on their front covers and breathed a sigh of relief.

Three years. That was all. Three years, three months, and nineteen days since he'd said his last goodbye to Ella. Three years was a long time for most people, but to Zac it was but a blink of an eye. Compared to the lifetimes he'd endured to finally be with her, three years was no obstacle.

He had to stay positive. First find Ella and then search for his mother. Zac was finally free from the control of Mikhael now that he and the Choir thought he was dead. No longer could they say that his kind shouldn't be mixing with hers; Zac and Ella could finally lead a life without pretence.

He'd died so he could be reborn for her, like his mother had done before him, finally free from his otherworldly restraints. There had been no other way for them to be together, he hoped Ella understood that. He was back now, and in this lifetime she'd loved him as madly as he'd always loved her.

Taking his mother's jewellery out from his pocket, Zac read the inscription on the back. '*The fallen shall rise again.*' That was exactly what he'd done.

He ran his finger over the date on the newspaper again and smiled.

'Oi, mate, you going to buy that bloody paper or just stand there rubbing your dirty paws all over it?'

Zac mumbled his second apology of the day and walked away as the newspaper vendor turned to the woman beside him.

'Bloody filthy tramps. I remember the days when Highgate was a respectable place.'

• • • • •

Five minutes later, Zac found himself at the impressive gates of the Fantz mansion. He'd never forget that warm September afternoon when he'd first spoken to Ella, how upset she'd been with her mother for having married Richard Fantz and dragging her away from Spain to live in London. Then weeks later she'd ushered him through the back of the house, embarrassed by the grandeur of her new family home after discovering that Zac had no home of his own—unaware then of what he really was. If only it had simply been his lack of wealth driving them apart.

This house was where he'd first kissed her, where they'd first made love, and where he'd nearly killed her stepbrother, Sebastian. After everything that had happened to Ella, would she still be living in Highgate?

He rang the doorbell and tried to still the swarm of wasps buzzing inside his chest.

'Ain't nobody home,' came a voice from overhead.

Two men in hard hats were on the roof of the house organising tiles. A long driveway separated them from the gate, so they had to shout down to him.

'The house is for sale. You not seen the bleeding great board next to you?' one of them said. 'No point ringing and ringing, all you're doing is winding us up.'

Richard was selling his beloved home?

'Do Richard and Felicity still live here? I'm looking for Ella Fantz.'

The builders turned to each other and laughed.

'Elephants? Does this look like a fucking zoo? We don't know who lives here. Our boss asked us to fix up the roof before they sell. Now piss off and go beg someplace else.'

Zac hadn't come this far to turn around and give up. He walked away from the main gates, out of sight of the builders, and sat with his back to the wall. He had to think. There was always the internet. He could search for her there, not that he had any idea how to use it or whether electricity would give him the same issues as before. Or he could try to track down Ella's friends; they might know where she was, but he didn't know their surnames or where to find them.

Thirsty and hungry, he was contemplating walking back to Highgate Village to wait for the café to open when he saw a familiar figure approaching him.

'What do you do here? This is private property. I call the police!'

The woman loomed over Zac as he sat on the pavement. Her blonde hair, now flecked with a few grey hairs, was scraped back from her face. She'd lost a little weight, but he recognised her immediately. The housekeeper. The woman who'd welcomed him to the Fantz home three years previously on the day everything had started to go wrong.

'Ylva. It's me, Zac.'

She looked at him, squinted, looked again, and then jumped back.

'Oh, Zac. I remember you. You're Ella's friend that came to tea. *Skenet bedrar!*'

He understood her! She was speaking Swedish, but he still knew what she was saying. So he'd retained his knowledge of all languages—another positive sign.

'Yes, looks can be deceiving,' he said.

'All the time all she say, "Zac, Zac, Zac." Why did you leave her? Ella never come back! And you look terrible. Like you've been dug up from ground and then run over again. What do you do here?'

'I'm looking for Ella. Or Mr and Mrs Fantz. Or anyone that can help me find her.'

'I cannot help, Zac. Sorry. I'm just here to clean before house sale.'

Much like the emptiness he'd experienced when he was unable to feel Ella from afar, he realised he could no longer feel the housekeeper's emotions or intentions either. Was Ylva lying or telling the truth? Did she know where Ella was? He'd never been a mind reader, but he *could* read a person's soul; he'd known what people needed and felt, regardless of what they were saying. But right now, with Ylva, he felt nothing.

'Well, can I come in and see if my belongings are still in her room? Look at me. Could I at least have a quick shower? Please?'

Ylva took in his filthy clothes and matted hair but avoided eye contact.

'No. I can't let anyone in. Please, just leave.'

It was futile, but something was making him stay. A vibration ran between them, a tangible force forming around him and pulling her closer. He'd lost some of his powers and retained others, but this, this fizzing between him and the Fantz housekeeper was a new sensation. Her soul was gravitating toward his; the energy was virtually palpable.

'Can I come in, Ylva?'

'No, Zac. I must go now.'

'Ylva, look at me.' He held her gaze, pulling her in and willing her to surrender. 'Ylva, may I please come into the house?'

The housekeeper smiled sweetly.

'Of course you can come in, Zac. I give you new clothes and feed you. Take anything you need; you know where Ella's room is. Then I tell you whatever you need to know. Nobody is home. Mr Fantz moved out, and we are starting the packing up…but Ella's room has not changed.'

Zac raised his eyebrows and smiled to himself. What the hell had just happened?

He followed her into the house, ignoring the stares of the workmen. This was interesting. Very interesting indeed.

7

ELLA'S ROOM WAS exactly as he remembered it. All her clothes were still in the wardrobe and so were her shoes and handbags. She clearly hadn't wanted anything sent on to her, wherever she was. As he'd hoped, Zac found the bag of new clothes Ella had offered him all those years ago—the catalyst for their first argument. This time he was not too proud to take them.

Standing in the shower, watching the water run black at his feet, he thought back to their only Christmas together. The day they'd made love in that very same shower after he'd told her what he really was. Would he have told her the truth had he known what would happen next—that telling her his only secret would change her destiny forever?

Emerging shiny and clean from the shower was invigorating, but his hair was a lost cause. No amount of washing or brushing could smooth out the clumps and knots that had formed. He tied it back with one of Ella's hair elastics and decided to address his matted mop later. First, he had to speak to Ylva.

• • • • •

'You must be so hungry,' she said as he sat at the kitchen table.

The room was empty save for a few groceries and packing boxes stacked in a corner. Ylva placed a bowl of steaming vegetable soup before him as well as a large plate of sandwiches.

Zac filled his mouth with as much as he could manage.

'Please. Join me,' he said between mouthfuls. It was the first time he'd felt such hunger. He'd never needed to eat before, did he now? 'I need to ask you some questions.'

Ylva smiled up at him passively, her face void of any emotion. Before he spoke, he made sure she was looking straight into his eyes. It seemed to be the only way to draw in her soul.

'Tell me everything that has happened since the New Year's Eve party at Cloud Ninety-Nine. Tell me what happened after Ella disappeared.'

Zac reached for a third sandwich. Whatever the housekeeper had to say would hold all the answers to his questions. After this conversation with Ylva, the next person he would speak to would be Ella. The thought was like a punch to his guts.

'After you left her that Christmas, she was so sad,' Ylva said. 'I don't live in this house, but I am here very early and very late and that child not leave her room; actually, she ban me from entering. She cry and cry so much I say to Mrs Fantz that we call doctor. Her mother even say remove sharp things from Ella's room and to keep feeding her, but the poor baby didn't get out of bed. She just hug your sweatshirt, the one you wearing now, and cried into it. You boys are bad, hurting nice girls like her!'

It took all of Zac's strength not to explain, to tell the housekeeper how he'd fought to be with her. How much he'd loved Ella and always would. All this had happened before they were last reunited, but he'd never heard someone else's account of the pain he'd caused.

'Luckily her mother make her leave the house,' Ylva continued, 'and she had her hair all cut new and went to New Year's Eve restaurant launch. I no idea what happen that night, ninety-nine floors high. I wasn't there, but the next day I turn up for work...yes, New Year's Day, I like my work...and all hell happen.' She shook her head from side to side, tendrils of greying blonde hair coming loose from their tie. 'I've been Mr Fantz's housekeeper for twenty years. I serve his family since his first wife die when he put little Sebastian in boarding school like he wasn't important. Poor Mr Fantz, such a nice man. A good man. I liked his new wife Felicity; of all the women Mr Fantz date she is the nicest, and I wanted them all to be a happy family at last, but she is...how do you say? Flighty? She wanted to be a new shiny Mrs Fantz, with the glamour and glitz. They marry very fast, and then after New Year party Ella doesn't come back, huge drama and Felicity goes. No call or email or nothing for one week! Me and my boss were so worried.'

Ylva had a paper towel in her hand that she'd twisted into a damp rope. Had Richard and Felicity ever realised how publicly they'd been playing out their business? Did Richard know that his housekeeper had been in love with him for all these years? Ylva appeared to be a private woman, but now she was talking non-stop—telling him every last detail about the events of that fateful night. Zac felt a twinge of guilt. It may have been useful to have the ability to extract information from her against her will, but it was morally wrong.

'Ella is a lovely girl. But of course you know that, Zac. She was a bit madam and rude back then, like many teenager, but she was also kind and good. Mr Fantz was all worry when she disappear like that. He adopt, you know, she was a daughter to him. And when her mother finally contact him she just say Ella is safe in Spain and Felicity stay there, too. Mrs Fantz needed to find herself. *She say that!* Find herself! She was forty last year. How can she find herself when she doesn't know what she's looking for? Felicity shouldn't be searching for *herself*, she should be searching for her *mind* because she lost it a long time ago.

Mr Fantz is wonderful, a lovely, kind, and very rich man. Who with the right marbles in her head would leave him?'

A woman who loves another, Zac thought, thinking back to Felicity and Leo, Ella's parents, reunited in that remote mountain cottage in Spain. Leo was a priest. He wasn't going to sweep Felicity off her feet any time soon, but when they had been thrown together again three years ago and Ella had finally met her real father, Zac knew Felicity would never go back to her old life. Least of all to the man whose son had attacked her daughter.

'So, Ella is still in Spain, Ylva?'

Zac was beginning to regret having asked her to explain every detail. He knew all of this already—none of it was helping him find Ella.

'I think so.'

'Where exactly?'

'I don't know; she never return.' Ylva dabbed at her eyes with the mangled paper towel. 'She sent email to Richard saying she didn't want her belongings anymore; she was starting fresh in Spain. I don't blame poor child not wanting to return to England. The newspapers are cruel. All silly gossip. I sometimes do the Google on the internet and it is full of lies, people saying they have seen her and know the big secret. There is no secret. She was just sad and went back home to Spain. I think Mr Fantz know Miss Felicity doesn't love him now. She come back a few times, and I hear them say about marriage counselling. I know she is only trying because he loves her. Stupid men! Her perfect body was here but her mind, her mind she left in Spain. So, Mr Fantz is very sad, so sad that he's selling the house and moving to St Lucia where he has more hotels.'

Zac nodded but his own mind was elsewhere. He'd only met Richard once, and as nice as he'd seemed, Zac hadn't come here to ask after his state of mind. He needed to find Ella, and there was no one at the house that could help him do that.

'Maybe I join Mr Fantz in St Lucia,' Ylva muttered. 'I have no husband, no children. My work is all I do. Mr Fantz and I, we have our own history from long ago.'

She giggled like a schoolgirl, and once again Zac felt the familiar pang of guilt. He shouldn't have forced the housekeeper to talk. He hadn't even learned anything new.

'Ylva, do you have any idea how I can find Ella?'

'No. If the bad newspapers and magazines can't find her, I think you struggle, too. Give me your telephone number and if she calls, I ask Mr Fantz to tell you. You are not the first man asking about her.'

Zac sat up and leant forward. 'What do you mean?'

'Two years ago, a handsome man was here. He ask for you and Ella.'

Nobody knew Zac was alive. Why would they be looking for him at Ella's old home? Why would they ask for her too? Did Mikhael suspect he would return?

'Was he very tall with long blond hair?' Zac asked.

He could hear the desperation in his voice and tried to steady his breathing.

'No, he was dark man with sexy cheekbones. Like a model. He say his name is...wait...long time ago. Maybe I write it down? Gary? Gabby?'

'Gabriel?'

'Yes! Gabe, he say his name is Gabe. Lovely man, so charming. Had something important to tell you and say you must contact him. Wait, I have the note. I think.'

Ylva rifled through folders that had been neatly packed away in the moving crates. She took out scraps of paper and receipts, peering at each one before replacing them back in the files.

Gabriel had been searching for him? But his friend had been there when Zac ended his life, when he'd told the realm the truth about Mikhael being his father. The look on Gabriel's face had said it all; it wasn't only Zac that Mikhael had lied to. Gabriel was as shocked and disgusted as the rest of them. Zac's head swam with a million questions. His friend had seen him die, so why would he be asking for him a year later? Had he worked out Zac's plan to return? His stomach twisted at the severity of what this could mean. What if Gabriel was now siding with Mikhael and checking if Zac was truly dead? Unlikely, but anything could have happened in the three years he'd been away. Zac couldn't risk being caught again, not now he was so close to getting back to Ella and discovering who his mother was. He rubbed his eyes. There were too many questions he couldn't answer.

'Ha! Found it. I never throw anything. Here it is.'

Ylva handed him a piece of paper with a simple mark drawn on it. It was Zac's sigil, an ancient sign, and there were words beneath it in beautiful calligraphy. He recognised his friend's handwriting immediately.

If you are reading this, then you are free, as I suspected you would be. I've been watching her from a distance, keeping her safe for your return, and she is well. I want to help you. Much has happened in your absence. As I can no longer feel you, my friend, I will be waiting for you where heaven meets Earth. Our home from home.

Zac nodded at Ylva and put the note in the same pocket as the jewellery.

'Thank you, you have been most helpful,' he said, kissing the housekeeper lightly on the cheek. 'Please go with Richard to St Lucia. I believe something special may just happen between you both.'

She smoothed the creases out of her apron and then put her hand up to her pink cheek.

'Oh no, Mr Fantz not like me like that.'

'Well, he may if I talk to him,' Zac said with a smile.

Once he found Ella, he would return to see Richard and repay the housekeeper for her help. He would make sure Richard and Ylva lived a happy, calm life together; it was the least he could do after dragging them into his sticky web of lies. Had Zac never entered Ella's life, none of these events would have happened—he'd altered Richard's life forever and for the worse, so it was only fair that he made amends.

'You will forget you ever spoke to me,' he told the housekeeper, staring into her eyes. 'You will forget about Gabriel, the man who gave you the note, and you will forget I was here. Is that clear? You are a good woman, Ylva. I promise Mr Fantz will see that one day.'

She nodded and walked away, humming as if he wasn't even there. His new mind-control trick both thrilled and scared him.

• • • • •

Zac walked toward Highgate Village, a rucksack full of food and spare clothes slung over his shoulder. He sat down on the same bench in Pond Square where he and Ella had talked all those years ago. For the first time in his existence, he had no idea what to do. If he found Gabriel, then maybe his friend could lead him to Ella, but if Gabriel was tricking him, it would lead him back to Mikhael and certain death.

There were so many unanswered questions. How was he going to find Ella? Was her stepbrother Sebastian still a threat? And what about Zac's mother—was she alive too?

Thousands of years had passed since he'd last seen his mother, but his memories remained clear and unwavering. The smell of her neck when she held him after a fall and the way she would wipe away his tears with her long dark braid. In the springtime, she would let him decorate her hair with forest flowers that would stay nestled among her curls all day. She used to carry him everywhere, saying it was safer to be up in the air than on the ground. His spindly legs wrapped around her waist, and he'd lock his dusty feet together and cling to her, so even when she let go of him, he never fell. But in the end, it was *she* who had fallen and spent centuries searching for her son. Now it was Zac's turn to search for her, to discover whether his theory was right, and to see if his mother was also walking this earth.

8

FINE YELLOW SAND burned Sebastian's cheek, but no matter how hard he tried to lift his head, he couldn't find the strength to move. Sweat trickled down his temples and into his eyes, which were cemented shut with blood and sand. He attempted to rub them, but his arms lay useless and limp beside him. Nothing but a low whimper escaped his parched lips. He needed help, but more than that he needed water. Slowly inching his tongue closer to his swollen lips, he tried to wet them, but his tongue was like a bloated corpse squeezed into an arid cave. Even his own blood had long ago dried hard and tight across his mouth and chin.

How long had he been in the desert?

The wind, carrying nothing but heat, howled and whipped the dunes, sending sharp pinpricks of sand into his face. His breaths were now coming in shallow fits and starts, his nose and throat burning with every inhalation.

So, this was how he was going to die.

• • • • •

A few days ago, Sebastian had been playing poker in a small village on the outskirts of the Moroccan town of Sidi Ifni; that much he could remember. The bar was a decaying art deco style building painted in blues and whites that overlooked the angry Atlantic Ocean. From the outside, it looked like a normal cafeteria, but once the sun had set, behind closed doors, it was a different place entirely. Those in the know referred to it as *The Gin and Pussy Palace*, and it didn't disappoint. At first, the locals had been wary of the foreign white boy with all the money, but he'd soon worked out how to buy himself protection and benefits. Everything was going so well, so why had those men turned on him and dumped him here?

When he'd left London three years ago—when he had been *forced* to leave his home by his bitch of a stepsister, Ella, and her wild exaggerations—he'd taken a ferry to France and slowly worked his way south of Europe. He was wanted by London's Metropolitan Police, and he'd heard his father was also trying to track him down. He had no intention of returning to England to stand trial for the things his spoilt sister had accused him of. No, he would keep travelling overland, avoiding airports and the tourist trail, and settle somewhere remote. Maybe Africa or India, somewhere cheap where people wouldn't recognise him, and his morals would remain unquestioned. He had access to money in accounts no one knew about. There had been no reason for his plan not to work. Until now.

Sebastian had spent a year in France and then in Spain, eventually crossing the Strait of Gibraltar. Plenty of locals had been happy to make the short journey from Spain to Morocco on their fishing boats for a fistful of euros, and so from there he worked his way down northern Africa. Over the last year he'd soaked up the delights of Fes, Marrakesh, and Casablanca—drinking the finest coffee and smoking the strongest weed. These cities provided the easiest hideouts if you knew the right people. He had a friend in Algeria who had been willing to get him a fake passport and papers, which meant he'd be free to finally get on with his life and disappear from the public eye forever. Six weeks ago, he'd stopped at an outpost near the Sahara, swayed by its rugged coastline, with the intention to simply stay two nights in a motel before heading further south.

That was until he'd discovered *The Gin and Pussy Palace* and its perky perks. Girls. Plenty of them at just the perfect age for the right price. They were hidden at the back of the café in the drinking and poker rooms where they would only be seen by those who would pay, and Sebastian was more than happy to part with his money for the right girl.

It had been a night like any other. The whisky was flowing, and he'd won the last hand of poker, so the drinks were on him. He was telling a story—the locals liked the stories of his travels and previously pampered life—but this time his words were not being received well.

'You must stop at once!' Hasim, the bar owner, had pleaded with him. 'No more talk like that.'

Sebastian had drunk too much but he was far from incoherent; in fact, he was holding court. The girl sitting on his lap pushed her skinny backside against his crotch, making him stir with desire, while another girl draped her arms around his neck and whispered in his ear, begging him to tell them the monster story again. He'd had them both before, and tonight he would have them both again. Probably at the same time.

'It's true.' Sebastian smiled, his tiny teeth glinting in the half-light of the bar. 'Demons. Magical beings with wings as big as cars. They can walk through walls and pin a man to the ceiling with one finger. I saw one sprout feathers out of his back and then vanish into thin air.'

Hasim looked nervously over his shoulder at a group of men in the corner who were cradling a bottle of gin between them. They were taking quick glances at Sebastian while whispering to one another.

'You will bring bad luck upon us,' the bar owner wailed. 'There is magic in this desert. You must keep quiet, Mr Sebastian. There is much darkness. You are not to shine a light on it or you will bring it closer.'

Sebastian hadn't listened to the frantic bar owner, and now here he was with a mouthful of sand, nothing more than bird food for the vultures circling above him in the pale blue sky.

A shadow fell upon him, and he relished the relief from the sun's incessant heat. Through the swollen slits of his eyes, he saw a woman's bare feet, nails painted a deep red. Wrapped around her slender ankles were dozens of beaded bracelets decorated with tiny silver bells and brightly coloured stones. He closed his eyes again and thanked a god that had deserted him a long time ago. He'd been saved.

9

SEBASTIAN'S EYES WERE still heavy but no longer felt scratchy with sand. As he slowly opened them, he was greeted with a kaleidoscope of colours dancing before him. There was something wet and thick dripping into his mouth. He swallowed, feeling a rejuvenating energy gradually seeping into his bones as the liquid ran down his throat. He sucked at the metallic ambrosia, regaining strength with every mouthful, until he found himself greedily gulping it down, his tongue finally free to lick and lap. He moved his arms up to clasp the source of his salvation, focusing on the sensation of soft skin against his palms and the tinkling sound of glass beads chiming against one another.

A woman's voice murmured in his ear.

'That's right. Drink it. It will heal you.'

She pushed his head hard against her neck, the source of the liquid, forcing him to run his mouth down her shoulders and past the necklaces at her throat. They clinked again as he moved them, nuzzling further down her wet body until he found her bare breasts. The liquid was trickling slowly from her throat to her chest. He ran his tongue over her nipple to catch the last drop. What was he drinking? It was red and sticky and smelled of old pennies and abattoirs. A different kind of strength was slowly building back up in his arms and legs. He blinked and attempted to focus, but her hand still held his head firmly against her chest.

'Drink!'

'What is this?' he asked, his voice muffled. He saw a flash of silver as she ran the edge of a knife along her jugular. More liquid ran down her chest and into his mouth. 'What am I drinking?'

'My blood. It will save you.'

Thick iron-tasting bile rose in his throat, making him choke. He used the little strength he had to pull his head back, staring into the face of the woman who'd saved him.

She was beautiful.

Not simply attractive like a girl from a magazine but ethereal, timeless. Her hair hung long and dark over her shoulders in thick bouncy curls held back by a colourful tasselled scarf. Her lips were full, her skin golden, and her eyes shone a deep green that were now fixed on his, her large pupils dark, round, and catlike. Around her neck were a multitude of glass bead necklaces, covering her bare chest that was now stained red with her blood. She was perched on the edge of a bed, her long gypsy skirt pushed up to accommodate Sebastian who was kneeling on the ground between her parted legs. The blood that he'd been drinking continued to ooze slowly out of a gash in her neck.

He went to stand, but she pushed his head harder into her chest while driving a small silver knife into the other side of her throat. Once more she guided him, this time to her other breast that was now slick with bright red blood. Her grasp on the back of his neck was too strong to fight, so he gave in to the warm, thick liquid. He no longer cared what he was drinking; it was working. He felt alive again. More than alive.

'It's only a day off,' she replied, screwing up her face at her assistant's excitement. 'I know they are rare but…'

'Go! Take him his breakfast and invite him out for the day. It will be worth it, I promise.'

Bewildered but hopeful, Ella had done as she was told, asking Josh to meet her when he was ready. An hour later, he'd found his way to the back of her ground-floor apartment via the garden entrance. And there he now was on her patio, hands behind his head and feet propped up on her patio table, yet again wearing nothing but a pair of shorts as if the idea of putting on a top had never occurred to him. Ella was beginning to grow accustomed to seeing him half naked. Well, perhaps not exactly *accustomed* yet, but her heart skipped fewer beats each time she laid eyes on his bare torso.

She joined him outside, and he gave her a slow smile.

'Hey, gorgeous. Ready to hit the beach?'

Gorgeous? Men like him flirted with everyone, and she'd be stupid to take him seriously. Ella had thrown on her cutoff jean shorts and worn a loose cropped T-shirt over her bikini. She'd lost a lot of weight since Zac had vanished, but her figure was slowly gaining its curves again. She'd noticed just that morning that her shorts no longer slid down her hips and her chest finally filled out her bikini top. Perhaps too much. Josh hadn't appeared to notice, though, as he was already heading for the back gate.

They picked their way down her garden steps to the private beach, Ella holding onto a picnic basket filled with food she had prepared that morning. Her camera was slung over one shoulder and bounced off her hip as they descended the stone steps from her house to the sand dunes below. Since she'd moved to Tarifa, photography had been Ella's only interest outside of work. The Costa de la Luz, where the hotel was situated, was famed for its clear light and huge skies. Taking photos of the waves and sunsets had been her form of meditation—a healthier way of forgetting compared to her binge drinking and one-night stands. Although, in the two years she'd owned the hotel, this was the first time she'd brought anyone to her tiny secluded beach.

Josh hovered beside her.

'What have you got in there?' he said, delving into the basket she was carrying. 'It smells amazing.'

'Get your mitts off.'

'Just give me a peek.'

'Don't you get fed in Hollywood?'

He grabbed the basket off her and ran toward the water's edge, sprinting in jagged lines and doubling up on himself as she tried to catch up with him. When he reached the rocks at the far end, he slowed and put it down, pushing Ella back with one hand as he took items out one by one.

'What are these?'

Ella was out of breath and swatted at Josh as he looked on, amused. She gave up and sat down on the rock beside him.

'You're a prat, de Silva.'

'I'm just admiring your handiwork. So, what are they?'

'Empanadillas.'

'Which means?'

'Tuna and red pepper pastry parcels.'

He nodded appreciatively and looked inside each individual Tupperware box. He then peeled the corners off the tinfoil parcels, smelling them and moaning in exaggerated delight.

'That's a Spanish omelette with potato and onions,' she said before moving on to the other selections. 'Garlic prawns, meatballs, bread, watermelon, some chorizo and Serrano ham, Manchego cheese, and that pot is full of olives. So, you know, we can suck them and spit them out.'

Josh grinned and broke off a piece of omelette, winking at Ella as he popped it into his mouth. He gave another dramatic groan of pleasure.

'Did you cook all of this yourself?'

'Stop eating it! You'll have to wait until lunchtime.' She took the basket from him and loaded up the food, glowing inside at the compliment while hoping he couldn't see how happy he'd made her. 'Of course I cooked it all. It's not difficult. Don't I look domesticated to you?'

He stepped behind her and peered over her shoulder. He was so close she could smell his aftershave and the sea air in his hair. Why couldn't he put a T-shirt on? He was such a bloody flirt. His arm brushed against hers and she shivered.

'Truth is, I've never met a woman who's beautiful, intelligent, and fun who *also* knows how to cook. How come no one has snapped you up already?'

'That is the most sexist comment ever, and you're easily impressed. Anyway, who says I don't have a boyfriend?'

He turned her around to face him and brushed a curl of hair away from her face.

'I know you don't. And I'm *not* easily impressed. I can just tell when someone's special.'

His sun-kissed face was inches from hers and the dimple was back on his cheek. Why was he staring at her like that? She wanted to laugh but nothing came out, so she screwed up her nose instead.

'Are you trying to seduce me, Josh?'

His eyebrows shot up in amusement.

'Damn it! If you have to ask, I'm obviously not as smooth as I thought.'

'You'll just have to try harder,' she called out, running to the other side of the beach.

Oh my God, were they flirting? She had no idea why she was bothering with Mr Vain, not to mention letting him chase her. She never ran anywhere, but it felt good to get some wind in her face—especially now that her cheeks were burning and the rest of her body was reacting in all sorts of other ways. Her heart sped up as she felt him gaining on her.

'Oh, you wanna play, do you?' he shouted out.

She squealed and ran faster. So, this was what it felt like to enjoy herself with a man. It had been such a long time since she'd been so carefree without worrying about the consequences. Her drunken flings had never had a fun prelude; they were quick and empty and over with before they'd even started. As for Zac, he'd always been so serious and intense; she couldn't imagine the two of them running around and acting silly. He'd been like no other man. Well, Zac hadn't technically even *been* a man, but he wasn't around anymore so there was no point comparing him to anyone else. She yelped as Josh wrapped his arms around her waist and pulled her down onto the sand.

'Stop it! No, I hate being tickled. Stop!'

She was laughing so hard that her words stuck in her throat and a stitch formed in her side. Josh was astride her, holding her arms above her head with one hand and tickling her waist with the other. She tried to move but his grip was strong, and no matter how much she attempted to stop him, her laughter was building up to hysteria.

Suddenly, she was back in her house in London three years ago—strong hands holding her down and fingers running up her thighs. Then it was six years ago on her mother's wedding day—a wiry man slick with sweat lying on top of her, her own body rigid with fear but too weak to move. Counting the cracks in the hotel ceiling. Crying out at the searing pain. Trapped under his suffocating weight, his high-pitched laugh and tiny-toothed smile mocking her as she sobbed.

'What the *fuck*, Ella!'

Josh was curled up on the sand, his face contorted in agony and his hands between his legs. Ella was on all fours, panting, tears streaming down her face and onto the sand. What had she done?

'*Fuck*, that hurts! I can't believe you just kneed me in the balls. Jesus, Ella, it was just a bit of fun! Can't you take a…Ella? Are you OK?'

She was properly crying now, her breaths rasping as she gulped in air, her hands over her face. She thought she'd got over all of that. She thought she'd moved on.

Her whole body flinched as she felt his hand on her shoulder.

'Ella, it's OK. Take a deep breath. I'm sorry. I didn't mean to scare you.'

She wiped her face, her fingers black with mascara.

'No, *I'm* sorry. I'm so sorry. God, I must look a real mess.' She sniffed and rubbed her eyes with the palm of her hand. 'Are you hurt?'

He shook his head. 'Just my pride. I'm fine. You? Are you all right? I…do you…shall I walk you home?'

His eyes were scanning her face, his brow etched with concern. Poor Josh, he'd only been playing; he'd had no idea how pinning her down would bring all the horror bubbling up to the surface again. He helped her back up to standing; his hand felt cool and soft—reassuring. She gave him a small smile, reluctant to let go. Her tears were still damp on her cheeks.

'Take a deep breath,' he said, giving her hand a small squeeze.

'Josh. I…'

'It's OK. You don't have to explain if you don't want to. Just tell me how I can help.'

She took a shaky breath and sniffed again. 'You could listen, if you have a minute?'

'I have all the time in the world.'

'Let's get back to our food first before the seagulls steal it,' she said, rubbing the sand off her knees and walking to the rocks at the far end of the bay. He jogged to keep up with her fast strides, purposely saying nothing—waiting for her to speak. He'd confided in her about his father, so maybe her biggest fears were safe with him.

'I reacted like that because…' She took another deep breath. She hadn't realised how difficult it would be to say it out loud. '…because of my stepbrother.'

'Sebastian? Did he hurt you?'

She breathed out and rubbed her eyes, focusing on the wet sand oozing between her toes as they walked through the shallow waters.

'He raped me. At our parents' wedding while I was still in my bridesmaid dress. I'd never had sex before; the more I cried, the more he laughed. I didn't tell anyone afterwards because he convinced me that it was my own fault. That I'd come on to him. I hadn't but...'

Josh's face was still, but she could see that his hands had clenched into tight fists.

'He went to work abroad straight after it happened,' she continued. 'I didn't see him again until three years later when I was home alone at Christmastime, a few days after I last saw you actually. He let himself in and tried to do it again. Luckily Zac stopped him and, to cut a long story short, the police now know what Sebastian did to me and he's on the run.'

Ella sniffed and swallowed down the ache in her throat. 'Every day I'm petrified he will find me again. I still get nightmares, especially now Zac is...I don't know where my stepbrother is, but I do know he won't stop until he gets his revenge on me for telling Richard and the police what he did.' She shrugged and ran her thumbnail over her teeth, nibbling at the skin surrounding it. 'So that's why I freaked out just now. I'm sorry, it wasn't you. I thought I was getting over it, but...'

'Don't apologise. Don't ever apologise.' He dried her tears with the back of his fingers. His own eyes were glassy, his jaw clenched. 'I had no idea. I'm sorry. You're safe now, I promise.' He pulled her to him, the second time in two days, and she felt his breath in her hair as he spoke. 'Maybe I shouldn't go to Málaga tomorrow. I don't want to leave knowing you're here dealing with this on your own.'

The last thing she wanted was Josh, someone she hardly knew, feeling sorry for her. She was already regretting opening up to him. Not even Mai Li and Kerry knew why she hated her stepbrother so much—and it hadn't occurred to her mum or dad that she was still suffering. She'd clearly been doing a great job of hiding her fears. She pulled away and dusted herself down, even though there was no more sand left on her.

'I'll be fine. Honest. I've managed three years on my own, haven't I?' She attempted a feeble smile and nudged him lightly with her shoulder. 'Anyway, today was meant to be a day off for me and a holiday for you, and I've totally killed the mood.'

Josh leant against one of the large rocks surrounding them, a strange expression passing over his face. The soft sun brought out the natural highlights in his hair, and lines creased around his eyes as he squinted down at her. She grabbed her camera out of the food basket and took a photo.

'Um, excuse me, young lady, you can't take pictures of me!' He laughed, pulling at the hem of her top until she was beside him. 'Come on, hand it over. Were you planning on selling my photos to the tabloids?'

'And blow my cover?' she replied in mock horror, passing him the camera. 'No way! I'm quite happy hiding away in my ancient monastery.'

'Wow, Ella.' He was flicking through the images on the camera's tiny screen. 'Is there no end to your talents? This is a bloody cool picture; they all are. You're really good, you know that?'

She rolled her eyes but was secretly pleased with the compliment. At least he wasn't tiptoeing around her like a fragile victim after her confession. Ella had always felt inferior around Zac. How could she not with him being who and what he was? But Josh made her feel clever and interesting.

Why did she keep comparing them? Anyway, even if she *was* beginning to fancy Josh just a teeny bit, he was going to Málaga in the morning and then back to his glitzy life. What was the point?

'Are you hungry?'

'Always.'

She reached for the picnic basket beside them and sat down on the sand. 'Hope you don't mind a bit of crunch with your lunch,' she said with a giggle, shaking the sand off various boxes and tinfoil parcels. There was a bottle of sangria in the bag too, which she poured out, handing Josh a plastic cup as he sat down next to her. He took it silently without looking at her.

'I want to tell you something,' he said, running his finger over a shell in the sand.

Ella downed the warm sangria in one gulp and turned to face him, the pit of her stomach lurching as if it were filled with a million fluttering creatures. She really didn't want him feeling sorry for her; she shouldn't have mentioned Sebastian.

He continued to look down at the shell on the sand, running his finger over its bumpy surface. 'I've wanted to say this to you since I saw you at that London club, Indigo, all those years ago. It's going to sound corny as hell, but I don't care.' He closed his eyes for a few seconds, like he was trying to brace himself, and then fixed his gaze on the sand again. 'I'm not religious or spiritual, but sometimes I feel like there's something out there. You know?' He glanced at her quickly, to check she was listening, and then went back to playing with the shell. 'The energy I feel, it's not in the things people say or do but in the white spaces; the silences and stillness. The unspoken moments. The first time I saw you in that bar on my birthday, I felt it, something I can't quite put my finger on. It's like...like I'm drawn to you. Every time I see you, I feel this crazy need to just be near you. Not in a sexual way, not that you're not sexy, I just mean...' He picked up more shells and added them to the first. 'I know I sound stupid and we hardly know each other, but it's been driving me mad and I just had to say something. You know what I mean? Or am I just talking a load of...?'

He trailed off, his eyes still avoiding hers. Of course she knew what he meant. He was describing their life path together. Destiny. It had always been there; even when her soul had yearned for Zac, Josh had always been at the back of her mind. But she didn't know how to explain it either without sounding crazy, so instead she watched him lining up the shells in the sand until eventually he rushed in to fill the silence.

'Ella, I promise this isn't a chat-up line. God, there are so many reasons why you and I wouldn't work. I respect that,' he said, finally looking up at her. 'You need time to heal after your loss, and I've got a girl in LA. She's a lingerie model and really lovely.' Ella bit the inside of her cheek. Why was he telling her? What did she care anyway? She stifled a sigh because she *was* beginning to care and it annoyed her. Lingerie model...nice one, Josh. So predictable. 'And we live in different countries. Continents!' he continued. 'So, we would never work. Anyway, I know you don't fancy me because I've lost count of the amount of times you've told me what an arsehole I am.' He laughed, but it sounded fake. 'I just care about you and needed to tell you. I don't know why or how else to explain it.'

Ella placed her hand on his arm and smiled. 'Josh, I get it. I know what you mean. Let's just have a drink and chill out, yeah?'

His shoulders slumped with relief as she poured him another glass of sangria. So he felt the vibration between them too, but he had a girlfriend. Well, what guy with his looks and success wouldn't? Josh was a nice guy, but he was right. Mutual attraction or not, their lives were never going to work. He was in the limelight and she was hiding from the world. He had an uber-amazing girlfriend and she had an addiction to bad decisions and dead exes. He may well be her destiny, but that was no reason to ruin his life or complicate hers.

'Cheers!' She tapped his plastic cup with hers. 'Here's to old friends and new beginnings.'

'I'll drink to that.'

• • • • •

The sun was setting over the water, and Ella's head rested beside Josh's. He was still asleep after ensuring every last mouthful of the picnic had been devoured. It had been the first time in a long time that she'd cooked for anyone, and she'd tried to hide her delight every time he asked for more. It didn't take them long to doze off in the afternoon sun.

She looked over at his sleeping face—why did he have to be so beautiful? They'd been taking photos of each other all day, and it saddened her to think she'd never had the opportunity to take a photo of Zac. She also felt a bit sorry for Josh's girlfriend; it was quite clear that he was never going to stay with just one woman. He was too gorgeous and too flirty, not to mention too vain, to say no to the countless offers he no doubt received every day. She'd had fun and he was easy to be with, but he wasn't the kind of guy a girl could get serious about.

'Hmm, that was one well-needed siesta,' he said, yawning and sitting up. She sat up too and he wrapped his arm around her shoulder, pulling her closer. 'Thank you. Hey, I never noticed that on you before.' He pointed at her thigh. 'Is it a scar?'

'A birthmark. It's more noticeable when I have a tan.'

'It's cool,' he said, running his sandy fingertip over the crescent mark, each stroke sending sparks up her leg. She took a deep breath, attempting to clear her foggy head. Too much drinking in the sun and too much Josh.

'Well, so much for showing you the sights of Tarifa,' she said, moving away from him. She began to pick up the empty wrappers from lunch and pack them away. 'I'm sorry we never made it past my back garden.'

'I've still had an amazing day,' he said, handing her a paper plate. 'I feel so relaxed. Thank you.'

His forehead and nose were bronzed from the day's sun. He already looked like a different man compared to the stressed, self-important actor she'd seen just a few days previously. She slung her bag over her shoulder, and they walked side by side along the wet sand, waves lapping at their ankles.

him in the shallow water. She found herself sitting astride him, taking her straight back to three years ago when she'd sat just like that with Zac on New Year's Eve, her ballgown soaking wet and his bare back in the snow.

Her hair dripped water onto Josh's face and their eyes locked, their fast breaths in time with one another. He swallowed, his eyes moving from her lips to her chest and back up to her eyes. Was he going to kiss her? She thought of his girlfriend and the fact he was leaving in the morning. She didn't need to add another notch to her bedpost or more complications to her life. Josh was fast becoming too important to lose among her empty conquests. She sat up and pushed her hair away from her face.

'You're right—we should call it a night. You have to get up early tomorrow,' she said, clambering off him.

He got to his feet too but was no longer smiling. 'Yeah, I need to pack and stuff. Anyway, thanks for everything. I promise I'll stay in touch,' he said, drawing circles in the sand with his toes. 'Looks like I'll be back in six months to film here anyway, so we'll have that night out then. OK?'

'Definitely,' she said, giving him a quick hug. His arms felt good around her, and she tried not to shiver as her wet T-shirt pushed against his bare chest. It would be too easy to look up into his almond-shaped eyes now and kiss him. She kept her face pressed against his shoulder, because looking at him was like looking directly at the sun.

'Will you be all right, Ella?'

'Me? Of course! I'm always fine,' she said, pulling away and straightening her top. 'Get on with your Hollywood life, de Silva. You don't need to worry about me. I'll see you when I see you.'

She could feel the touch of his stare travelling up her back as she climbed the beach stairs to her apartment. She wouldn't let herself turn around because if she did, she knew exactly what would happen. She would run to him and he would catch her.

If it was meant to be, then it would happen no matter how much they fought it. Zac had said Josh was her destiny, and Zac never lied. She'd just have to wait and see.

But she could already feel the wheels of fate in motion.

11

THE BRIGHT SPRING sunshine did nothing to lighten Zac's mood as he walked down Highgate Hill toward Archway. His time with Ylva had taught him very little. She didn't know where Ella was, and by the sound of it Richard wouldn't have known where to find her either. It wasn't time completely wasted though—Zac had learned that Gabriel was looking for him, and he'd also discovered that he now had a new power. What was it even called? Mind control? Brainwashing? He shuddered at the thought, although the April weather was far from cold. If he could make others do his bidding, then in theory he had no need for money or any other supernatural abilities. He shivered again. That kind of power could be lethal in the wrong hands.

It wasn't until he passed the quaint shopfronts of Highgate Village that Zac realised he was retracing the first steps he and Ella had taken together—but in reverse. If only rewinding time could be that easy. The sight of Waterlow Park made his chest ache, thinking back to his tiny shed and the way Ella had looked at him when she'd realised that he wasn't like her, not yet realising just how different they really were. He passed the green dome of St Joseph's church, the view of central London running hazily along the horizon, then the Whittington Hospital on his right, until he was right back at the beginning. The bus stop where they'd first met.

What was his next step going to be? Zac always had a plan. He never made mistakes. But for the first time in his existence, he had no idea where to start. Would his friend Gabriel know where to find Ella? He'd said he'd been watching over her—but could Zac trust him? And would it lead him back to his mother? He had no idea if she was even alive or if his impulsive decision to end his life had been a silly risk. Was the ability to return to life limited to just him? Until he found Ella, he wouldn't know if his gamble had truly paid off.

He ran his hand through his hair and stopped as his fingers snagged in his matted mane. Well at least he knew what his first step was—a haircut. Across the road from the bus stop was a parade of shops, their fronts tinged grey from exhaust fumes and their window displays old and tired. How different Archway was to Highgate, just a few minutes' walk from each other but miles apart. He ran his eye over the shop frontages. A laundrette, an off-licence, a fried chicken takeaway, a corner shop, and a tattoo place.

He crossed the road and peered into the grimy window of the tattooists, its display photos faded to shades of grey and green. His reflection stared back at him mockingly. Someone else was looking at him too—a young woman. She was standing behind the counter, her hair cropped short and dyed a turquoise blue. Zac smiled. Maybe he wasn't quite ready for a hairstyle as dramatic as hers, but there was no reason why he couldn't make a few adjustments. His appearance hadn't changed in two thousand years, and perhaps it was time to celebrate his newfound freedom with a new look. He grinned, not caring who saw, feeling positive for the first time since he'd left that airless tomb.

• • • • •

She flinched as he ran his finger over the ugly raised scar slashing her cheek in half.

'It's nothing,' she said, turning her head away from him. 'I was born with it.'

He turned her face until she was staring straight into his eyes. Her throat constricted as she swallowed.

'What happened?' he asked again.

'Love happened.'

Zac rubbed his thumb gently over her cheek, and this time she didn't move.

'Tell me,' he said.

Zac was no stranger to tales of love and loss, he had experienced plenty of both over the years, but even his own heart dipped a little as she told him her story. A pretty English backpacker had stolen her heart, stuffed it still beating and bloody into her bag and returned to London as if her trinket was nothing more than a cheap souvenir.

'Charlie was the most beautiful, vibrant, fun girl I'd ever met,' she told Zac. 'I promised her that I would save up and come to London one day. That we would be together again. She laughed at me, but I did it. I left my dusty little town and came to London. This huge city was crazier than anything I'd ever imagined, but I eventually tracked her down. She was with a guy in a pub. A *man!* We argued, me, her, him, a bouncer. Someone threw a bottle, and then this happened.' She pointed at her face. Zac was still stroking his fingers across her cheek, but she didn't seem to notice.

'It's been over a year now, and I never saw Charlie again. I had no travel insurance and no way to pay for any treatment, so I left the cut to heal itself. I found a tiny room to rent above this shitty tattoo shop, and the owner agreed to hire me. I've been trying to figure out what to do with my life since then. Although with this face, I don't stand a chance of finding a decent job…let alone the girl of my dreams.'

Zac removed his hand from her cheek and smiled.

'You're beautiful.'

'No, I'm not. The scar made a mess of my face.'

'What scar?'

Tara stepped out from behind the counter and walked over to the full-length mirror by the door. She stared and stared, her eyes unable to believe her reflection as silent tears rolled down her perfect cheeks. Her scar was gone.

'How did you...?'

Zac was still smiling.

'You look happier now.'

'Who are you?'

The question remained unanswered, suspended like a light mist between them, as he joined her at the mirror. Relief was etched across his tired face; relief that he'd retained his ability to heal others as well as himself. He hadn't liked controlling her mind or using her as his guinea pig, but he'd at least been able to change her life for the better. Healing others had been one of the many things he'd been forbidden to do before, back when he was in constant fear of altering people's life paths. But now he no longer cared if his actions threw fate's plans off course. He just wanted to help. Tara's reflection stared back at him; a lot of his own pain was there in her eyes.

'Do you know how it feels to be searching and hiding at the same time?' he asked. 'To hate your differences but also be excited by the possibilities they hold?'

She nodded. He cocked his head to one side, the muscles in his jaw twitching.

'I thought you would. That's why I came into the shop and why I wanted to help you. When I saw you through the window earlier, your scar, I knew it would have a story. You didn't deserve to lose out on love, Tara, but sometimes love isn't enough...life takes over. I've been given a second chance, which is why I wanted to give you a fresh start, too. It's time we take back control and go after what really matters. You in?'

No brainwashing spell this time. He was just asking her for help, one desperate person to another, hoping she would trust him and not ask questions.

'Yes, of course. I owe you…I guess. What do you want?'

Zac didn't blame her for being so hesitant and wary of him, but she'd trust him soon enough. He planned to tell her everything. He needed to hear himself say the words that he'd been forbidden to speak for so long.

'I lost something special,' he told her. 'I need you to bring them back.'

'Bring what back?'

'My wings.'

12

'SO, YOU'VE NOT seen her for three years, but you've been in love with her in every one of her lifetimes? I'm guessing you mean that in a figurative sense?'

'No, I mean it literally.'

Tara had been tattooing Zac's back for twelve hours, and during that time he'd done nothing but speak about Ella, now and in her past lives, spanning two thousand years. He could see by the battling expressions on Tara's face that she thought he was crazy, or possibly deluded, but he didn't care. It was the first time he'd been able to speak freely of his past and his love for Ella, and it felt good. Tara understood all about unrequited love, to desire someone who would never love you back with the same intensity. So even though she was probably judging him, she kept her thoughts to herself.

'Sorry. This may sting a little,' she said, her face set in concentration as she focused on his back.

'It's fine.'

12

'SO, YOU'VE NOT seen her for three years, but you've been in love with her in every one of her lifetimes? I'm guessing you mean that in a figurative sense?'

'No, I mean it literally.'

Tara had been tattooing Zac's back for twelve hours, and during that time he'd done nothing but speak about Ella, now and in her past lives, spanning two thousand years. He could see by the battling expressions on Tara's face that she thought he was crazy, or possibly deluded, but he didn't care. It was the first time he'd been able to speak freely of his past and his love for Ella, and it felt good. Tara understood all about unrequited love, to desire someone who would never love you back with the same intensity. So even though she was probably judging him, she kept her thoughts to herself.

'Sorry. This may sting a little,' she said, her face set in concentration as she focused on his back.

'It's fine.'

After having him describe to her in detail exactly what he wanted, Tara had sketched ideas until they settled on an intricate design—large impressive wings arching over his shoulder blades with loose feathers floating down the tops of his arms. There was a mirror in front of him, and he watched her hard at work. With every feather she painted he felt himself return, as if he'd never been away.

'What will you say to Ella when you see her?' Tara asked.

She was humouring him, but he continued anyway.

'No idea. Problem is, I don't know what she's been up to during the last three years. We weren't together that long before I left, so she probably moved on. I've loved her all my life, but I've only known her a very short time.'

'That doesn't make any sense.'

'It was never me she was meant to be with anyway. She should be with her fated love by now. Am I boring you? I apologise for my incessant talking. You're a good listener.'

Tara laughed. 'No worries. I've worked in bars all my life. I'm used to people telling me their problems. So why couldn't you get in touch with her over the last three years?'

'I've not been around.'

'Where have you been?'

'Dead.'

Her eyes widened but she didn't comment.

'Sorry,' he said. 'It's four in the morning, you've not eaten since I came in and I'm forcing you to do this. Maybe I should come back tomorrow?'

Tara switched off the hum of the needle and walked around to face him.

'What you did back there,' she said, pointing to the front of the shop. 'When you asked me to cancel my appointments and I did. That hypnotic trick? You were a prick for doing that—out of order. But tattooing you in exchange for that magic you did on my scar? I'm happy to do that and I'm happy to listen. So stop being a whinging Pom with all your "sorrys" and tell me about Ella.'

Zac gave her a half smile, and she nodded in return.

'I'm scared, Tara. I think that's what it is. Scared that I'll find her and she won't want me anymore.'

She rolled her eyes and switched the machine back on.

'You don't strike me as a pussy, Zac. Toughen up. It doesn't matter what Ella's been up to. As long as she still loves you and understands why you've…been away…then I'm sure she'll take you back. God has a plan, or so they say.'

Zac snorted, a half laugh and a half sneer.

'God is a fallacy. He was made up by man to keep the masses sated. There's no God, Tara.'

'OK. Well, fate then. Let fate decide. Surely you believe in that?'

Zac laughed again.

'I used to. Except fate and destiny, they aren't beliefs; they aren't something you choose to have faith in. They just are. They are the forces that push us forward and that hold us back. Destiny is the lazy man's religion. When it comes to fate, you don't have to do anything to make something happen. You don't even have to pray. All you have to do is wait.'

'Sounds good to me,' Tara said. 'I've never liked the idea that life's a haphazard series of events, not after I met Charlie and felt the pull between us. There has to be a point to everything. I'd started to lose my faith in fate until you walked in here this morning.'

'Why's that?'

She laughed, a small quiet chuckle that matched the delicacy of the flowers tattooed on her arms.

'You looked more broken than I've ever been, but you healed me and not just physically. I can feel something growing inside me now that's been gone a very long time. I don't know what you did to me, but

I feel stronger now, like good things are coming. Hope. That's what it is. You've given me hope.'

He smiled, the guilt from having brainwashed her and Ylva this morning slowly easing.

'Tell me, Zac,' she continued, 'if you don't believe in God and you don't believe in fate, what *do* you believe in?'

He looked down at his lap and was quiet for a long time. What *did* he believe in? When he finally looked up, he saw his blue eyes in the mirror shining as dark as the wings of a bowerbird. He blinked quickly.

'I don't believe in anything anymore. Somebody, a long time ago, said they believed in me. She called me a god, but I don't think she believes in me anymore. I don't even believe in myself. I no longer know what I am.'

Tara put down her tattoo needle and walked to the back of the shop. She opened a cupboard, took out a box of bandages and numbing creams, then retrieved a large bottle of rum from the back.

'Here.' She handed it to Zac. 'You'd be surprised how many big strong men like you need a bit of a pick-me-up in here. Drink it. You're getting maudlin.'

Zac took a swig, groaned, and then took another.

'You're right, Tara. I've been given a second chance. Call it a miracle or luck or magic, but whatever it is, I came back.'

'Exactly! If fate or God can't control you, maybe you're like a glitch in *The Matrix?*'

'I don't understand.'

'Like the film. The idea of life being as insubstantial as a computer game. That some people can see through the illusion and make their own way in life, control it as they see fit. Those that know don't walk *in* the picture, they walk *through* it.'

She was right. Zac stood alone now—no longer governed by the laws of anything or anyone. He was free.

'Yes,' he said under his breath. 'I can do what I want now.'

'Of course you can.' Tara dabbed the excess ink off his arm and stepped back, admiring her work. 'And you're all done.'

Zac stood up and rolled his shoulders. Walking slowly toward the full-length mirror, he turned to the side, marvelling at the way Tara had created each individual feather. Every single one was unique and shaded in hues of blue, grey and black. He didn't recognise the man before him. His long hair used to soften his features, but now he looked hard, angular and older. His jaw was stronger and more prominent, and his eyes, no longer framed by soft dark curls, shone with a determination that scared even him. He turned from side to side, studying the images on his back from every angle.

'It's a work of art.'

Tara's face beamed in response. 'Lift up your arms,' she said, holding a long mirror up behind him so he could see the full effect in the reflection before him. He did as he was told and gasped as the muscles in his back rippled and his wings transformed into those of a majestic angel taking flight—each feather splayed over the shoulder blades, cascading under his arms and across his rib cage.

His eyes shone silver with gratitude. She had no idea what she'd returned to him.

'Thank you. This is a masterpiece.'

'It's the least I could do. You gave me back my life,' she said, touching her face. 'I don't think I could ever thank you enough, Zac.'

'In that case, want to do me a little favour?'

He rested his hand on her shoulder briefly and then left the room, returning a moment later with a pen and a scrap of paper. In his hand was one of the many flyers littering the coffee table at the front of the shop. This one listed London attractions on one side and a Tube map on the other. Zac ripped it in half and drew a circle on the map side as well as a strange 'I' symbol.

'Are you familiar with a bar called Indigo in Camden?' he asked her.

She shook her head. 'I don't know anywhere in London that isn't a five-minute walk from this crappy shop.'

'Don't worry, I'll give you directions. I would really appreciate it if you could deliver this tomorrow night to a man that works there.' Zac handed her the piece of paper and folded his hand over hers. 'Can you do that?'

Tara nodded. He wasn't forcing her this time, but she was still willing.

'Who do I ask for?'

'Gabriel. He also goes by the name of Gabe. He's my only true friend. He'll be at Indigo from nine o'clock in the evening, but you mustn't show any fear or apprehension; this could be the difference between me getting help or getting killed.'

'Killed? Look, I owe you, but I don't want to get involved in anything dodgy. If this is about guns or drugs or…'

'No, Tara, this is just about love and fate. That's all.'

'You promise it's that straightforward? I just go to a bar and hand over a piece of paper?'

'Yes,' he said. 'But I think I may need to perform that hypnosis thing on you again before I leave to make sure you get it right. To make sure you are calm and don't raise suspicion. Do you give me permission?'

She nodded.

'Thank you. Here,' he said, reaching into his pocket and handing her a handful of crumpled bills. 'Some of it is sterling and some of it is in euros. I hope it's enough to pay for the tattoo.'

Tara counted it, ironing out the scrunched-up notes on the tattoo bed, her mouth moving silently as she added it up.

'This is way too much; it's more than double what your wings cost.'

'Keep it. I don't need money,' he said.

She raised her eyebrows and shrugged.

'Thanks. So, what are you up to now?'

It was Zac's turn to shrug.

'Not a lot. I need to find a hotel room and get a phone so I can call you later and check how you got on at the bar. I should probably grab some dinner too,' he said, looking at the clock on the wall. 'Breakfast, not dinner. I can't believe it's nearly morning.'

Tara pointed at the plastic bags on the floor filled with the food she'd bought earlier. Then she pointed at the bottle of rum on the counter.

'I'm in no rush to go home. Keep me company and we'll eat shit food and get drunk until the sun comes up. You can tell me more stories.'

Zac grinned and sat up on the tattoo bed.

'You're not bored with me talking about Ella?'

'Nope. Whoever this girl is, she's one lucky lady. I hope you find her. You got any other stories about amazing women?'

'Yes,' Zac said, smiling as he thought of his mother. 'I'll tell you a tale about a beautiful enchantress who once ruled the world until an evil winged demon took away her son and left her for dead. But she never gave up searching for her boy.'

'That sounds like an incredible story,' Tara said.

'It is, but I don't know the ending yet. I'm hoping it's a happy one.'

13

IT WAS EVENING and everything in the room was bathed in a pale pink glow. Sebastian had no idea where he was, yet again, and he was quickly tiring of waking up in unfamiliar surroundings. The room was round, and he was lying on a bed draped with brightly coloured scarves. The walls and ceiling were made of cream canvas with wooden poles holding up the sides, and it tapered into a point in its centre. Fairy lights were strung around its beams, and there were old Moroccan rugs on the sandy floor. The air was hot and dry, but there were no windows or fans in the room.

He'd been dying in the desert, but someone had rescued him. A woman. Had she brought him here?

He sat up and tentatively touched his face, relieved to find that his hands now worked and his face was no longer bloody or swollen. There was a thick metallic taste in his mouth and pictures flashed before him; long dark hair, the clinking of glass beads and blood…lots of blood running from a gaping wound and down a woman's breasts. Blood in his mouth, a thick, cloying warmth as it trickled down his throat. The sickly stickiness of it as it smeared over his cheeks and dried on his chin. Had it been a dream? A nightmare?

There was a faint sound of rhythmic sighing and, through the gauze of the mosquito net surrounding him, he could see the blurred shape of another bed in the room. He parted the net and slowly stood, aware he was clothed in unfamiliar cotton yoga trousers and a loose top.

Crossing the room he saw her, the woman from his visions. She was propped up on a mountain of brightly coloured silk cushions on a large bed. Her breasts were uncovered, and around her neck she wore the dozens of glass beads he'd remembered. Her dark hair tumbled over her shoulders, and her head was thrown back, eyes closed, throat exposed as if waiting for the blade of a knife. He couldn't see any sign of where the bleeding wound had been. Sebastian followed the contours of her body down to her long pleated skirt adorned with tiny mirrors along the hem. She was grasping at something beneath the fabric. It was a head, the shaven head of a naked young woman whose hungry groans were getting faster and faster as the dark-haired woman pushed her face deeper between her legs.

Sebastian padded silently across the room until he was beside the bed, scared of interrupting them, the familiar warmth of arousal creeping upon him. He shouldn't be there; it was wrong to watch. He didn't know these women, and he had no idea where he was.

'Come closer.'

The bare-chested woman was looking at him with eyes half closed in sleepy euphoria. Her hips writhed as she moaned; her eyes locked onto his.

'I need to talk to you,' she said. 'I won't be long.'

She pushed the woman's head down harder, allowing the girl's hands to slide up her torso to her breasts, her eyes still focused on Sebastian's as he walked toward the bed. He couldn't take his eyes off the two women. Was she expecting him to do something? Join in? He could feel himself stiffen now that he was beside them; he didn't want them to stop. The woman's breathing was getting faster now, and the girl removed her hands from the woman's chest and returned them beneath her skirt. The dark-haired woman gave Sebastian a slow smile and opened her mouth slightly, running her tongue along her lips. Suddenly, she threw back her head and a low cry of ecstasy coursed through her body, hips bucking and fingers entangling in her own thick curls. She laid back on the bed and laughed, reaching out to stroke the side of Sebastian's leg.

The girl emerged, her pupils black with passion and her lips glistening wet. She didn't acknowledge Sebastian, as if having a stranger watch them was nothing unusual. She wiped her face on the woman's long skirt and climbed up her lover's body, kissing and licking her breasts until she reached her mouth, but the dark-haired woman shook her head.

'That will be enough for today.'

The girl picked up a long dress from the floor, slipped it over her head and nodded at the woman on the bed.

'Thank you,' she said, exiting through a curtain in the side of the tent. A shaft of sunlight temporarily illuminated the room, and then Sebastian and the woman were once again plunged in the semi-glow of evening.

'Sit down,' she said to him, straightening her skirt and plumping the cushions up beside her. 'We have already met. Do you remember me?'

He nodded but didn't move.

'I presume you are wondering where you are and why you are here?'

He nodded again.

'Then stop standing there like a mute idiot and sit down. I won't ask again.'

'I'm sorry if I disturbed you and your girlfriend,' he answered, sitting beside her.

She gave a small laugh. 'She isn't my girlfriend. I don't even know her name. Did you like her?'

Sebastian nodded.

'And do you like me?'

Sebastian nodded again. She ran her hand up his leg and let it rest on his groin, raising her eyebrows at his obvious excitement.

'I saved your life, you know. You've been asleep for three days.'

He attempted to piece together the fragments of memory that were slowly returning. Had he really drunk this woman's blood? He swallowed down the bile rising in his throat. Fear and uncertainty battled with the delicious heat emanating from her touch.

'How did you rescue me?'

'I have my ways,' she said, smiling and gently squeezing him. 'So, now that you are no longer dying, you have to do something for me.'

'What?'

The woman was beautiful, although at least fifteen years older than any of the schoolgirls he normally desired.

'I need you to take me to your stepsister,' she said.

'My sister? Ella?'

'Is that her name this time? How pretty.'

'What do you want with her?'

She positioned herself so that she was sitting behind him. Her lips were by his ear, her hard nipples brushed against his back, and he could feel the heat from her naked crotch burning through the thin cotton of his trousers. She pulled at the string around his waist and loosened his waistband. Reaching inside, she ran her hand along his hardness and spoke softly in his ear.

'I need her, Sebastian. I've been searching for someone for a very long time, and she is the only one that can lead me to him.'

Her hand moved over him, long strokes getting faster and faster until he could no longer think clearly. How did this woman know about Ella?

'What about my sister? Do you need her as well?'

His mind was foggy, and her grasp was getting tighter. She was talking about Ella. Thinking of his stepsister as the woman touched him made his breathing ragged.

'No. I don't care about Ella,' she said. 'She's all yours. You can do what you want with her when I'm done.'

'When you're done?'

'Yes, we have unfinished business.'

He had no idea where his sister was. All he knew was that if he ever saw that wanton whore again, he would kill her. Fuck her first and then kill her. If it hadn't been for that bitch, he'd still have his life, his family, his friends, and his secrets. He'd feel her squirm beneath him once more, and then he'd watch her take her last breath—but first he had to figure out who the hell this strange woman was.

'Stop, I can't think…you're…'

'You want me to stop, Sebastian? Really?'

She was getting faster now, her breathing hot in his ear. Her other hand reached up beneath his top, her fingers trailing over his chest as she groaned softly into his neck. He couldn't hold back the release any longer and cried out as he succumbed to her touch.

'OK, yes, I'll help you.'

She wiped her hands on his trousers and stretched out on the bed.

'Good.'

A bell sat on a carved wooden table beside her. She rang it and a young man, wearing nothing but loose cotton trousers, entered the room. He walked up to her and placed a tender kiss on her lips.

'Yes?'

'Show Sebastian where the showers are and get him fresh clothes. Feed him, give him whatever he wants, and then bring him back to me. We are not to be disturbed.'

The man nodded and signalled for Sebastian to follow him. He did as he was told. She didn't seem like the kind of woman that you said no to.

14

IT DIDN'T TAKE Sebastian long to discover he was in a former yoga retreat, a collection of Bedouin tents in the middle of the Sahara Desert. This was no secret; the other people in the camp were happy to tell him all about it. He was sitting at a rough wooden table beneath the shade of a tarpaulin. Beside him sat the man who'd brought him clean clothes, and opposite him was the shaven-haired girl and two other women. One was in her fifties with dreadlocks and a ring in her nose; the other was younger with dark skin and a rough accent he couldn't place.

'She just appeared,' said the older woman after Sebastian had enquired about the mysterious woman. 'We all signed up for a two-week Yoga retreat run by a small tour company in the UK, and we arrived here by camel. It was all very exotic. The next day, she turned up. The yoga teachers,' she pointed at a dishevelled couple talking at the entrance to one of the smaller tents, 'they said she was going to join us, but then we stopped doing any yoga. That was about a month ago. We've all decided to stay—we won't return to our lives until she releases us.'

'Releases you?'

'Oh, it's not like that.' A dark-skinned girl with a serious face handed him an apple and cut slices off another with a small penknife. 'We love her. We all do. We'll do anything for her, and we'll stay here as long as she needs us to.'

The others nodded in unison.

'Do you know her name?' he asked.

They shook their heads.

'Has she spoken to you yet?' the girl with the shaved head asked.

'Yes, actually, we did a bit more than speak,' Sebastian answered, taking a bite out of the apple before looking around him. Everyone was in a stupefied state with beatific smiles on their faces, their actions slow and languid. He had been in some strange places while on the run the last three years, but none had made him feel as uneasy as this place.

'So, you've been in the middle of the desert for a month? Where do you get your fresh water and food?'

They shrugged and smiled.

'What do you do all day?'

'Whatever she needs us to do,' the older woman replied, pushing her dreadlocks back from her face. 'Tarquin here,' she said, nodding at the man beside him, 'he took one of the camels out to pick you up three days ago. You were in a bad state, but she healed you. She has healed us all, one way or another.'

'She made me drink her blood,' Sebastian said.

They stared back at him blankly.

'Don't you find that strange? I was about to die and then I drank her *blood* and went to sleep. When I woke up, I was fine. In fact, I'm more than fine. I feel amazing. Who *is* this woman?'

They all smiled at him, but nobody answered. He grabbed another bottle of water and stood up.

'Fine. I'll find out myself.'

• • • • •

There were five tents in the compound positioned in a circle. At their centre was a large space covered with rugs, with dozens of lanterns dotted around the perimeter. A firepit filled with dry wood was at the far end, away from where everybody slept, and three camels stood tied up in the shade behind the largest tent. Beyond that, there was nothing, no cars or toilets or electrical devices. Sebastian had showered in an outdoor contraption constructed of hoses and a cold-water tank. There was no way out of the compound and nowhere to go. He quickly realised he was completely alone except for a group of stupefied people and a never-ending expanse of sand and sky.

The woman was in the largest tent. He stood in the doorway and watched her apply red lipstick to her full lips. No longer half naked, she'd taken off her beaded necklaces and now wore a short vest top and a similar skirt as before. He wondered whether she was wearing any underwear this time. He doubted it. She was watching him in the reflection of the dressing table mirror.

'Come in. Close the door.'

He lowered the flap of canvas so they couldn't be seen from outside.

'You're dressed now; that's good,' he said.

'That's not what most people tell me.'

She didn't turn to look at him. Instead, she put in long earrings and tied her hair up in a bright silk scarf.

'Who are you?' he asked.

'I'm Luci.'

He took a bite of his apple. She remained with her back to him.

'Three days ago, I was dying in the desert. Today, I feel healthier and stronger than I have ever felt in my life. Look!' He lifted his top. 'I have a six-pack. How is that possible? Those weirdos out there said *you* healed me and made me like this. Is it true?'

'Yes.'

'How?'

'My blood, Sebastian. I healed you by feeding you my blood.'

'Like a vampire?'

Luci laughed and turned to face him. Her lipstick shone bright red and Sebastian felt sick at the thought of her blood in his mouth. He took another bite of apple to mask the taste of iron that still lingered.

'Do you believe in vampires, Sebastian?'

'No, of course not.'

'Good, because they aren't real.'

'So why did you feed me your blood?'

She shrugged. 'I can also heal with my hands.'

'Why didn't you?'

'Because I…' She stopped, her mouth remaining open while she rethought what she was going to say. 'Because I have a certain flare for the dramatic.'

She tightened the scarf around her head and walked to the bed, collecting more scarves and adding them to a basket on the floor.

'What's the matter with those people out there?' he asked.

'Nothing.'

'Don't lie to me! Are they high or something? This place is creeping me out. Is this a cult? It's like they're under your spell.'

'Do you believe in magic, Sebastian?'

'Of course not.'

'I've been called a witch in my time, you know. Do you think I'm a witch?'

'Look, if you don't want to answer my questions, then fine. I don't have to stay here. I'm not your bloody prisoner.'

Luci blinked slowly and gave a tiny smile.

'If you want to go, be my guest.'

He flung open the canvas door and stared out over arid sand dunes. The sun was now a puddle of orange on the horizon, and the only light visible was from the firepit that had been recently lit. The wind was picking up and howling through the tents. Sebastian had nowhere to go and no way of getting there. He threw his apple as hard as he could through the gap in the tent and it ricocheted against the wooden table where the others were still sitting. Not one of them blinked as it smashed into tiny pieces.

'I'm not like you, and I'm not like them,' Luci said, pulling the tent flap down again. She motioned for him to sit on the bed, but he shook his head. 'Are you scared, Sebastian?'

He shook his head again.

'Pity. You should be. Nobody here is under a spell; they simply choose to serve me. I find people gravitate toward darkness.'

'Well, you won't see me doing that.'

'That's because your heart is darker than mine.' Luci swayed a little as she spoke, like a cobra ready to pounce. 'Tell me where Ella is.'

'I haven't seen her in years. Why do you need her?'

Walking around him, Luci ran her finger up the back of his neck. He shivered. She moved like an underwater dancer.

'I'm searching for my son. Ella knows him.'

'Why would Ella know a child?'

'My boy is no child.'

'How old is he then? He can't be older than ten or twelve. You're not that old yourself.'

She smiled.

'Oh Sebastian, how little you know. I'm older than the moon.'

Her beauty was beguiling, and it unnerved him. He wanted to run his tongue over her scarlet lips and feel his fingers slip inside her again. He also wanted to get as far away from her as possible.

'I don't understand.'

'My son is in love with your stepsister. He has been for two thousand years. If I find her, I will find him.'

Zac? Sebastian felt the colour drain from his face. This was how it had all begun, the day he'd been attacked by that monster. It was because of Zac that he'd been running for so long. Three years of fear and nightmares, all that time knowing the world—a place he had once been so sure he understood—contained monsters like Zac, was slowly shifting the ground beneath his feet. A world of beings so powerful they could lift a man off the ground with their mind. And she was one of them?

The air inside the tent was getting thinner. He couldn't breathe. He pulled at the neck of his T-shirt, but it didn't help. He'd been talking of Zac and his magic the night he'd been beaten and left to die in the desert. Did Luci have a part in that? If she was really Zac's mother, then she was right—he should be scared. Very scared.

'Your son is Zac?'

'Is that what he calls himself in this world? Yes, Zadkiel's my boy. I want him back.'

Sebastian was not getting involved in this. It was dangerous. He'd already felt the force of Zac's anger; he wasn't going to seek him out again.

'I can't help you,' he said, turning away from her and attempting to lift the canvas door again. It was now as heavy as lead. Suddenly, he was thrown to the ground, his face hitting the ornate rug below with a thud. He was dragged backwards by an invisible force until he found himself at Luci's feet. She looked down at him, her face radiant in its stony glory.

'Don't fuck with me, Sebastian. Sit down.'

He felt himself being pulled into a standing position by his waist as the chair from the dressing table hurtled toward him, slamming into the back of his knees until he was sitting in it. One by one, Luci's silk scarves wound their way out of the basket on the ground and slithered toward him like multicoloured serpents. Climbing up his legs, they snaked up his body and then wrapped themselves around his wrists and ankles until he was secured to the chair. Luci's smile shone blood red.

'You have no idea who I am, do you?'

Sebastian shook his head.

'We met a long time ago.'

'When we were children?' he stuttered.

'No. When you were Sabinus, a Roman soldier in Tuscany.'

What the hell was she talking about? She was definitely one of them, a monster like Zac. He had to free himself from the chair and get the hell out of there.

'You're saying we met in a *past life*? Is that what this is about? What has that got to do with Ella and Zac?'

'I have whisperers all around the world. They tell me what they hear. They watch people and listen—my eyes and my ears. They tell me you talk of winged beings, that you have seen our kind. Two thousand years ago I asked you to help me find my son, but you didn't want to help me back then. This time you *will* do as I say.'

Sebastian closed his eyes, wishing he'd died in that desert and never been found. This woman was even crazier than Zac.

'Two thousand years ago?'

'My son was born in Fiesole, Tuscany, in 25 BC. He is Zadkiel, the Path Keeper, Angel of Mercy. And I'm his mother.'

Angel of Mercy? Zac was an *angel?* Sebastian thought back to the day Ella's boyfriend had pinned him to the ceiling without touching him before growing wings and disappearing. He hadn't wanted to believe what he'd seen, but it was clear the guy wasn't normal. He wasn't even human. But an angel? There was nothing angelic about the way he'd kissed his sister! Sebastian tried to move his arms, but the scarves only wound around him tighter.

'If witches and vampires don't exist, then neither do angels. This is ridiculous. How could you have given birth to an angel thousands of years ago?'

Luci leant in closer, her breath warm on his cheek.

'Because I'm the original fallen angel, Sebastian.'

He swallowed as an icy chill ran down his spine. Surely, she didn't mean she was…

'I was there before everything,' she continued. 'I brought light to your world and life to your souls. After Zadkiel was born, I had my wings ripped out by his father and was left for dead. Except I quickly learned that archangels cannot die—instead, we stay in your world forever.' She laughed softly. 'But his father didn't know that. The realm doesn't know I'm still alive.'

Realm? Sebastian cleared his throat, unsure if he wanted to know the answer to the question forming on his lips.

'Who's Zac's father?'

A shadow passed over her face. 'Mikhael, the most powerful angel there is. You probably know him as Archangel Michael. Evil bastard.'

If Sebastian hadn't been strapped to a chair by magically controlled serpent scarves, he would have scoffed at what Luci was telling him. Instead, he was terrified.

'So, you're the original fallen angel?'

Luci smiled and nodded, her mouth as scarlet as a bloody gaping wound.

He knew exactly who she was. He'd been to Sunday school and read the Bible. He'd studied works by Blake, Dante, and Milton, and he'd seen their ancient paintings and read their gory descriptions of hell and purgatory. He tried to keep his voice from shaking as he uttered three terrifying words.

'You're the Devil?'

Luci rolled her eyes.

'I wish people would stop calling me that. The Devil, Satan, Beelzebub. Those words were invented by Mikhael.' She spat out his name like he was poison on her lips. 'I was never any different than the rest of them. I just said "no" to him.'

'So, you're not evil?'

She threw her arms in the air and sent Sebastian's chair flying backwards until it hit the bed with a thud. He groaned, and the scarves tightened the more he attempted to move.

'Zadkiel's father always had me described as demented!' she screamed. 'The reason for all the bad things in the world—the antithesis of your make-believe God. Every myth and evil wrongdoer in folklore has been based on me: witches, mummies, vampires. People have seen me rise from the dead, perform magic, and feed humans my blood, so they made up characters that are inhumane. But I'm not against your kind. I *died* to stay on Earth among your people.'

Luci stood very still and stared at Sebastian, her eyes glowing a bright green.

'You'd never believe how much Mikhael once loved me, but as soon as I defied him and decided to stay here with our son, he turned on me and told the world I was bad. See what tainted love can do to a man, Sebastian? Do you see? It makes them dangerous.'

'Why are you telling me this?'

'Because I can. Because people need to know! Anyway, do you think anyone would believe you if you told them?'

Luci was pacing the room, her breasts bouncing up and down beneath her thin cotton top as she waved her arms in the air. Her thick hair swayed in time with her hips. Why was he noticing these things when this woman—this creature—wasn't even human?

Luci stopped, turned to him and put her face close to his, her lips still shiny and dripping in red. Sebastian swallowed. He no longer wanted to do bad things to her.

'I am Lucifer,' she whispered. 'I am the morning star and the bringer of dawn. The ruler of Venus and the angel of light. I am also one very pissed off mother who wants her boy back. Are you going to disobey the maker of all creation? Or are you going to help me?'

Sebastian had no choice. He was about to make a pact with the Devil.

'How far away the stars seem, and how far
Is our first kiss, and ah, how old my heart!'
~ William Butler Yeats, *Ephemera*

PART TWO

ARABELLA MIDDLE OF THE BEGINNING

TUSCANY, ITALY
5 BC

I.

THROUGHOUT MY CHILDHOOD I had often heard the story of the blue-eyed boy. They called him a demon, the magical son of secrets. As a child, I was warned about the bad spirits in the woods and told not to venture further than Fiesole's high walls, or the witches and winged monsters would get me. But, even at that young age, I knew it was impossible for there to be anything worse beyond those stone walls than what already resided within.

The first time I saw him was a hot day. The kind of day that made the insides of my thighs stick and chafe, forcing me to tuck the rough fabric of my tunic between my legs so I could walk without the sting. The air was dead; nothing moved. Even the flies no longer buzzed. Days like those were the longest kind. The sharp, dry grasses scratched my legs as I picked my way through the outskirts of town. I'd made that journey many times before, but this time I didn't intend to turn back. This time I wasn't seeking excitement—I was fleeing from it.

There was a section of the city wall that had been damaged in a storm and was missing some stones. It was easy enough to climb as long as I pulled my skirt up above my thighs and pushed my toes through the gaps in the fallen rubble. I used the elbow of my left arm to hoist myself up, gripping tightly with my right hand. I had long forgotten that I wasn't normal, quickly growing used to the pitying stares and the way other children in my street would flinch when they saw my gnarled, twisted hand. I had been that way since birth.

'You were jinxed by your father's lover,' my mother told me one night after too much wine. *'My punishment for loving that cheating rat was to give birth to a useless daughter.'*

I reached the top of the wall and sat astride it to catch my breath. Perhaps I was imagining it, but the air felt cooler up there, like there was the possibility of hope and freedom that I was yet to experience. Reaching for the cloth sack around my waist I pulled out a chunk of bread and a tough piece of rabbit my mother had cooked three days before. She never asked me where I found the animals, and I never told her, although they were rarely fat enough to feed her and my younger brother for more than a day or two.

I chewed slowly, wishing I'd brought some water with me, and kicked the heels of my feet against the wall. The houses on this side of town were made from straw and wood, built out of the very land that sustained them. There were a few stone buildings and walls that jutted out of the ground, but it was mainly round huts with thatched roofs. There was no one to be seen. Most women had already left for the market or were resting inside their homes after lunch away from the heat, preparing themselves for an afternoon's work. Even the fields, normally busy with farmhands, were unusually empty. My mouth was so dry it was a struggle to swallow my bread. I clambered off the wall and headed toward a run-down shepherd's hut, hoping to find a well nearby. In the distance, I could hear goats bleating, but the thick blanket of sunshine beating down upon my aching head was too blinding to allow me a good view of what lay beyond the small holding. I followed the sound of the animals, hoping they would lead me to a stream.

Instead they led me to my destiny.

The scent of wild jasmine clung to my clothes as I pushed through shrubs and ducked under a wooden fence toward the dilapidated hut. Sitting on the ground with his back against its rough wall was a boy chewing on a piece of straw that bobbed up and down between his lips. He was a little older than me, perhaps eighteen or twenty; I wasn't very good at telling people's ages. I didn't even know my own age, but I had started my bleeds three winters ago, so I knew I was already a woman.

I crouched behind a large lavender plant and stared at him, my heart hammering inside my ribcage. I recognised him straightaway as the one the townsfolk spoke of, the demon boy. Even though he was at least ten meters away, I could see his eyes shining like moonlight on still water—the eyes I'd heard didn't belong to any man. He was sitting against the low stone building, moving his head from side to side as he hummed a tune, the sunlight making those feared eyes of his glitter a sapphire blue. As he hummed, he moved his hands up and down as if he were instructing the grasses, the birds and the trees to join in with his song. I followed the line of his bare arm to his fingertips and up to the clear skies. And that's when I saw them—flying goats. Five of them, with mottled brown on white markings, hovering high above the ground. Their hooves paddled in tiny motions, up and down, searching for the dry grass that belonged beneath their feet. They looked down at the ground far below them in disbelief, their straight mouths moving from side to side as they chewed and pondered their predicament.

I gasped. The boy turned his head in the direction of the lavender bush, and immediately the goats plummeted to the ground. Realising his error, he lifted them up with a swipe of his hand moments before they hit the ground, and then he set them down gently on the grass. As soon as their hooves touched the ground, they ran bleating in the opposite direction, their spindly legs shaking and slipping beneath them.

I held my breath and waited for the boy to settle back down again and continue watching his herd. Instead he stood up with a frown, brushed the red earth from his behind, and looked around him. His shoulders were broad, and his rough tunic had ripped a little beneath his arms where he'd outgrown it. His hair, lightly curled and already damp from the midday heat, stopped just above his shoulders, and his bare arms and legs were strong and brown from the sun. He took a step closer to the fence and stood towering over me, casting a shadow over the lavender bush and bathing me in ice. My face was now level with his waist. He wore a leather belt that held a small knife and a money pouch. The pouch was empty. His hands were working man's hands, large and calloused, but his nails were cut neatly. On his wrist, he wore a frayed bracelet made from knotted cloth.

I still hadn't taken a breath, and my head felt so light it threatened to float away from my shoulders. What would he do if he caught me? Would he throw me through the air like his flying goats?

I watched as his face softened, his eyes widened, and a small smile played on his lips. Satisfied, he returned to the hut wall, placed another piece of straw in his mouth and sat down to resume his humming. The goats were now huddled at the back of the field beneath an olive tree, glancing at him warily with their yellow sideways eyes. He reached beneath a woollen rug at his side, took out a bottle made of animal skin and drank from it.

'Want some?' he said, staring straight ahead.

Who was he talking to? His animals? I'd never much liked goats, with their strange mouths and demonic eyes. There was no one around but the boy and I—we were completely alone. My breaths came in shallow bursts barely deep enough to fill my lungs. I wanted to run away but I couldn't move, couldn't breathe, and I couldn't take my eyes off the blue-eyed demon.

He turned his head in my direction and spoke again.

'Are you thirsty?'

I tried to swallow but my throat was too dry and my tongue, which seemed to have swollen to double its size, felt like it was made of wood. He began pouring water into his mouth from a great height, letting it dribble down the side of his jaw until it disappeared down his neck and into his hair. Was he teasing me? I still didn't dare move.

'Come! Stop hiding behind that plant and join me. I know you need water.'

Would he hurt me if I didn't obey? I stood up slowly, squinting as the sun hit me in the face. I shielded my eyes with my good hand, my sack of belongings hanging off the crook of my other arm. I kept my gaze fixed on my broken sandals and focused on the flapping sound they made upon the parched earth until I reached him.

'Sit, it's shady here. You're tired.' He passed me the bottle without looking at me and then reached back under his blanket and produced a green pear, which he rolled along the ground until it hit my foot. 'Sit.'

I did as I was told and brought the animal skin to my lips, groaning with pleasure as the cool water worked its way down into my stomach. I then bit into the pear, savouring the crunching sound it made, not even stopping to wipe away the sticky juices that dribbled down my chin. I'd eaten nothing but stale bread and a handful of cold rabbit in three days, and the sweetness of the fruit was almost too much to bear. I mumbled my thanks but kept my eyes focused on the goats at the end of the field. I dared not look at him. I'd seen the magic he could do, and I'd heard of the dangerous things that could happen if you made eye contact with him.

Legend had it that the boy had been born to a witch; a beautiful, evil woman who would entice the villagers' husbands with her beguiling ways. They said she possessed healing powers that people would pay all their gold to receive. She'd been both feared and revered, as was her illegitimate child. He was never allowed to play with the other children and had remained by his mother's side, or firmly clasped to her bosom, day and night. The story I'd heard was that the two lived an undisturbed life, alone in the woods, until one day a giant winged god arrived and whisked the witch away, leaving behind her bastard demon child. The boy had walked the town for days, crying and begging for food, searching for his mother, until an elderly shepherd who had no family of his own took pity on him and gave him shelter. And there the boy stayed, wandering the countryside with his goats years after the shepherd had died, never once venturing into town.

I wasn't one for fantastical fables—but I wasn't one for taking risks either.

'Why are you scared?' he asked.

I could see out of the corner of my eye that he was facing me, but I directed my gaze at what was left of the pear in my hand.

'I'm…I…no, I'm fine. Thank you.'

He placed his hand on my arm and I jumped, my breaths shuddering in my chest. I screwed up my eyes and waited for the magic. My teeth squeaked as I clenched my jaw and tensed my body, preparing to take flight.

'Look at me, please. I won't hurt you.'

His voice was barely a whisper, both soft and strong. I opened my eyes and glanced at his hand on my arm. It felt warm and heavy, not the touch one would expect from a demon. I took a deep breath and turned to him. His eyes travelled all over my face, as if searching for the source of my fear and pain. As my breathing returned to normal and my jaw slackened, his gaze finally met mine and a look of relief appeared on his face, making his eyes go from sparkling indigo to the colour of a summer sky. I returned his smile, and he placed his hand back onto his own lap.

'That wasn't so bad, was it?'

I shrugged and smiled again.

'I'm Zadkiel.'

He waited for me to reply, but now that I had finally found the courage to look his way, I was too captivated by him to speak. His face was immaculate. Yes, it was handsome, but it was more than that. It was rare for anyone to reach adulthood without a broken nose, a missing tooth, or at least a scar or two—especially a man who worked the land and lived such a poor life—but Zadkiel's entire body, including his arms and legs, was perfect. Not a mark on him. He was as flawless as one of the bathhouse's frescos of men with perfectly straight noses, olive skin, and wine-red lips. He looked like a god. I could see why women feared him.

'What's your name?' he asked.

I gave my head a little shake.

'Can you tell me why you are here, then?'

I swallowed and tried to find my voice.

'Arabella. My name is Arabella, and I am running away.'

'Where are you going, Arabella?'

I shrugged. 'I don't know. I only planned as far as climbing the city wall, and then I got thirsty and I saw you. I haven't given it much thought beyond this point.'

He nodded, glanced quickly at my lap where my crippled fist lay, and then stared straight ahead. I hid my hand behind my back and followed his gaze over the fields. Some of the braver goats were beginning to leave the shelter of the trees and gingerly make their way back toward us. Zadkiel ignored them and continued to look out over the hazy horizon made up of nothing but red earth, olive trees, and small wooden houses as far as the eye could see. He squinted and stared, the piece of straw bobbing up and down in his mouth, and we stayed like that for a few minutes. Perhaps it was hours. I occasionally took a sip from his bottle and looked over at him. Once or twice our eyes met, but I quickly turned back to the goats. The air began to cool, vibrating with the chatter of cicadas as the day neared to evening.

'I must go,' I said, standing up.

'Where to?'

'I don't know.'

I sat back down. Zadkiel turned his head to one side, his face stony in concentration.

'You can stay here until morning. There is enough hay to sleep on, and I'll make sure you are safe.'

I looked at the hut behind me, the floor littered with goat pellets and its rough walls coated in cobwebs. Then I thought of my own warm bed that I shared with my mother and brother. I thought of the stories I told him every night to help him sleep, stories about powerful beings and winged horses. I thought of the fireplace where I cooked every morning and evening, and the small garden where I tended my vegetables. It was a tedious life, one I was tired of living, but did I hate it enough to abandon those I loved?

'I think I'll go home.'

Zadkiel nodded and returned to staring out over the fields. I stood up again, taking my time collecting my sack and making sure nothing had fallen out. There was so much I wanted to ask him about the legend that was his childhood—about the magic I'd watched him perform with the goats and the strange colour of his eyes and why he kept himself hidden—but I didn't dare. As I turned away, he reached out for my arm and I jumped.

'Arabella, will you return?'

His tunic was the same colour as the earth on which he sat. Zadkiel was as much a part of the landscape as the dry fields, the stones, and the trees. He was dark and still; only his bright blue eyes remained incongruous, too unnatural to belong in the arid Tuscan hills. I crouched down so we were level again.

'Zadkiel, are you always here on your own?'

He nodded. 'Some days I take the goats to new pastures and spend a few weeks roaming, but this is where I return. There's also a man that I sell the goats' milk to; he makes cheese and sometimes takes a young goat or two for meat, but this is my life. It's very peaceful.' He cocked his head to the side. 'I'm sensing you may need some peace in your life.'

I watched his beautiful mouth as he spoke, his words soft and gentle like the rustle of the tall grasses around us. He was right. Running away wouldn't have helped me—I just needed to breathe again. I needed to be able to empty my mind and not worry about when we would next eat, what our neighbours were saying about my mother, or what would become of my brother if I had to go away to work.

'I do,' I said.

I felt shy suddenly, more so than when we'd met hours earlier. He nodded and looked away, but he was smiling—a large smile that lit up his whole face and made the evening seem like morning again.

I ran all the way home, my steps lighter and my limbs like liquid, vowing that as soon as it was light the next day, I would escape back to the blue-eyed boy.

II.

As I clambered back over the wall and ran through the dark streets leading me home, I constructed a story about where I'd been and why I was late. I repeated it like a mantra in my head until I was certain I could say it with conviction.

I've been out hunting. I followed a large hare, but I got lost. I fell asleep, and when I awoke it was already dark and the hare had gone.

I wasn't sure my mother would believe me, but I had no choice. If I told her the truth about running away and spending the day doing nothing, I'd be beaten. Neither did I want her nor anyone else knowing about Zadkiel. He was my special secret. My private escape.

Home was one of many stone dwellings in a cobbled street on the outskirts of town. There was no moon that night, and I had to feel my way along the narrow alleyways until I reached the front door. I expected my house to also be in darkness, but a candle burned in the bedroom, a dull orange glow like a beacon…or a warning.

I let myself in and stumbled over something in the doorway. My brother, curled up in a tight ball on the sandy floor, covered in an old tunic of mine. It was a humid night and the remains of some stale bread and a half-eaten apple laid beside him. He mumbled in his sleep and rolled over as I moved him away from the door. I headed for the bedroom we all shared, but my mother wasn't alone. Before I reached the door, I heard soft thuds followed by the telltale grunts that had haunted my dreams for years. Bile rose in my throat and I swallowed it down, sharp and bitter. I'd told her she didn't have to do that anymore, that I'd find us food and work. I should have tried harder; I shouldn't have been standing there empty-handed. The grunts got louder and faster and were followed by her cries and gasps, as familiar to me as the gentle snore of my little brother, who thankfully never awoke when mother had visitors. I stepped back outside and sat with my back against the house to wait. It never took long.

Whoever the man was didn't see me as he erupted out of the front door and into the warm night air. He held out his arm to steady himself against the wall as he headed in the direction of town and the taverns that never closed. I could tell by his sway that he was already drunk and, now that he'd got one need out of the way, he was on his way to satisfy another type of hunger.

'Mamá?'

She was crouched in the corner of our bedroom with an earthenware pot at her feet filled with water, using the hem of her dress to wipe down her body. Her small, drooping breasts shone creamy white in the dull glow of the candle. She kept her eyes down and continued to scrub in the same place, red blotches appearing on her thighs and chest.

'Mamá.' I stood in front of her and she looked up. Her eyes were void of any light. She had been drinking, too, and the tops of her arms and her buttocks were dark red and turning purple. 'Not again! What did he do to you?'

I knew what had happened. It was never enough for these men to empty themselves of their forbidden desires and fill my mother with shame and disgust. They had to make sure she knew who was in charge. They took their anger out on her so they could return to their wives sated and calm.

She nodded at the low table beside the bed where a pile of bronze coins sat.

'Perhaps tomorrow you can go to the market and buy us some meat and eggs? It has been a long time since we ate something you didn't have to catch.'

I gave her a tight smile and bit down on my lower lip. I wouldn't let her see me cry. For too many nights, I'd heard her muffled sobs and prayers to the gods for help and guidance. Sometimes she would accept wine from the men instead of money. She said it softened the edges of her world, but wine couldn't clothe us or pay our rent.

'Mamá, I think maybe it's time I went to work. There is a respectable family in Florence advertising for a maid. I could send you money?'

Her eyes cleared and she looked at me properly, like she could finally see me.

'Arabella, no one will hire a servant with a crippled hand.'

'We need money, Mamá. You can't sell yourself forever.'

'I won't have any daughter of mine be a slave.'

'I wouldn't be. I'm sure I could work in the kitchens where no one would see me, and they would allow me a few hours a week to visit and give you money.' I thought of my brother lying on the floor with an empty stomach and an emptier future. 'Tommaso is smart, Mamá. Maybe he could study a little longer so he doesn't have to toil the land like all the other men around here. Maybe I will meet a rich man in town and we can get out of Fiesole. Maybe…'

'Enough "maybes,"' she said, dabbing at her eyes with the dirty hem of her dress. 'I am the adult, and I will do what I must to bring in money. The women in the bathhouses said soon the soldiers will be marching through Fiesole on their way north. They will be looking for a place to rest and someone to cook for them. I need you here to help. They prefer younger girls.'

There was talk of Rome conquering Germania. I remember as a child watching the legionnaires march through town, their bright red tunics and shining armour easy to spot among the crowds in the street. With soldiers came work and money…but there also came trouble. The soldiers rarely stopped for long, but when they did it was for wine and women.

'Don't look at me like that, Arabella,' she said, straightening the sheets on the bed. 'There will be a town full of strong young men in need of fun; one of them may even be desperate enough to overlook your flaws and take you off my hands. Make yourself beautiful and available.'

• • • • •

I couldn't sleep that night. Even though it was hot in our room, Mamá insisted on closing the shutters on the windows and locking the doors. My brother was fitful beside me and the bed sheets smelled of wine and sweat—male sweat. I lay staring into the darkness, wishing for it to swallow me up. I didn't want the same job as my mother. She said it was easy and quick and good money could be made, but I wanted a normal life. I thought about the blue-eyed boy on the other side of the wall. Who was Zadkiel? *What* was he? I had to see him again and get as far away from this house as possible.

III.

The next morning, I lied to Mamá—I was getting good at saying untruths. As soon as the sun rose, I slipped the coins she had earned into my pocket and told her I would head to the market and return with a chicken or a duck. Then, as soon as she shut the front door, I ran in the opposite direction.

It was another hot day, but this time I'd remembered to fill an animal skin with water. Even though my heart was heavy, I smiled at the thought of seeing Zadkiel again. We had hardly spoken the previous day, but just sitting beside him had filled me with hope. I didn't know how, but he felt like the answer to our problems.

I clambered over the wall again and ran all the way to the shepherd's hut, my heart hammering in my chest. I expected to see him sitting with his back against the wall again, staring at the goats or seeking shade from the nearby cluster of trees, but he wasn't there. In his place was an eerie silence that unnerved me. The goats were gone, and the dry grasses hummed with the deafening sound of crickets. I stood motionless, afraid to take another step. Where was he? And where was his herd?

From inside the stone hut came a solitary bleat of a goat. I walked hesitantly into the enclosure, deeper and deeper into the building, until my eyes grew accustomed to the dark.

It was a massacre! I recoiled at the sight of the rough white walls of the hut streaked in red. There were scarlet splashes on the ceiling and puddles of thick blood pooled at my feet. The smell of hot metal was intoxicating. A goat lay on the ground, the contents of its stomach spilling out onto the dusty earth as a fat fly buzzed around the body, looking for a place to land. A baby goat collapsed beside his dead mother and butted her with his head, bleating in confusion, while two other goats stumbled and fell as they attempted to get back on their feet. All around me lay animals at different stages of despair, and at the back of the hut was Zadkiel, his face wet with blood and his hands dripping red.

I backed away, my legs threatening to collapse beneath me like those of the injured animals. So, it was true what they said about him. He *was* a demon. A murderer like his witch of a mother, not to be trusted.

'Arabella?'

I refused to look in his direction as I edged my way out of the hut.

'Arabella! Stop.'

I said nothing.

'Please,' he cried. 'I don't know what to do.'

The desperation in his voice pulled at something deep within me. I dared myself to glance up. His eyes were not those of a monster, unless monsters wept. As I continued to slowly back away toward daylight, the blue-eyed boy raised his hand and the door behind me slammed shut. We were in complete darkness now, save for the dim glow of sunlight streaming through the shuttered windows.

'You're scaring me, Zadkiel.'

He carefully stepped over the injured goats. Once he reached me, he leant over and opened the door again.

'I'm sorry. I didn't want you to leave.' I flinched at the stench of blood that emanated from him. 'It was the wolves. After you went home yesterday, I left the goats for a few hours while I delivered some milk to the market trader. It was getting dark, but I thought I had enough time to get there and back before I had to move the goats inside. I was wrong. When I returned, there were five wolves and they had struck down every single animal from my herd. I spent the night dragging them back to the safety of the hut. I tried to help them, but it was too late. None of them will survive.' He wiped his bloody face with his arm. 'Look at them! These creatures were good and innocent—they were all I had. My only friends. My livelihood. What do I do?'

It was clear he wasn't lying. It was rare for wolves to venture so close to town but not unheard of. Although I was no lover of goats, neither would I stand by and watch them die. I picked up one of the tiny animals; he looked more like a fluffy rabbit than a goat. He had scratch marks along his back and blood seeping from a wound on his head. I cradled him in my arms just as I had done with Tommaso when he was born. My mother hadn't been interested in my brother from the moment she birthed him. She didn't know who his father was but told our neighbours that Papa often returned home from work trips. I think she'd started to believe her own lies, although nobody else did.

The baby goat rested his head on my shoulder, his stomach rising and falling beneath my hand. His tiny puffs of breath, warm against my neck, were getting shallower by the second.

'There's nothing you can do now, Zadkiel. Perhaps you should simply comfort them.'

He crouched down beside a large white goat who attempted to raise her head. He placed his hands on her stomach and closed his eyes. A tear escaped and ran down his bloody face, like a stream working its way through the burnt earth of the Tuscan hills. I hugged the baby goat to me, thinking of how much I wanted to take Zadkiel in my arms and comfort him too. His grief filled the room as thick as the stench of death.

Then it happened.

The magic.

'Zadkiel, the goat is trying to get up,' I whispered, struggling to get my words out. We watched the animal get to her feet, slowly at first, and then shake her head and scamper out into the field. She ran in circles, bleating and bounding from rock to rock. I laughed and Zadkiel stared at me, his bloody face etched with confusion.

'I think you healed her,' I said.

He looked down at his hands and then at the goat.

'Try again,' I continued excitedly, handing him the baby goat in my arms. It began to kick out and bleat as soon as Zadkiel took hold of him. Then, within less than a minute, the goat wriggled out of his arms and ran out into the field to join his mother. This time Zadkiel laughed.

'I can heal?'

I thought back to the legend of the blue-eyed boy's mother and how according to local history, people from the surrounding villages travelled for days to beg the witch to cure their ailments. Maybe she did. Maybe it was more than a legend.

We set to work, and one by one Zadkiel got the goats back on their feet. Not only were they healed, they appeared shinier and healthier than they'd been before the attack. After a couple hours we were left with just one animal, the goat with its stomach ripped open. I pointed at the poor creature at our feet, my hands and clothes soaked with blood and sweat.

'You can't save them all,' I said to him.

He shook his head and wiped his brow on the crook of his elbow, the only clean part of his body.

'You can have the meat. It's fresh. I will cut it up for you to take home.'

'I can't, Zadkiel. You must sell it. A whole goat is worth a lot of money.'

He gave a sad smile.

'I don't need money, Arabella. But I do owe you my thanks.'

I helped him carry the dead animal to a table at the back of the hut where he cut into its flesh with the small knife he kept in a pouch at his waist. I swept away the blood-soaked earth and opened the remaining windows until the hut no longer smelled of suffering.

He placed the meat in three cloth sacks and handed them to me. There was enough to feed us for weeks if I preserved it well, and maybe there would be some spare meat I could sell to the neighbours.

'We don't need to attract any more wolves,' he said, heading into the woods with the animal's carcass. 'I need to bury this first, and then I will show you the stream so you can wash yourself.'

I looked down at my hands, one dark red with blood and the other a useless gnarled lump. My crippled hand didn't worry me often, but then I rarely spoke to anyone that mattered. The boy hadn't remarked on it yet. Did he pity me? Did he find me repulsive like the other men in town did?

I was still staring at my hands, lost in thought, when he returned.

'You have nothing to worry about, Arabella. You are beautiful.'

It was the first time anyone had called me beautiful. Yet what did Zadkiel know about beauty? I doubted that he'd seen many women on his travels.

'That's kind of you, but it isn't true,' I said, my head bowed. 'I'm a cripple. My mother has always said no one will want me as a wife or a worker. I know she's right.'

Zadkiel went to take my twisted hand but I hid it behind my back. He looked at me. He had a way of holding me down with his gaze that should have scared me but didn't. His eyes were a different shade of blue every time they met mine. This time they were the colour of the sky before a storm.

'The stream is this way,' he said suddenly, pushing his way through a cluster of trees.

It was past midday, and the sun was at its hottest. My frayed sandals were but a few strips of leather held together with thread, and they were rubbing my ankles. I hobbled behind him until we reached a clearing in the woods and a rough wooden fence. Beyond it stood a cottage made of mud and wood with a thatched roof. The garden surrounding it was well maintained, and in the distance I could see fruit trees and a row of vegetables in a neat line. I couldn't see the stream, but I could hear it.

'Is this where you live?' I asked as he held the gate open for me.

'Yes. Most people don't venture this far into the woods. It was where my mother lived; she built this house with her bare hands. When the old shepherd who adopted me died, I decided to search for my childhood home. I have rebuilt it in places and planted a garden. It's good enough for me.'

It was lovely. I thought about what Zadkiel's life must be like, to wake with the sun and tend to his herd, to eat the plants from his own garden and the meat from his own animals. He had no reason to ever leave this clearing. Most townsfolk feared or pitied the legendary demon boy, but I was beginning to envy him.

I followed him into the house. There were three rooms, and the first one had an open fire and a few pots and plates. Another smaller room contained sacks of grain and dried chickpeas alongside terracotta bottles of oil and some dried fruit. The last served as a bedroom. The bed was simple with a wooden frame, a hay base, and cotton sheets topped with animal furs.

'Your home is like a palace,' I said, walking around the rooms and running my hands over the thick glass in the windows—something I'd only ever seen in the larger houses in town.

'I want for very little. Any money I make I spend on my home. At first, I imagined that my mother would come back. I wanted it to be perfect for her. Now, I'm not sure she will ever return.'

'Was the house empty when you found it again?'

'Yes, but it had been ransacked. All that was left was a sack of my childhood belongings that I'd hidden in a hole in the wall after she disappeared. Among them was an old shawl of hers from which I made this.' He lifted up his arm to show me the tattered braid wrapped around his wrist. 'This way I get to keep her close at all times. It's all I have left of her.'

I'd heard some wicked things said about his mother, but I didn't know if Zadkiel was aware of the rumours the village folk had been spreading for years.

'I know what they say about me,' he said, as if reading my mind again. 'There's no need to be polite. I know the people of Fiesole fear me. I, too, have heard the stories about her. My mother the enchanting whore. My mother the witch. My mother the child abandoner.'

'Do you remember her?'

'Not everything. I remember her long hair feeling like silk. I would wrap it around me like a scarf while she carried me on her hip around the garden. I remember the smell of her neck as I fell asleep in her arms at night and…' a muscle twitched in his jaw as he looked out of the window, 'I remember the sound of her laughter when she taught me how to swim in the stream. She loved to watch me have fun. She had such a wonderful laugh. My mother was a powerful woman who wouldn't let anyone cross our threshold, but she wasn't dangerous. She was just a normal loving mother.'

I don't know what possessed me to ask, but the question was out of my mouth before I had time to think it through. 'What happened to her?'

His handsome face fell as he turned it away from me, staring out of the window as if he could see all the way back to the past.

'One day, when I was about six years old, she sent me to the forest to gather firewood. We had plenty already and it had been raining the day before, so I found it a strange request. But I was an obedient child and did as I was told. When I returned, she was no longer there. The house was exactly as I'd left it, but instead of my mother waiting for me with open arms, there was nothing but a few giant feathers caught up in the jasmine plant.' He pointed outside at the green-and-white bush that grew along the perimeter of the cottage. 'I picked them up and hid them in a sack along with a clay doll she'd made me and her old shawl, which I stuffed in a hole beside the fireplace. That's all I remember. After that, I spent weeks searching for her and begging for food until a local shepherd rescued me and took me in.'

'What were the feathers like?'

I didn't know how much he knew or believed about the winged gods taking her away, but I wasn't going to mention that part of the story.

'I have them here somewhere. Ah, here they are.' He reached inside a clay urn and lifted out a handful of feathers. I had never seen a creature with plumage as magnificent as these. They were larger than the feathers of any bird and very full, one full and jet black and the other like a sharp white blade dipped in blood, its tip a deep scarlet. He placed them back inside the urn, a look of sorrow passing like a stormy cloud over his face.

I placed a hand on his cheek; I couldn't help myself. I'd never touched a man's face before and was surprised to feel such smoothness and warmth beneath my fingers. The sensation contrasted wildly with the sharp angles of his cheekbones and jaw. This time I wasn't afraid to stare into his eyes. He smiled and tucked my hair behind my ear.

'You hide away too much, Arabella. Beauty like yours should be allowed to shine.'

My face was burning red while his was still black with dried goat's blood.

'We are both filthy. I can't return home like this,' I said.

He walked into the smallest room and returned with two tunics, handing me one.

'We can bathe in the stream. Wear this while your clothes dry. It shouldn't take long in this heat.'

He picked up a clay bottle of oil from a shelf along with a strigil. I'd seen women in the bathhouse use the same curved metal instrument to scrape themselves clean; it was a luxury I'd never possessed. I followed him outside, but before I had a chance to ask him which part of the stream I should bathe in, he'd already taken off his tunic. He was naked beneath. I'd never seen a naked man before. Considering all the men that frequented our home, my mother always made sure the bedroom door was kept firmly shut.

Men were a mystery to me, although I'd seen plenty of naked women at the local bathhouse where my mother and I visited regularly. She said it was a good place to be seen as respectable members of the community, although I knew it was where she gossiped and discovered which neighbour was unhappy in her marriage. It was easier for her to collect dissatisfied husbands than to hunt for desperate men in the street.

The baths were attended by the men in the morning and the women would follow suit in the afternoons, bathing in their dirty water. It was only the big-hipped, round-stomached bodies of women I saw there. The soft curves of their full bodies were not as enchanting as the sight I was witnessing right now. A woman's body didn't undulate with strength and power such as Zadkiel's back did as he waded into the water. When the stream reached his waist, he used his tunic to scrub his face. It was as if I wasn't there. I stood mesmerised, watching the blood wash off him and his skin slowly reappear like light through the darkness.

'Go ahead and bathe,' he said without turning around. 'I won't look.'

I chose a spot that was partially hidden by a low hanging tree and peeled off my sticky clothes. The stream was cold at first but was also light relief from the relentless heat of the sun. I waited until the water reached my shoulders before rubbing my body clean. I kept my eyes on Zadkiel's back to ensure he didn't turn around, but he kept to his word. My hand moved beneath the water as I rubbed at the sweat and dust that had gathered under my arms. I continued to stare at the boy, the touch of my fingers on my skin feeling illicit as I rubbed my breasts and between my legs, all the while watching him bathe. The muscles of his back rippled like water as he moved, and I wondered what they would feel like beneath my own fingertips. Maybe I could be as perfect as him one day? Perhaps Zadkiel could help me after all?

I rinsed out my tunic and beat it against a nearby rock to get it clean, turning the water around me a light shade of pink, and then hung it up to dry on a nearby branch.

Zadkiel was rubbing his arms with oil now and scraping them clean with the strigil. I called out his name and he turned quickly, as if he'd forgotten I was there. I crouched down further into the water until it reached my neck, keeping my eyes focused on his as he waded toward me. I was afraid to glance down for fear of seeing his naked body beneath the clear waters. He too kept his eyes locked on mine.

'Zadkiel, may I be so bold as to ask a favour of you?'

He smiled and turned his head to the side, his eyes searching my face for clues.

'Of course.'

I slowly lifted my left hand out of the water and did something I had never done before—I held up my crippled fist to the sunlight like the Goddess Ceres holding up her torch before venturing into the underworld.

'Will you heal me?'

He stroked the gnarled, twisted roots of my fingers with his, and I shuddered at his light touch.

'Arabella, you are already perfect. I don't need to heal you.'

'Please,' I begged. He was my only hope. 'I'll do anything you want.'

Then I did what I'd seen my mother do a hundred times before: I ran a finger down his neck, along his collarbone and down his strong, tanned arm. 'I'll do anything you want.'

I heard his breath catch in his throat.

'No, Arabella. You don't need to do that.'

'You don't want me?'

He didn't have to answer; I could see that he did. His eyes were getting darker and his body tensed beneath my touch. He rubbed his thumb against my crippled fist again until his whole hand was caressing mine. I had never let anyone touch me there. Now I wanted him to touch every part of me.

'If I heal you, will it make you happy?' he asked.

I nodded.

He took my twisted limb in both hands and began to peel back my fingers one by one. Like the petals of a flower unfurling under the warm gaze of the sun, my hand opened and my fingers straightened in response to his touch. He stroked my palm with his, and as he caressed my hand, my entire body filled with something bright and powerful. He was giving me a strength I'd never felt before. I attempted to move my fingers and to my surprise they followed my command, stretching and moving as if they'd always been able. I held my left hand up and Zadkiel threaded his fingers through it, his hand the first that had ever held mine. I laughed, tears of joy streaming down my face.

'You're happy,' he said. It wasn't a question.

'I am. Because of you. Thank you.'

I reached for his other hand and held them both, and that is how we stayed for a long time—our fingers intertwined beneath the water, our bodies naked and our souls fusing together.

'Do you know how special you are?' I asked him.

He shook his head and lowered it.

'Zadkiel, look at me.' His hands held mine tighter. 'You have saved my life today and the lives of all those poor animals. You are a god. Everyone has been wrong about you. They shouldn't fear you… they should worship you.'

'I don't believe in gods.'

'Well, *I* believe in *you.*' He gave me a faint flicker of a smile but still wouldn't meet my eye. 'Have you always had this power?' I continued.

'I always knew I was different,' he replied with a sigh. 'My mother would tell me that people wouldn't understand, that they all feared the unknown, which was why we had to keep away from the townsfolk. I didn't like crowds anyway; there were too many emotions. I am very susceptible to the feelings of others. It becomes overwhelming at times, so I keep away.'

He stepped back but I moved closer, our bodies now inches apart and our hands beneath the water still clasped tightly to one another. I willed him to continue.

'My childhood, after my mother left, was a lonely one. It was just me, the shepherd, and the goats. He taught me everything I needed to know about tending to them and milking. He was fast becoming blind with old age though, so during my twelfth summer he took me to the market to sell with him. People knew I was the lost boy, the one whose mother had abandoned him, but until that point all they'd done was pity me. There was no fear. Not yet. A few months after my first trip to the market, the shepherd died and I continued his business. I was sad to lose him, but I'd grown accustomed to loss. Four summers later, in my sixteenth year, I was at the market when one of the women I was tending to began to scream. I had no idea what I'd done wrong, and it took a lot to convince the crowd that had formed around us that I hadn't touched her. Then they too began to stare at me in horror.

'His eyes!' one woman cried.

'He's a warlock like his mother!' another shouted, pointing at me.

'One by one, the market traders took one look at me, left their stalls, and rushed home. I was left alone with my urns of milk and my head full of questions.

'That was the day everything changed.

'When I got back to my cottage, I ran straight to the stream, sought the still, shallow waters, and looked at my reflection.' He closed his eyes and sighed again. 'Arabella, I wasn't born with eyes this colour. They were hazel, maybe a little green in the sun, but not like this. When I saw they had turned a vibrant blue I immediately washed my face, but of course they stayed the same. I had no idea what was happening to me. I'd never seen anyone with eyes this colour—this unnaturally bright.'

As he spoke, I stared into those magical eyes. I could see why the village folk had been scared. I was getting used to them now, but set against his dark hair and olive skin, they shone like stars. They were not of this world.

'I think your eyes are exquisite,' I said. Zadkiel had done more than heal my hand; he'd emboldened me. 'So, then what happened?'

'I was worried, of course. Word of my unnatural deformity spread quickly. Villagers invented stories about me being possessed by a demon, saying I would eat their babies and take over their souls. I was known as the "blue-eyed boy," and no one dared buy milk from me at the market anymore. I had to sell it cheap to traders who had stalls outside of Fiesole. I grew angry, but there was nothing I could do but keep to myself. I didn't want to risk the locals turning on me.

'Then one night, while checking on the goats, I heard a growl outside of the hut and there stood three wolves as tall as my waist. They approached me slowly, their haunting yellow eyes trained on mine while they padded silently closer. I was afraid, so I waved my hand at them to push them back—but instead of scaring them, I sent them flying through the air. All three of them. One landed on the branch of a tree, and the others fell from quite a height and limped off. I was stunned. I had no idea that I had such power. I was never the same after that. Since then, my eyes have looked like this and I've had certain…abilities. I don't know why I'm different.'

With his fingers still intertwined in mine, he placed his hands behind his back so I was pulled forward toward him. My heart began to quicken but in a pleasant way that was new to me. He looked at me, really looked at me, and smiled. It was like he knew what I was thinking, which only made my heart quicken faster. His lips were by my ear now, and his words came out like a breathless whisper.

'It pained me to hear you call yourself useless, Arabella. To me, you are perfect. It's me who's the freak. I wish I could be normal.'

I wanted him to feel normal. I wanted that more than I'd ever wanted anything before. I lifted my head and brushed my lips against his, feeling his chest freeze and his breaths mix with mine. He let go of my hands and placed his own on my naked waist, his eyes boring into mine, asking permission. I gave a small nod and slowly, so slowly, he ran his fingers up my body. His fingertips didn't stop their fiery trail up my body until they reached my face, which he cupped in his cool hands. I stood as still as one of the marble statues in the bathhouse, my skin giving light shudders and my centre clenching in anticipation. He then lowered his beautiful face and softly pressed his lips against my own. A groan of pleasure escaped from somewhere deep inside me, the sound of hope that I had never dared bare. Then he kissed me again, harder this time, his fingers getting lost in my hair and his hard body pressing against mine. When I eventually pulled away I was struggling to breathe, my lungs desperate for air like the first time I saw him. I took a shuddering breath.

'Now do you feel normal, Zadkiel?'

He smiled, and I could have sworn that a bright white light emanated from every inch of his being.

'No. I feel like a god.'

IV.

Zadkiel and I spent the afternoon together doing as lovers do. We held hands, and I insisted it was my healed hand that he grasped in his, afraid the miracle wouldn't last. We talked about our childhoods and our dreams. We embraced, we ate, and most of all we laughed.

'I've never kissed anyone before you,' he said as we sucked on figs from his tree. I licked at the honey-like juice running down my hand, and he grinned as if he had never seen anyone eat fruit before.

'You're my first kiss, too, Zadkiel.'

I thought back to how he'd touched me in the water, the way he'd known what would give me the greatest pleasure. He'd certainly not been acting like a man who had never seen a woman naked before, let alone a man who'd never been kissed. We'd stopped ourselves eventually—he said it wasn't right to go any further no matter how much I pleaded with him. I knew these pleasures were only to be experienced by married couples, but I also knew that one day we'd be together forever.

'I don't believe I'm your first lover,' I said. 'You seemed to know exactly what would please me.'

He bit into another fig and stared at me for an eternity. It was impossible to fathom what he was thinking.

'There are things I have not yet told you about my abilities.' I waited. 'Along with healing and moving objects without touching them,' he explained, 'there is another skill I possess.'

My stomach clenched in anticipation.

'I'm able to sense your emotions,' he said.

I laid my hand on his and he picked it up and kissed it, making it sticky from the fig juice on his lips.

'You know what I'm thinking?' I asked.

'No. It's deeper than that. I can feel what you are feeling, the sensations you cannot even hide from yourself.' I must have looked confused as he continued with earnest. 'Like I mentioned before, as a child I sensed everyone's emotions all the time. It was overwhelming and made for a very lonely life. I've known how you feel about me since the first day we met; I sensed you before I set eyes on you. What another feels, I experience tenfold.'

I looked down at the ground, a red heat climbing up my chest and neck.

'There's no need to be embarrassed, Arabella. You are the first person I've met who's seen me as more than a creature to fear. I initially sensed your apprehension and then your raging thirst, but once you sat down beside me, I felt something greater…something I hadn't known since before I lost my mother. I realised you cared about me.'

He pulled me onto his lap, and I laid my head on his shoulder as he stroked his hand up and down my arm.

'Your emotions deepened when you returned this morning and, by the time we entered the stream, I knew you and I had been brought together. We are meant to be one.'

He wrapped his arms around me and I kissed his sweet, sticky lips.

'You think this is love?' I asked.

'If it is, then I believe in the gods after all. This is my heaven.'

I grinned. This day had been cut out of our lives and placed far away from any existence I'd ever known, a gift that was just ours to enjoy. Reality could no longer touch us—and neither did any of my old woes matter. Zadkiel was normal, I was beautiful, and our world held no hardship nor troubles. Then my heart sunk, thinking of Tommaso and my mother and the promise I'd made to return with food.

'I need to get back to my family,' I said. 'I'm meant to be at the market right now, and my mother will begin to fret. I shall return tomorrow.'

Zadkiel kissed the back of my neck, and I sank deeper into his embrace. I didn't want to leave; I could have stayed in that idyll forever. Had I been strong enough to stay, perhaps I would have avoided the horrors that awaited me.

'Of course, family is everything,' he said. 'Please, let me fetch you the goat meat. Take some dried fruit and dried beans too. Please, I have more than I need.'

He stood and pulled at a lilac rose in the shrub beside us. It smelled divine.

'Here, this is for you. The rose is called Angel Face.'

I clasped it in my two healthy hands and smelled it.

'It's a beautiful colour.'

'Lilac roses signify love at first sight.'

I blushed again, my heart racing with the knowledge that Zadkiel was experiencing the same emotions as I in that moment.

'You saved my life today,' I said.

'And you, mine,' he replied. '*In aeternum te amabo.*'

• • • • •

The sun was sinking fast, the sky a scarlet blanket torn with gold. My day had been filled with nothing but blood and brilliance. As I neared my house, I saw the wide-open door and Tommaso sitting on the doorstep playing in the dirt. He jumped up when he saw me and ran into my arms.

'Did you buy a chicken?' he squealed. 'I'm hungry. Can I have an egg? Mamá said today we will have eggs!'

It had been a struggle to carry the sacks of food over the wall, but the joy of being able to use both hands for the first time made the task a pleasure. Zadkiel had offered to help me, but I insisted he stay with the goats in case the wolves came back. I managed to arrive at the market just as the stallholders were packing up and, with all the food my new love had given me, I'd been able to spend my coins on other necessities.

'Here,' I said to my brother, strapping new sandals onto his dirty feet.

'My first shoes!' He hugged my leg and jumped from foot to foot. 'Arabella! Look, your hand! How did you make it work again?'

I scooped him up into my arms with ease, something I hadn't been able to do since he was small, and then tickled his belly.

'It was magic. I think the gods answered my prayers. But, Tommaso, please don't tell Mamá about my hand. Please? I want it to be a surprise,' I lied. I still hadn't decided how I would explain the miracle to her, not without mentioning Zadkiel. I refused to have my beautiful secret sullied by my mother.

Tommaso nodded and scrambled out of my arms to sit back on the doorstep.

'What's that you're playing with?' I asked.

He held up a small horse coarsely carved out of wood.

'The soldier gave it to me.'

The army was already passing through Fiesole?

'When were the soldiers here?' I asked.

'Mamá invited some of them to the house. One went to the bedroom with her, but the one with yellow hair sat and waited with me and gave me this. I wanted to call it Pegasus, but it has no wings, so the soldier said he will make me another with wings and bring it tomorrow when he comes to visit you. Mamá told him that you had something he might want.'

My skin exploded with a million goose bumps. How quickly I was reminded that my life was not the carefree paradise I'd tasted that morning.

'Where is she now?' I asked.

'Sleeping. Arabella, I'm hungry!' Tommaso pulled me toward the house. 'What food do you have?'

I ushered him inside and shut the door behind us, making sure to lower the bolt in place.

'Have you eaten anything today?'

'Just some bread the baker gave Mamá this morning. He was here, too. Then she was with her soldier friends all day and they were drinking wine, which they wouldn't give me, so I went outside to play with my horse and wait for you.'

In that moment, I hated my mother with every ounce of my being. I was also stricken with guilt and remorse. My time with Zadkiel meant my brother had gone hungry. I wanted to run straight back to my blue-eyed boy and get as far away from my mother as I could, but what would become of Tommaso if I left?

I found her asleep in her room. An empty wine goblet sat beside her bed along with five copper coins. The tattered sheet barely covered her naked body. Her lips were stained berry red. She looked like a monster, a hungry desperate monster that wouldn't stop until she'd consumed her young and dragged them down to hell with her. I returned to my brother and cooked some meat and vegetables for him before putting him to bed with a full stomach. Tomorrow I would return to Zadkiel and seek his council; he would know what to do.

V.

'You are up early, Arabella,' my mother said as I poured some oats into boiling goat's milk. I had already made a fire and cleaned the house. 'Where is your brother?'

'Playing outside.'

I told myself I would go to Zadkiel once Tommaso was fed. I reached for the wooden spoon with my left hand, my right still holding the sack of oats, and then remembered that my mother knew nothing of my healing miracle. The soldiers were in town. If she knew I was no longer a cripple, she would be sure to tell them of my increase in value. Tommaso said they would return today. I prayed I could keep up the pretence, knowing a deformed girl would be of no interest to them.

Roman soldiers were forbidden to marry during their service, but that didn't stop them from taking up women to satisfy them during their travels. I'd heard horror stories of poor young girls kidnapped from villages and kept in battle camps as sex slaves, used and abused until their disease-riddled bodies eventually killed them. I would not succumb to such a fate.

'Where did you get all this food?' my mother asked, peering into the sacks of grain and the basket of vegetables. I'd placed the meat in salt to preserve it, and there was also goat's cheese wrapped in cloth and milk in a clay bottle.

'I bought it.'

She hadn't yet noticed the new sandals Tommaso and I were wearing.

'The coins I gave you would not have bought you all of this.'

'I have a friend who gave me some meat and cheese,' I said, keeping my eyes on the milky porridge.

'You dirty whore! Have you been fucking and keeping the money?'

Without thinking, I swung around and slapped her hard across the face. How dare she accuse me of lowering myself to her level! What

I felt for Zadkiel wasn't her filthy lust; it was pure. Fated. Even though our love was deep, I had still refrained from giving myself to him until we chose to marry. I would never sink to such depravity, numbing my senses with wine and taking money off my neighbours' husbands so they could empty themselves inside of me. All I wanted was to make an honest living and look after my brother—live a quiet life with a husband and children of my own. Instead, I was left picking up the pieces of my broken home. Yet I had never lashed out at anyone, and I truly hadn't meant to hurt her.

I waited for her to cry out, or hit me back, but she just stood there, her cheek glowing red. Then she walked to her bedroom and shut the door quietly.

I was in serious trouble.

'Arabella, Arabella! Look!'

Tommaso ran into the kitchen, nearly knocking over the two bowls of porridge I was pouring out. He thrust a small wooden horse in my face; this one had wings and had been sanded down to a smoother finish. Whoever had made it had put a lot of effort into it.

'I have two horses now. Aethon and Pegasus. Neigh, neigh!'

Tommaso galloped out the door, hitting the knee of a soldier that was leaning against the doorframe.

'You must be Arabella,' he said, smiling and displaying a row of tiny teeth. He wore a dirty red tunic beneath his armour, and his helmet was tucked under his arm. I stood and wiped my hands on my dress.

'My mother is not available,' I said, my voice high and uneven.

He continued to lean against the doorframe, his eyes travelling from my feet, up my legs, and over my chest until they came to rest on my lips.

'I came to see *you*. Your mother was right. You are young and very pretty, but she told me you were disfigured.'

I screwed up my left fist so he could see that I wasn't what he was looking for.

'I am. I'm a useless cripple.'

'My name is Sabinus,' he said, running his tongue over his bottom lip. He took my screwed-up hand in his, turned it around, and then dropped it again. 'Why don't we get to know each other a little better? You can still do a lot with just one hand; it's not the only part of your body that interests me.'

'I don't want to,' I mumbled, avoiding his eyes. I walked to the door and ushered my brother in from outside, handing him his bowl of porridge.

The soldier looked like he was about to leave until my mother glided into the room wearing her best dress with her hair in a long braid. She took the second bowl of porridge off me and placed it on the table before the blond man.

'Sabinus, thank you for returning. Please, eat with us.'

She smiled at him, but when she looked in my direction her eyes were cold. I noticed her cheek was still red and blotchy. I placed a jug of water and two cups on the table, and the soldier began to slurp at his porridge, ignoring my brother staring up at him in awe.

'Arabella, I need you to get us some bread,' my mother said. She sat on the bench beside the soldier and rested her hand on his knee. 'Take Tommaso with you. Sabinus and I need to talk.'

He leered at me as my mother's hand disappeared beneath his tunic. I took the coin from her open palm and left, my brother trotting behind me. The last thing I heard as I left the house was my mother's laughter as she led the soldier to her bedroom.

• • • • •

We had plenty of bread at home, but I was happy to be outside and away from the soldier and his intentions. I bought a small loaf and the stallholder gave me a bunch of grapes to share with my brother. We sat beneath the shade of the cypress trees, spitting out pips and watching the slaves build the amphitheatre. The Romans had taken Fiesole eighty years previously, and with them came great buildings and monuments. The townsfolk said the new amphitheatre would make Fiesole famous, but all I wanted was to get away from the crowds and be with Zadkiel. The thought of his pretty house in the woods made my chest blossom like a rose opening her petals for the sun.

I sat my brother on my knee and rested my chin on top of his head. He wasn't a baby anymore, but his hair still smelled like wildflowers.

'How would you like to come with me and see my friend?' I asked. 'We could swim in his stream and pick pears. He has baby goats. He could teach you how to feed them.'

Tommaso's eyes lit up.

'Could I take Aethon and Pegasus with me?' he asked, holding out his hands and showing me the wooden horses.

I thought of the soldier in my house with the tiny-toothed leer and my mother's hands inside his tunic. I took a deep breath. What would my punishment be for striking my mother? Hopefully Sabinus had paid her well and got her so drunk she passed out before we returned and I found out.

Too afraid to face my mother, I decided to head straight to Zadkiel's house with Tommaso. The sun was already high in the sky, and my true love would be waiting eagerly for me. I'd told Zadkiel all about Tommaso the previous day and I was excited for them to meet, although getting to his cottage via the crumbled wall meant passing my house first. I wasn't concerned though because I knew my mother would be too busy or drunk to notice us.

As we neared our street, I spotted a horse and cart outside our building, Mamá walking back and forth loading furniture into it. Three sacks of clothes and bedding were already piled on top of pots and pans. We had very little, and the cart was nearly full. Two men were helping her with the table and chairs.

I ran as fast as I could, dragging Tommaso behind me.

'What is going on? Where are we going?' I shouted.

She didn't smile when she saw us. Instead, she lifted up my brother and placed him beside the driver of the cart. Tommaso looked down and grinned at me.

'Do you think this horse has wings, Arabella?' he said, reaching forward and stroking the horse's tail.

'I'm leaving for Rome to find your father,' Mamá said, pulling herself up onto the cart beside my brother before nodding at the driver. 'I'm taking Tommaso with me.'

'No!' I shouted up at her, pulling at her dress. 'You can't go!'

My brother, startled upon hearing my cries, began to sob and call out my name.

'Leave him here. You can't take him away from me,' I cried.

'You will be too busy to worry about us, Arabella. I got a good price for you.' She held up a small leather money pouch. 'You've always been useless; at least now you can serve a purpose. I'm sure Sabinus will take good care of you as long as you do as you're told.'

At the sound of his name, the soldier appeared in the doorway. He stood behind me and put his arms around my waist.

'Let's hope you fuck as well as your mother does,' he muttered into my ear, his breath thick with the scent of what was to come. 'You're mine now, little girl.'

It all happened so fast. I called out to Tommaso and lurched forward, intent on pulling him away from our mother, but the soldier had too strong a hold on me. The cart pulled away, sending clouds of dust into my face. My brother was still calling out my name, his tiny hands reaching out to me like little white butterflies in a thick fog. But my mother didn't turn back.

'Tommaso!' I screamed.

I attempted to run after the cart, but the soldier pulled me back, wrapping his arms back around my waist.

'Get off me!' I cried. 'I don't consent to this. I want my brother.'

As the dust cleared, I noticed two small wooden figures on the mud-caked ground. Tommaso's little toy horses. Sabinus noticed them too and stepped on them with his heavy boots, grinding them into the dirt and reducing them to a pile of splintered shards—the same shards that were now embedded deep into my heart. I sobbed as I watched my family become a dark speck in the distance. How could my own mother have done this to me?

The soldier swung me around to face him. He grabbed my right arm and tied a red scarf tightly around my wrist.

'This means you belong to me. The other soldiers won't touch you unless I say they can. Your crippled hand will never be able to untie it so don't even try. We leave for Germania in the morning, and you will be by my side throughout the journey. You will be light relief at the end of a hard day's marching.'

I shook my head in tiny motions. I didn't understand. I wasn't for sale; my mother had no right to sell me off to the highest bidder like a donkey in the market. His dirty fingers began to unbutton my tunic, his goose-like teeth flashing as I attempted to swat his hand away.

'Don't panic, little one. We can practice tonight. I will try to be gentle.' His hand reached into my top and cupped my breast. 'But I can't promise anything.'

As he turned toward the house, I took my chance. I pried my arm out of his grasp and ran as fast as I could in the only direction I knew. Toward my destiny.

15

JOSH HADN'T WANTED to return to Tarifa. In fact, all he'd wanted to do was get back to LA and forget about Ella. But he couldn't. She'd got under his skin and he had no idea why. It wasn't like he was short of women in his life, but Ella was...What was it about her that drove him so crazy? She was fearless and clever and funny and completely fucked up. Did he really need to complicate his life?

But it was more than that. He knew something about Ella that he hadn't told a soul about, something he wouldn't even admit to himself. She'd lied to him and he hadn't blamed her.

The only reason he was returning to Tarifa was because Billy, the location manager, had announced earlier that morning that he needed to spend the last day by Tarifa's beach checking out the old castle and gothic weather station. Two locations he'd missed on the day he'd been ill. Of course, Josh could have stayed in his hotel and met Billy at the airport the next day, but there was a part of him that wanted to test fate. If he bumped into Ella, he would tell her the secret he'd been keeping for three years. If he didn't, then he would forget about her. Either way, he wasn't going to go to her hotel to search for her—he knew better than to seek out trouble.

'I'm going back to the hotel now,' Billy announced, slurring.

They'd just finished dinner by the castle and the sun was beginning to set, turning the little blue-and-red fisherman's boats into cutout silhouettes against the inky water. Billy had a piece of rice stuck to his chin, and his mouth was stained red from the copious glasses of Rioja he'd drunk.

Josh tried not to grimace at Billy's filthy face.

'Marbella's over an hour away. It will cost a fortune.'

'Since when have you cared about money, Joshy? Planet Pictures are paying anyway. Come on; let's go back to the hotel. Just you and me. We've hardly had any time alone.'

It wasn't easy to mask how he felt about *that* suggestion. Sober Billy was bad enough, but drunk Billy was a creepy letch.

'I might hang out here.'

'On your own? You're crazy! You'll get papped and molested by teen fans.'

'Look around you, Billy,' Josh said, throwing his arms up. 'No one knows who I am here. In fact, I can't even see any women under the age of fifty, unless you count that stoned surfer chick and her boyfriend over there. I'll be fine. I'll meet you at the hotel in the morning.'

Billy drank the dregs of his wine and gave a small burp. 'Maybe I'll hang out here with you and we'll hit the bars.' He stood and stumbled a little, and then he put his hands on his hips and began to wiggle his behind. 'I still have the moves. Wanna dance with me, Joshy? I bet you have fantastic rhythm.'

'No. Definitely not. Let's get you to the taxi rank.'

Josh left a bundle of notes on the table and allowed Billy to put his arm around his shoulders as he led him up the steep, cobbled streets to the main road. Billy was still begging him to join him, shouting out of the window, as the taxi pulled away.

Breathing a sigh of relief, Josh walked back through the Moorish arch into town past the painting of a naked Jesus with far too much pubic hair and the quaint shops selling shell necklaces and crochet bikinis. He grinned. After four days in Marbella, with pervy Billy on his case and Ella on his mind, he was finally free to have a quiet drink alone and enjoy the sights.

Then he saw her.

Josh stopped and rubbed his tired face. This couldn't be happening.

Across the narrowed cobbled road, leaning against the wall of a bar, was Ella talking to a Spanish man looming over her. Josh walked closer until he could hear their conversation. He didn't understand Spanish, but judging by the look of desperation on the man's tanned face, whatever he had to say to Ella was very urgent. She, on the other hand, didn't look the slightest bit interested. In fact, she was trying to push his arm away as he leant beside her.

Josh tapped the man on the shoulder.

'Everything OK?' he asked.

Ella beamed up at him and ducked under the man's arm.

'Josh! Ha, fate. See? I knew it. I *knew* I'd see you again. Did you come looking for me? Or was this a conin...condinci...' She held up her index finger at him as she struggled with the word. 'Coincidence! S'OK. I'm fine. I've had a few drinks but I'm fine. I was just saying to Pablo here...'

'Paulo,' the Spanish man said.

'Yes, Paulo. I was just saying that there's no such thing as coindi...whatever. He wants to be my chef.' She leant in closer to Josh's ear and whispered loudly, 'I think he wants to be more than my chef, but you know, I'm not *interesada.* I'm turning over a new leaf. No more random men. *Nada.* Not even you, Josh...and every girl in the world wants *you*, right?'

Paulo was already shuffling from one foot to another. Josh recognised the look of a man who'd just realised who the actor was and that he didn't stand a chance.

'*Hasta luego, Ella*,' the Spaniard mumbled, nodding at Josh and joining his friends further down the road.

'Who are you here with?' Josh asked.

Ella swayed a little and then laughed. 'No one. All my real friends are in London. But who cares? You're here now. Come on, let's go inside! I'll get you a drink. You can be my friend tonight.'

'No thanks. Look, Ella, I was just passing by and…'

'Come on!'

She pulled him into the busy bar and clambered onto a stool, signalling the barman over. The seat slid from under her and Josh caught it.

'Chodding sair. I mean, sodding chair!'

Josh helped her back up, trying not to laugh. The barman placed a margarita in front of her, but Josh moved it to one side, ordering a glass of water instead.

'Don't be a knob, Josh! I'm not drunk. These stools are slippery little duckers. I mean…'

'I know what you mean.'

He couldn't leave now, not with her in this state. He ordered himself a beer.

'You have fans,' she said, nodding her head to the side and making a kissing face at him.

There were a group of giggling girls standing by the pool table. He raised his bottle at them, causing a flutter of excitement. One of them screamed and started jumping up and down. Normally, he'd go over and lap up the attention, but with Ella beside him the whole fame thing felt stupid.

'Come on, you lush, time to get you home.'

'No way, it's still early.' Ella batted him away and reached for her margarita.

'Have another drink. I am!'

'I have to be at Malaga Airport at the crack of dawn. I'll get you home, and then I have to go.'

'Don't be a wimp, Josh. Let's do shots. It's my birthday in two days, so legally you can't say no. Tequila! Tequila! Tequila! *Dobles.*'

She banged her fists on the bar top and called the barman over by name, who dutifully lined up four shot glasses and filled them to the brim.

'Happy birthday for Saturday, but I'm not doing tequila.'

'Suit yourself, Mr Boring.'

Josh laughed. He couldn't help himself. She was so…so many things. When he'd been with her on the beach the week before, there had been at least three occasions where he'd nearly kissed her. Why her of all people? And why had he told her the way he felt, the whole *being drawn to her* thing? That was his only rule when it came to women—don't tell them what you're thinking.

As for the 'model girlfriend' thing, that was a lie. He *had* been dating models, more than one, but none that mattered. The lie was a way of keeping Ella at arm's length because, if he was totally honest with himself, this strange pull between them scared the hell out of him. What if she liked him back? She didn't deserve to be hurt again. Not after what her bastard brother had done to her, and then her last boyfriend dying.

Ella was completely oblivious to Josh's tumultuous tangle of emotions. Dressed in ripped jean shorts with cowboy boots and a white T-shirt, she was the very epitome of laid-back local girl. Her hair hung past her shoulders in large curls as if it had been left to dry naturally in the sun, and her face was also sun-kissed and glowing. He couldn't even tell if she had make-up on. The girls in LA would never have been seen dead on a night out without at least lip gloss and heels, yet here was Ella perched on a bar stool looking more radiant and vibrant than any Hollywood starlet. Her leg jangled up and down as she knocked back a shot, her crescent birthmark flashing at him like a smile. He breathed in deeply, attempting to control the growing ache in his chest.

With a loud slurp, she sucked on a slice of lemon then wiped her mouth on the back of her bare arm. This girl had no agenda, no fear, and definitely no shame. How was he going to find the courage to talk to her about what he'd seen three years ago? How could he admit what he knew about her?

'What you thinking?' she asked, leaning closer. 'You know what *I'm* thinking? I'm thinking how I don't like perfect things or perfect moments. Know what I mean? Perfect things make me nervous, like the unexpected is just around the corner.' She slipped off the stool, moved it closer to him and clambered back on. 'When things are going well, or someone is extra amazing, I get this feeling like I'm being tricked. It's like turning the handle on a jack-in-the-box, waiting for the nasty thing to jump up at you. Anyway,' she said, running her finger over his jawline, 'your face, Josh, I can't fault it and it's been making me nervous since you randomly turned up at my hotel last week. But just now, I noticed this tiny, little chip here.' She stroked her thumb over his lips until the tip made contact with his front tooth. 'And I realised you weren't perfect after all. Which made me like you more.'

She turned back to the bar and drained the rest of her margarita, following it with another tequila shot. Josh ran his tongue over his teeth until he could taste her touch. He wanted to taste more; he wanted her thumb back in his mouth.

He smiled at himself in the mirror behind the bar, trying to see if the chip was obvious from afar. 'My agent says I should get my teeth capped, but I didn't think the chip was that obvious. Should I get my teeth done? Does it show?' he shouted over the noise of the bar.

'It makes you sexier and you know it. God, look at you, you're so full of yourself. Here.' She handed him a shot of tequila.

'No, seriously, I have to leave soon.'

'For fuck's sake, Josh. Stop being a killjoy and have a bloody drink with me!'

She shrugged and drank it herself, sucking in air through her gritted teeth and chewing on another piece of lemon. Then she started laughing and swiped his arm.

'Will you leave your bloody hair alone! Three times I've caught you checking yourself out since we sat down.'

'People are always taking photos of me. I don't want to look like crap.'

'Josh, no one is even looking at you anymore. Actually, I think most people are looking at me.'

She was right. How had Josh not noticed? Paulo the chef was back, and another man with shoulder-length hair was glancing over at her from near the pool table. Was this her local pulling joint?

The DJ said something into the mic and Ella jumped up.

'Karaoke!' she cried, ruffling his hair.

He fought the urge to look back in the mirror and straighten it again.

'Josh, Josh, Josh, do you sing? I'm going to sing. Come on, you boring bastard, let's have a singsong.'

She pulled at his hand, but he stayed firmly seated at the bar.

'I can't...I have to go. My flight leaves at eight o'clock tomorrow, and the airport is miles away. Let's get out of here.'

It was too late. Ella already had the microphone and was standing on a small stage at the back of the bar. There were only a handful of people left drinking inside, and even the giggling girls Josh had smiled at earlier had begun to lose interest. He considered leaving, hoping Ella would follow, but she'd already started singing the words to "You're So Vain."

Josh put his head in his hands and laughed. What the hell was she playing at? She was walking toward him slowly, pointing as she belted out the lyrics to the Carly Simon hit.

While people clapped along, she sang about being naïve and how he'd had her several years ago. She had her back to him now, writhing up and down and leaning her head back onto his shoulder as she sang into the microphone.

Josh stayed on his bar stool as Ella danced around him, seductively flicking her hair and running her hands over his chest. She was pretty well coordinated for a girl that ten minutes earlier had been too drunk to stay on her chair, although unfortunately her singing was not as good as her dancing.

He knew this song and what came next—the air guitar. Right on cue, Ella was on her knees giving it her all, much to the amusement of their fellow drinkers. The bar was now filling up fast. Those who had been drinking and smoking outside came back in, and those walking past, upon seeing Ella cavort around a guy that very much looked like '*that one in that film,*' entered the bar, too. There was not much Josh could do but let her finish her number and smile graciously.

She ended the song with a flourish and swayed unsteadily on her feet. Josh caught her and dipped her, giving her a light kiss on the lips. The bar went wild, and he laughed as his audience applauded and took photos on their phones. The pictures would probably be all over the internet by morning and he'd have his agent shouting at him on the phone about being seen in the wrong kind of bar with the wrong kind of girl. He didn't care though. This was Ella, and she was different.

He lifted her up over his shoulder in a fireman's lift, threw a one-hundred-euro note at the bar and called out, 'Drinks are on me!' as he headed to the taxi rank. Ella was laughing so hard that he prayed she wouldn't be sick over the back of his new Paul Smith shirt.

• • • • •

'That was fun,' she said, giggling, as Josh took her front door keys off her and led her into her apartment. She attempted to take off one of her boots but fell on the floor.

'Oh my God, I'm going to piss myself if I keep laughing this hard. Josh, that was bloody hilarious. Your face! And you kissed me. I can't believe you were so desperate to leave you actually kissed me.'

She gave up on taking her shoes off, and he watched her weave her way to the bathroom. She came back out a few minutes later, toothbrush in hand, wearing nothing but her underwear and cowboy boots.

She had absolutely no idea about the effect she had on him. He had to get out of there before she took off any more clothes.

'Ella, I've got you some water and I found some aspirin in your kitchen. They're on your bedside table. I've got to go now.'

'Don't go. Stay.'

He tried not to stare at her body, but she was inches away from him now. This girl was something else.

'I told you, I have to get back to Marbella and get my luggage. I leave early tomorrow. We'll keep in touch, OK?'

'Josh, I know you want me.'

Did he? Of course he did, but if it was going to happen it wasn't going to happen like this. Not with her drunk and him worried about missing his flight.

'Ella, you're wonderful, and yes, I fancy you but this…this…' He pointed to her and himself. 'This isn't going to happen.'

'It is.'

'Listen, I know it's been hard for you since Zac…'

'You know? You *know?* You know what you know, Josh? You know *nada.* Absolutely nothing.'

Except he did; he knew more than she realised.

'There's stuff you'll never understand,' she said, 'things that don't even make sense to me after all these years. You and me, as stupid as it may seem, we're destined for each other. Don't look at me like that; I mean it. Destiny, fate, written in the stars, meant to be, whatever the fuck you want to call it. We don't have a choice, Josh. It's not me that wants it. It just is. Haven't you noticed how many times we've been thrown together this past week? All those weird coincidences? You even said yourself that you're being pulled in my direction. Life is never going to give up on us until we give in. So, just kiss me again, properly. Let's get this over with.'

What was she talking about? He'd heard some come-ons in his time, but she wasn't making sense. She was stinking drunk and probably angry he was turning her down.

'I have to go, Ella. I'm sorry. Good night.'

He kissed her forehead, and she sat on her bed with a thump, her unused toothbrush still in her hand.

'You won't make it to LA. The universe isn't going to let you walk away this easily. You'll be back.' She laughed a dry, sad laugh. '*You* were meant to be my true love, Josh. Can you believe that? Not Zac, the man I *actually* love...but you. I didn't believe it either when I was told. I didn't want to, but I can see it now. It's our path. So, I guess I'll see you soon.'

Josh nodded and let himself out of her apartment. By the morning, he would be on a flight back to his life in LA, away from this surreal place and Ella's crazy talk. There was no way any more coincidences would make him stay in Tarifa. He'd bottled out of telling her his big secret, but it didn't matter anymore. It wouldn't change anything.

He opened the apartment door and glanced back at the fiery girl whose ember was beginning to dim. She was on the bed, looking down at a large framed feather in her hand, her knuckles white from the strength of her grip.

He shut the door firmly behind him and told himself to forget about her.

16

WATER. SHE NEEDED water. What the hell had she been drinking last night?

Ella scrambled out of bed and tripped over something—her cowboy boots. Beside them were her bra and lacy knickers. She was naked. *What the fuck?*

She shielded her eyes against the bright glare of the sun shining through the French windows. What time was it? It had to be close to midday. What time had she got to bed? She couldn't even remember getting home last night. Oh, wait, had Josh been there last night? She had a faint recollection of him carrying her out of the bar and bundling them into a cab. Yes! He had definitely been there, but why? He was meant to be in Marbella.

Thank God she didn't work on weekends. It was going to take more than a shower to get rid of this hangover and piece together her memories of the night before.

'*Joder*, my head!' she muttered to herself.

A packet of painkillers was propped up against a bottle of water on her bedside table. She knew she hadn't put them there; she was never that sensible. She sat on the bed, took two tablets and washed them down with half the bottle of water. She then took two more and drank the rest of the water. Who had left her headache tablets? Had Josh come back to her room last night?

Oh no. No, no, no, no, no! What if she'd had sex with him? What if he'd left without leaving a note or kissing her goodbye? She picked up her phone. No messages. *Bastard!*

She checked her packet of contraceptive pills. She'd taken one. Good. Plus, no matter how drunk she got, she always used a condom. She had a drawer full of them, not that she could see whether any had been taken out.

She *must* have had sex with Josh de Silva. She remembered him bringing her home, and why else would she be naked? She'd shagged a famous Hollywood heartthrob and couldn't even remember the details. What was the point of that? Fuckety fuck *fuck!* How embarrassing! She'd dropped her knickers like every other desperate fangirl. She didn't even know if she liked him that way. Oh, who was she kidding? Of course she liked him. He was gorgeous. But if she'd been sober, she would never have given him the satisfaction of knowing how she felt about him.

She stumbled to the bathroom and brushed her teeth, trying not to wretch as the toothbrush touched the back of her throat. Her mouth tasted vile. Had she been drinking tequila last night? Why did she always do that? And why did she have that annoying song stuck in her head?

'Oh no!' she said, groaning out loud.

Friday was karaoke night at her local. Had she been singing in front of Josh? She had sex with him, possibly while wearing cowboy boots, after having sung karaoke in her local bar. Could she be any more shameless?

She contemplated having a shower but then did what she always did when she woke up feeling ill and full of remorse: she slid open the back door and jumped naked into her swimming pool. None of the hotel rooms overlooked her apartment; her own little slice of paradise was completely private.

The initial cold of the water hitting her skin woke her up, and she groaned again at the thought of Josh being halfway to LA by now. At least she wouldn't have to avoid him in town like all her other mistakes.

Nope, she didn't need Josh in her life. She didn't need *any* bloody man! According to Zac, Josh was her destiny—but Ella controlled her own fate. Josh was on his way back to Hollywood, and her family and friends were arriving the next day to celebrate her birthday. She was turning twenty-three, old enough to get her life in order and stop fucking around with the wrong guys. Yep, that was that. Josh was but a blip, a wrong turn. From now on she would determine her own path.

17

JOSH HAD NO idea what he was doing. He could have got a flight elsewhere or booked into a hotel for a few days to await further news, but instead he was back in the lobby of the same hotel from which he had left just seven hours earlier.

He rubbed his face and sighed. What was it Ella had said to him as he'd left her room that morning? *The universe isn't going to let you walk away this easily. You'll be back.* And there he was, returning to the girl he couldn't shake off.

Josh yawned. He hadn't slept all night. He'd had a long cab journey from Tarifa to Marbella and then an hour of packing and answering work emails. Then he'd booked a taxi and headed straight to the airport, planning to sleep on the plane. He had a packed schedule ahead of him—Malaga to London and then on to LAX, followed by weeks of meetings and castings and press events. He liked his life. No, he *loved* his life but, after having bumped into Ella, his lifestyle was beginning to feel vacuous and ridiculous. Why did she make him feel that way, as if being with her was real and everything else was just pretend?

He'd been sitting in the first-class lounge reading through the *Bite Night* script, finally seeing it for the pile of crap it was, when the BBC Breaking News logo flashed up on the television screen in the corner. A terrorist threat at LAX Airport had been thwarted and California was on red alert, with all US airports evacuated and all planes grounded.

Josh hadn't had time to process what that meant for his travel plans before Billy came rushing into the lounge, his round face puce and sweat forming rings beneath his arms.

'Thought I was going to be late,' he said, coughing. 'I can't believe you got here so early. I threw up five times this morning and…' He looked up at the television screen, his face turning a deeper shade of scarlet. 'What the hell is this?'

Josh laughed, although he wasn't sure if it was the news or the state of Billy's face that was amusing him the most.

'A terrorist alert. It's hilarious.'

There were only two other businessmen in the lounge and they both looked up from the television, startled at Josh's reaction.

'Hilarious?' Billy shouted.

'Yes! Do you know what this means?'

'I know exactly what this means. We're going to have to stay in London for a bit. It's fine. We can conduct the meetings from there. The studio has offices on Baker Street. Then maybe we can fly to Canada and drive over the border if the airports don't open up soon. Perhaps it's just the LA ones. I'm sure we can fly into…'

'I'm not leaving Spain,' Josh said.

Billy began to cough again. He doubled over and rested his hands on his knees.

'Yes, you are!' he spluttered. 'I've had your manager and PR people on the phone. They aren't happy with you as it is. You have plans, and you have to see them through.'

'No, I don't. I'm looking at the bigger plan, Billy. First, you decided to shoot the film in Tarifa, of all places, then my room flooded and I had to stay at an unknown hotel, then you got ill and I had to stay longer in Tarifa, and finally, guess who I saw last night? Ella. And now this?'

Billy was staring at him, eyes narrowed in confusion.

'What the hell are you blabbering on about?'

'She was right, Billy. Ella was right. This is my destiny!' Josh collected his belongings and pushed his way past a crowd of people gathered around the large TV screen in the departure lounge. He didn't even care that his luggage was already checked in; he'd get his people to sort that out later. He had to get back to Ella.

'Wait!' Billy shouted as Josh pushed past him. 'You're not making any sense. You just need some sleep. Joshy, come back! Where the hell are you going?'

'I have a date with fate!' he called over his shoulder, and Billy was too busy coughing again to chase him.

Josh ran all the way to the airport exit. Not only was Ella permanently branded on his mind, her face coming into sharp relief every time he blinked, but he'd started to notice her everywhere. Every woman in the airport looked like her, the duty-free shop smelled of her perfume and as the taxi pulled up outside the airport its radio was playing the same song she'd sung the night before. He laughed. He was getting the message loud and clear.

'*Donde vas?*' the cab driver asked him.

'*Torre de los angeles,*' he answered, giving the taxi driver the name of the hotel. Then he laughed out loud, realising what the name meant. Tower of Angels.

Angels? His stomach clenched. He had to tell her his secret. Since that night three years ago, he'd convinced himself that not believing in something meant it couldn't be real. He'd definitely been proven wrong. Today, he would tell her everything. Today he believed.

• • • • •

A two-hour cab ride later and Josh was back at Ella's hotel, heading straight for her apartment. He had no idea what he was going to say to her, or exactly why he'd come back, but her comment about destiny had haunted him all night. She was right—coincidences didn't exist.

His hand was shaking as he knocked on her apartment door three times. Paloma, the receptionist, had been elated to see him and insisted he go straight to her room. She'd said Ella was home, but there was no answer.

Was she still asleep? He checked his watch, saw it was nearly midday, and knocked again. No answer.

Perhaps she was out in the back?

When they'd spent the day on the beach, she'd told him how much she loved taking photos of the sea. Maybe she was on the beach. Even if she wasn't, he could wait for her on her patio. He wasn't going to put it off any longer, even though he had no idea how he'd find the words to speak the unspeakable.

He left the hotel via the side entrance and walked around the perimeter of the grand building. The back of her apartment was silent save the distant hum of cicadas and the calm waves lapping the sands of their little beach. The sun was hot and high now, and he pulled up the sleeves of his shirt before climbing the stairs to her patio garden. As he reached the top, he could hear the gentle lap of the pool.

Then he saw her.

Like a mermaid, she glistened beneath the water, her long golden body swimming effortlessly below the surface. When she reached the end of the pool, she took a deep breath and dived back under, her arms by her side and her legs hardly moving as she glided from one side of the pool to the other. Josh stood transfixed, staring at her naked back and the way the sun glinted off the curves of her hips and her perfectly pointed toes.

She reached the other side, stood up, took another deep breath and then screamed.

'What the fuck! Josh? Oh my God, you scared the crap out of me! How long have you been standing there like a weirdo?'

He snapped out of his reverie and held his hands out in front of him.

'Sorry, sorry, I got here a few seconds ago. I didn't realise you were home. I knocked but you didn't answer. I needed to see you. I was going to wait for you out here.'

Ella swam to the edge and climbed the steps out of the pool. Her dark hair, much longer when wet, reached down to her waist and dripped onto the patio as she stood before him. She was completely naked. He reached for a towel on the chair beside him and offered it to her while shielding his eyes, but she swatted him away.

'Don't look so uncomfortable, you creep. I'm sure you had no problem with my body last night before you did a runner. I can't believe you didn't even say goodbye or leave a note.'

Of all the things he'd expected her to say, that wasn't one of them. During the entire journey from the airport to the hotel, Josh had struggled to understand why he was running back to Ella. Now, as she stood before him, water dripping into tiny puddles at her bare feet, he knew exactly what he wanted. He wanted her. Not in the obvious way he'd wanted other girls in the past; this time he wanted *all* of her—mind, body, and soul. Forever. It was so clear now.

They were meant to be together; they always had been. Ella had known it before he'd even admitted it to himself.

'Well, then say something!' she said, whacking the top of his arm. 'I thought you had a plane to catch? Or did you forget something last night? Like respect and manners?'

'I'm not going to LA,' he muttered, keeping his eyes fixed on the puddle of water at their feet. 'LAX Airport is closed. Terrorist alert or something.'

After a long silence she spoke.

'So, you still believe in coincidences?'

'Not anymore.'

'Why are you here then? Fancied another quickie, did you?'

Josh stepped forward and wrapped the large towel he was holding around her shoulders. He gently lifted her hair and placed it over the back of the towel, enveloping her body within it. Her arms were pinned to her side as he held it closed.

'I never slept with you last night, Ella. We didn't even kiss. Not properly.'

'Not properly?'

'You sang at me at the bar, and I gave you a quick peck on the lips as part of your embarrassing show. We had quite an audience.'

Ella made a strangled sound and turned her head. He took her chin and gently moved it back until they were facing one another.

'Hey, I had fun.'

'It was you who put me to bed and left me water and headache tablets?'

He nodded.

'And you didn't undress me?'

'What? *No!* The first time I saw you naked was two minutes ago when you stepped out of the pool like an angry siren straight out of a teen sci-fi fantasy.'

Ella swore under her breath and tried to walk away, but he held the towel tighter. He was scared to let go, scared of what would happen next. Ella wasn't just some girl. Whatever he did next was going to lead him straight to his future. Right now he was more than happy to stay in this tiny pocket of time, holding on tightly to her towel. Nothing but him and Ella.

Her wet face was inches from his, so close he could see the water droplets on her eyelashes glinting as the sun beat down on them. The air was silent. It was just her breath and his. A heartbeat. The earth paused, waiting, fate resetting its path.

'What are you doing, Josh?' she asked.

'I don't know. You tell me. You seem to have all the answers.'

With a shake of her shoulders she freed her arms from the towel. She stepped forward, making him stumble backwards until his back was flat against the wall of her apartment.

'You believe me now?' she asked, her wet body inches from his. 'You believe there's an "us?"'

He placed his hands on her waist and felt her shiver beneath his fingers.

'Yes.'

'Tell me. What am I to you?'

His hand slid past her waist and over her hips, pulling her closer to him. Her cold chest was now pressed flush to his. This was it—his first step into a future that had already been mapped out for him.

'You're someone I want to fall in love with.'

Ella ran her hands through the back of his hair and pulled him closer until her lips were brushing against his.

'That's all I needed to hear.'

Josh had kissed a lot of women in his life, whether for acting or for real. There was never any shortage of actresses or fans he'd thought he cared about, and they had all been more than happy to be kissed. A kiss was a kiss after all. When the script said the kiss took his breath away, he'd act out the part—looking stunned and misty-eyed—but he'd never truly believed a kiss could be that powerful. He had no idea that a kiss could render you speechless, useless, and completely and utterly spent.

When Ella kissed him, his whole world imploded and everything disappeared. There was no her or him, just a them. Everything was condensed into a tiny pinprick of time that lasted an eternity.

When she pulled away, he saw she'd felt it too.

'I told you,' she said, struggling to find her voice.

He pulled her back and kissed her again, harder and more urgently. He wrapped his arms around her waist and pulled her toward him until there was no space between her damp body and his.

'Ella,' he said. Her name sounded different now, more familiar than even his own. 'Ella, I need to talk to you.'

She stared at him, her eyes struggling to focus.

'Yes, we need to talk.'

She stepped back and he pulled her forward again, their mouths hungry for one another.

'Sorry. Go!' he said, laughing. 'Go and get dressed. If you don't, then we're not going to get any talking done today, and there's a lot I need to tell you.'

She smiled hesitantly, wrapping the towel around herself again and walking slowly back to her apartment. When she reached the patio doors, she looked back at him. Her eyes met his and it felt like a punch to the stomach. Ella had always been his destiny. Why had it taken him so long to see it?

18

ELLA PEEKED OUT of her bathroom window at Josh. He had his back to her and was leaning over the garden wall, watching the kite surfers on the horizon. What the hell had just happened? She'd kissed him because she was trying to prove to herself that Zac had been wrong, that Josh wasn't anything special. But that kiss! That wasn't a normal kiss. That was…What the fuck *was* that?

She put on a long cotton dress and roughly dried her hair. That kiss had changed something. It had realigned her when she hadn't even realised she'd been derailed. The world appeared differently now—it was finally the right way up. Neat. Easy. Like everything was going to be OK. She hadn't felt like this since before her mother married Richard seven years ago. Had she been struggling against her life path for seven years?

She picked up a hair elastic and headed for the garden while brushing her wet hair.

'Hey,' Josh said, turning around at the sound of her footsteps.

She felt shy and could see he did, too. No more full-of-himself de Silva. He took the hairbrush and elastic out of her hand and twisted her around so she was facing the sea.

Without saying a word, he lifted her hair from her damp dress and gently combed it through, his fingertips brushing the back of her neck with each stroke. A light shiver ran down her spine at his touch. He parted her hair and started braiding it from one side to the other.

'Are you doing a French plait?' She laughed. 'Where did you learn to do that?'

'My mum. When I was a kid, she used to like me brushing her hair. She's always been an anxious person; she said it relaxed her.'

'Tell me about your family,' she asked, realising she knew very little about him aside from teen magazine gossip.

'Well, you've met my dad. Portuguese, larger than life, successful film director, arsehole. My mum was a Miss America finalist back in the day, and they got together when she was about eighteen. He said he'd get her into the movies, but he never did. They lived in Portugal where I was born. Apparently, they spent a summer right here in Tarifa when I was a baby. My grandfather had a small hotel. Then we moved to London and things turned to shit.' He'd stopped braiding her hair. All she could hear was the sound of his gentle breathing on the back of her neck and the soft swish of the waves. 'The bigger my father got, the smaller my mother became, until eventually she was nothing but a watery smile. The more fragile she got, the more he disliked her—it was a vicious circle. He didn't care. In the end, it was me who was up in the night dealing with her panic attacks and picking up her meds from the doctors.'

'I'm sorry.'

'It doesn't matter. Someone had to be there for her.'

'Do you have brothers or sisters?'

'One brother.'

'Is he an actor, too?'

Josh laughed.

'He's two years old. He's a cute kid, but I don't see that much of him. In the end my dad's affairs caught up with him and one of the women told the papers she'd had his kid, although who knows how many more brothers or sisters I have out there. Mum was never the same after he left; it ruined her. He now lives near me in LA with a woman not much older than I am, and my mother's in London trying to remember how to breathe again. I travel back and forth quite a bit.'

All this time Ella had thought that Josh was just a spoiled brat, a rich kid with the perfect life. He had the looks, talent, money, a beautiful mum, a successful father, and not a worry in the world. How wrong she'd been.

'It's why I was such an idiot in uni,' he continued. 'Things between me and my dad were pretty messed up back then. He still directs some of the films I'm in, but he knows I hate him. Although I do my best to keep it out of the media—you know how these shitty gossip magazines love a scandal.'

Josh finished the braid, swung it over her shoulder and then kissed the back of her neck.

'Thank you,' she said.

'Come.'

He took her hand and led her back to her apartment. Her clothes and underwear were still scattered all over the floor from the night before, her bed unmade, but the only thing Josh was looking at was her.

'Sit down,' he said, signalling to her bed. 'There's something I've been meaning to tell you for a long time. I'll feel better once you know.'

'About your girlfriend?'

'What? Oh, that. No. I don't have a girlfriend, not a serious one. I was just...I don't know why I told you I had one. This is much more important.'

Ella raised her eyebrows at the news but said nothing. No girlfriend was a good thing—wasn't it? She perched on the edge of the bed and watched him walk to her bedroom wall that was adorned with photos and paintings. He lifted one down. It was the largest frame there, containing a giant feather that was as long as a peacock's but was also wide and bright white. Ella's heart skipped a beat.

He sat down beside her and handed her the frame.

'What's this?'

She swallowed, but her throat was so dry it hurt.

'It's a feather.'

'From where?'

What was he playing at? She could feel her hands getting clammy. She placed the frame beside her on the bed, scared she would drop it.

'I don't know. I just thought it was pretty.'

'It's not from a bird, is it?'

Why was he doing this? Josh couldn't possibly know; only her mother, father, and stepbrother knew. They had seen Zac for what he was, what he used to be before he...She bit down on her lip but couldn't help her eyes filling up with tears. The feather was all she had left to remind her that Zac had been real.

Josh took her hand in his. One of their hands was trembling; she wasn't sure whose. Perhaps both.

'Ella, if whatever we have between us is going to grow, then we need to be honest with one another. And I need to be honest with myself.' He breathed out and looked up at the ceiling. 'I know what this feather is, and I have known for a long time. I didn't want to believe it, but when I saw it in your room the other day, I had to finally admit it to myself.'

'What do you know?'

'I know what Zac is.'

They stared at each other for a long time, neither of them wanting to make the first move. Ella hadn't spoken the truth about Zac in three years, no one except her parents whom she'd bored rigid with her 'will he, won't he come back' conversations until they'd both told her to move on.

But she couldn't stay numb any longer. She was back on her path with the man she was destined to be with, yet here he was talking about the one person she needed to start forgetting. A single tear trickled down her cheek. Josh wiped it away, but more tears fell. He pulled her into his arms and held her.

'He isn't coming back,' she said, sobbing. 'He's dead. He said I was meant to be with you and he was right. There's nothing between Zac and me, Josh. Not anymore. He's gone…forever.'

'Shh, it's OK.'

'How did you know? No one knows.'

She sniffed and rubbed her eyes. Josh leant over to her bedside table and handed her a box of tissues.

'I saw something three years ago, something extraordinary,' he said. 'I was desperate to talk to you about it, but you'd gone. Your disappearance was all over the news. They were saying that you'd had a family drama and run away, but I knew the truth. I'd seen it with my own eyes but was struggling to believe it, so I tried searching for you. No one at uni had seen you, so I went to your house and your dad—I mean Richard—wouldn't tell me where you were, either. I was going crazy because I knew you were the only one with the answers. But I couldn't find you.'

Ella screwed the wet tissue up into a ball. He'd been searching for her? All these years he'd been wanting to talk to her?

'What did you see, Josh?'

'New Year's Eve, the night your stepdad had the grand opening of his new restaurant. Do you remember?'

She nodded. How could she forget? It was the night that had changed everything.

'I was having a crap time at home,' he continued. 'My parents were on the verge of splitting up. I had tickets to the hotel restaurant opening. My dad had given me some spares, but I had no intention of going. I was at some girl's New Year's party not far away in Islington, and I was getting drunk and miserable, so I decided I had to see you. I felt terrible about the last time I saw you, when I was a creep to you on the bus. I needed to apologise face-to-face.'

He'd been at the New Year's Eve party? Ella didn't remember seeing him.

'I got to the hotel about ten to midnight and London was heaving,' he said. 'You know what it's like in town that time of year. Fireworks were going off already, and everyone had had too much to drink. I showed my invite to the doorman and he let me in. I was a bit drunk, and to be honest I was also nervous about travelling up the side of the building in a glass lift. The restaurant is on the ninety-ninth floor, right?' She nodded. 'People told me the view is amazing, but it's bloody scary that high up. I was lucky I didn't have to queue for the lift as everyone was already at the top of the hotel, counting down to midnight. As the lift doors opened, some guy rushed out and pushed past me. I think it was your stepbrother. I don't know him, but I recognised him from the newspapers and stuff. Anyway, I got in the lift. It had just started to snow, so I couldn't see anything but white. It was like floating in the middle of a cloud for ages, which made it less scary. How long does that lift take to get to the top floor?'

'About three minutes.'

'Right. I was nearly at the top when, through the mist, I could make out a blonde girl on the roof. She was standing on the ledge and there was a pair of hands pulling at her dress. I thought it was part of some show they'd put on at the restaurant. I couldn't see her face; I wasn't close enough.'

Ella had dyed her hair lighter that day, which meant very few people had recognised her. She knew what was coming next and it pained her to listen to him—she'd never heard anyone retell the story. Up until now, she and Zac had been the only two people who'd seen what had really happened.

'So, there I was in that glass lift climbing toward the world's highest restaurant, wondering if I was drunker than I thought because there was a girl in a long, sparkly dress standing on the wall, looking like she wanted to jump. There were these hands trying to reach her, but no one was stopping her. Fireworks were already going off below me and, even from the lift, I could hear singing and laughing. Then the girl jumped. I was shouting, banging on the glass, and as I reached for my phone to call the police, I saw it.'

Josh looked down at the large frame that Ella had placed on the bed.

'Saw what?' she said, her voice a faint croak.

'Feathers. Huge bright white feathers hit the side of the lift and blocked my view. There was a lot of white, and then something shot past me. A pair of enormous wings beat through the fog and cleared it away long enough for me to see just how high up I was. The girl was falling through the air and this winged creature swooped down and caught her in his arms. As he came back up, his face full of panic and fear, he flew past me and I saw who it was. I saw Zac, and I saw you in his arms.' He swallowed. 'I thought you were dead, Ella. You tried to kill yourself, didn't you?'

She nodded. 'He saved me.'

'What is he?'

She couldn't say it. She'd never said the words out loud to anyone who didn't already know.

'Ella, what is he?'

'An angel. He was an angel.' She covered her face in her hands and sobbed. 'But he doesn't exist anymore.'

He pulled her hands away. His eyes searched hers, waiting for her to say it was all a big joke, wanting to make sense of what he had seen. He looked like he was struggling to breathe. Ella placed her hand on his knee.

'Josh? Are you OK?'

'No. What you just said, it doesn't make sense. Angels aren't real.'

'You saw him yourself.'

'I don't know what I saw. I was hoping you would tell me that it was, I don't know. That he was…'

'Josh, there's no other explanation. Zac was an angel. I was only properly with him for about two weeks, if that, but he'd been in love with me for thousands of years during all my past lives. It was so intense; since the day I first saw him, things between us were really full-on. He was only meant to be on Earth to guide me—to bring me to you, actually—but I fell for him. Then he literally fell for me.'

Josh rubbed his face.

'Do you have any idea how fucked up this is?'

She sniffed and laughed through her tears.

'I know. It's been three years since I lost him, and I'm still totally screwed up. I'm a mess.'

'So…Zac told you we were meant to be together? Even though you were in love with each other?'

'Yes. Which is even more fucked up.'

'Very.' Josh dried her face with his shirt sleeve. 'Ella?'

'Yes.'

'I don't know if I can handle this. How do you get your head around it all?'

She shrugged.

'I mean, think about it, what's the point of us?' he said. 'How can I ever compete with an angel? How can I ever give you anything close to what he gave you?'

She sidled up closer to him and placed her hand back on his knee.

'There's no competition, Josh. You are here; he's not. You were always meant to be part of my life; he never was. He and I were forbidden to be together and…now he's dead.'

'I didn't think angels could die. How do you know he's dead?'

'Because I watched him cut off his own wings.'

'That's...what? God, that's insane. I can't believe we're even having this conversation.'

He placed his hand over hers and held it tight.

'Are you OK, Josh? Do you want some water or...?'

'No, I'm far from OK. I'm terrified.'

'Of what?'

'Of just how crazy I am about you.'

Ella closed her eyes, her racing heart gradually slowing back down. The man she was meant to be with knew her darkest secret and still wanted her. She threw her arms around his neck and kissed him, grinning as his eyes widened in surprise.

'You're right,' she said, laughing. 'You're totally crazy...but I'm not complaining.'

She pushed him back on the bed and sat astride him, kissing his mouth and neck and cheeks. Her face was damp with tears and she could taste their saltiness as he kissed her back, his hands around her waist and on her behind, pulling her closer. Sod her no-man ban; this thing with Josh was meant to be. It was right. Everything from now on was going to go as planned.

'Ella, stop. Just a minute. Stop.'

She didn't want to stop. She never wanted to stop. She reluctantly sat up, her legs still around his waist.

'What's the matter?' she asked, out of breath.

'I have to go.'

'Josh, the angel thing doesn't have to change anything between us. We should still give it a try.'

He smiled. 'Don't worry, I'm not running away. Quite the opposite. What time do the shops shut down in town?'

'What? I promise souvenir shopping is not going to be as good as what I'm about to do.'

'I'm serious. What time do the shops shut around here?'

She wouldn't blame him for running a mile—who would want to get involved with a girl who had a past like hers? Sebastian, Zac…she had a lot of baggage.

'It's Saturday, so they shut early, around two in the afternoon. What are you up to?'

Josh kissed the tip of her nose. 'Your birthday's tomorrow, right?'

She nodded.

'And your family and friends are coming?'

'Yes. You've just reminded me that I have to call my mum and check what time she arrives.'

'Great, you do that. I'll see you tomorrow then.'

Ella jumped off him as he clambered off the bed.

'Tomorrow? Where are you going?'

He gave her a half smile and shook his head.

'If I stay here, I'll never leave, and I have to sort stuff out. It might take a while. I'll see you in the morning.'

'What are you sorting out?' she called after him as he headed for her front door.

'I'm cancelling everything, Ella. My whole life.'

'What? Why?'

'I don't want it anymore. You're the one, and I'm going to stay here with you.'

She grinned. Was this really happening? *The* Josh de Silva was declaring his undying love for her and throwing away his career and everything he cared about for her? She couldn't let him do that.

'Josh, wait! Don't do anything drastic. Maybe we should discuss this first?'

He stopped at the front door and turned to her. His face was glowing.

'I know what I'm doing, Ella.'

'Well aren't you at least going to ask whether it's OK with me?' she said, although her heart was soaring.

'I don't need to,' he replied with a wink. 'It's written in the stars, remember?'

19

WHERE HAD JOSH gone? And what did all this mean?

Ella perched on the edge of her bed, her head in her hands. She didn't know if she should laugh, cry, or vomit. Her hangover was battling for attention against her sheer exhilaration and panic.

Josh had kissed her, and it wasn't just a regular, normal kiss! And he knew about Zac! And he said he wanted to change his life for her!

She ran to the bathroom and threw herself against the toilet, dry retching into the bowl. Oh God, this was too much. Tequila and destiny were *not* a great combination. Did all this mean she was finally back on her path? Or did it mean her life was one big, messy joke?

She heaved three more times, drank some water straight from the tap, and then splashed her face with cold water.

She stared at her grey reflection and then groaned, remembering that she had to call her mother. Great. That was the last thing she needed right now—but it was her birthday tomorrow, and she had to know what time everyone was arriving. Talking to Felicity was difficult at the best of times, so Ella reasoned that she may as well tackle the call before having a much-needed lie-down. Not that she had any idea where in the world her mother was.

Felicity had gotten bored of the hotel renovation game within a year of buying the monastery and, although she'd been the one to throw all the money into the project, she'd spent the last year 'finding herself.' Which, as far as Ella was concerned, was a glorified way of running away from her problems.

She scrolled through her mobile phone until she found her mother's number, took a deep breath and waited for the connection.

'Darling! Sweetheart!'

Ella winced and held the phone away from her ear. Why did her mother's voice have to be so comically shrill and dramatic?

'Hey Mum, where are you?'

'I'm still in India, darling.'

'At the Ayurvedic resort? Aren't you bored of brown rice and being teetotal?'

Ella heard the slurp of a drink, and her mother gave an exaggerated sigh.

'Oh no, it's magical. I've completely gone back to nature. I feel like I'm finally finding myself. Darling, have I been a terrible mother the last few years? I've been contemplating on that—lots of meditation. I've been wretched, haven't I? You do forgive me, don't you sweetie?'

Ella closed her eyes and willed her nausea to pass. She was too hungover for this shit.

'For the millionth time, Mum, *yes* you're forgiven. I was a stroppy teen and you were a selfish cow. We've gone over this. We're starting afresh, remember?'

'Namaste, my darling. I've finally found peace.'

Ella laughed. 'Well hallelujah, it's been a long time coming. Can we get back to normal now please?'

'I don't understand, darling.'

'Honestly, Mum! Since you buggered off last year and left me to deal with the hotel *alone*, you've been to every hippy dippy place there is. A meditation retreat in Thailand, past life transgression therapy in San Francisco, a yoga workshop in Bali, and that shamanic nonsense in some Californian mountain.'

'Mount Shasta. It was very cleansing.'

'Whatever.' It was always like this, her mother making her sway between exasperation and laughter. 'It's nice to know you're happy, Mum, even if you're acting like someone half your age.'

'Hmm, pardon?'

Ella could hear the murmur of a male voice in the background as well as her mother's muffled talking and tinkling laughter—as if she were covering up the mouthpiece.

'Sorry, Ella. Yes, I'm happy.'

That was definitely the sound of clinking ice cubes. She wasn't entirely sure how much her mother had gone back to basics or how much 'alone time' her mother was getting, either. There was no time to get deep and personal with her now anyway. Josh was back, he knew about Zac, he loved her and...She was going to be sick again. She had to get off the phone and eat something.

'Mum, what time are you getting here tomorrow?'

'Our flight is early this evening, so we land around one in the afternoon—taking into account the stopover in Madrid.'

'We?'

'Pardon?'

'You said "we."'

'Oh, I meant us at the resort; we all leave together. Some of them are heading back to Spain, too. Yes, I meant us. The gang. My friends.'

Ella sighed. Her mum was definitely up to something, but she didn't have the strength to deal with it right now.

'You've made friends? Doesn't sound like you. OK, so you'll make your way from Malaga Airport on your own? It's just that I have to pick up Mai Li and Kerry from Gibraltar.'

'It's fine. Honestly, darling, don't worry about us. I mean me. I'll be there with bells on. My baby girl turns twenty-three tomorrow. My God! I feel positively ancient. I've bought you some beautiful silk scarves from the markets here, and the jewellery is just beautiful. You'll love it.'

Ella felt guilty for wanting to get off the phone; her mother was clearly trying. Things hadn't been easy the last few years; *Ella* hadn't been easy, to say the least. She sometimes forgot that her parents had witnessed Zac die too. That her father was struggling, having lost his role as angelic expert now that the Choir wouldn't talk to him. Not to mention that he'd only just started to get to know his daughter and Felicity again after twenty years. Plus, her mother and Richard had broken up, something her mum was clearly dealing with in her own unique way. Everyone was battling their own issues, and it wasn't as if Ella's self-medication of drinking and sleeping around had done her any good either.

'You going to manage dinner tomorrow, Mum? You have a seventeen-hour trip, and you're going to be really tired.'

'I can sleep on the plane, sweetheart. It's your father I'm worried about. He'll be exhausted.'

Ella still found it weird that her mum and dad were friends now. Sometimes they even met up without her. Felicity hadn't mentioned Leo for a while; in fact, Ella hadn't heard from her father in ages either.

'You've spoken to Papa? When? I've been trying to get ahold of him for days, but his phone is always off.'

'Oh, yes, I spoke to him last week,' Felicity said, sounding flustered. 'He's at a work function—a church thing, I think. He's been working very hard, but I know he's very excited about seeing you tomorrow.'

Perhaps things would be easier now that she was back on her life path. Maybe things would straighten out between her parents too. Although, Richard had been her mother's destiny and look what had happened there!

'Mum…' Ella hesitated and took a deep breath. 'About you and Papa.'

'There is no me and Leo, darling. He's still a priest and I'm still legally married, for a bit longer at least. You and I have talked about this before. I'm not in a good place right now.'

'I know, I know. I just wanted to ask you a question. It's kind of relevant to something that's happened lately. It's about Zac.'

'Zac? He's not back, is he? Have you heard something?'

'No! Nothing like that. It's just that he once told me everyone has a soulmate, the one we always feel is missing from our life. Yet we also choose "the one" before we're born, the one we're meant to be with during a specific lifetime who enables us to fulfil our journey. We can go lifetimes without finding our soulmates; he told me they can reincarnate as a different person in each lifetime—maybe a friend or brother, or we simply have only a fleeting encounter with them. However, "the one" is the person who is part of each individual life path. The one we're destined to fall in love with.'

'That's true, sweetheart. I learnt a lot about that when I had my regression therapy and found my spirit animal.'

'Right, weird. Anyway, I just wanted to ask, who was Richard to you?'

Silence. When her mother returned, her voice was a lot quieter.

'Richard was "the one," Ella. The man I was destined to love that would help my life progress. But sadly, he no longer has a role to play in my future.'

Ella didn't know what to say. She could hear her mother's gentle breathing at the other end of the line. Waiting.

'Mum, I've always wanted to know something,' she said eventually. 'That night, when you met Richard on my sixteenth birthday, what did you say to him that made him kiss you straightaway? How did you *know?*'

Felicity let out a small laugh that sounded more like a sigh. 'Remember in those letters you read when I described first meeting Zac?'

Ella still found it strange to imagine her mother at nineteen, talking to Zac while pregnant with her.

'Yes.'

'Zac told me I would recognise "the one," that he would be searching for me and would give me back my life. He said I would have appeared in his dreams.'

'Yes, I remember you writing that.'

'Well, on your sixteenth birthday you got lost and Richard brought you back to me. Richard did exactly what Zac said he would do: he brought me back my life—you. When I ran up to him, I knew it was my one chance to see whether Zac was right, so I asked him if he'd been dreaming of me. If he recognised me. He did. Apparently, he'd been dreaming of a blonde woman for years but hadn't realised what it meant. It all sounds ridiculous and far-fetched, a big and silly coincidence, but it didn't feel silly at the time. It felt magical.'

So that was why Richard had looked at her mother that night like she was something from a dream—because she had been. Zac had been right, as always, and Felicity had had the courage to believe him.

'Why didn't it work out then?' Ella whispered, a lump forming in her throat.

'I think Richard and I would have been happy forever, as fate had foreseen, had Zac not entered your life and created waves that turned into one god-awful tsunami. I did a workshop all about the chaos theory when I was in San Francisco. The concept is that a little butterfly can flap its wings, and over time that butterfly creates a storm. Zac was that butterfly. He wasn't meant to be in our lives. If he hadn't started that chain of events, I would never have known what Sebastian did to you. I would have lived in blissful ignorance with my chosen husband, and you would have taken a different path. As for your father, he's always been my soulmate, Ella. In every lifetime. I loved him before, and I always will—that will never change. I have no idea if we were fated to be reunited in this lifetime though; once again, it was Zac who decided that. If it hadn't been for him, who knows what life we'd be living right now?'

Ella knew exactly what life she'd be living, and she was certain it would include Josh.

'Mum, Zac told me I would fall in love with someone else,' she said. 'Someone that wasn't him.'

'Well, maybe you'll find that special someone soon, or he may find you.'

'You think another man could make me as happy as Zac?'

'Of course!' Felicity trilled. 'We all get a second chance at happiness, sweetheart. Zac isn't coming back.'

'You don't know that.'

'No, but you can't wait forever. Your forever isn't as long as his.'

Ella closed her eyes. She'd done enough crying for one day. It was time to pull herself together and face her future head on.

'Mum, do you think you can be in love with two men at the same time?'

Her mother went quiet. She heard her take a sip of her drink and the same murmuring sound of a male voice talking in the background before Felicity hushed him.

'If you can't have the man you truly love, yes you can be in love with another at the same time. There's more than enough room in your heart to love both your destined partner and your soulmate. I did. It's time to lock away the pain, sweetheart, and step into the sunshine. A wise friend once told me "*If a woman can no longer fight, she must wear her armour well.*"

'You make it sound like love is a battle.'

'Well, it isn't easy, Ella. No part of life is. You have to learn how to survive what it throws at you and remember to enjoy yourself. Starting with your birthday tomorrow.'

Felicity was right. Soulmates, 'the one,' past lives and all of that stuff didn't have to define her. She should have left it all behind the moment Zac chose to leave her.

'Are you happy, my darling?' Felicity asked, her voice unusually quiet and urgent.

'Yes, Mum. I think I'm finally happy.'

20

IT WAS STILL dark outside and Zac was walking around the edge of Trafalgar Square in the vain hope of finding a taxi. At that time in the morning it could take a while, but he didn't mind waiting. He was good at it.

As soon as he'd left Tara the week before, his tattoos healing in seconds, he'd booked himself into The Savoy. He'd always liked the look of London's most famous hotel but had never ventured inside. The last time he'd stayed by the banks of the River Thames was when he chanced upon Chaucer writing *The Canterbury Tales*. The writer had been working as a clerk in the Savoy Palace, England's grandest of buildings at the time and where its namesake hotel stood today. Zac had been tasked with the simple mission of talking to the writer. Sometimes, it took nothing more than one tiny word or action to create something beautiful—in this case a revered piece of literature.

What a shame Zac would never have the opportunity to do that again—to change history in a matter of seconds. Zac had been the muse and the catalyst for some of the world's greatest pieces of art and music; he wondered whether he could still make a difference in the lives and paths of others.

Yet the question that had haunted him since his reawakening was: Did he still care? Was it still his job to shape and mould the future, or was it OK to focus on what he truly wanted for his own life? Zac's new mind-bending abilities meant he could finally do as he pleased. He'd never even stayed in a hotel before, but now he could live a life of luxury without ever needing a penny. Did morals apply now that he was straddling two worlds? Surely he was permitted a little pampering after his return from death? Could he be deemed a criminal if he didn't even exist?

Zac had bought a mobile phone the day after receiving his tattoo and called Tara straightaway. As promised, she'd already delivered the note to Gabriel and confirmed that his friend had been both shocked and delighted to hear that Zac had returned.

'Did he say when he'd meet me?' Zac had asked, trying to keep the relief and excitement out of his voice. Tara had been vague, remembering very little of her interaction with the man behind the bar, preferring instead to talk about a woman called Kat who'd been talking to her in the nightclub.

'I'm quitting my job and spending the weekend in Liverpool with her,' Tara told him. 'It's all thanks to you, Zac. Being healed by you has given me the confidence to start afresh. The money you gave me meant I could walk away from my shitty job, and then you sending me to Indigo meant that I met Kat. She's amazing. I can't believe how much you've changed my life. It's like you have a magic touch or something.'

The more she spoke the more Zac smiled until, by the time she rang off, he was positively grinning. So what that he was no longer the Path Keeper, the mightiest of angels and the bringer of mercy? He still had the ability to steer others toward joy. He just hoped he'd get his happy ever after too. Gabriel had the note, which meant Zac was now one step closer to seeing his friend and discovering where Ella was.

Lucky for Zac, he was a patient being. For three days in a row, he'd taken the same cab ride to the same place to wait for the archangel, and each evening Zac had returned to an empty hotel room enveloped in a sense of despair.

What if Gabriel never showed? How long should he wait for his friend? The archangel was his only hope of finding Ella. The note the angel had left with Ylva clearly stated he'd been watching over his girl, so Gabriel *had* to know where she was.

Zac had tried everything to track Ella down. He'd looked up her mother's business name and called her office. He'd intended to meet Felicity and bend her mind until she told him where her daughter was, but her assistant said she no longer owned the company. He made someone in the hotel show him how the internet worked—he even requested his own laptop—but after a thorough search, it was clear Ella hadn't been spotted in years. He also went back to her old university and forced the receptionist to check her files for an address abroad. Nothing. His only chance of finding Ella was talking to Gabriel, so he would have to do the same journey every morning until his friend showed up.

• • • • •

The bright yellow glow of a taxi cab shone through the darkness. Zac held out his hand and it slowed. He peered through the window and smiled at the driver, recognising him straightaway. Was this fate again or just a coincidence? And what did it even matter now that Zac was, as Tara had put it, off the grid?

'Where you off to, mate?' the driver asked. 'I normally end my shift around now, but if you're heading north I'm going that way.'

He got in and told him the destination. Was Zac really untouchable? Would he spend the rest of eternity walking through the thinly woven tapestry of life? Would he spend a lifetime picking his way among the threads that bound everyone together, his presence still affecting the world without fate including him in her tightly knit pattern?

'Here, you remind me of this bloke I had in the back of my cab once,' the driver said to him through the reflection of his rearview mirror. 'It's the eyes. Yeah, they was bright blue just like yours. Don't suppose you're friends with that Fantz girl, are you? Ella, was it?'

Zac stayed silent.

'Lovely girl. Had her in the back of my cab once, too, the night of the New Year's Eve drama. Remember that? Was in all the papers. I took her and a bloke what looked a bit like you to the airport that night. He had longer hair, mind. You look a bit rougher than him. I never said nothing to no one about where I took them. Newspapers were all offering a pretty penny for people to slag her off, and my God how they did. She had mates from school and her old life in Spain saying she was a bitch and sharing photos of her, but I kept shtoom. She was a nice girl, and them two was really in love. I always wondered what happened to 'em.'

Zac smiled to himself. Today was Ella's birthday. If his life were a movie, then Gabriel would turn up today; he would tell him where Ella was, and Zac would arrive just in time to surprise her and carry her off into the sunset. Unfortunately, Zac had been part of enough stories to know that in real life the happy parts are rarely at the end.

'I hate gossip, though, hate it,' the driver continued. 'You'll never hear me chatting about any of my fares. You come in my cab and you want to talk, it's all good, but it don't go no further. You ain't very chatty, are you?'

'I'm afraid I won't be paying for this journey,' Zac answered, their eyes meeting in the rearview mirror. 'And you won't remember having seen me tonight.'

'Not paying? Rightyho, mate. No problem. Here we are, Angel station.'

21

ZAC HAD BEEN sitting at the far end of the station platform for an hour. Turning up to the same place day after day hoping to meet Gabriel was reckless. If Gabriel was being watched by Mikhael, then Zac was leaving himself wide open, but it was the only way he could be certain the archangel was on his side. Zac hadn't given a time on the note, but he knew his friend well. If Gabriel truly wanted to help, then he would come alone and in secret, meaning he'd be there at dawn when angelic powers were at their weakest and the Choir wouldn't pick up on his absence.

The hairs on the back of Zac's neck stood on end and goose bumps began to rise on his arms. The archangel had finally arrived. All angels had an aura, but Gabriel's was so strong that when he entered a room, the air went out. Throughout history, Zac had seen the way people reacted to him—breathless and confused. He closed his eyes and steadied his nerves. This was it.

The London Underground jacket Zac was wearing wasn't the most creative of disguises, but if his hunch was right and Gabriel couldn't sense him, then at least his friend wouldn't recognise him immediately, either. After all, the archangel was looking for a fallen angel with long, wavy hair, not a short-haired Tube worker. If Gabriel hadn't come alone, then Zac's vague disguise would at least give him enough of a head start to run for his life.

The archangel looked up and down the platform, his steps measured and languid. He glanced at Zac leaning against the wall in the distance, and then he doubled up and walked to the southbound platform opposite.

Gabriel had come alone *and* he hadn't felt him. Zac let out a long breath he hadn't realised he'd been holding.

After a few minutes, Gabriel appeared again.

'You came,' Zac said softly.

The angel turned quickly at the sound of Zac's voice. His eyes narrowed, the dim light of the platform casting shadows over his razor-sharp cheekbones.

'I don't believe it. My boy did it,' he said quietly, not moving. He gave Zac a lopsided smile and shook his head from side to side as his friend walked toward him. '*You did it!*'

He held his arms out wide and threw them around Zac, pulling him into a bear hug. 'Look at you! Where's your pretty hair gone?'

Zac laughed and struggled out of his friend's embrace. Gabriel was still beaming as they walked to the bench at the far end of the walkway and sat down. The station hadn't yet officially opened, so they were the only ones on the platform. The archangel sighed and looked up at the ceiling. Were there tears in his eyes?

'I wasn't sure if you'd show. I came every morning,' Zac said, not quite believing he was finally sitting next to his friend—as he had done a million times before over the centuries. Zac was no longer alone. It was as if nothing had changed, as if no time had passed at all and he was still who he'd always been.

Except he wasn't. He never would be.

'Sorry it took me so long,' Gabriel replied. 'I had to wait a couple of days until the others weren't watching. I couldn't risk being followed.'

'So, you knew the note was from me?'

'Yeah, Angel station. Subtle.' Gabriel's grin was so wide it showed every one of his teeth. His light green eyes shone like polished jade. 'Remember that wild night we had at the inn around here? When was it? Three...four hundred years ago?'

'We were playing cards to see who would get to name the public house.'

'That's right, and you wanted to call it Arabella Inn. Honestly, when you get obsessed with a girl, you really get obsessed.'

'Well, you wanted it named Gabriel Inn after yourself. That's even worse!'

The angel laughed. 'Yeah, well, in the end the owner named his pub after us both, The Angel Inn. And now look, the whole area *and* the station are named after us. Don't you just love it when a card game changes the face of London?' Gabriel looked at Zac for a long time. 'I miss those days. Things were easier back then, when people knew who we were. *What* we were.'

'It's good to be back,' Zac said.

In all the years he'd known Gabriel, his one true friend, the archangel had never had his wings ruffled. His existence was effortless. He bent and swayed to life's ebbs and flows, never changing but always adapting. This was the first time Zac had ever seen him look less than calm.

'I can't believe it's really you,' Gabriel said. 'I had no idea what craziness was going through your mind back on that mountain, but when you hacked off your own wings, I thought that was it. Over. Yet here you are, sitting here looking all fine like nothing happened. I could kill you again for what you put me through!'

Zac wanted to smile, too, but he couldn't. It wasn't relief he was feeling—it was a deep shame for his rash actions that rainy night in

Spain. He couldn't forget the look of horror on Gabriel's face as he'd ended his own life, let alone poor Ella's reaction. Had he been selfish? It had felt like a grand gesture of love and defiance at the time...but maybe he *had* been selfish, leaving his girl and his Choir behind without an explanation. It was the first time in his existence that he'd ever experienced guilt, and it wasn't a nice feeling.

'How did you know I'd make it back?' Zac asked, looking down at his trainers. They'd been in the bag of clothes he'd taken from Ella's old room. They didn't fit properly. He'd acquired a phone out of necessity, but he still hadn't been able to bring himself to brainwash a shop assistant and get new shoes for free.

'At first, I didn't know you'd be able to come back. How could I?' Gabriel replied. 'I'd seen what happened to the other angels when Mikhael took their wings. They died and disappeared forever, which is why none of us could understand why you killed yourself. Why, when all you wanted was to be with the one you loved, did you throw away your life for hers? So I visited Leonardo, the priest. He always had the answers. I wasn't sure if he'd want to see me though, not after the way Mikhael and the rest of us treated his daughter.'

'You spoke to Ella's father?'

'No, I didn't in the end. I arrived at his apartment an hour before I knew he would be home. I wanted to look through his books and files about us. The priest and I had talked a lot over the years, but I never realised he had such interesting things about our history in his home. Then I found this.'

Gabriel reached into his jacket and produced a small oil painting. Zac recognised it immediately; he'd seen it before in Leo's house. It was all the proof he'd needed back then that cutting off his own wings could possibly bring him back. It had been a massive gamble, but so far it had paid off.

'That's my mother,' Zac said.

'I know, but I was unaware you were her son. Luci and I go way back.'

'Her name was Luci? What was she like?'

'She was perfect in every way.' Gabriel's eyes changed from clear jade to something stormier, a deep green like the troubled waters of a tropical sea.

'Leonardo said I was born to two archangels. Was she one too, then?'

'Yes, the very first.'

Zac screwed up his eyes and rubbed the back of his neck; it felt cold and naked now that his hair was short. The priest had been right. His mother had been a powerful archangel. Why had nobody ever told him about her? And what had become of her?

He opened his eyes and blinked a few times until Gabriel was no longer blurred around the edges. 'What was her full angelic name?'

'Lucifer.'

Lucifer? *The* Lucifer? Zac rubbed his face. It didn't make sense. The Choir had only ever spoken of the evil Archangel Lucifer in hushed tones, as if the very mention of its name would bring bad luck. How could his sweet, kind mother be the same being?

'Are you saying my mother was the original fallen angel?'

'Yes, she and Mikhael were the first of our kind to come to Earth. Our leaders. He has been obsessed with her since eternity began.'

'I don't understand,' Zac said. 'So why did Mikhael kill her then? If she was so powerful and he loved her so much, why take away her wings?'

'Because she defied him and got pregnant. Basically, she loved you more than she could ever have loved him. It was the first time any angel had managed to carry a child. He feared your power, Zadkiel, and the fact that you were greater than him in every way. Greater than the two of them combined. He had already lost her to you; he couldn't risk losing his throne too.'

'Is that why he told me that my mother was a whore and my father was a lesser angel? That I was just a half-angel—a Nephilim? So that I wouldn't know my true heritage?'

'It appears so. I'm still trying to work it out myself. You didn't die in Tuscany during your first life; it was all a lie. You're a pure angel, but he wanted you to believe you had lived like a normal man. That's why when you were killed, he treated you like we treat all humans when they die—Mikhael brought you Home. We accepted you into the Choir, as we have done with countless other Nephilim before you, and you were just another half-angel joining us. None of us realised you were Luci's child, let alone his. He told us that her baby hadn't survived, that female angels would never be able to have children on Earth. Doing so had made her crazy and that was why he'd killed her—to save the world from her evil. I never saw Mikhael rip out her wings, but he delighted in telling us the details of the massacre. He used her punishment as a warning to us all.'

Zac shook his head. He hadn't died in Fiesole? He could have stayed with the girl he loved all along? Stars swam in front of his eyes as he shook his head in tiny motions, slowly realising he'd been living a lie for two thousand years!

He clenched his jaw, his nails digging into the palms of his hands.

'I wanted to return to Arabella, to be born again like other Nephilim choose to do, but Mikhael forbade it,' Zac cried. 'But Mikhael told me that I had a job to do, that I was to be a Path Keeper. I get it now. He only said that because I wasn't able to be human again, was I?'

Gabriel shook his head.

'No. You're a pure angel, Zadkiel. The only one of your kind. Nobody knew but him, so he destroyed the truth and your mother. Except Luci never really died.'

Zac's hand shot out, grabbing his friend's arm. 'You've seen her? My mother's alive?'

'Sorry, kid. I haven't.' Gabriel's eyes had cleared to a smooth jade again, although this time they were shining brighter than ever. 'But I've always struggled to believe that Lucifer was that easy to kill. Your mother, she was something special—strong, clever, mesmerising and formidable. It took me a long time to get over her death, to get over thinking of her being eradicated so easily like some lesser angel. I couldn't bear it. But now I know that she outsmarted us all.'

'How do you know that for certain, though?' Zac thought of his own risks, cutting off his wings based on nothing but the painting of his mother and a powerful hunch.

'I first suspected the truth when I saw her beautiful face again,' Gabriel said, holding up the portrait. 'This was painted centuries after her death. I figured you must have seen it too, and that's why you killed yourself. It was the only explanation I could think of for you being so impulsive. You've never made a mistake, Zadkiel.' Gabriel's eyes shone with tears that he blinked away. 'Losing you was incredibly hard for those of us who witnessed it. Especially me.'

Zac swallowed down the guilt that was building up inside of him again. He had to find Ella and his mother; he had to ensure that his recklessness had not been in vain.

'I was convinced that you'd left us for a good reason,' the archangel continued. 'So when I saw this portrait of your mother, I took it as a sign that you were both still alive. I didn't wait to speak to Leonardo the priest; I took the painting and refused to mourn you. From that day on, I spent my time searching for evidence. I travelled the world, sifting through old newspapers and hundreds of books. I even went to the Vatican and ancient libraries—desperate for anything that would prove my theory that your mother had survived. I was convinced that if she was alive, then you would return too. It took me months and I had to do it in secret, afraid Mikhael would discover the truth too.' Gabriel rested his hand on his friend's shoulder and tilted his head to look at him, his mouth settling in a straight line. Nothing but love and sadness shone in his eyes. 'Your mother is definitely alive.'

Zac couldn't move. His breaths were now coming in shallow fits and starts. He had been right all along.

'She's appeared throughout history many times as a variety of different women,' Gabriel continued. 'Always powerful and undefeatable, most recently going by the names of Lucia, Lucinda, and Luci. I've seen photos of her with politicians, paintings of her leading men into battle, and accounts of mysterious women throughout history doing extraordinary things.'

Zac's voice was hoarse when he asked, 'So we're the only ones that know she's alive? No one else has worked out that all these women are Lucifer?'

His friend nodded. 'We're the only ones. I'm sure of it. Mikhael is so certain of his strength that there's no way he suspects. He truly believes that he came out on top, and he's never spent enough time with humans to discover this himself—to see the things I've seen and make the connections. He's always hated humans for stealing Lucifer from him, for her loving you and her life on Earth more than she did Home. The only involvement he's ever had with their kind was to ensure that they continued peddling lies about the fallen angel. For over two thousand years, from Eve and the Whore of Babylon right through to Lilith the Jewish temptress, Mikhael ensured that women in religion were either virgins or whores and either gentle wives or evil, sex-mad bitches. He hates and fears strong women, so he made sure that humans did too. This is why Mikhael created the concept of God, so that he could also create a Devil, an antithesis to all that is good. Lucifer was rebranded as all that is evil. She became a warning to both humans and our kind that if you are not compliant, you will die a Death Eternal.'

Zac's poor mother. Had she really been searching for him all this time, two thousand years, all while being loathed and vilified? There was still one question he had to ask before he could run the risk of looking for her. A question he wasn't sure he wanted to hear the answer to.

'Gabe…does all this mean that my mother…?' He took a deep breath. 'Is she dangerous? Is she as terrible as the stories tell us she is?'

Gabriel's grip on his friend's shoulder tightened. 'No!' he cried. 'I've just told you that was all bullshit; it was part of the pro-God propaganda Mikhael helped create. Now that I know how deeply in love with her your father must have been to…well, to create you, it makes total sense. You can only hate someone that much if they have the ability to hurt you. There's a thin line between love and hate. By having the world fear her, he was still controlling the memory of her and remaining the good guy. Mikhael lied to us all—the human world and his Choir. Only you, me, and your mother know the truth. We need to find her.'

Saliva began to pool in the corners of Zac's mouth. He swallowed and took another deep breath, willing himself not to vomit. Not only had their leader taken Zac away from his mother, but he'd also taken him away from the only girl he'd ever had the chance of loving. Mikhael would pay for this.

With a sigh he turned to Gabriel, who looked as exhausted as he felt. 'What did you do once you realised all of this? What happened after I died?'

'A lot has happened since you left us,' the archangel replied with a short burst of sardonic laughter. His hands were back on his lap, but his knee was jiggling up and down in tiny motions. Zac didn't like to see his friend so agitated. It made him nervous, too.

'After you hacked off your wings, your father was broken. We all were. You were right about your death being his punishment, but instead of repenting he became angrier than ever. We couldn't take you Home. I'm not sure why, but your body without wings wouldn't allow us to bring you back up. You had broken the number one angelic rule, and your body was stuck on Earth. Fallen in every sense of the word. Mikhael said that the same thing had happened with Lucifer, that he'd dumped her wingless body in the forest, so we returned your body to the Spanish mountains and buried it. Only we archangels knew of its location.' His knee was still bouncing up and down, his foot making a tapping sound on the floor. 'Mikhael was really suspicious of your actions. He couldn't understand why you hadn't killed him instead. A few of us wish you had. I think he was scared you weren't really dead. Of course, once I discovered the truth about Luci, I realised he must have been worried that she was out there, too, and that you knew something he didn't. Which you did.'

He laughed.

'Archangel Raphael hates him as much as we do, but we never talk about it. We don't dare. Your body was buried under huge rocks not far from where you'd died, and every day Mikhael would send Raphael and me to check on your grave and report back. Your wings we took back Home with us, but I'm afraid they disintegrated within days.'

Gabriel looked away from the pained expression on Zac's face. Every angel's wings were individual, like a fingerprint. Losing them was like losing your soul.

'After about a year, Mikhael was satisfied it had worked and you were truly dead. No one could feel your presence, and your body was decomposing as any human body would.' He blinked slowly, his jade eyes misting over again. 'Sorry, I know it's difficult to hear, but believe me, it wasn't much fun to watch, either.'

'So how did I end up in a tomb?'

Gabriel smiled. 'Yeah, you like that? Well, once I discovered the truth about your mother, I was convinced you would return too, so I took your body and replaced it with a rotting carcass I dug up from a nearby graveyard.'

'Nice.'

'Yeah, sorry. Then I flew you in the dead of night to Highgate in London, put a T-shirt on you since you were still half naked, and hoped you wouldn't look like a decomposed zombie if you *did* wake up. I also figured if I left you in North London you'd know where you were, and hopefully Ella wouldn't be too far away.'

'Thanks, and all that, but you barricaded me in.'

'Of course. I wanted you to stay safe.' Gabriel made a sucking sound through his teeth. 'I did the same for Jesus after he died, and *he* found his way out of the cave without moaning about it.'

'You could have left a few tins of food and some wet wipes or something.'

Gabriel punched him playfully on the arm and grinned.

'You found me, though, didn't you? It worked.'

'Yes, thank you. And, luckily for the old widow who saw me smash my way out of the tomb, my body still heals itself and I'm no zombie… even if my hair was a disaster.'

Gabriel made a shocked face. 'Oh no, not your pretty hair!'

Zac tried to hide his grin but he couldn't. Gabriel was the closest thing he'd ever had to a brother, his best friend, and it felt good to be back with him.

'You said Mikhael got angry after I…did what I did. That Raphael and the rest of the Choir began to hate him too. What happened? Did any of them turn against me for putting a human before the angelic realm?'

Gabriel frowned and shook his head.

'Turn against *you?* Hell no! It was way worse than that. Things got ugly. The rest of the angels were *furious* with Mikhael. He let you die! We all love you, and we were heartbroken. So, when word got out that Mikhael had done the one thing he'd forbidden us to do, make love with another angel and create a child, a son he let *die*…well, the shit hit the fan. Big time.'

'What happened?'

'An almighty…' He hesitated and then smiled. 'A fuck-fest, that's what happened. About a year ago, nearly all the angels came down to Earth and started going at it like rabbits. Not with each other—they saw what had happened to your mother, and no one wanted to lose their wings—but there's never been any rules about sex with humans. Last year, hundreds of us came down to the UK and hung out at university campuses, music festivals, and basically anywhere humans were up for a bit of fun. Look at us, Zadkiel, we're not exactly ugly. It was too easy and exactly what we all needed to let off some steam, so we had our own celestial summer of love. You know that having the odd lusty fling is fine as long as we don't get women pregnant—but the angels weren't following that rule either.'

'Nephilim have been born? Half-angels exist again?'

It wasn't the first time Gabriel had fathered an earthborn child. His love affair with a woman named Mary over two thousand years ago had led to the most famous Nephilim being born.

'Yeah, some half-angels were conceived,' Gabriel continued, his face suddenly serious. 'It was stupid of us; we should have known how Mikhael would react. My boy Jesus was the last official Nephilim and look what happened after he died—the end of the angelic reign and the beginning of the God fallacy. After that, we were warned not to father children. But that was then; this time, no one was listening to Mikhael.'

Zac couldn't believe what he was hearing. He knew all about Jesus, he'd even met him, but he couldn't believe the angels had been stupid enough to defy Mikhael's law after all this time and procreate again.

'So what happened?'

'The boss found out and put a stop to it, of course. He's killed a lot of babies in the last year, Zadkiel. *A lot.* It got nasty. We all know human lives come and go, but who kills babies?'

Zac closed his eyes. He knew Mikhael was evil, but this? It was all Zac's fault! If he hadn't been so selfish, then the Choir would never have rebelled and innocent lives needn't have been lost.

'It's like the birth of Jesus all over again,' Zac said. Mikhael had been the one to help King Herod with the 'firstborn son cull.'

'Yeah, well, that was only ever going to end in trouble,' Gabriel said. 'The Romans still got my boy in the end, eh? The only thing people and angels have ever agreed on. Ain't nobody got time for another messiah. Best to keep the politicians and the rich in power. Who wants a do-gooder spiritual being telling everyone to be nice to each other?'

This was Gabriel's favourite subject and one they'd secretly spoken about at length many times before: the God myth and Mikhael's ban on angels chasing after humans. Sex was fine but falling in love wasn't.

'So, all the shagging about has stopped then?' Zac said. 'Has the slaughtering stopped? Has everyone got their fill and gone back to normal now?'

Gabriel shrugged. 'Probably. Raphael was the first to break the rules; he's been seeing a girl in Glastonbury for a few years now. He really likes her, and he's managed to keep it from Mikhael—so she's safe. I heard she gave birth to his son last year and has another on the way. You have an ally in Raphael when you're ready.'

'Wow,' Zac said under his breath.

The archangel of healing had been successful in having a human relationship, something Zac had wanted with Ella for two thousand years. How had he kept his earthbound family safe from Mikhael? If Raphael could do it, then maybe there was hope for him and Ella after all.

'And you, Gabriel? Did you break the rules?' he asked.

Gabriel shrugged again. 'Not as much as the others. I was too busy hanging out in dusty research libraries and moving your body around.' He laughed. 'Don't get me wrong, I've had a bit of fun. There was a Japanese student in Brighton, clever and really cool, who I had a thing with. In fact, I could have sworn I saw her at the club a few days ago when I talked to the girl who delivered your note. Freaked me out. She was identical to her. But I could feel it wasn't her and her hair was different; maybe they were related. Anyway, there was her and a few others, but no, I didn't set out to have children with them, and eventually the angels either got bored or scared of Mikhael and stopped. I did too. I couldn't risk him murdering any more of my babies. Not after Jesus. Mikhael is one mean motherfucker, and he had the cheek to tell the world that Lucifer was the evil one.'

'Do you miss her?'

'Who? Your mother? Yeah, every day.'

'No, I mean Mary. Jesus's mum. Don't you ever wonder who she was reborn as?'

Gabriel sighed. 'Look, I've been around for eons. Lucifer and Mikhael came first, then me and Raphael, then the other archangels and so on. We arrived as soon as the first ape turned human. Do you know how many women, and men, have come and gone in my life since then? How many Nephilim were created before Jesus was killed and things got complicated? Mary was the last special one, but she wasn't the first. Yeah, I think of her sometimes. She looked great in blue.'

Zac rolled his eyes, and his friend laughed. 'But you're the only one I know who has ever got hung up on just the one. Even Raphael isn't that obsessed with the mother of his kids—he only sees her every few weeks, sometimes months. That's why he's kept it under the radar so long; he doesn't hang about. This obsession you have with Arabella, or whatever she's called now, is not healthy. All that time you spent with her three years ago, that's why Mikhael got scared and kept dragging you back. He must have thought he was going to lose you to the human world like he did your mother.'

'She's my everything,' Zac hissed. 'I've died twice for her, at the very beginning and as an angel. And I would do it again.'

Gabriel looked up at the ceiling and sighed. 'I've got to hand it to you, kid. When you love someone, you don't muck about. But look at you. Look at what you are now! You're going to live for eternity, and she won't. So, then what will you do?'

Zac had spent two thousand years pining for Ella and their forbidden love, longing for her in whatever form she'd taken in each of her lives, but he'd never once appreciated the incredible life he'd shared with Gabriel as an angel. If he could even call it a life. But he no longer had his angelic friends, a job or any form of identity. What *was* he going to do now with his second chance? Would he spend the rest of his existence courting every version of Ella for eternity? Was that even possible?

'I'm not sure what I'll do next,' Zac replied.

Even if he did get Ella back and they got to stay together forever, it wouldn't be for long. As an angel, he'd known every single one of her birth *and* death dates—and this time, her life was a short one. She had eleven years left. Zac had always known Ella was going to drown and die at age thirty-four. If he didn't push her back off her path and stop her heading toward that date, he could lose her again. Then what would he do? How long would he have to wait until she was reborn and grown up and he found her again? It could take dozens, if not hundreds, of years between lives. He couldn't risk meeting up with Gabriel regularly; the others may find him, and who knew what his father would do? No Ella, no friends, and no security. Perhaps he hadn't thought this through properly after all.

People were starting to stream onto the platform. London rush hour had started. Although it was April and still cool outside, the swarms of commuters in their thick coats were making the platform heat up. Zac took off his jacket.

'What is this, brother? You got a *tattoo?*' Gabriel pushed up the sleeve of Zac's T-shirt to reveal the images of feathers floating down his upper arm. 'New hair *and* ink? What we got here then, some new-life crisis or something?'

A ghost of a smile flickered on Zac's lips.

'I got my wings back. Take a look.'

Gabriel peered down the back of his friend's T-shirt and let out a low whistle.

'You're crazy. Any specific reason why you coloured yourself in?'

Zac laughed. 'I wanted to feel complete again. I missed the feathers. Anyway, the tattoos will fade and the hair will grow back. I wanted to look different for a short while because I'm a different person now. Well, not even a person or an angel. I don't know what to call myself anymore. One of the fallen? I guess when I fell in love, I fell good and proper.'

Ella. He'd been wanting to ask about her from the moment he saw Gabriel. He couldn't wait any longer. Zac looked down at his feet, his voice dropping to a whisper.

'Do you think she'll still want me?' he asked.

'Who?'

'Ella.'

'Who's Ella?'

Zac tutted. This was a game they played. Gabriel, the nonchalant big brother, and Zac, the kid he enjoyed winding up. Gabriel was trying to keep his face indifferent but was failing.

'You know who. Arabella. Ella. Is she OK? You said in your note that you'd been looking out for her. Is she back on her life path? Does she miss me?'

Gabriel couldn't keep a straight face any longer. He looked up at the ceiling and let out a light laugh.

'Chill out. I saw her two weeks ago. Don't worry, she's never seen me. I watch from afar, and no—she's not back on her path yet.'

Zac allowed a glimmer of hope to blossom in his chest.

'So, she's still in mourning for me?'

'She's stuck in the monastery most of the time, but she's kept herself busy.'

'She's become a nun?'

The archangel laughed so loudly it reverberated through the tunnels and bounced off the grimy, tiled walls. A couple of people on the platform turned to look at them. Zac felt twitchy. He didn't want to be seen, although he knew Gabriel would sense anyone dangerous. Zac was safe as long as he remained with the archangel.

'Boy, get a grip! You think Ella's a *nun?* Believe me, your girl is far from being a nun. This isn't the eighteenth century anymore. No, she's converted an old convent in Tarifa and is running it as a hotel. I saw her two weeks ago, and there was no serious boyfriend hanging around, if that's what you want to hear.'

Zac thought about Josh and fate and wondered whether life would bring them together as it should have done by now. As long as Zac got there in time, he could get in the way of destiny again and cut off her path. He could change everything—including who she loved and when she died.

'So she's been alone for three years, pining for me?'

Gabriel raised his eyebrows.

'Not totally alone, no. She's kept…active. What's your plan? Are you just going to barge right in and take her back?'

'Of course. That's why I did this. It's why I killed myself, so I could be resurrected with eternal life on Earth. I want my girl back, Gabriel, and this time I won't let her go.'

'Man, you are one intense brother. I remember the time when they used to call you the Path Keeper. You went about making sure people *followed* their path, but now you want to just live your own life even if it destroys hers? You're not her destiny, Zadkiel. You know that.'

'I don't care; it doesn't matter anymore.'

Gabriel sighed. 'It's getting busy in here. I better get going.'

He went to stand but Zac pulled him back down.

'You can't go without telling me where she is. Please.'

Gabriel turned to his friend and placed both hands on his shoulders. 'Zadkiel, you know you're like a brother to me, but you need to leave Ella alone. It isn't fair to her—nothing good will come from stepping in the way of fate.'

'No way. You're crazy! Nothing's going to stop me. You know how much we love each other.'

Gabriel let go of Zac's shoulders and sighed. 'You've been around long enough to know that love means much less than people realise. What's the point of having a relationship with her? None of us archangels can sense you, but Mikhael *can* feel *her.* She will lead him to you. Plus, what's the point of winning her back in every one of her lifetimes over and over again? What can you even offer her? An eternally young guy to hang out with? You can't even give her children, Zadkiel. They would be Nephilim, and they wouldn't survive Mikhael.'

'Raphael has managed.'

Gabriel raised his eyebrows. 'Mikhael didn't try and kill Raphael's woman. He doesn't even know about her. But he *does* know about Ella. He blames her for your death, and he'll be watching her. Chasing her will get you both, and any future children, killed. Death Eternal for her means no more lifetimes for either of you.'

'Maybe I could convince him to leave us be? Or fight him?'

Gabriel snorted. 'As long as he has his sword, he has all the power. You'd have to kill him and destroy his sword. You know how to do that?'

'No. Of course I don't.'

Zac stared at all the commuters scattered around them, oblivious to Gabriel and him being anything more than just two men talking. He never thought he'd envy humans but he did. Every single person on that platform had the freedom to love whomever they wished. All he wanted was to be with the woman he belonged with, do normal things with her and have a family.

'Maybe Ella and I could adopt a child.'

'And what, you stay looking like a hunky twenty-something-year-old while your kids grow to be grandparents? How will that work?'

'We'll muddle through.'

'You're not going to stop, are you? Fine. I'll take you to her, but you better get your shit straight. If Mikhael finds you it means I'm going down too, and I'd like to keep my pretty wings, thank you very much.'

Zac grinned and patted his friend's back.

'Maybe I should call her and let her know I'm coming. I bought a mobile phone yesterday; electricity doesn't seem to be affected by me anymore. Do you have her number?'

Gabriel rolled his eyes.

'No, funnily enough I haven't had the chance to ask for her business card yet. Are you for real? Just look up *Torre de los angeles* in Tarifa.'

'*Tower of Angels?* She named it after me?'

Zac hoped that Gabriel couldn't hear the quickening of his heart. Ella was still thinking of him. She hadn't forgotten—she had been waiting all this time—and even the name of her hotel was a sign, a beacon, calling for him. This was going to work. He wasn't too late after all.

'OK,' he told his friend. 'I'll look it up and call her straightaway. Did you know today's her birthday?'

Gabriel looked at him incredulously and shook his head.

'So?'

'So we need to get there as quickly as possible. Let's go!'

Zac was already walking toward the exit, but Gabriel placed his hand on Zac's chest, stopping him from going any further.

'Slow down, Romeo. We'll go tomorrow.'

'What? But I have to…'

Gabriel raised his hand and Zac stopped talking, letting out an angry breath through his nose.

'Zadkiel, I need to plan this properly. Dawn tomorrow will be safer. Can you travel like before?'

'No. I lost some of my powers, including teleportation and the ability to feel what others feel.'

'You can't feel people?'

'No, otherwise I'd be with Ella right now. Things have been tough. Anyway, I'll call her, and you can go on ahead and tell her I'm on my way. I'll catch a flight tomorrow. I've never had the need to fly in a plane—should be interesting.'

'You have a passport?' Gabriel asked. 'Last time I checked, angels couldn't even have their photo taken.'

'I have something much better than a passport.' Zac gave his friend a lopsided smile. 'I can make people do anything I want them to do.'

'For real?'

'Yep. I lost some abilities but gained others. I now have this kind of hypnotic power over the minds of humans.'

'Really? Is that how you got that girl to deliver the note to me? I couldn't feel anything off her; she was so calm. It was weird.'

'Yes, exactly. I just ask for whatever I want, and I get it. I can even wipe people's memories. I think that's how my mother has survived for so long.'

'Figures. Go on then, show me your magic trick.'

Zac walked over to one of the smartly dressed commuters and pointed to his wrist. A moment later, he presented Gabriel with a gold watch.

'Here you go. A thank you gift for everything you've done for me since I died.'

'So, now you're a thief too?' Gabriel said, frowning and smiling at the same time.

Zac shrugged. The archangel let out a loud laugh, putting his arm around his friend's shoulder.

'Come on, you crazy fool. Let's go get your girl.'

22

'I DON'T UNDERSTAND why we had to get the Tube when we can ride taxis for free,' Sebastian muttered.

It was the morning rush hour, and he was seated beside Luci on a Piccadilly line train. They'd caught the Tube at Heathrow Airport and managed to secure a seat. Sebastian wasn't used to London's public transport; the smell and heat emanating from the other passengers was making him nauseous.

'I like to be surrounded by people. It makes me happy. I've spent far too long on my own over the years,' she answered, staring up at the Tube map opposite them. 'We need to change at King's Cross station. Didn't you tell me Ella goes to university there?'

Sebastian shook his head.

'That was over three years ago,' he said quietly, leaning into Luci and avoiding eye contact with the other commuters. He'd bought a baseball cap at the airport, but he was still worried about being recognised. 'She will have finished her degree by now. Let's stick to the original plan and go to Highgate. My father will know where she is.

Maybe you can convince him to forgive me while you're there and then find a way to get the Met Police to drop the charges against me.'

'Maybe. Oh! Look at that,' Luci cried, pointing at the Tube map in front of them. 'We're close to Angel station. I came here four hundred years ago. My whisperers had heard there were two angels at an inn, one with long, wavy hair and the other with dark skin. I knew they were talking about Zadkiel and Gabriel, but I got there too late. I'm always one step behind my boy.'

Luci's voice was so loud that people were starting to stare at her, a woman dressed in crazy, skimpy hippy clothes, talking about angels. Sebastian looked the other way and closed his eyes, hoping it would make her stop. He was tired. The journey from the Saharan settlement to London hadn't been an easy one.

After her big reveal to Sebastian back in Morocco, Luci had left him tied to the chair in her tent and ridden into the main town on a camel with one of the yoga teachers. She'd returned an hour later driving a Jeep. The next day she'd announced they were leaving.

'You're free now,' she'd told everyone at the campsite.

Sebastian had watched as people queued outside her tent to say goodbye. She'd looked each person in the eye and placed a hand on their shoulder as she spoke. Some had hugged her, and some had cried. The young girl with the shaved head had begged Luci to take her with them and had kissed the fallen angel until Sebastian had begun to stir. Why did they all love the crazy bitch after being treated like slaves and being held captive in the middle of nowhere?

'You won't remember me. You will only recall a wonderful time at your yoga retreat,' she said to the girl. 'Now go on and do good things and be happy.'

They'd all smiled at her and returned like sleepwalkers back to their tents. That was the last Sebastian had seen of the others. It was a shame. After having witnessed the bald kid in action with Luci, he would have liked to have had her for himself. Bloody waste of a firm young body, letting her go like that.

The journey from the camp to Marrakesh had taken five bumpy hours. The Jeep had no air conditioning, and the air outside was hotter than inside, so opening the window hadn't helped either.

'Is this all you packed?' he asked Luci, rummaging in the beaded cotton bag at his feet.

'When you move around as much as I do, you learn to survive with just the essentials.'

Sebastian rubbed his wrists where the scarves had been wrapped around him. They still stung after two days, although the red marks had disappeared instantly. He grabbed one of the four bottles of water at his feet and noted the contents of the bag—a change of clothes for her and a couple of apples. That was it. Sebastian was too scared to question her further; not only did he fear what her next torture trick may be, but she was easily distracted when driving and they'd already had some near misses. He'd shouted out the first time they'd nearly had a head-on collision.

'You think I care if I turn the car over?' she'd laughed, putting her foot down harder and forcing Sebastian to grip the handrail above his window. 'Not being able to die is a wonderful thing.'

At Marrakesh Airport, Luci had disappeared and returned ten minutes later with boarding passes to London Heathrow.

'But I didn't give you my details,' Sebastian said.

'When you have my abilities, you don't need passports or ID. As long as you stick with me, you'll be fine. We're going first class; it's the only way to travel.'

She'd smiled, and he'd shuddered.

Sebastian had slept on the plane all the way to England as well as a little on the lengthy Tube journey from the airport to Highgate. After a five-minute walk from the station, they were finally outside his former home.

He'd forgotten how big his father's house was. After living off the beaten track in motels and guest houses for so long, the mansion was positively palatial—but not as pretty as he remembered. The driveway was littered with piles of bricks and a cement mixer, and the gate had been changed back to a traditional one with an old-fashioned lock instead of the fingerprint scanner it used to have. Sebastian couldn't see any of the usual staff, the gardeners, or Ylva the housekeeper. The only people there were two builders on the roof.

Luci placed her fingers in her mouth and let out a long, piercing whistle. The builders turned around and, at the sight of a partially clothed woman displaying impressive cleavage and not enough clothes for a British spring, they quickly scampered down the ladder.

'You all right, love? How can we help you?' the first builder asked, directing his question at Luci's chest.

He had a goatee, three earrings in both ears, and a dark blue smudge of a tattoo on the side of his neck. Sebastian sneered. What the hell was his father doing employing people like that to work on his home? He stepped forward.

'I'm Sebastian Fantz, Richard's son. Let us in.'

The builder frowned at him. He was joined by his work colleague, an older man with glasses and greasy hair who looked Luci up and down like she was a cold pint of beer on a hot day.

'All right, gorgeous. Who you looking for?' the second builder asked.

'My father, Richard Fantz,' Sebastian replied.

'Who the fuck was talking to you, mush? He ain't here anyway, and you ain't his son. I've seen photos of his boy in the house.' He turned to his bearded friend. 'This bloke's too skinny and ratty to be Mr Fantz's son, dontcha think? They're having us on.'

'Now you listen to me. I demand…'

'Stop,' Luci said, placing a hand gently on Sebastian's arm. 'Our friends here clearly need a little more persuasion.' She beckoned them over with the crook of her finger, and they stepped closer to the gate. 'Now, you delicious boys, will you be so kind as to let us onto the property?'

'Yeah, course,' the older builder said, producing a set of keys from his pocket. 'This house don't belong to the Fantz lot no more though. It was sold last week. There's some removal people inside filling up boxes.'

Sold? Sebastian pushed past the builders toward the front door. He instinctively looked up at his bedroom on the top floor and wondered whether any of his belongings had been packed away.

'Where's my father?'

'Maybe *I* should ask these nice young men instead of you, Sebastian. Gentlemen, could you please tell us where Mr Fantz can be found?'

'No idea, love. Sorry.'

'What about Felicity?' Sebastian asked.

'I ain't answering to you, posh boy.'

Luci repeated the question and the builders shrugged.

'Rumour has it they're getting divorced. Never seen her around here anyway, and me and the lads have been here months fixing the roof and converting the wine cellar into a game room for the new owners.'

'Who bought the house?' Luci asked.

'No idea,' the builders answered in unison.

Sebastian sighed and walked up the stairs to the front door, closely followed by the builders. The house was swarming with workmen and people packing boxes.

'Luci, if you want my help, then get these disgusting plebs out of my house. I can't search for anything when the place is full of dirty men in overalls.'

Sebastian busied himself rummaging through kitchen drawers, looking for any clues that would lead them to Ella, while Luci instructed all the workmen and packers to vacate the premises and not return until morning. Within five minutes, the house was empty except for the two original builders. The one with glasses was staring at Luci's behind as she absentmindedly peered into the half-filled boxes.

'Wouldn't mind a piece of that,' the older builder said to his friend quietly but loud enough for Luci to hear. She plucked some cherries from a fruit bowl on the kitchen table and then picked up a banana.

'Something amusing you?' she asked.

The builders sniggered.

'We just wondered what you're gonna do with that, love,' the younger one replied, nudging his friend and pointing at the banana. 'You look like the kind of bird that likes long, hard things in her mouth.'

Both men were laughing loudly now and completely ignoring Sebastian. He continued searching through boxes while watching the scene unfold from the corner of his eye. His thin lips twitched into a smile. He'd spent enough time with Luci to know this was going to be worth waiting for.

Without breaking eye contact, she began to slowly peel the banana.

'I was simply going to eat it,' she said to the builders. 'But perhaps it would be more fun to imagine it's your cock.'

The two men smirked and moved closer to her.

'Go on then, show us what you'd do,' the bearded one said, running the tip of his tongue along his top lip. 'That's it, slide it in. Nice and easy does it.'

Luci waited until almost the entire banana was in her mouth before glancing up at them and biting down hard on the fruit and then spitting it back out. Sebastian jumped at the cries of the two men who were now rolling on the ground, doubled up in agony. Crimson patches, like roses blooming in slow motion, were growing on the crotches of their beige overalls.

'What the fuck!' the younger one cried, cupping himself. His high-pitched wail increased in volume as he stared in horror at the blood dripping through his fingers. 'It's gone! Where's my dick gone?'

The older man started to vomit, colour draining from his face.

Luci threw the rest of the banana at their feet and headed to the back of the house, Sebastian following quickly behind her.

'I can't believe you just did that! Are they going to be OK?'

'I doubt it.'

'What are you going to do?'

'Nothing. I don't need them anymore.'

'But won't people wonder what happened to them?'

Luci stopped. 'Sebastian, this is London. Strange things happen in London all the time. Luckily for us, everyone in this city is too busy and too selfish to give a shit.'

'What will they do now?'

She narrowed her eyes. 'What will they do now? Other than bleed to death? Oh, I don't know, maybe those pathetic men will think twice next time they make a woman feel uncomfortable for eating a piece of fruit. I guess that's what they'll do now—learn, then die.'

Sebastian glanced at the workmen bleeding all over his kitchen floor and then back at Luci, who was taking cherries out of her pocket, eating them, and then spitting the stones out in the direction of the two writhing men.

'This isn't right. You can't leave them like that.'

'Why?'

'Because I'm already wanted by the police, and two dead men in my old home is going to be a bit suspect.' He glanced back at the builders, who had both grown worryingly pale. '*Please.* Luci! This isn't a game.'

She sighed and walked back into the kitchen, looking down at the men groaning in a puddle of their own blood.

'What would you like me to do, Sebastian?'

'I don't know. Stick their penises back on or something!'

The builders flinched as she crouched down and placed a hand between their legs. They instantly stopped moving.

'There, all better,' she told them. 'You won't remember we were here. Now sleep.'

As they slumped unconscious at her feet, she unzipped their overalls, pulled down their underwear, and laid them in a spooning position.

'Now what are you doing?'

'I'm amusing myself, Sebastian. You made me heal them, so as their punishment I'm giving them something a little confusing to wake up to. Their nasty, bigoted minds won't be able to cope with this scenario—plus the copious amount of blood and vomit will add to the suspense.'

'All of this because of one little banana comment? You're unhinged! They didn't mean anything by it.'

Luci's eyes were a piercing green as they bore into Sebastian's. He flinched. Her lips parted as if she was going to say something further, but instead she shook her head slowly.

'Men never mean anything, do they? Until they do, and then it's too late.'

'You *are* the Devil,' he muttered.

Luci wiped her bloody hand down his T-shirt and whispered in his ear.

'Never mistake a strong woman for an evil one, Sebastian.'

• • • • •

There was hardly anything left in the house. Sebastian was dismayed to find not only his father's bedroom empty but his own suite on the top floor completely cleared away; there was nothing but a few faded porn magazines in the corner and an empty plastic lighter. There remained just one room left to check—Richard's office. Sebastian rattled the door handle, but it wouldn't open. It made sense that his father had left this room for last.

'It's no use,' he said to Luci. 'The door's locked.' He barged it with his shoulder. 'His computer is in there. I bet if I can find that little notebook where the old fool keeps his passwords, I can get into his emails. There must be a message from Felicity or Ella in there.'

Sebastian threw himself at the door again and winced at the pain. Luci rolled her eyes.

'You really are pathetic.'

Moving him gently to one side, she laid her hand on the lock. There was a small click from inside the door's mechanisms, and it swung open silently.

The office was immaculate. The antique mahogany desk shone, and beside it was a large bookshelf displaying old volumes of encyclopaedias in alphabetical order and a framed photo of Richard and Felicity's wedding day, their children by their side. Ella was the only one in the photo not smiling. Sebastian stirred as he remembered what had happened an hour before that photograph was taken. He had to find the bitch and give her what she deserved. Little cocktease had been asking for it, and now everyone thought he was some kind of monster!

Yanking open drawer after drawer, he rifled through files and paperwork until he came across a diary. Would that hold his father's passwords or offer an explanation as to everyone's whereabouts? There were scribbles in the margin about meetings with his accountant and lawyer, along with a completion date for the house and a note about a conference in St Lucia. Maybe that was where Richard's new hotel was going to be? Sebastian made a mental note to look it up online later. He was secretly relieved his father wasn't around. Sebastian wasn't sure if he was ready to talk to him yet, but it helped to know where he was. He turned to today's date in the diary and laughed.

'No passwords, but looky here.' He showed Luci the diary, pointing at the date circled in red. 'It's my baby sister's twenty-third birthday today. If we can figure out where she is, maybe we'll get to her in time to give her a special surprise?'

'I don't care about your petty nonsense, Sebastian. Just help me find her.'

'But how great would it be to interrupt her birthday celebrations and…'

Luci sighed and held up a small address book. 'Is this what we're looking for?'

He snatched it out of her hand and flicked through it. This was too good to be true. Not only was he going to finally get his revenge on the little tramp, but he was going to do it on her birthday, too. Then Luci could help him get away with murder. Literally. He grinned and turned to E for Ella and then to F for Felicity. All that was listed were websites and passwords but no addresses.

'This is useless. We may need to call my dad's office or Felicity's work. If *you* call, they won't recognise your voice. I can't take the risk.'

He picked up the office phone and then put it back down.

'Forget it. The phone line's already been cut off.'

He couldn't call his father on his own mobile phone or even Luci's. If the police found out, they would track them down. He flicked through the address book again and turned to H for Hotmail and then to G for Google. Finally! There was the password to his father's private email address.

'His password's "Felicity." Predictable old fool, I could have guessed that,' he said, punching in the letters.

There were only fifteen emails from his father's wife and Ella, but they were all over a year old and were nothing more than 'Hi, how are you?' messages. There was no mention of an address or where Ella now lived.

'I don't understand—she went to university down the road. She must be living somewhere in London, but there's no mention of her anywhere. Maybe she changed her surname?'

'Is this her?' Luci asked, running her finger over the wedding photo.

'Yeah, that's the whore. Although the photo's seven years old.'

Luci looked at him steadily.

'She has a nice face. I doubt my son would risk coming to Earth for a...whore, as you put it.'

'I thought you didn't like her.'

'I never said that. I don't know the child.'

'But I can still do what I want with her when we find her, right?' he asked over his shoulder as he continued to search through Richard's emails. 'That's what you promised me.'

Luci stared at him for a long time, her eyes like slits and her lips settling into a straight line. He looked away, scared that she would try brainwashing him too. After a while she sighed and turned to the bookshelf, her back to him.

'Sebastian, do what you want with Ella,' she said eventually. 'Just find my boy.'

He could hear her pushing books to one side and flicking through their pages. After a few minutes, the sound of light laughter made him look up. She was holding a card in her hand.

'Well look at this!' she said, waving it in the air. '*Torre de los angeles.* Ella has a sense of humour.'

'What's that?' he asked, taking the card off her. 'Looks like an invitation from last year. Tarifa? Isn't that in the south of Spain?'

'Yes. It's also where Ella has her hotel.'

'A hotel? Let's go now and catch the next flight. Zac is bound to be there if it's her birthday.'

'No, Sebastian. If we do that, we won't get there until this evening, and that's when the angels are at their strongest. I can't take the risk of them watching her and seeing me arrive. Plus, she'll probably be out celebrating. If Zadkiel doesn't want Mikhael to know he's with her, then he'll go at dawn too—if he hasn't already seen her today. We'll leave at first light. Even if he isn't there tomorrow, he'll come running if he senses she's in danger.'

Sebastian huffed with disappointment; there was a certain poetic romance about ending her life on her birthday. Then again, if this

Mikhael creature was more powerful than both Zac and Luci, he didn't want to bump into him either.

'Fine. Wait up, isn't Tarifa across the water from the north of Morocco? We could have got a bloody boat there. If we'd known that, we could have saved ourselves the hassle of coming to London!'

Luci snatched the invitation back from him and smiled. 'London is *never* a waste of time, stupid boy. I'm off to Bond Street for a spot of free shopping before tea at Claridge's and a stay in their penthouse. Coming? My treat.'

He didn't exactly have a choice.

23

EVERY ITEM OF Ella's wardrobe was heaped in colourful piles on her bed. She'd tried everything on and hated it all. Nothing looked right. She checked her phone again. No messages. Josh had said he would see her on her birthday, so at first light she'd been up and showered. She'd arranged her hair ten different ways before finally twisting it in a loose plait over one shoulder. She'd made up her face, then wiped the lipstick off, then added smoky eyes, then took it all back off again and finally settled on something more natural. She was wearing a simple sundress and sandals but was still thinking about changing into jeans.

Oh, what did it matter? What if he didn't even call?

She looked at the time on her phone. It was nearly ten in the morning. She smiled at the photo on her screen. It was an old one of her and her mother on her sixteenth birthday. Felicity was wearing her treasured gold-and-amethyst necklace, and for the millionth time, Ella wished it hadn't been lost when Zac died. He'd been convinced it was a sign, that it was somehow connected to his mother and was proof he would return if he killed himself. What a load of crap that turned out to be.

She groaned out loud. She didn't want to think about Zac anymore! She had more pressing matters to deal with, like the fact that she only had three hours left until she had to leave to pick up her friends from the airport and Josh hadn't called yet. What on earth was she going to say to Mai Li and Kerry about him anyway? Were her and Josh an item or…?

She had to stop worrying about it. He made her feel happy; that was enough for now. She smiled. She *was* happy. Thanks to Josh, for the first time in three years she hadn't had a cold, sharp rock of grief and sadness nestled behind her ribcage as soon as she'd woken up.

The previous day, after she'd spoken to her mother when Josh had left, Ella had run upstairs and called an emergency team meeting. The hotel was small and there were only ten staff members: Paloma the office manager, a receptionist, two girls in housekeeping, three in the kitchen, a doorman, a gardener, and an odd-job man.

'Tomorrow is my birthday,' she'd announced. 'We have no guests booked until the end of the week, so I am closing the hotel for the next six days. Full pay. Go home and enjoy yourselves. I'll see you Friday morning.'

They'd all looked at her with wide eyes.

'But Mr de Silva asked for his room again this morning,' Paloma remarked. 'We have *one* guest.'

'Don't worry. I'll look after him.'

Paloma smirked, and Ella raised her eyebrows at her in warning.

'Have a great birthday!' her team shouted as they rushed out of the hotel, not needing to be told twice.

After sending the staff home that evening, Ella had been tempted to knock on Josh's bedroom door and check if he needed anything. After all, he'd left his luggage behind at the airport, and he didn't even have a toothbrush with him. But no, it was late evening and he'd told her they'd see each other the next day—she wasn't going to crowd him and ruin whatever it was they had before it had even properly started.

She blushed at the thought of him having seen her naked that morning, not to mention what he knew about Zac. It was all too surreal. How had he gone from being a cocky fool to…to *this!*

Memories of the kiss they'd shared filled her stomach with molten lava. Zac's kisses had been like water, trickling into all her empty spaces and filling her up—both soothing her soul and setting it on fire. But Josh was different; kissing him had felt like coming home after a long, hard day and never wanting to leave again. Did that even make sense? Could kisses be that different? Could comfort be better than passion?

She'd gone to bed that night and, for the first time in three years, she hadn't imagined that her hands were Zac's. Instead, she'd closed her eyes and remembered the touch of her naked body pressed against Josh's, remembered the taste of his mouth as his tongue caressed hers, and remembered the way his fingers felt on the back of her neck as he'd plaited her wet hair and planted tiny kisses on her bare shoulders. She'd climaxed quickly, instantly falling asleep, her chest heavy with both apprehension and excitement.

• • • • •

A shrill beep from her phone made Ella's heart leap.

It was a text from her mother saying her overnight flight had been on time and she was already in London about to board her connecting flight to Malaga. She said she would stop for lunch after hiring a car so, all things considered, it would probably take her five or six hours. Straightaway, there was another beep. Her mother's message was closely followed by a text from her father saying he was held up in a work meeting and he'd be with her in about five hours, too.

Ella frowned. That was conveniently weird. Had her mother been lying to her about being alone in India? Had Felicity and Leo been…? No. She pushed that thought to the back of her mind—she had enough issues with her own love life without having to worry about what her mum and dad were possibly up to.

She stuffed her unwanted clothes back into the wardrobe and leant against the doors to force them shut. Her phone beeped again. She sighed and glanced at it quickly. This time it was from neither of her parents. It was Josh.

HEY BIRTHDAY GIRL, TAKE A LOOK OUTSIDE. X

Ella made a sound that was a cross between a giggle and a yelp and ran to the back door that led to the patio. She peered over the low garden wall and there he was on the beach, a bottle of champagne in one hand and two glass flutes in the other. He was wearing a crisp blue shirt with his jeans rolled up, his bare feet half buried in the sand. Beside him was a huge pink box with a ribbon tied in an elaborate bow on top. The box was so large it came to his knees.

She ran outside and bounded down the stairs to the beach. His grin grew wider and wider with each step she took. In her head, she planned to walk up to him seductively and give him a teasing peck on the cheek, but as soon as she reached the bottom step she kicked off her sandals and ran as fast as she could, wrapping her arms around his neck and her legs around his waist, her lips locking onto his as he tried to hold her up without dropping the glasses.

'What a welcome.' He laughed as she finally let go, and he laid the bottle and flutes down on the rug beside him.

'This is the best birthday surprise ever! How did you know that's my favourite champagne?' she said.

'Ah, yes. I woke up early for breakfast and to go shopping, but the hotel doors were locked and I couldn't get out. I went to reception but there was no one there, so I went to the kitchen and that was empty, too. In the end, I took this bottle and some glasses from the bar, figuring that since you're the boss, it's not technically stealing. Where is everyone?'

'I sent them home. I closed the hotel.'

'You left me with no breakfast?' he said with a smile.

'That was my cunning plan. Starve you out so you would track me down.'

'It appears to have worked,' he said, taking her face in his hands and kissing her again.

Her knees nearly buckled beneath her, but with his strong arms circling her waist he held her up. What the hell was happening to her? He was literally making her weak at the knees. She nearly laughed aloud, but instead she pulled away and attempted to catch her breath.

'Are you hungry?' she asked.

'For what?'

He was staring at her lips, which were still buzzing from his kiss. He lifted her braid away from her shoulder and kissed the crook of her neck, making her shiver. How could kissing him get her more worked up than all those empty one-night stands she'd had, all those desperate attempts to lighten her nights of sadness?

'So, you closed the hotel for me?' he asked, his breath hot on her collarbone.

His hands were nowhere near her body, and yet she was struggling to focus.

'Don't flatter yourself. My friends and family arrive today.'

'I know. I'm looking forward to it.' Did he just say that? He was actually serious about her! 'By the way, the phone was ringing in reception earlier but there was no one there to answer it. You might want to check your answering machine,' he said.

'I don't have one. It was probably a booking enquiry. They'll send an email or, if it's urgent, they'll call my mobile. Don't worry about it.'

'You're so Spanish. Not a care in the world.'

'Well, it's true. I don't care about work right now.'

'What do you care about then, birthday girl?'

What *did* she care about? This. Just this, and him, and the fact that the future was looking a lot more colourful than it had a few days ago.

'My birthday present. That's all I care about,' she said with a grin, pulling away from his embrace. 'Is that box for me?'

'Of course not. I carry my big pink box everywhere with me.'

He reached down for the glasses at his feet, handed her one, and popped the champagne.

'But first, a toast.'

'It's a bit early for champagne, isn't it?'

'It's your birthday. It's totally allowed.'

She giggled as she slurped the froth off the top of the glass, which was now dribbling onto her hand.

'A toast to what?'

'To us,' he said, clinking his glass against hers.

'There's an *us?*'

'Of course.' His eyes locked on hers and she held her breath. 'And it's going to be amazing.'

She felt the colour rise in her cheeks. Maybe it was the champagne on an empty stomach, or maybe it was the sun heating up the sand between her toes, or maybe it was him. Josh, her apparent destiny, the man she'd never even considered because Zac had always cast his beautiful shadow over him, obscuring everyone else in darkness so he was her only light. Well, there were no more angels left in her life, there was only Josh—and he was very real indeed.

He placed the box at her feet.

'Happy birthday.'

When was the last time anyone had made a fuss of her? She couldn't remember. Attempting but failing at hiding her delight, she pulled at the ribbon and peeled the paper off. Inside the box was another box. She opened it and inside was a pair of gold Louboutin heels, which she recognised by their telltale red sole. She didn't even realise shoes that beautiful existed in Tarifa. Maybe Josh had travelled all the way to Marbella to get them. She slipped them onto her bare feet—they fit her perfectly. How had he known her size?

'I feel like Cinderella. These are gorgeous.'

Josh's face was serious. Was he nervous? She wobbled as her feet sank into the sand. He held her steady as she took them back off and handed them to him.

'Now you have to take me somewhere fancy. I won't be wasting these amazing shoes at my crappy, local bar.'

'I'll take you anywhere you want. There's more,' he said, nodding at the large box.

Inside was another box. Ella laughed.

'More? Is this the box inside a box game? OK, let's open the next one.'

She pulled the tissue paper out and unwrapped another parcel, revealing a professional make-up kit filled with bottles, brushes, tubes, and little boxes. This man was pure Hollywood.

'Amazing. I've no idea where I'm going to go around here this glammed up. I'll be the best dressed hotelier in town.'

He gave her a small smile, but the rest of his face was still stony. He nodded at the box again.

The next item was a small, shiny black box. Inside, nestled in white tissue paper, was an ornate hairpiece encrusted in tiny pearls and diamonds. She gathered up her braid, twisted it, and clipped the hairpiece in place.

'How do I look?'

Josh stared at her, his face void of any expression. Even though the sky was a cobalt blue and the sun had climbed ever higher, the waves still crashed against the rocks in the distance as if a storm was coming. Ella couldn't tell if the deafening roar was the waves or her heart beating with nerves.

He stepped forward and took out the final gift, a small, dark blue velvet box, so small she hadn't noticed it among the tissue paper. He opened it slowly and dropped to one knee, the box in one hand and the other holding hers.

Ella's eyes widened. What the…? Surely he wasn't…

'Ella, I meant what I said yesterday. I want you in my life forever. I know this is crazy. You probably think I'm mad for even doing this, but you said it yourself…we're meant to be together.'

'Yes.'

'If fate is real and life is only going to keep throwing us at one another, then why fight it? I know this is impulsive and you probably think I'm mad, but it feels right. I want you to think about how good this could be.'

'Yes.'

'Will you do me the honour of being my…?'

'Yes. Yes, Josh. Yes!'

'Really?'

'Definitely!'

'You don't think this is a crazy idea?'

'Of course it is! It's totally ridiculous and we hardly know each other—but let's do it anyway. For such a long time, I've been waiting for things to start feeling right, and I've been waiting to feel happy again. Then you suddenly appeared out of nowhere, and we had that kiss and…This might just be the least absurd decision I've ever made.'

Josh's hand shook as he took out a pink diamond ring with tiny stones encrusted around its sides. He placed it on her wedding finger. Like the shoes, it fit perfectly. She pulled him back up to his feet; his smile was as shaky as his trembling hands. He kissed her lightly and then stepped back to look at her.

'OK. Wow. So now what?'

'I don't know,' she said, grinning, wondering what the bloody hell she'd just done. Had she really agreed to marry Josh after spending just a few days with him and sharing nothing but a few heated kisses?

'Your father's a priest, right?' he said. 'Your friends and family arrive today. You have an empty hotel with its own chapel and everything a girl needs for her special day, except a dress. How about we get married tomorrow, and then we can live happily ever after?'

He was even more insane than she was. It was a stupid idea, an impulsive, crazy, irresponsible, wild idea. She loved it. Throwing herself in his arms again, she kissed him hard. With that kiss, she gave him everything she had; every last drop of hope, trust, and belief she'd been harbouring. In that kiss, Ella handed Josh her fragile glass heart, knowing it would never crack again, knowing that with him it would always remain whole and protected. He wouldn't hurt her; he couldn't—he was her destiny.

This was exactly what she needed to draw a line beneath her past. She and Zac were over. This was going to be her new future, and it was going to be a wonderful one.

24

GIBRALTAR AIRPORT WAS an hour's drive from Ella's hotel, and Josh had insisted he accompany her to meet her friends.

'I've booked that restaurant you mentioned for after the ceremony,' he said, squeezing her knee as she drove around the winding mountain roads. The sky was clear, and sailing boats glimmered like tiny, triangular specks of white in the distance. The world felt good. Too good.

Ella pushed away the feeling of apprehension that always loomed as soon as life appeared to be going well. So what if things were finally amazing? It didn't mean anything. Disaster was *not* imminent.

'Oh my God, this time tomorrow I'll be Mrs de Silva, and we haven't even told anyone yet! I'm warning you, my friends are going to flip when I tell them we're getting married in twenty-four hours.'

'Do you think they'll like me?' he asked.

She tried not to laugh. He had no idea how much her friends used to fancy him back in uni.

'I doubt it. What's there to like?'

'I can show you, if you like,' he whispered into her hair. His hand travelled further up her thigh and he nuzzled her neck, planting light kisses on her collarbone. His touch was maddening. She wanted him with an intensity that shocked her, but they would have to wait. They'd decided, for the sake of just one measly day, it was worth waiting until the night of their wedding day.

His hand was on the inside of her thigh now.

'Stop it, I'm driving!' she said, giggling.

'But I want you.'

'I mean it! This is hard for me, too, Josh. You're driving me crazy, but I'm sure you can wait until tomorrow.'

'I don't think I can. You might have to pull over.'

She swatted his hand away, and he pretended to be mortally wounded. She laughed and he revelled in it—he really did love an audience.

They passed a sign for the airport, and Ella turned off the main road.

'Is that the queue into Gibraltar?' he asked.

'Yes, but I won't bother driving in. There's no point. I told Mai Li and Kerry I'd park on the Spanish side and meet them at the border. It's much quicker. You can wait in the car. I can't be dealing with all your fans today.'

He looked smug, and she laughed to herself. He really did love being famous. She had no idea what he'd said to Billy or anyone else from the film studio the day before, but he hadn't mentioned work once, so she was making the most of his undivided attention.

After ten minutes of circling the back streets, Ella finally found a parking space even though it was nowhere near the border control. She was running a bit late and it would take a few minutes to get there, but there were always crowds of people crossing into Spain, so she figured her friends would still be queuing.

As she went to open the car door, Josh pulled her toward him. 'Hey, wait up.'

She climbed over to his side and sat astride him, her arms around his neck.

'Can I help you, fiancé?'

He gave her a half smile and ran his tongue over the tiny chip in his tooth. God, he was so hot. She was even beginning to like his cockiness.

'I'm crazy about you, Ella,' he said, his hands on her behind pulling her closer. 'I'm so madly in love that I just can't stop smiling. I'm so happy. I just wanted to tell you.'

It was the first time he'd told her that he loved her—it was all too unreal. She could feel him hard against her, and she used all her willpower to open the car door and clamber out. She leant over, kissed her fingers, and placed them on his lips.

'Cool yourself down, de Silva. I'm locking you in my car in case you change your mind and run away.'

He pulled her arm again, and she kissed him for a long time.

'I love you, too,' she said quickly, shutting the door.

She hadn't said those words to a man since Zac. But it was OK; it felt right. She grinned all the way to the border crossing.

• • • • •

'Look, there she is! There she is!'

Mai Li and Kerry were waving at her from the queue. Kerry was holding a giant helium balloon with the words 'Birthday Girl' stamped on it in neon writing. It was bobbing in people's faces as she jumped up and down, completely oblivious to the havoc she was causing. Ella held up her hand to show she'd seen them and tried to keep a straight face as Kerry tottered over to the border guard with her passport. Her friend was built like a Barbie doll, and she dressed like one, too. The guard waved her through, checking out her round bottom and tight skirt as she ran over to Ella. Mai Li struggled to keep up behind her, the balloon bouncing between them.

'Oh. My. God! Look at you. You're so, like, mega gorgeous. Happy birthday, girlfriend!' Kerry said, squealing and hugging Ella, preventing Mai Li from getting closer.

'Get that balloon out of my way, Kerry. I told you at the airport not to buy it. Ella! It's so lovely to see you. Happy birthday!'

The three girls embraced, and her friends chattered excitedly about how great she looked, asking about her birthday plans and commenting on how hot it was for April. Ella wanted to wait until they'd calmed down before mentioning Josh, but it looked like it was going to be easier said than done.

'The car's this way.'

They followed behind, talking nonstop. She had to say something before they saw Josh. She took a deep breath. 'Mai Li? Kerry? *Girls!*' They finally stopped talking. 'Um, I've got something I need to tell you. Some good news.'

Shit! This was harder than she'd imagined. It had seemed so natural and exciting talking about it in the car with Josh, but now that she was saying it out loud, she realised how crazy the idea sounded. She was marrying a famous Hollywood actor tomorrow after being with him for just a few days. There was no easy way of making that sound sane.

OK, short and sharp—like ripping off a plaster. She could do this.

'Well? What is it?' Kerry asked. 'Spit it out.'

'I'm getting married.'

'What?' They both screeched and stopped in their tracks.

'I'm getting married. Tomorrow.'

'But I didn't even know you had a boyfriend,' Mai Li said.

'Well, I don't. I have a fiancé.'

She held out her hand, and they screamed at her light pink diamond ring. Ella continued walking. She could see the car already, and the idea of them meeting Josh any moment was making her feel dizzy. Her friends followed—three girls, two suitcases, and a balloon took up the entire pavement, forcing people to walk around them.

Ella stopped as they neared her car, her friends still clustering around her and the ring.

'It's so pretty,' Mai Li cooed.

'It's so big!' exclaimed Kerry.

Mai Li peered closer. 'Is it Tiffany's?'

'Yeah,' Kerry said. 'Who *is* this guy?'

'Me.' Josh took off his sunglasses. 'I'm the lucky man.'

He was leaning against Ella's car and her heart flipped as she saw him through the eyes of her friends. T-shirt tight over his muscular shoulders, strong jaw with two-day-old stubble, designer shades—he was 100 percent teen pin-up material.

Nobody moved. Mai Li's suitcase fell to the ground, but she didn't pick it up. Josh walked over to Ella and put his arm around her waist.

'Hi, I think we met a few years back at Indigo.' He held out his hand for them to shake, but they remained frozen still.

'Right, let's get back to the hotel then,' Ella said as cheerfully as she could. 'I bet you're both starving.'

Her friends still hadn't moved. She looked at Josh and widened her eyes in a silent plea. Were they really that shocked? She would have to do something drastic to snap them out of it.

'Errr, girls, would you both like to be my bridesmaids? You can help me choose a dress this afternoon. I rang up ahead, and the shop is opening late just for us. I'll also buy you both a new dress and shoes, and we'll need to choose flowers of course. *Hello!* What do you think?'

Kerry turned to her, her mouth still agape.

'Is that Josh? Like, Josh de Silva?'

Ella nodded.

'You're marrying Josh de Silva? Like, for real?'

'Yes.'

'Tomorrow?'

'Yes.'

'And we're going to be your bridesmaids?'

'Yes.'

'Oh my fricking God!'

Kerry let out a high-pitched squeal that snapped Mai Li out of her reverie. They both ran at Ella and hugged her, jumping up and down, before turning to Josh and smiling shyly.

'Hi,' Mai Li said, shaking his hand. 'I'm sorry about that. We're a bit surprised. We thought Ella was still madly in love with Zac and…ow!'

Kerry had hit her arm and stepped in front of her.

'Hi, we've met before. I'm a huge fan. I have a photo of you in my purse, look!' she rummaged in her handbag and showed him a picture she'd cut out of a magazine. It was Josh wearing nothing but swimming trunks. 'I guess that's a bit weird now, what with you marrying my best friend who never tells me *anything!*' She shot Ella a dark look and put the picture back in her bag. Then she took it back out and handed it to Ella. 'I suppose you better have this, seeing as you've just made everything really awkward.'

Ella glanced over at Josh, who was doing a great impression of finding the entire interaction totally normal.

'Shall we go?' he said, opening the car doors.

The girls clambered into the back, battling with the helium balloon that kept trying to escape. Ella had only been driving a few minutes when Kerry's head appeared in the space between her and her new fiancé.

'So, Josh, you got any brothers?' she asked. 'Seeing as you're off the market now?'

'Yeah, I have a brother,' he said. 'But you might have to wait a while. He's only two years old.'

Kerry's smile faded and she sat back down, the balloon bobbing around where her head had been.

'I can't see out the back window, Kerry,' Ella said. 'Do you mind just…'

Kerry stabbed her long nails into the balloon, making it explode with a loud bang. Ella and Josh both jumped and looked at one another with a grimace.

'Well, that didn't go *too* badly,' Ella mouthed at him. 'My parents next.'

25

JOSH SAT IN the hotel library and sipped at a whisky. Ella had told him to help himself to whatever he wanted, so he'd headed straight to the bar. He needed all the liquid courage he could find.

Just over a week ago Tarifa had been just another work trip in another country, following creepy Billy around some cool locations. A few days ago he'd simply planned on getting some sunshine and rest; he'd wanted to take his time looking at film scripts he'd been sent. Yet here he now was, madly in love and marrying a girl he hardly knew. About to meet her parents. On his own.

Ella hadn't wanted him to talk to Leo and Felicity without her, but Josh had insisted. He wanted to ask her father for his daughter's hand in marriage, the traditional way. He'd told Ella to enjoy herself at the wedding dress shop with her friends and not worry about him. But the truth was, he didn't want her to see how terrified he was. Ella always seemed so certain of every decision she made, so sure of herself, but Josh wasn't. Proposing to Ella and not flying back to LA was the most impulsive thing he'd ever done in his life. It felt right, but it still terrified him.

His mobile phone has stayed turned off since the day before when he'd kissed Ella for the first time. Josh had emailed Billy as soon as he'd left her room, plus his agent and PR team, and said he'd be taking a few weeks off. He didn't care what lie his team told the studio bosses or the press about his absence; they'd probably say he had a family crisis or that he was in rehab. Whatever. He told them he simply needed to get his head straight and that they were not to disturb him. It would send them into panic overdrive, guaranteed, but he didn't care. Fifteen minutes later, he'd received thirteen missed calls and twenty-eight emails. He hadn't even looked at them; instead, he'd turned off the phone and thrown it into his suitcase.

Was he doing the right thing? This wasn't a part in a movie. This was real—yet he'd never felt more certain about anything in his entire life.

A car pulled up on the gravel drive, and Josh peered out the window. A tall, Spanish-looking man stepped out, walked to the passenger door, and held his hand out to an elegant blonde. This had to be Ella's parents. He'd met Felicity briefly at a party three years ago, but she looked different now—older, yet calmer. They hadn't spotted him watching, but he could hear them talking as they took the cases out of the boot.

'I can't believe our baby's twenty-three already!' Felicity was saying as they carried their bags to the hotel entrance. Her heels were making it hard for her to totter over the gravel, and Leo held out a hand to steady her.

'Lily, *por favor,*' he said, taking the suitcase off her.

Josh wasn't bilingual like Ella's family, but he could understand the basic Spanish he'd learned at school.

'Will we tell her?' Leo asked.

Felicity shook her head and kissed his cheek.

'Not on her birthday, *cariño.* Maybe tomorrow.'

She placed a hand on his cheek, and Josh ducked back into the library, embarrassed to have witnessed such a tender exchange. Ella had told him her father was a priest and her mother was in the middle of a divorce. Were her parents getting it on? He sighed and ran his hands through his hair. While they were worrying about telling Ella their big news, he was about to ask for their daughter's hand in marriage. He rubbed his eyes and took another gulp of whisky.

'Where is everyone?' Felicity's voice echoed around the empty foyer.

Josh stepped out of the library and held up his hand in greeting. 'Hi. Ella's just popped out, but she'll be back soon.'

'She's not here to meet her own mother? I haven't seen her in months!'

'She asked me to wait for you,' Josh said. He hoped he didn't sound as nervous as he felt. 'You must be Mrs Fantz and…'

'Oh! I know you, don't I?' Felicity said. 'Joshua de Silva, Pascoal's boy? I used to know your father. What are *you* doing here?'

He took their bags off them and gave Felicity what he hoped was his most charming smile.

'It's a long story. Ella gave me strict instructions to greet you and make sure you were both comfortable. Ella has booked a suite for you, Mister Santiago de los Rios, and Mrs Fantz—you know where your apartment is, I imagine.'

'Of course. This is *my* hotel!'

'Yes. Sorry. Please, this way.'

Ella's father was frowning at him. Josh took their suitcases upstairs and pretended not to notice as Felicity elbowed the priest lightly and gave him a look. Josh deposited Leo's suitcase outside the door of a large suite, and Felicity made her way to the end of the corridor where her private apartment was. Like Ella's, it was never rented out to guests.

'Thank you, Joshua,' Leo said with a strong Spanish accent.

'Josh.'

'Thank you, *Josh.* Now that you have shown us to our rooms, would you be kind enough to tell us where our daughter is? And why the hotel is empty? And who you are?'

Felicity was watching them both from the door of her room opposite them. Josh cleared his throat and thought of his tumbler of whisky downstairs.

'Yes...Ella's fine. It's all good. Why don't we leave the bags here and go down to the library? We can have a drink and a chat, and I'll explain everything. Much more comfortable there.'

Ella's parents looked at one another again and followed him back downstairs. He poured them all a glass of whisky and then nodded at the sofa. Leo sat beside Felicity, who was giving Josh a look that said, 'Nice to see how comfortable you've made yourself, in what is still technically *my* hotel.'

'So...' Josh took a deep breath, attempting to give them a smile that wasn't too shaky. 'Ella has shut the hotel for a week because she wants to spend her birthday with both of you and her friends Kerry and Mai Li, who we picked up from the airport this morning. Right now, Ella is...' He tapped the toe of his foot against the marble floor, keeping his eyes fixed on his drink. 'She's with her friends buying a wedding dress,' he said quickly, all in one breath.

He looked up, meeting Felicity's eyes. She appeared calm, but by the tilt of her head it was clear she was waiting for him to continue before she decided how to react.

'Mrs Fantz, Mr Santiago de los Rios, I need to ask you something.' He took another deep breath, his vision now wavy—either from the alcohol or the nerves that were about to engulf him. He shouldn't have poured himself that second whisky. 'Would you grant me your permission to marry Ella, please?'

Leo and Felicity stared at one another. Her eyes were wide, and she was shaking her head slowly. She covered her mouth with both hands, muttering something. It sounded like a succession of 'No, no, no.'

'What are you talking about, Joshua?' Leo barked. 'I've never even met you before.'

'I proposed to Ella this morning and she said yes. I wanted to do it properly and ask for her hand in marriage from her parents, too… and to also ask you, Father, to perform the ceremony. If possible. Tomorrow.'

He swallowed down the sharp taste of whisky rising in his throat. Leo's frown was deeper than ever, and Felicity had gone a deathly pale.

'Is this a joke?' Felicity asked, looking wildly around the room. 'Are you hiding in here, Ella, ready to pounce out? Hmm, sweetie? Because I don't find this remotely funny.'

Josh closed his eyes and counted to three before opening them again. He hoped he wasn't going to faint. On set he did most of his own stunts. He was regularly interviewed on live TV and encouraged to do ridiculous things, and in one film he even had to fight with a real shark—but this was by far the scariest thing he'd ever done. Ella had been right; they should have spoken to her parents together. He was stupid for thinking he could break the news to them alone.

'This isn't a joke, Mrs Fantz. I'm very serious about wanting to spend the rest of my life with your daughter.'

'Who are you?' Leo asked, his voice a lot kinder than the expression on his face.

Josh bit down on the inside of his lip, aware that his underarms were getting damp. He hoped there weren't dark patches on his shirt.

'I'm Joshua de Silva. I'm an actor, but I used to know Ella from university, back in London. I came here completely by chance a week or so ago and fate kind of threw us together.'

'Fate?' Leo said.

Josh rubbed his face.

'I'm aware that what I'm saying sounds strange and crazy, Father, but I know…I know everything. I know it's the right thing to do.'

'What exactly do you know, boy?'

The priest was losing his patience. Ella had said that her father was easy-going and calm, but right now the Spaniard looked like he was going to punch him. Josh spoke quickly, desperate to tell them everything he knew before they stormed out of the hotel and called their daughter.

'I know about Zac. I know what he was. I know he's dead now and that Ella's been trying to get back on her path. I'm the guy she's meant to be with. Three years ago, in London, we kept getting thrown together. Even Zac told her it was meant to be me. I felt it at the time, of course I did. To be honest, I've been crazy about your daughter since the first time I met her, except back then she only cared about him. When I found myself here for work, at her hotel of all places, all my feelings came rushing back, and we both finally gave in to our path. We decided to just go for it and see what happens.'

Leo was glaring at Josh, his arms crossed.

'Marriage is not something you just *go for!*' he shouted. 'You don't just blow caution to the wind because a girl is getting over the death of an old flame and is on the rebound. You don't know if you love somebody that quickly.'

Felicity's face was stony, but her eyes were smiling. She placed her hand on the priest's knee.

'Is that right, Leo? Did you not, twenty-four years ago, drive for hours through the night looking for me while clutching a wedding ring in your hand?'

The priest shook his head. 'That was different.'

'Was it? Did *you* not know within an hour of meeting me that we were destined to be together? Except we weren't as smart as these two—we listened to reason and not our hearts. Look at him.' Leo wasn't looking at Josh; instead, his attention was on Felicity's hand on his knee.

She took his face and turned it toward Josh. '*Look* at him! That is the face of love.'

They both stared at Josh. He was still biting down on his lip, his foot tapping a rhythm on the marble floor.

'He's doing the right thing, Leo,' she said. 'He's been brave enough to ask us face-to-face, and to have said yes, Ella clearly loves him. I never thought my baby would find happiness again after what she's been through. Josh, you say you know about Zac?'

Josh nodded, and Felicity blinked three times in quick succession.

'Good. The Zac situation has not been an easy thing for *any* of us to get our heads around...but clearly there are no secrets between you and our daughter. We've been urging her to let go of him for a long time now. That union was never going to end well. In my opinion, you're both far too young to marry, but at least you are...well...human and alive. Don't hurt her.'

'Never.'

Felicity turned back to Leo and whispered in his ear. The priest sighed, his face softening.

'Do you *really* know about Zac? Are you *sure* you understand?'

Josh nodded. 'The night of the New Year's Eve party at Cloud Ninety-Nine, when you and Ella argued,' he said, looking at Felicity, 'I was there. I was in the lift on my way up to the party, and I saw her jump. I also saw Zac fly through the air and rescue her. I know what he is, I mean, what he *was*, and to be honest it's a relief to finally be able to talk to someone about what I saw. I thought I was going mad.'

Felicity jumped up and threw her arms around him, which shocked them both.

'You saw her? You saw her fall?' she whispered. 'Nobody believed me. Even *I* doubted my sanity, especially after I got home and her dress was on the floor of her room, and I realised she'd miraculously survived. It wasn't until I discovered what Zac was that it made sense. But to be honest, even now the whole angel thing is, well, surreal. Even after we saw the wings and the other…creatures…and witnessed the awful way Zac died.' Felicity dabbed at her eyes. 'It has affected us all deeply.'

Leo reached out for her, and she peeled herself off Josh.

'So, you're her chosen one for this lifetime, Josh?' the priest asked. 'Is that what Zac told her?'

Josh nodded, still chewing his lip.

'And she loves you?'

Josh smiled. 'Yes, and I love her so much. I adore her. I promise you both I will spend every day of my life making her happy. I've never met anyone like her before—it's as if being with her is the only time I feel like my true self.'

'OK, OK, we get it.' Leo laughed. 'Fine. Who are we to argue with fate? Welcome to the family, son. Looks like we have a wedding to plan.'

Josh stood up, shook the priest's hand heartily, and then hugged Felicity again.

'Thank you! Ella will be finished around eight. She's booked us all a table at a tapas bar in town and said we're to meet them there. I think she was worried about telling you both in person. Or maybe she was testing me.'

He laughed nervously, and Leo patted his back.

'Well, you passed the test. Our daughter will be celebrating her birthday and engagement in one night. I should probably go and freshen up but first, pour me another drink.'

• • • • •

'Today has definitely been my most memorable birthday yet,' Ella said to Josh.

It was two o'clock in the morning, and they had finally managed to get her friends and family back to the hotel and to their rooms. Felicity had spent the evening spontaneously bursting into happy tears, Leo had watched Josh like a hawk throughout the meal, and Mai Li and

Kerry had bickered all evening as to whether it was worth going out dancing or not. Ella had convinced them that it wasn't.

It was a quiet night and the sea was still. The moon was so bright and swollen, it was as if the beach was made of silver. The only sound for miles was the gentle swoosh of the waves lapping at their toes. Josh and Ella walked hand in hand along the shoreline, their feet sinking into the fine sand.

Neither of them had wanted to say goodbye once they'd returned to the hotel. A mix of emotions swirled in the pit of Ella's stomach—fear, excitement, love, nerves, joy. A kaleidoscope of vibrant colours tumbling over one another. There was no point in going to her room yet; she wouldn't be sleeping much anyway. Nights were still cool in April, and Josh had draped his suit jacket over Ella's shoulders. It was too big for her and made her look like a child playing dress-up, the sleeves flapping over her hands as they walked.

Ella loved the beach at night. When she was alone and couldn't sleep, she'd walk along the bay, ankle-deep in the water. She'd fill her lungs with salty air, breathing in the same rhythm of the waves. In. Out. In. Out.

'I love my parents and friends,' she said, 'but they were a bloody handful tonight. Still, at least they know about us now, and they seemed genuinely happy.'

'Kerry wasn't. She's not happy at all. I think you have competition there.'

Ella hit him playfully on the arm and laughed.

'She'll come around. She's had the hots for you for years. You'll have to palm her off on your cousin or one of your sexy actor mates. If you don't, she'll probably cut out more photos of you from the gossip magazines and stick pins in them.'

Josh laughed and kissed the top of her head.

'I was kidding. Your friends are cool, and your parents are lovely. I can't believe in ten hours we'll be man and wife.'

'*Husband* and wife.'

'Yes, sorry, husband. Wow, I'm going to be your husband. Shit, that's so grown up.'

'You know, it's not too late to back out,' she said. 'If you think we're being too impulsive. I mean, you haven't even spoken to your own parents yet. What will they say?'

'I don't care what they say. My mum's happy if I'm happy, and my father is a selfish prick who's done crazier things in his life. We can do the big Hollywood bash back in LA if you really want to. We can honeymoon here in Spain, have a road trip and ignore everyone for a few weeks, and then afterwards face the music and the inevitable onslaught of my agent, family, and hordes of teen fans.'

She buried her face in his shoulder. 'Oh God, the fans. Now I'm scared.'

'Don't be. You can be as in or out of the limelight as you want. You can even stay here if you prefer, and I'll only act in European films. I don't expect you to...'

'Shhhh, Josh. We have plenty of time to make plans. Right now, I just want to think about you, me, and this quiet beach.'

He stopped walking.

'You know what I want to do?' he said.

'I told you, not until tomorrow night.'

'No. Well, yes, of course, but that's not what I meant. I want to shout. I want to tell the world how much I love you. I want to scream it up at the stars and out to the sea and wake up the whole of Tarifa. I love Ella!' he shouted.

She laughed. Could he be any more dramatic?

'Go on, try it,' he said.

'I love Josh de Silva.'

'That wasn't even loud enough to wake up that seagull over there. Louder! Wake up the moon.'

She couldn't stop laughing. This was stupid and wonderful and fun. Was life always going to be like this with him? She hoped so because right now she wanted the whole world to know how happy she was.

• • • • •

Gabriel watched the couple on the beach and shook his head. This was not good, not good at all. Even though he was too far away for them to notice him, he could still feel what they were feeling.

Up until now, when he'd watched Ella with others, he'd sensed the constant heaviness within her. Her despair seeped out of every one of her pores like thick black tar, her sadness cloying and suffocating. Ella may have occupied herself with the odd fling, but her heart had remained true to Zadkiel since the day he'd left her.

Until today. Ella's soul was now as bright and light as a feather.

Gabriel had promised Zadkiel that he'd let her know her love was on his way—but now he couldn't because she was back on her path. No one had been expecting that.

The man was swinging Ella around in his arms, her feet in the water and the hem of her long dress trailing in the waves.

'I'm getting married tomorrow!' she shouted. 'I'm so excited!'

She wrapped her arms tightly around his neck, and he bent down to kiss her.

'I love you, Mrs de Silva!' the man shouted up at the stars.

They both turned and, hand in hand, ran back up the beach toward the hotel.

Gabriel thought of his friend and sighed.

Had Zadkiel called the hotel that morning like he said he would? If he had, then Ella had clearly not received the message because the girl in the distance now kissing her fiancé goodbye on her patio wasn't a woman who longed for her lost love… She was a free soul on the brink of a new life journey.

All angels were Path Keepers at heart; they could sense when a person had slipped off their path, and they knew when they were back in the arms of fate. The stars were already realigning, creaking overhead like the cogs in an ancient machine—and there was absolutely nothing Gabriel could do about it.

Zadkiel was too late, and the archangel had no way of tracking him down or letting him know. He sat down on the sand, his back resting against a large rock, and put his head in his hands. Hadn't he told that crazy kid that Ella would bring him nothing but trouble? But Zadkiel wouldn't listen. He never did.

In the morning, the fallen angel would arrive at the hotel and discover that the only woman he'd ever loved, the one he'd died for, had been snatched away from him and would never be his again.

And it wouldn't be the first time.

'O, I am fortune's fool!'
~ William Shakespeare, *Romeo and Juliet*

PART THREE

ARABELLA
END OF THE BEGINNING

TUSCANY, ITALY
5 BC

VI.

THE STREETS WERE a blur. I could no longer tell the difference between a house or a person as I weaved my way through the narrow alleyways to the city wall. Twigs scratched my feet through my new sandals, and small stones worked their way into my shoes, digging into my flesh and wedging themselves between my toes. But I kept running because I was too afraid to stop. Sabinus was gaining on me. I could hear his terrifying, heavy footsteps thumping as loud as the beating of my own racing heart. He was a Roman soldier. Why had I ever thought I could outrun a soldier? All I had achieved by escaping was to make him angrier, and I didn't want to think of what he was capable of when angry.

Finding myself at the broken section of the wall, I scrambled up its side. As I reached the top, I could see Sabinus pushing his way through the busy streets. He may have been stronger than me, but I was small and I knew the town better than him. It was easier for me to navigate my way through the alleyways and crowds. He could see me on the top of the wall, but he hadn't yet reached the base; this was my chance to get away.

I jumped.

It was a desperate and reckless move. The ground below me was rocky and, as I landed, I twisted my ankle and fell against a jagged tree stump, which ripped through my tunic and cut open my thigh. A pain like a thousand knives stabbing me shot down my leg from the tear in my flesh—a curved gash like a crescent moon smiled up at me, black and bloody. How was I going to get away now? I was too injured to run, and a fast escape was impossible. But I could still hide.

I limped over to a gnarled oak tree and pulled myself into its branches, climbing until they thinned out and I couldn't go any further. I'd been used to climbing with just one good hand, so two working hands made the ascent much faster. From the safety of the tree's thick leaves, I kept my eyes trained on the top of the wall, waiting to see whether Sabinus would follow me beyond the town. From that great height, I was also able to see the clearing in the woods where Zadkiel's house stood, as well as the hut where he kept his goats. Would my love be at home or in the fields with the goats? I couldn't risk running to an empty building and letting Sabinus find me alone, not while I was this injured. My thigh throbbed and burned, the entire leg now crimson with blood. I tore at the hem of my tunic and wrapped it around the top of my thigh to stem the bleeding.

Zadkiel had told me that everything I felt, he felt tenfold. Would he feel my fear and pain from so far away? I prayed he would. If he didn't, then at least the tree would shield me long enough for Sabinus to get bored and hunt for me elsewhere. I held the branch tightly and peeked out through its leaves.

The soldier was now standing on top of the wall, silhouetted against the bright blue sky. His cape blew in the breeze, and he held a dagger in his hand.

'I will find you, Arabella!' he roared, placing the weapon back in its sheath and climbing down the wall in my direction.

When he reached the other side, he stood still and looked around, his eyes squinting against the sun. He took in his surroundings: the peasant huts, the rolling hills, and the huge expanse of forest. Sabinus was a soldier, which also made him an experienced hunter and a trained killer. I knew I stood little chance of surviving if he found me. He stopped at the broken tree stump where I'd fallen and ran his hand over it, inspected his glistening red fingertips. Holding his hand up to his nose, he licked his fingers and smiled. He knew I was hurt and that I couldn't have got far. He found the tracks I had left in the dusty earth, and I held my breath as he passed beneath my tree, looking at the flattened, dry grass around it.

Where was Zadkiel? Why hadn't he heard my silent pleas?

There was a rustling noise, and then the bushes beside the soldier parted. My heart began to hammer so loudly I feared he would hear me. Alas, it wasn't Zadkiel.

'Signor?'

A woman stepped out of the undergrowth. I was too high up to see her face clearly, but I could tell by her wavering voice that she was scared. She stumbled toward Sabinus, her trembling arms reaching out to him. Her thick, dark hair was matted with leaves and moss, and her dress, which had once been a thing of splendour and possibly white silk, hung off her like a tattered rag. Sabinus glanced up and momentarily forgot about my tracks on the ground. He walked toward the woman and then stopped directly beneath me. I could only see the tops of their heads, but I could hear every word they uttered.

'*Signor?*' she said again, her voice louder and more urgent this time. 'Can you help me?'

Sabinus's head moved from side to side as he took in the dishevelled woman before him.

'What do you want?'

'My boy. I have lost my boy. Have you seen him?'

'No,' he answered, dismissing her with a wave of his hand.

'Please!' She was on the verge of tears. 'I don't know how long I have been gone, but I have lost my boy. Can you help me?'

She laid a hand on the breastplate of his uniform. As he swatted her arm away, the thin wisp of fabric that held up her filthy dress tore, exposing her breasts. The only clean part of her body, they shone a creamy gold in the sunlight. She pulled at the fabric of her dress but only managed to rip it further. Sabinus's cruel, high-pitched laugh sent slivers of ice down my spine.

'You are that desperate to find your son that you unclothe yourself before a soldier?'

'No!' she cried, crossing her arms over her chest and backing away. 'I don't know where I am. I need help.'

Sabinus pulled her arms apart to reveal her breasts again.

'This town is full of nothing but disobedient whores.'

The woman gathered up the fabric of her dress and turned away, but Sabinus pulled at her long hair, making her yelp in surprise. He didn't let go.

'Where do you think you are going, whore?'

'I need to look for my son. He is young and scared. I have to go.'

'You'll go when I say you can go.'

I wanted to stop him, truly I did. He was directly below me; I could have fallen on him and broken his neck. But I may have missed and broken my own. Or worse, he may have captured me. I stayed behind the safety of the leaves and prayed Zadkiel would hear me and save both me and the poor, wretched woman. She was naked from the waist up, and now that Sabinus had hold of her long, matted hair, I could see two dark lumps on her back between her shoulder blades.

'Please, *Signor*, let me go.'

'You know what's wrong with all you whores?' he spat, pulling at her hair harder until she buckled to her knees. 'You aren't like us soldiers; you don't know how to take a command. You don't know your place. I'll show you what I think of you and your wanton ways, you dirty plebeian.'

He pushed her to the ground and pulled at her flimsy dress until it disintegrated in his hands. She was on her back now, and I could finally see her face. She was beautiful. Confused, scared, and filthy, but beautiful.

Sabinus pinned her hands to the dry forest floor, one on either side of her head.

'If I wasn't so weak, you'd never be able to get this close to me,' she hissed.

'You whores are only good for one thing. Go on, keep fighting. I like it.' He slapped her hard across the face and laughed. 'First the peasant girl runs away from me and now you offer yourself to me like a desperate crone. This town needs to control its women better.'

He kneed her in the stomach to stop her from struggling, and her head snapped back in pain. That's when her eyes met mine. They widened, realising I was the girl the soldier spoke of.

Sabinus continued to fight against her, oblivious to me perched in the branches above. The skin on her bare shoulders peeled and bled as he attempted to hold her down. It was clear that her green eyes, though dull and distant, once belonged to a strong woman. Somebody who was used to greatness.

We stared at one another, my eyes widening as hers narrowed in anger and pain. Was she asking me to help her? I had no idea how to stop Sabinus without us both getting killed. Then she began twitching her head to the side, and I realised what she'd been trying to tell me. I had to use this opportunity to escape.

She was saving my life.

Sabinus didn't notice me slide down the other side of the tree and hobble away; he only had eyes for his latest victim. I didn't even want to contemplate what he planned to do to her. Every step I took felt like a searing knife was being plunged deep into my thigh, but I nevertheless stumbled forward as fast as I could.

Then I saw him. Zadkiel. Looking around like he was searching for something—the source of my pain.

I was safe.

I ran faster, tripping over branches and falling to the ground, until suddenly my feet felt like they were hardly touching the ground. Then they weren't. I was floating, flying, faster and faster toward him. Zadkiel was making me fly! I laughed, laughter that merged with sobs of relief as his beautiful face got closer to mine and I was suddenly wrapped up in his embrace. He ran back to his cottage with me in his arms as I buried my head in his neck, trying to control the convulsions of both fear and relief coursing through my body.

I was safe.

I was safe.

I was safe.

But what if Sabinus found me with another man? And what about the poor woman in the forest? Would she be reunited with her son, or would the soldier kill her before she had a chance?

Zadkiel sat me down on a stool in his kitchen and shut the doors and windows, putting a bolt across the front door. He didn't have to ask me why I was running; even a person with no powers could have seen how scared I was. He crouched beside me, held my hand, and waited patiently until I was ready to speak.

'My mother has left for Rome and taken my brother,' I said, words mixing with racking sobs. 'She sold me to a legionnaire called Sabinus who, right now, is in the forest hunting for me. I've just seen him attack another woman. I…I…didn't…' I took a shaky breath. 'I didn't know where else to go, Zadkiel. I'm sorry; I didn't know what to do.'

'Hush. You're safe now. You did the right thing.'

I pulled at the soldier's scarf tied around my wrist, trying to undo the knot.

'What's this?' Zadkiel said, taking a knife and releasing my arm from the tight fabric.

'Sabinus put it there. It means I'm his.'

A dark cloud passed over his face, and his eyes turned from blue to a deep indigo.

'You don't belong to anyone. Did he…?' The muscles in his clenched jaw began to twitch as he fixed his stare to the ground. 'Has he touched you?'

I shook my head, thinking of the woman in the forest who had saved my life and the terrible things Sabinus was probably still doing to her. It could just as easily have been me being attacked on that forest floor.

'I can feel you're in pain. Where are you hurt?'

I lifted the edge of my ripped tunic, and he winced at the sight of the gash on my leg. Small pieces of bark were embedded in the curved wound, which Zadkiel pulled out one by one. Then he placed his hand over it. It stung at first until nothing—no more pain. He took the red scarf he was still holding, dipped it in a clay pot of water, and wiped it over my thigh. The wound had disappeared, leaving nothing but a faint curved mark. He'd healed me once again. My blue-eyed god.

'Thank you,' I said, kissing him softly on the lips.

'This is your home now, Arabella. You are not to leave these walls unless you are with me. If he paid for you, I doubt he will let you go that easily. I will make plans, sell everything, and then we will leave Fiesole.'

'There's no need. Sabinus has to go to Germania tomorrow,' I told him. 'He wanted to take me with him, so I only have to hide until then and then I should be safe. He will be forced to go, with or without me. We don't have to run away.'

Zadkiel kissed my forehead and passed me a cup of water. I took it in my trembling hands and sipped it, my breathing slowly returning to normal.

'What about my brother?' I asked.

'We'll find him. I don't care what I have to do to make you happy, as long as we are together.'

I stood up, my leg no longer hurting, and wrapped my arms around his neck.

'I promise to love you forever, Zadkiel. *In aeternum te amabo.*'

He bent down to kiss me then stopped and whipped his head around.

'He's coming.'

Through the cottage window we watched Sabinus running toward us, his red cape flying and his face contorted with anger.

'That's him. That's the soldier,' I said, my hands still shaking as I pointed to the figure in the distance. 'Do something, Zadkiel. Throw him through the air. Kill him. I don't care. I've seen what he is capable of.'

Zadkiel's face was set as still as marble, but his eyes burned with an intensity I'd never seen before. I looked back out the window, but Sabinus was no longer there.

There was a knock at the door. I froze, shaking my head at Zadkiel.

'I will not hide in my own home,' he said, cupping my face in his hands and kissing me. 'I love you, Arabella, and I promise we will always be together. Nothing is stronger than love, not even an angry soldier. Whatever happens, he can't have you.'

He opened the door, and I hid out of sight. I could see Sabinus standing in the threshold, smiling like nothing had happened.

'Good afternoon to you,' he said to Zadkiel. 'I am looking for a woman. She came running this way and is partially clothed with long, dark hair. I have been sent to search for her. She is ill of mind and a danger to herself.'

He was talking about the lady in the woods—that poor mother who had saved my life. She'd got away! But why was she running to *this* house? There were others closer where she could have sought help.

'I'm sorry,' Zadkiel said. 'There is no one else here. Just me.'

Sabinus's frown turned to a chilling smile, his tiny teeth flashing as he pulled the red scarf out of Zadkiel's hand.

'You're lying. Let me pass, goat-boy.'

'No. Please leave my property,' Zadkiel said, blocking the door. 'There's no one here.'

'You have my girl. Move!'

'No. I shall not ask you again. You need to leave, or I will not be accountable for my actions.'

Sabinus's laugh was hollow and held no joy or spirit. It filled me with dread. Why wasn't Zadkiel picking him up with his magic and throwing him across the field?

'I have a proposition for you,' Zadkiel said, stepping outside and shutting the door behind him.

A few seconds passed, and then I heard a grunt, a cry, and an almighty crash. Had Zadkiel killed him? I stepped out of my hiding place just as Sabinus kicked the door open. Splintered wood shattered around me as I flung myself back into the corner. The soldier stood in the doorway, his huge frame blocking out all the light, and scanned the room until his eyes rested on me. I could no longer see Zadkiel. Where was he? I cried out his name, but my words were drowned out by the soldier's high-pitched laughter.

'I lose one whore and gain another. This town is infested with wanton women like a rotting piece of timber is with termites.' He pulled me up by my hair and tucked me under his arm like a farmer would a hen. I kicked out, scratching and biting him, but it only made him laugh louder.

My head turned this way and that, desperately seeking out my love as Sabinus marched us out of the house.

And then I saw him.

Zadkiel lay on the ground, the soldier's dagger protruding from his chest. Even in death, he was perfect. No blood stained his tunic or the dry ground beneath him. His aquamarine eyes stared blankly up at the clear sky.

'No! Zadkiel! No!' I screamed. I sank my teeth into the soldier's arm. 'Let me go to him. Please.'

Sabinus didn't say a word as he bent down and pulled at the dagger in Zadkiel's chest, stepping on Zadkiel's body to gain a hold as he yanked it out of his ribcage. With me still under his arm, facing backwards so my hands had nothing to thrash out at but his broad back, he chuckled and wiped his dagger on my behind. It was over; there was nothing more that could be done. Zadkiel was dead, and I belonged to a soldier who could do to me whatever he pleased.

My body went limp and, through the haze of my tears, I stared at my lover prostrate near the doorway of what I'd dreamed would one day be our home. No blood, no death cry, just a yawning chasm between me and my perfect blue-eyed boy, widening with every step the soldier took away from the cottage and my shattered future.

Sabinus moved fast, the cottage getting further and further away. I squinted against the harsh midday sun, unwilling to take my eyes away from the place I had dreamed of calling home.

Something was moving in the lavender bushes. It was the dark-haired woman—and she was weeping. She moved toward Zadkiel and then hid again just as quickly, her face stricken with fear as she stared up to the heavens. Sabinus was unaware of the events unfolding behind him, intent on returning to town and finally taking me as his own. But as the soldier strode away from the cottage, I watched the terrifying scene play out. I saw the winged gods come down from the sky and surround Zadkiel. I saw the woman tremble as she hid from them. And I saw them take away my only love.

That's when I realised who the woman was, who her lost boy had been, and why she would never see him again. My tears left a trail from Zadkiel's cottage to Fiesole, where my fate awaited me.

VII.

There was nothing left inside my mother's house but a few utensils and a bed; she'd taken it all. Sabinus held my arm tightly as he stormed through the house, screaming at me about the need to be compliant and that my bitch of a mother had lied to him about how dutiful her daughter would be. His hold on my arm was leaving a scarlet welt, but I couldn't feel it. I felt nothing at all. I was no longer there; my heart had been sliced in two along with Zadkiel's.

Sabinus threw me down on the bed and snarled.

'I should have done this when I first laid eyes on you. Maybe then you wouldn't have wasted my time running away.'

He tied the tatty red scarf to my right wrist again and held my arms down against my hips, pinning me onto the bed. With his other hand, he used his knife to cut away my tunic until I lay before him naked. He smiled and raised his eyebrows at the sight of my frail, shivering body.

'Well, at least this isn't a disappointment.'

He put his knife down beside me and went to take my other arm, flinching at the sight of my left hand, which I still held in a tight fist. I didn't struggle or cry out; I'd detached my mind from my body as soon as he'd carried me away. Now I wanted my soul to escape, too.

'Don't put your deformity anywhere near me. That pathetic excuse for a hand is the only reason I got you so cheap. Your dirty slut of a mother robbed me; she should have given you away for free. You're useless.'

Still holding me down with one hand, he used the other to lift up his own tunic and untie the folded fabric shielding his manhood. He pulled my right arm toward him and rubbed my hand against him. I didn't want to look at what I was doing, what my life had become. I turned my head away, and that was when I noticed his dagger was within easy reach of my left hand. Sabinus hadn't worried about leaving the weapon beside me. I was too deformed to take it, after all. He'd only ever seen my hand gnarled and useless.

Sabinus was now running his rough hands over my breasts and pulling at my nipples, squeezing them too hard, wanting me to cry out. I didn't. I laid there limp and lifeless, my body numb to his torture.

'Can you feel me, little one?' he said, rubbing my hand faster against him. 'You'll be loving this soon enough, just wait and see. Then you'll be begging me in the night to take you. You may dislike me now, but I'm doing you a favour. I'm taking you to see the world, where you'll be surrounded by *real* men, strong fighting men. Want to feel what a strong fighting man can do?'

His hungry eyes were still on my body and hadn't noticed my left hand reaching out for his dagger. He pushed my knees apart, smiling at what he saw.

'I have conquered many places, and I've always taken what I wanted. It's time to make you mine.'

He pulled me by my hips until my legs were on either side of him. I had seen him do the same to the dark-haired woman in the forest. I'd watched her face as he'd thrown himself on top of her. I already knew what pain and humiliation looked like, but I was not going to allow this to be my life—this was not going to be my destiny.

The soldier wasn't looking at my free hand as I grasped the handle of his knife and lifted it high. I could kill him. I could drive his bloody blade through his neck and be done with him, avenging Zadkiel and freeing myself. Except I'd never be free. His comrades had been inside my home, inside my mother. If the body of a dead soldier was found within these walls, the army would know where to look. I would never be safe and neither would my family. What would become of my little brother if they suspected my mother? How would I ever be free to enjoy my life again?

Sabinus had positioned himself between my legs, and I could feel the tip of his manhood nudging against me. He was enjoying himself, savouring my fear, watching my face to see at what moment I would admit defeat and plead for him to stop. But it didn't matter. I was no longer there; my soul had gone in search of its mate. I brought the blade higher still.

Sabinus leant down low over me and pulled back my hair until my throat was exposed. His mouth grazed mine, and he ran his tongue over his tiny teeth, his breath smelling like the sweet stench of rotting flesh. His armoured chest was cold and heavy against my breasts, making it difficult for me to breathe beneath him. He was like a snake teasing its victim, waiting for the right time to pounce.

'Are you ready, my little whore? This will hurt, Arabella, and I'm going to enjoy every second of it.'

I raised my hand, holding his dagger, just as he pushed himself inside me.

'Now you're mine,' he said, his face inches from mine.

With all the strength I possessed, I thrust the blade of his dagger through the side of my neck.

'I'll never be yours,' I whispered.

Blood sprang forth like a fountain from my slashed throat. The last thing I saw was the soldier's mouth fill with my blood as he cried out my name.

VIII.

I was free. Then I returned.

IX.

My soul has never forgotten what my mind has never known, not my first love nor my greatest enemy. In every lifetime, we play our role.

The world is our stage, and we act out our scripts. We follow our paths. We do what feels right, what carries us forward to our destiny.

I began my time on Earth as Arabella and went on to live many lives as many women, each time meeting the people I had to meet to continue my journey through life. I've married good men and bad men, and I've had happy lives and sad lives, but I've always been searching, waiting, expecting to meet the one that gave me everything and the other who took it all away.

A story began that hot day in Fiesole, a story that never reached its end. Me, Sabinus, Zadkiel, and Lucifer were forever searching for each other, forever bound to one another until our invisible threads could be severed.

Then one day, over two thousand years later, the four of us were reunited. It was time to complete the circle...one way or another.

26

THIS WASN'T ZAC'S first time flying, but it *was* his first time in an aeroplane. He stared out of the window at the billowing clouds, pink in the light of dawn, and thought back to how it had once felt to soar among them. As an angel, he'd had the ability to appear and disappear, but sometimes he would fly instead. Who wouldn't fly if they could? He smiled to himself as he remembered how his giant wings would change the shape of the clouds, turning them from fluffy cotton wool to fine wisps of smoke, and how it felt to have their cold mist settle on his face as he hid among them—forever afraid that those below would see him.

Flying across London with Ella in his arms had been his last and most reckless flight. Although it had been a snowy night, he had taken a risk that had ultimately cost him his life. Darkness can't hide you when your wings shine as bright as a million stars as they move against an inky, silent sky. Now he would never fly again.

Zac shuffled in his seat. He was used to being still, sitting for long periods of time with nothing to do had never been a problem for him, but what he wasn't used to was being surrounded by so many people. Not for the first time, he was thankful he could no longer feel the emotions of others. This many people in such a confined space, their heads full of where they were going and what they were escaping, would have made for an overwhelming journey.

The woman beside him coughed far too close to his face and he turned away, pressing his head against the cold plastic window. She sat on the edge of her seat, her large bulk unable to squeeze into the small economy seat. He shouldn't have settled for a budget airline. He could have flown business class, but he'd been too eager to see Ella as quickly as possible, taking the first flight available.

The large woman beside him smiled, and he smiled back. Her left thigh was spilling out under the armrest and inching onto Zac's seat, making his leg numb. He was being forced to position himself at an uncomfortable angle and didn't know where to put his right arm. He wasn't going to sit like a contortionist for the remainder of the flight.

'Excuse me,' he said. The large woman turned to him. 'There's a seat three rows back…' He stopped. What was he doing? Was he really going to force the woman to sit elsewhere against her will? He unbuckled his seat belt and smiled at her again. 'I think I'm in the wrong seat. Would you mind letting me pass?'

She nodded, and he squeezed his way past the businessman beside her, heading for the seat where he'd originally intended to make her sit. No one had noticed he'd swapped seats, and the woman would probably be more comfortable now, anyway. No longer having the ability to feel what others felt didn't mean he had to be a selfish bastard. He'd had powers before and had been careful as to how he used them; he didn't intend to abuse his powers this time, either.

He stretched, reclined his seat, and closed his eyes. Ella. He was going to see Ella in a few hours. If only he'd been able to get to Spain in time for her birthday, but it had been early afternoon by the time he'd finished speaking to Gabriel and that would've meant arriving in Tarifa in the evening; he wasn't prepared to take the risk of getting caught by Mikhael. Mornings were a safer time to travel; angels rarely watched people in the morning. They preferred the magic of dusk.

Zac had already decided that, as soon as he landed, he would hire (or more accurately, acquire) a motorbike and two helmets from the rental desk. It was technically theft, yes, but he intended to balance out his bad deeds with good ones, to justify his new existence. He imagined riding off into the sunset with Ella sitting behind him. He could practically feel her arms around his waist and her legs pressing against his. What he'd give to feel her kiss on the back of his neck again. Not long now.

All night he'd tossed and turned in bed, his mind swarming with questions. What would she say when she saw him? Would she be excited, relieved, angry, confused? He did know one thing—she'd be happy to see him. As Gabriel had told him the previous day, Ella had missed him terribly. The archangel would have spoken to her by now, and she'd be waiting for him, for her true love.

He and Ella were finally going to be reunited, and this time nothing was going to stand in their way.

27

'I CAN'T BELIEVE that's what you chose to wear to sit on an aeroplane for three hours.'

Sebastian had to run a little in order to keep up with Luci as she headed toward baggage collection.

'You don't think I look nice?' she asked.

'Of course you look nice. You look incredible. But a long, tight red dress and stiletto heels doesn't look very comfortable.'

She stopped and turned around, making him run straight into her chest.

'Do I look like a woman who puts comfort before first appearances, Sebastian?'

He shook his head and followed her to the luggage carousel. His hands hadn't stopped sweating since they'd boarded the plane in London. He wiped them on his trousers.

'So, what's the plan?' he asked. She was pulling a small black case off the conveyor belt, her back to him. As she marched toward the exit, he had to break into a jog to catch up with her. 'Luci. Stop! What's the plan?'

'You're getting tiresome, Sebastian. We go to Ella's hotel, you point her out to me, and then you fuck off once and for all.'

He hated airports, and now his nerves were making Luci angry. She'd told him at least ten times on the flight that it didn't matter if he was recognised on their journey. As long as he stayed with her, she could convince the authorities he was someone else. But he'd been on the run for over three years; looking over his shoulder was second nature to him.

They stepped out into the glare of the sunlight, and Luci put on a pair of large sunglasses she'd bought in London, seemingly oblivious to the confused stares of the people in the street. It was early morning and she was dressed like a cabaret singer who hadn't yet been to bed. Sebastian wished he'd found the courage to ask her to get him some new clothes while she'd been on her Mayfair shopping binge. He was still wearing the same shirt and loose trousers she'd given him in Morocco, although the London hotel had been happy to clean and press them.

With a father that owned some of the world's most exclusive hotels, staying in luxury had been something Sebastian had taken for granted all his life. But after three years of sleeping in motels, cars, and tents as he'd made his way through Europe and northern Africa, Claridge's hotel had offered a level of comfort he'd forgotten existed. Luci had managed to get them the most luxurious of penthouse suites with rooftop views over London. Their bedrooms were at separate ends of the vast apartment. She'd told him to order whatever food he wanted, and she'd make sure they got away without any consequences. He'd been both exhilarated and petrified since the day he'd met her, and he was finding it increasingly difficult to differentiate between the two.

He'd bathed in the large marble bathtub and ordered room service—intending to watch a couple of movies he'd missed out on while hiding in Morocco. He was quite happy keeping his distance from Luci. If he was honest with himself, he would admit he'd been too afraid to leave the bedroom. He never knew what that woman would do next.

There was a loud knock. Sebastian opened his bedroom door, but Luci was already answering the front door, dressed in lacy red underwear and high heels. He stood transfixed as she pulled two porters in by their collars. They set upon her like hungry wolves, a flurry of hands and mouths and tongues. Did Luci know he was watching? She was up against the wall now, pushing their heads to different parts of her body and laughing her deep guttural laugh as they ripped and pulled at her underwear. The front door hadn't been shut properly, and after a few seconds there was another knock, this time more tentative. A young blonde girl wearing a housekeeping uniform was peering into their suite. Sebastian still didn't dare move. He waited for the girl to apologise and rush off, but instead she stepped in, shut the door, and began to kiss Luci full on the mouth while the men pawed at her, too.

Sebastian closed his bedroom door quietly and locked it, unable to keep out the cries of pleasure that continued in the hallway.

What the *fuck* was the matter with her? Everywhere Luci went, she gathered hordes of adoring fans. He'd never met such a salacious woman. She was an insatiable, dirty whore who did what she wanted with whomever she wanted without giving it a second thought. Was she doing this to him on purpose? Was she trying to turn him on or scare him off?

He wasn't interested in watching, not now that he knew who she was. *What* she was. He would just lead her to Ella as agreed, and then he would take his stepsister away and give her what she deserved. Luci had promised him that, after all.

• • • • •

Sebastian shielded his eyes from the glare of the early morning sun. The airport was a small one, positioned along the only strip of land available between the mainland of Gibraltar and Spain.

'What the hell's all this?' he shouted over the sound of seagulls squawking overhead and the distant roar of an aeroplane. Luci was walking across a large expanse of tarmac, the Rock of Gibraltar looming behind them like a giant shark's fin. 'Why are we crossing a bloody runway?'

'It's the only way to reach the border.' She pointed at a long queue of people snaking alongside a line of cars.

'I can't believe all that time my father had a house in Marbella and I never visited Gibraltar. Is it nice?'

'Of course. It has cheap gin and monkeys, what's not to like? Come on, it won't take long to cross into Spain. Stay close to me and no one will question you.'

Luci pushed her way through the queue of people clutching their passports, her hips swinging from side to side and her heels clicking along the tarmac. Sebastian scuttled behind her, turning his head away each time he passed an armed policeman.

She reached the front of the line and smiled at a young British guard. He looked at the raven-haired woman in a strapless gown and the furtive scruff beside her like he was waiting for the punch line.

'Passports.'

'We don't have them, but you will let us pass,' she said, laying a hand on his arm and staring deep into his eyes.

He smiled back at her and nodded for them to continue. No matter how many times Sebastian watched the devil woman work her magic, it never ceased to unnerve him.

'Who's the other guy?' he whispered to her.

'Spanish police. We're still not in Spain.'

'*Pasaporte,*' the second guard barked.

Luci did the same as before, speaking softly to him in Spanish, giving him a big smile and a view of her cleavage for good measure. The guard looked her up and down and frowned.

'*Pasaporte!*' he repeated.

For the first time since he'd met her, Sebastian saw a flash of panic pass over Luci's face. She made sure to look the guard in both eyes as she spoke again, but even Sebastian could see the man was getting angry and impatient. Why wasn't it working?

'Bollocks!' she muttered.

'What? Why isn't he letting us go?' Sebastian wiped his hands on his trousers again. His shirt was sticking beneath his armpits; he pulled at it, trying to cool himself down. 'For God's sake, Luci! Make it work.'

The guard raised his hand at them, signalling not to go any further, and said something into his radio. Luci sighed and drummed her fingers against her thigh.

'Glass eye. He must have a glass eye. This is rare. It doesn't happen often.' She sighed at the expression on Sebastian's face. 'I used to struggle a lot with pirates, back in the day when eye patches were all the rage. This thing I do is useless unless both of my eyes focus on both of theirs.'

What? Was she for real?

This was it. He was going to be arrested and, as he was still officially on British soil, he'd be dragged back to England and charged for the things Ella had accused him of. The police already had all the evidence they needed to put him away for a very long time. He pulled his damp shirt away from his chest again and tried to steady his breathing while the guard continued to talk into the radio. The queue of people behind them was getting restless as two more Spanish guards joined them, hands hovering over the guns at their hips.

'Start walking,' Luci hissed to Sebastian.

'What? No way! They're armed.'

Luci was already heading toward the border into Spain. Sebastian quickly followed.

'Alto!'

All three guards pointed their guns at Luci's head, but she didn't slow down. Neither did Sebastian; he knew better than to disobey her orders. The Spanish police continued shouting, but they were already on the other side.

Shit! The guards were running toward them now, but Luci carried on walking, unconcerned by the danger they were both in. What the *hell* was she doing? He was going to have to give himself up. Prison was better than a bullet to the head. He glanced to his side, but Luci was still staring straight ahead as she marched on, her fingers twitching beside her. There was a yell. He quickly looked back and saw all three policemen tumble into a heap on the pavement. Luci smiled. Had she done that?

'Stop or we'll shoot!' one of the guards shouted from his position on the ground.

'Keep walking,' she murmured. 'They can't hurt us.'

Cars had begun to slow down to let the woman in a bright red ballgown and her scruffy companion cross the road. The armed guards were now back on their feet. Outside the fast food chains in the Spanish border town of La Línea, crowds of people began to form, chatting in a mix of English and Spanish—asking each other who the '*loca*' was.

Suddenly, there was a loud crack and a woman screamed; a shot had been fired, sending the people in the street running for cover. Sebastian had never heard a gun being fired before. It never sounded that loud in the movies.

'They're shooting at us!' he shouted.

'I know.'

'We're going to die. Oh my God, they're shooting again. Luci, they're going to kill us!'

'No, they won't,' she replied, a smile flickering on her lips. 'Keep walking. We're the bad guys, remember—the baddies never run.'

Sebastian's legs buckled beneath him as he felt a sharp punch in the back of his calf. A dark red stain bloomed on his light cotton trousers. Had he been shot? He'd expected it to hurt more than that.

'Luci, slow down! They got me. I'm going to bleed to death!' he shouted, hobbling behind her.

'No, you won't.'

The sound of footsteps gaining on them got louder. Luci finally stopped, gave another loud sigh, and turned around to face a team of armed police running at them, their weapons ready to fire again. She raised her hands up in the air slowly, as if she was conducting a sermon, and then brought them down in one fast, fluid movement.

A shadow formed at their feet. Growing darker and darker, the sky was suddenly filled with hundreds of seagulls squawking so loudly it was as if the air itself was screaming. Sebastian ducked as hundreds of birds launched themselves at the guards.

'It's a cheap trick, but it always works,' Luci shouted over the commotion. She opened the door of a nearby car and instructed the driver to get out.

Sebastian couldn't move, transfixed by the grisly scene playing out before him. The gulls were relentless, a flurry of feathers and beaks. Three guards lay on the ground, their heads a bloody mess as the birds pecked where their eyes had once been. The gulls' wings beat their way through the hysterical crowd of people now curled up in balls on the pavement.

Luci leant out of the car window and pointed at some children nearby, her magic forcing them to the ground and rolling them beneath parked cars to safety. Then with a shake of her head, as if clearing her mind of the hell she'd just created, she turned to Sebastian, who was still looking on in horror.

'Come on, let's go!' she shouted.

He scrambled in beside her and fastened his seat belt. As if the seat belt made any difference. Sebastian would only ever be safe if Luci decided he was.

28

IT DIDN'T TAKE long for them to get out onto the open road and head northwest for Tarifa. Sebastian turned around in his seat for the tenth time that minute and looked out the back window. They weren't being followed; they'd got away with it. Of course they had.

'What the hell was all that about?' he said, his breathing slowly returning to normal.

Luci laughed but kept her eyes on the road. She didn't have a hair out of place.

'Oh, just a little bird magic. It came in very useful during the seventeenth century when I was accused of witchcraft. Never fails. Luckily for us, it's not only the minds of *people* that I can control.'

'You talk to animals?'

'Of course.'

'You're unbelievable. You're like the villain from every film ever.'

'Where do you think Walt and Alfred got their ideas?'

'Who?'

'Disney and Hitchcock. The bird thing, the evil mothers and beautiful princesses talking to animals—I gave them all those ideas. I've been the muse for many great minds over the years.'

Sebastian rolled his eyes but said nothing.

The scenery was getting greener now, and to his left the mountains gave way to a ravine where below the Mediterranean shone a deep turquoise. It was nice to be back in the sunshine after dreary London. Sebastian had never ventured this far west of the Costa del Sol. Giant wind turbines loomed up over the hills before them, doing nothing to take his mind off the new, fantastical supernatural life he appeared to be living. He liked it here. He could easily settle in southern Spain. Maybe he would.

Turning to Luci, he marvelled at how her beautiful face glowed with such serenity. The crazy bitch had just killed and maimed dozens of people at the click of her fingers and yet there she was, dressed like a 1950s movie star and driving calmly, seemingly without a care in the world. What the fuck had he got himself into? Fallen angel or not, Luci *was* the Devil—she was impulsive and heartless, and she'd nearly got him killed. He'd even been shot!

He rolled up his left trouser leg, the fabric crusty and dark red with a round hole in the back, and braced himself for the mess that lay beneath. He touched it gingerly, but it didn't hurt. Spitting on his fingers, he rubbed at where the bullet had entered—there was nothing there but a smudge of dried blood. It didn't make sense. Had he been scratched by a flying bullet? Would it have bled that much?

'What you did back there was reckless,' he said to Luci.

She didn't answer.

'You could have got me killed!'

'I didn't take any risks.'

'Of course you did! Maybe *you* can't die, but *I* can.'

'No, you can't.'

She overtook the car in front of them on a blind bend, turning the wheel at the last moment as a lorry hurtled toward them. Sebastian closed his eyes and then opened them again slowly.

'What did you say?'

'You can't die.'

Her eyes were fixed on the road, and her long hair flowed in waves over her bare shoulders, blowing in the breeze from the window. She was mesmerising, and he hated her.

'You're not making any sense.'

'You're immortal, Sebastian. You drank my blood. I had to make sure nothing happened to you before we found Ella. You can't die at the hands of anyone but me now.'

Immortal? He was *immortal?*

They sat in silence for the rest of the journey.

29

ZAC PULLED UP outside the old, converted monastery and took in its ornate architecture and majestic turret dating back to the time of the Moors. He remembered that era in Spain's history well. It had been exciting in terms of science and architecture, but the battles had been bloody.

So this was Ella's new hotel. It was impressive. A long balcony ran around its perimeter with arched stone doorways and windows looking out over the dozens of orange trees dotted around the cobbled entrance. Zac had seen many Spanish monasteries in his time, but this one was exceptionally pretty. Just one wall stood between him and Ella. She was inside that building, and it was taking all his strength not to break into a run and smash his way in.

Leaving his motorbike parked beneath the shade of a tree, he headed for the entrance and pushed at the hotel door. It was locked. He peered through the glass, but no lights were on and there was no one behind the desk. His stomach curled up into a tight ball—where was she? Five times he'd called her the day before, but no one had answered and there had been no answerphone. Sending an email had been an option, of course, but what would he have said? After three years of being absent, finding the right words had been impossible—he just wanted to see her and explain everything face-to-face. He hadn't even considered that she may not be home. The idea of not seeing her today made his head swim.

He placed his hand over the lock. It gave a satisfying click and swung open. His shoes didn't make a sound on the stone floor as he peered in each of the downstairs rooms. They were all empty, although there was a light on in the library. A pair of slippers lay beside an armchair where a book and some reading glasses sat. The hotel may have been closed to the public, but someone was there.

He wondered where Ella's room would be. Would she have chosen the penthouse apartment at the top with the best view or something around the back and out of sight? He thought back to her home in London; her room had been in the extension hidden away from the rest of the house. He walked down the stairs and noticed a sign reading 'Staff Only.' He was on the right track. As he neared a door at the far end of the corridor, he could hear three excited voices. He didn't recognise two of them, but Ella's voice hit him like a punch to the guts.

He was so close. All he had to do was walk in, and he would be with her. This was it. He turned the door handle slowly, opening it a crack so he could see who she was with before making an entrance, but of all the scenarios he'd been dreaming of on his flight over, he hadn't thought for a moment he'd be greeted with this.

Ella was standing before a full-length mirror with her back to him—and she was wearing a wedding dress.

'The veil or the hair piece?' she asked a couple of identically dressed girls beside her, whom he recognised as her friends Mai Li and Kerry. 'Josh gave me the hair clip for my birthday yesterday, before he proposed, but I think the veil is more appropriate for a church wedding.

What do you two think? Oh God, this is crazy. Twenty-four hours isn't long enough to plan a wedding!'

'Don't worry, it's fine,' Mai Li said, placing a hand on her arm. 'Wear the veil for the ceremony now, and then this afternoon I'll do your hair for dinner and we can pin it up with the clip. How's that?'

'Errr, no!' Kerry said. 'I think *I* will do her hair. I trained in beauty before my degree, remember? Honestly, Mai Li! I mean, like, you hate fashion and I live for it. I'm doing hair and make-up, and you can take the photos or something.'

Zac watched the girls bicker, unable to move from the crack in the doorway. Ella was getting married to Josh? Had fate worked that quickly? But Gabriel was meant to have delivered his message to her yesterday. The only reason he wouldn't have was if…Ella was already on her path. He was too late.

Swallowing down the lump in his throat, Zac gazed on at the only woman he'd ever loved. She looked so beautiful. He wanted to walk right in and kiss her, pick her up and run away with her as fast as he could. Her simple dress was tight and fitted with a lace sash and a long train fanning out behind her. Her hair cascaded over her shoulders, and on her left hand she wore a large pink diamond ring. She really was getting married…and it wasn't to him.

'Ella, come into the bathroom where I have my curling tongs,' Kerry said, pulling her by the hand. 'I think romantic waves will suit you better than just boring blah hair. Come on, we only have ten minutes before we have to meet your mum in her room.'

'Where's my dad?' Ella said.

'I think he's already in the chapel with Josh. Mai Li, get in here. I need someone to hold the bobby pins.'

Ella's parents were here too? Zac bit down on his lower lip. His confidant, Leonardo, was aware of the wedding and hadn't urged his daughter to wait for Zac to return? Had none of them had any faith in his plan? Or did they think Josh was a better match for Ella?

Zac had told her to get back onto her path because he hadn't wanted her to grieve or spend her life waiting in vain, especially as he knew she would only live until she was thirty-four. But he hadn't imagined he'd return so fast or that she'd marry Josh so quickly. *Marry!* Maybe Ella was simply doing what Zac had told her to. If so, did it mean she didn't really love Josh? Was she marrying him because she thought Zac was dead and was never coming back? Or was Josh the better man, the true love of her life? He ran his hands through his short hair, his head heavy and spinning with questions.

The three girls headed into the bathroom. As soon as they shut the door, Zac entered the apartment. He had to find out more information before he made himself known. As much as he wanted to announce himself and stop the wedding, he wasn't going to. He'd ruined Ella's life enough times. He had to make sure she still wanted him—but first he had to find somewhere to hide.

Silently, he used his powers to open the wardrobe and cupboard doors and peeked inside, but they were all too full or too small to squeeze into. The curtains weren't long enough to stand behind either. This was farcical! If he wasn't so shocked by the unforeseen turn of events, he'd be laughing at the absurdity of the situation right now.

Then he spotted Ella's bed. It was old, wooden, and it was raised high above the ground; there was plenty of room under there. He slipped under and strained to listen. The bathroom door wasn't shut properly. He pointed at it and made it creak as he opened it a little wider so the voices of the three girls could still be heard.

'Are you nervous, Ella?' Mai Li asked.

'Not really, it feels...I don't know...natural.'

'I'm not surprised!' Kerry screeched. 'I have no frigging idea how you bagged the hottest guy in the universe in under a week. No offence. So, what's he like in the sack? I'm not going to pretend I haven't thought about him when I've been...'

'Kerry! That's Ella's future husband you're fantasising about. You can't say that!'

'It's fine.' Ella laughed. 'It all happened really fast. I get it.'

'I was just saying I bet he's good in bed, that's all,' Kerry mumbled.

'I wouldn't know,' Ella replied. 'We haven't slept together yet.'

'What?' both friends shouted.

'He was only here for a couple of days. Then he came back after a week and proposed yesterday. I don't want to rush into anything.'

'Says the girl who's getting married the day after getting a ring on her finger,' Kerry said.

'Well, I think it's really romantic,' Mai Li said, passing Kerry another bobby pin. 'True love can't be planned.'

'Mai Li's right, Ella. Josh is so frigging crazy about you, but then he always was. Remember that night in Indigo, like years ago, when I first pointed him out to you? He was obsessed with you even then. It's rare for me to get turned down you know, but he wasn't interested one bit. You two match. I always said you two matched.'

Zac closed his eyes, ignoring the growing ache in his chest, and tried to piece together the sequence of events. If Josh had just appeared on the scene then Gabriel hadn't been mistaken. Ella had only recently stepped back onto her path. But did it mean she really loved Josh? Could she fall in love that quickly? He knew the answer—everything was easier when it was preordained.

It was dusty under the bed. He moved his head away from the ground to avoid sneezing and felt something dig into his stomach. Shifting to the side he pulled the object out from under him; it was a large frame and inside, between two pieces of glass, was a huge feather. Not just any feather. *His* feather. How many of his feathers had he scattered to the wind that night on the Spanish mountains? If Ella had kept it all this time, why was it now under her bed? He turned to his left and looked up at a wall filled with dozens of framed paintings and photos. In the centre was a big square space. She must have had it hanging up in her room and then hid it for some reason. Or did she no longer want a reminder of Zac now that Josh was in her life?

He turned his attention back to the bathroom again. The door was wide enough to just about see the three girls inside. Ella's hair now hung in large waves down her back, and Kerry was adding extra blusher to her cheeks. Kerry cleared her throat.

'Ella, I know it's your wedding day and everything, but...Mai Li and I were talking about it last night and we have to ask. What about Zac?'

'Kerry! We agreed not to mention him!'

Zac held his breath, his body as heavy as stone.

'Oh shut up, Mai Li. You were the one who was worried. Ella's done nothing but talk about that hot barman we met years ago, someone she dated for about five minutes, since we've known her. Honestly, no offence, Ella, but it was getting a bit full-on. Then, suddenly, you're getting married to Josh, a guy you were never interested in? In fact, back in our uni days, you used to laugh at how vain and boring he was. It's weird.'

Ella didn't answer for a long time. Why wasn't she saying anything? Zac wished he could feel her. He wouldn't need to hear what she said if he knew how she truly felt.

'You've made her upset now, Kerry!' Mai Li hissed.

Ella sighed. 'It's OK. I've been thinking about Zac a lot too, lately. Ow! Kerry, please don't make the curls so tight. I'm going to look like Little Bo-Peep.' She went quiet again and then turned to face her friends. 'Zac's out of the picture. He's never coming back.'

'When did you speak to him?' Mai Li asked.

'I haven't; it's been over three years since I last had contact with him. If he wanted me back, he would have come for me by now.'

This was his moment. All he had to do was walk into the bathroom. Of course Ella still loved him. How could she not? She was only doing what he'd told her to do as he lay dying at her feet. She was following her path, but she couldn't possibly be happy. Could she? He shifted beneath the bed, ready to stand, and then he heard her voice again.

'I'm finally happy,' she said, and she sounded it. 'Zac wasn't good for me. Every time we got together, there was drama and problems. I just want an easy life. Josh is a good man, and I love him.'

'Plus he's hot, famous, and rich,' Kerry added.

Ella laughed. 'Yes, that too. But that's not why we got together. When I'm with him I feel, I don't know, like everything's going to be OK. Obviously, I fancy the pants off him, but life seems easier with him beside me. He says the same thing. It's fate.'

'So, you're over Zac?'

He held his breath, waiting for her to answer. He couldn't see her face; she had her back to him. If only he could see her beautiful face, he'd know what she was feeling. Ella stayed silent but nodded her head in agreement. Zac's heart sunk. That was all he needed to see. She was over him. It was that simple. Fate had captured her at last, and she was marrying the right man—just not the one who loved her the most.

The three girls stepped out of the bathroom, and Mai Li applied some extra mascara to Ella's eyelashes.

'Anyway, let's not talk about Zac anymore, OK?' Ella said. 'This is a new beginning. I'm happy, Josh adores me, I have my friends by my side, my parents are waiting for me, and the sun is shining. Shall we go and get me married then?'

They all squealed and embraced one another. Kerry opened the door, Mai Li picked up the train, and all three girls walked into the corridor.

Zac couldn't move. That had been his one chance, and he'd blown it.

• • • • •

Outside the hotel, the sun shone and there wasn't a cloud in the sky. It was the perfect spring day for a white wedding. The happy chirping of the birds in their branches mocked Zac as he walked to his motorbike.

Was he really too late? He could turn around right now and make a big, spectacular gesture like they did in the movies. He could use his powers to slam open the chapel doors and make her fly into his arms, like he had two thousand years ago when she was fleeing the Roman soldier. But what was the point? In every lifetime he'd held back, watched from afar, and let her live her life. Why should this life be any different? She only had eleven years left; she may as well spend them in peace with the man she was destined to love.

She'd said it herself—all Zac ever gave her was drama and pain.

As he reached inside his jean pocket for his motorbike key, his fingers closed around his mother's amethyst necklace and rings—the jewellery he'd intended to give to Ella. He already had his crash helmet on, but he was considering turning back to leave the jewellery in her room when he saw a young, Spanish-looking woman approaching him. She held a magazine in one hand and a set of keys in the other.

'Are you here to make a delivery?' she asked, pointing at his bike.

'*Si,*' he said, his voice muffled by the helmet. He handed her the jewellery. '*Para Ella.*'

She frowned and looked down at the palm of her hand, and then she nodded and entered the hotel.

Zac would give it ten minutes. If Ella didn't appear, he'd take that as his cue to get out of her life forever.

30

ELLA TOOK A moment to compose herself then knocked on her mother's bedroom door. This was it. In a few moments, she'd be standing at the altar beside her husband saying 'I do.' Husband. The word sounded so strange and final. She pushed away the creeping doubts that had been trickling into her mind all morning and opened the door.

'Oh! Ella!' her mother yelped, springing apart from Leo and tucking a loose tendril of hair behind her ear.

Ella's eyes narrowed, darting between her parents. Surely not? Not on her wedding day! A light flush travelled up her mother's neck.

'Darling, you look beautiful,' Felicity said, straightening her pastel pink shift dress and hugging her daughter. 'We didn't hear you. Your father was just here to…'

'Pick up Josh's buttonhole. And mine,' Leo said, pointing to the rose pinned to his chest. 'Your mother was just putting it on for me.'

He cleared his throat and joined Felicity beside his daughter.

'You look radiant, *mi niña,*' he said, stroking Ella's cheek with the back of his hand. 'You know your grandmother's going to be very sad she missed this. She loves you so much.'

Ella blinked away tears. Three years ago, her only blood relative was her mother, but now she had a loving father and grandmother, too—the family she'd always wanted. This wouldn't have happened if it hadn't been for Zac. Ella meeting her father, Felicity leaving Richard, Sebastian on the run, her and Josh getting together—all because of Zac. If he hadn't stepped into her life back then, who knows where she would be today? Would she still be in London? Would she and Josh have found their way to each other regardless?

Leo cleared his throat again.

'I'll see you at the chapel shortly, then. I better not leave Josh waiting any longer; he's a bundle of nerves. He may have already fainted.'

Leo, avoiding looking at Felicity, gave Ella a peck on the cheek and then rushed past the bridesmaids standing in the doorway.

'Papa, Josh's buttonhole?' Ella said, holding it out to him.

He scurried back, took it, and ran back down the stairs.

'Awkward,' Kerry whispered to Mai Li, who stifled a giggle.

'Isn't this wonderful? My baby is getting married!' Felicity trilled, linking her arm through her daughter's. 'There's no rush, darling. We'll just walk slowly. Always good to keep a man waiting.'

The irony of her mother's comment wasn't lost on Ella.

The chapel was on the ground floor, accessible via the large courtyard in the centre of the hotel. Ella lifted the skirt of her gown so it wouldn't trail along the marble steps, and Kerry and Mai Li picked up the train. The four women descended in silence, all of them lost in their own thoughts. Ella's mother absentmindedly playing with her empty ring finger. Was she thinking about Richard or Leo? Was she right to have married "the one"—or had she always been destined to return to her soulmate?

Their footsteps echoed on the white stairs, the hotel silent save for the sound of water cascading from the large stone fountain in the courtyard. The door to the chapel came into view, and Ella's heart leapt at the thought of what lay beyond.

'There you are!' Paloma was running up the stairs toward them.

What was her assistant doing at the hotel on her day off?

'Oh, thank goodness you're here,' she said, out of breath. 'I couldn't find you. I wasn't sure if you'd…oh my God. *Que guapa!* Why are you wearing a wedding dress?'

Ella felt the colour rise in her cheeks. *Own it!* she told herself. Nobody knew about the wedding apart from her parents and two friends—but it wouldn't be long before the media caught wind of the fact that the delectable de Silva was off the market, and then she'd have to get used to more than a few shocked faces.

'I'm getting married.'

'I didn't even know you were dating. Who are you marrying?'

'Josh.'

'The hotel guest? Joshua de Silva, the actor? *Por dios!* That is why I came.'

She handed Ella a magazine she'd been clutching in her hand. 'I wanted to show you this. It's a picture of you in the British press. There you are singing at that bar in town, and in that photo, he is kissing you. I read the article. They are asking who the mystery girl is.'

Ella inspected the grainy images. The drunken karaoke night. So that's what had happened! How embarrassing.

Kerry peered over her shoulder. 'O. M. G. You made it into *HELLO!* magazine. Ella, you are, like, *already* famous and you're not even married to him yet.'

'I don't want to be famous!'

'Well, I just wanted to show you,' Paloma said. 'I apologise for the disruption. Oh, and there was a courier at the front of the hotel. He gave me this for you.'

A necklace and two rings laid in the palm of her hand, their lilac stones winking in the daylight of the courtyard. Ella gasped. She held them up to the light, tears pooling in her eyes. She blinked and looked up at the ceiling to stop them from falling.

What was Paloma doing with Felicity's amethyst necklace? Ella had been the last one to wear it before giving it to Zac the day he'd died. It was this jewellery, which he claimed had once belonged to his own mother, that had carried the clues as to who he was and what he had to do.

'That's my necklace!' Felicity said, taking it gently off Ella.

Felicity sat down on the steps, pale beneath her perfect make-up. Ella joined her. Neither of them had seen that jewellery since the day Zac had killed himself. He'd put it in his pocket. Ella's heart was racing, her mouth too dry to speak. Was he here? Was Zac in her hotel right now?

'What's going on?' Kerry said. Mai Li put her finger to her lips, and they both sat down beside the bride.

Felicity looked up at the Spanish girl. 'Who are you, and who gave these to you?'

'Mum, this is my assistant,' Ella said. 'Paloma, what did the courier look like?'

'I'm not sure.' Paloma was very still, as if she were listening for something. She was making Ella uncomfortable. Why was she staring like that? Paloma's eyes grew wider as she looked between Ella and her mother. 'He was young with tattoos on the top of his arms.'

'Long hair?' Ella asked.

'No. He had a crash helmet on, but I saw no hair.'

'And his eyes?' Felicity asked, reading Ella's mind. 'Were they blue?'

'I don't know—his visor was down.'

It didn't sound like Zac. It couldn't be him. Surely if he'd returned for her, he would have stopped the wedding. Also, Zac didn't have tattoos or short hair.

'Are you OK, Ella?' Mai Li asked, shuffling closer to her on the stairs. 'It's just Kerry and I don't speak Spanish.'

'Yeah, like, what the frig is going on? You two look like you're going to pass out!' Kerry added.

'Nothing,' Ella whispered. 'Thank you, Paloma, for bringing this to us. Would you like to stay for the wedding?'

Now it was her assistant's turn to look uncomfortable. Her expression had changed from one of confusion to pure panic.

'I have to go.'

'Honestly, it's no trouble. Stay for the ceremony and a drink afterwards? We're going for a meal in town this evening.'

'No, thank you. There is something urgent I must do.'

She ran down the stairs two at a time and down the corridor toward the foyer. This all felt wrong—the mysterious courier, Paloma's reaction. Ella had to get to the bottom of this. Josh could wait another five minutes.

She ran after her assistant, calling out her name. Her long dress slowed her down, making her stumble, and by the time she reached the hotel exit, Paloma had disappeared. Ella scanned the grounds for the mysterious courier too, but there was no one there, nothing but the distant sound of a motorbike engine.

31

'LUCI, WATCH OUT!' Sebastian grabbed the handrail above the car window and checked that his seat belt was fastened. The sooner he got out of this blasted car the better. 'You nearly hit that guy on the motorbike. Look! He had to swerve onto the grass, and now his bike's fallen on top of him. Shall we see if he's OK?'

'Don't be ridiculous, Sebastian. We're here now.'

The wooded entrance to the hotel opened up into a large gravel drive surrounded by cypress trees. Sebastian had never been to a monastery before, not in Spain anyway, especially not one that had been so expertly converted into a hotel. He had to admit his sister had done a good job; it was an impressive place.

'*Torre de los angeles* was once a monastery named after the patron saint of the town—they called it "The Virgin of the Light." It's Tarifa's prettiest and oldest building. Isn't it glorious?'

He nodded, taking in the tall tower with its arched windows and the weathervane atop a tall steeple shaped like an angel blowing his horn. In the centre of the drive, serving as a mini roundabout, was a statue of two fighting deer, their antlers locked in battle.

'That's new,' Luci said, getting out of the car and walking toward the entrance. The door was already open, but there was no one around. 'Not much else has changed, though.'

'You've been here before?'

'Oh yes, years ago, in the late eighteenth century. It was full of monks back then. I went through a stage of de-Goding people.'

'I'm going to regret asking this, but what do you mean exactly?'

'It's a long story but, as you know, I have an issue with God. Mainly because he's made up.' She leant against the monastery wall, inspecting her long red nails. 'After Archangel Mikhael thought he'd successfully murdered me, he decided to form an alliance with humans. In accordance with the world leaders at the time, he created an omnipotent being who would govern both the angelic realm and the human world—God. You look confused, Sebastian. Keep up. So, along with a God, he created a Devil…me. That way, everything good was down to God, and everything bad was, well, my fault. Even though Mikhael believed I was dead, he wanted everyone above and below to fear and hate me as much as he did.'

Sebastian nodded. As terrifying as Mikhael sounded, he was beginning to like the sound of this Machiavellian warrior angel.

'I was at the crucifixion of Jesus, you know,' Luci continued. 'It wasn't long after my own resurrection. I knew he was a Nephilim; he looked a lot like his father. I was hoping Gabriel would be there, that he would help me find Zadkiel. But no one turned up to watch the so-called "son of God" die at the hands of his own people. I washed his feet and told him he would rise again. They called me a whore back then, too. For centuries, I've stood by and watched humans use God as an excuse to start wars, to dominate women, and to decide what happens to the weak and vulnerable—and Mikhael started it all. So, after thousands of years of his bollocks, I decided to show God's followers that they were serving a fictitious entity.'

'How did you do that?'

'Mainly by fucking them. You'd be surprised how easily a man can change his mind about anything once he gets the taste of a woman.'

'Charming. And the nuns?'

'Oh, they were insatiable. They were worse than the men. They couldn't get enough of me, and it got quite sordid toward the end. Fun times. I emptied this monastery of its believers three times over during that century.'

'What you're basically saying is that you know your way around this old building because you once shagged everyone that ever resided within it?'

'Yes. There's a secret library in that turret.' She pointed at the tower. 'I spent quite some time in there, reading and having sex. Two very undervalued pastimes.'

She winked at him and stepped through the hotel's doorway. Sebastian couldn't wait to find Ella and get as far away from Luci as he could.

They walked along dark, winding corridors leading to cobbled internal patios and covered walkways, but there was nobody there. Lucy unlocked room after room with the touch of her hand, but they were all empty. A few bedrooms had clothes in the wardrobes, so people were clearly staying there, and whoever was in the penthouse suite had enjoyed a wild night, as there were bottles of beer floating in the hot tub and a half-eaten box of chocolates on the bed. But no Ella.

'She's not here,' Sebastian said for the third time.

'She has to be. I'm not leaving until I've searched every room. Perhaps they're in the restaurant or…' She smiled. 'Is today Sunday or Monday?'

Sebastian had no idea.

'It doesn't matter. Let's try the chapel anyway. I had so much fun beneath that altar with those saucy monks. I wonder if it's changed much.'

Sebastian trudged behind her, impatient to get to his stepsister. His breathing quickened at the thought of how Ella would react when she saw him. Would she cry and try to run away? He hoped so. It was always a lot more fun when girls struggled.

They were back outside the building now. At the base of the tower were large wooden doors with a cross above them.

Luci rested her head against the door and smiled.

'I hear voices inside. Sebastian, it's time to make our grand entrance.'

32

ELLA TOUCHED THE necklace around her neck that her mother had insisted she wear and thought of Zac. She felt guilty, standing at the altar with the angel on her mind, but how could she not? Where had the jewellery come from, and who had that courier been?

She jumped at the feel of Josh's hand in hers. His kind eyes staring down at hers, and the beaming face of her father, made her push away all thoughts of fated angels. This was it. She was marrying the handsome Josh de Silva. But did she really love him? Could she with thoughts of Zac resting so heavily on her heart?

Everyone was looking at her expectantly. Were they waiting for her to say something? She hadn't been listening to a word her father had been saying.

'Sorry, Papa. Could you repeat that?'

'I said do you, Arabella Imaculada Santiago de los Rios, take Joshua Joseph de Silva to be your lawfully married husband?'

It was strange to hear her full name. Nobody ever called her Arabella, not even her parents. She realised she was marrying a man without knowing his full name, either.

'Joseph? Is that your middle name?' she whispered.

He scrunched up his nose and nodded.

'Sorry, Papa,' she said. 'I mean yes, I take…'

Suddenly, there was a loud bang at the back of the church as the wooden doors slammed open, hitting the stone walls on either side. The sun shone into the chapel, creating a silhouette of the two figures standing in the doorway. They walked toward the altar, stepping through the rainbow of colours the stained glass windows threw across the aisle.

Her heart leapt. Was it Zac? No, she could tell right away by their body shapes that neither of them was her angel.

'A wedding? Oh, I do so *love* a wedding,' a female voice said. 'I'm so glad I dressed up for the occasion. Don't mind us; we're just looking for somebody.'

Josh put his arm protectively around his bride, and Leo stepped down from the altar. As the strangers got closer, Ella could see one was a dark-haired woman and the other was…

'Sebastian?'

'Hello, little sis.' He turned to the pew beside him. 'And mummykins. Look at that, my father's bimbo wife is here, too. Where's Richard? Oh, no! Wasn't Daddy invited?'

This couldn't be happening. What the hell was Sebastian doing at her wedding? She'd thought she would never see him again. How had he got into Spain without being caught? And who the fuck was that stunning woman beside him? She looked familiar.

'OK, let me guess,' the woman in red said. 'The blushing bride must be Ella, the priest is her father—how very modern—and the confused blonde must be the mother. And what about those two girls in the hideous burgundy dresses? Never mind, it doesn't matter; I doubt they're important.'

'What do you want?' Josh said, standing between Ella and the brunette. 'This is a private wedding. We don't want any trouble.'

The woman smiled.

'Ah, the dashing groom. Yes, with your chiselled features, I can see why a girl would want to have you between her legs, but I'm not so sure why she would want you beyond that.' She ran her hand over his chest and moved it down to his stomach. 'My goodness, you're very hard down there, aren't you? Now be quiet.'

Josh stood stock-still. Why wasn't he pushing her off him? Was she an ex-girlfriend or a crazy groupie? And what did Sebastian have to do with any of it? Ella's first thought was to cry out for Zac, which was ridiculous. Fat lot of good that would do this time.

'That's quite enough,' Leo bellowed. 'Get out, whoever you are.'

The woman faced the priest and cocked her head to one side.

'Are you not Leonardo?' she said. 'The famous angel expert they speak of in the Vatican? I've heard your name. I know you know my people.'

Angels? Why was the woman talking about angels?

'You,' she said, pointing to Leo, 'and you, you, you, and you,' she continued, nodding to her mother, Josh, and her friends. 'Go to your bedrooms and stay there. It's Ella I need to talk to. If you do as I say, no harm will come to you.'

Much to Ella's horror, they all walked single file down the aisle and out through the side door that led back to the hotel without a backwards glance.

'Stop!' Ella cried.

Why were they ignoring her? She went to run after them but invisible hands held her back. She swung around and faced the woman in red.

'Who the hell are you?' she shouted. 'And why can't they hear me?'

'Oh, I do apologise, Ella. How very rude of me. I'm Luci and this here is Sebastian, but I believe you two have already met.'

Sebastian flashed his tiny teeth. He was thinner than when she'd last seen him and his hair was longer, but his smile was as creepy as ever.

Luci peered closer at Ella's neck and inspected the pendant on her necklace.

'Where did you get this? This is my necklace,' she said.

'No, it's not. It's mine. It used to belong to my great-grandmother, and then my father gave it to my mother.'

Why did the woman think the necklace was hers? Then it dawned on her. Ella knew exactly where she'd seen that beautiful woman before. A painting, the necklace, a face that looked just like Zac's…

'Give it to me!' Luci shouted.

Ella did as she was told, her trembling fingers struggling with the tiny clasp behind her neck. She removed the rings off her right hand, too, and passed them over.

'You have the full set? You have no idea how long I've waited for the planets to align themselves like this. These metals and stones were especially made to bring him to me. So where is he?' Luci twisted her head around wildly. 'Where is my boy?'

'Zac was right, then,' Ella said. 'You're a fallen angel.'

'He knows about me?'

Ella swallowed, struggling to find her voice. Zac's mother was still alive? But that would mean that he…

'Speak, girl!'

'My father…he had your portrait in his house. He'd found it in the Vatican and saw you were wearing the same necklace his grandmother gave him, so he asked to keep it. When Zac saw the painting, he recognised you straightaway. We worked out that, to still be alive, you would've had to have been one of the original fallen archangels.'

What had the woman said her name was? Luci. Ella's stomach sunk to her feet. Of course! Why hadn't she worked it out sooner? Had

Zac? She took a deep, shuddering breath before forming a sentence she never thought she'd hear herself say.

'So is Luci short for…?'

'Lucifer. That's right. I'm Lucifer, but don't believe everything you hear.'

Zac's mother was the Devil? How could that be? How could she have walked the earth for so long without anyone knowing?

'What did Zadkiel do when he saw my picture?' Luci said, gripping the top of Ella's arm.

'Well, when he realised you were still alive, it gave him hope. It made him do what he did.'

'What did he do? *Where is my son?*'

Ella stared down at the ground. His mother had no idea, and Ella didn't want to be the one to tell her.

'Look at me!' Luci screamed. 'Say it. Where is my boy?'

A single tear escaped down Ella's cheek. Out of the corner of her eye she could see Sebastian grinning, but she didn't wipe her face. If this was Zac's mother, then where was he? Why hadn't he survived, too? If he'd lived, surely he could feel her fear right now?

'Zac's dead,' she said.

Luci gripped her arm tighter.

'No. That's impossible. What do you mean?'

'Luci, you got your answer. Zac's dead,' Sebastian said, stepping forward. 'You said I…'

'Shut it and stay where you are!' she shouted at him without taking her eyes off Ella. 'What happened? You know what my son is. He can't die. Don't lie to me.'

Ella sniffed and let another tear fall.

'You think I would be marrying Josh if Zac were alive? I haven't seen him since January three years ago. He saw your portrait, realised you were a fallen angel, and decided if he died, then he too could return and be with me forever—no longer under his father's rule. Except it didn't work. He never came back. He hacked off his own wings with Mikhael's sword for nothing!'

Ella was sobbing uncontrollably now. She knew how much Zac had wanted to see his mother again; she also knew angels were never wrong. Zac didn't make mistakes. So why had it worked for his mother but not him?

She tried to free herself from Luci's grasp, but the fallen angel gathered her into her arms instead and held her tightly. Was she hugging her? Ella allowed herself to relax into her embrace. Whoever this crazy woman was, she was still a mother—someone who was hurting who clearly loved Zac as much as Ella did.

'You haven't seen my boy in three years?' Luci asked.

Ella shook her head against her shoulder.

'Come on, this is a waste of time,' Sebastian said. 'Ella's no use to you now. I did what I said I would do and brought you to my sister. I'm going now, and I'm taking her with me. You promised I could have her.'

The two women turned slowly to face Sebastian.

'Have me?' Ella spat. 'Fuck off, Sebastian! I'm not going anywhere with you, you evil bastard. You ruined my life. I have no idea how you even found me!'

'I like you,' Luci said, wiping Ella's tears off her face. 'I can see why my son was so obsessed with you.'

'What?' Sebastian spluttered. 'Don't let her talk to me like that!'

Luci ignored him and continued talking to Ella.

'Did you know I once saved your life from this creep? It's true. Two thousand years ago, during your first life with Zadkiel. You were Arabella, and Sebastian was a Roman soldier called Sabinus. Do neither of you remember?'

They shook their heads in unison.

'What a pity. No wonder you humans never learn. Well, Sebastian was a disgusting man back then, too. He bought you as a sex slave. I'd just awoken in the forest, years after Mikhael had ripped out my wings and left me for dead, but instead of helping me look for my son, this vile creature raped me. Then the piece of shit killed my boy.'

Sebastian stepped back from the two women, his hands held up in surrender.

'This is preposterous. I can't be accountable for something I supposedly did in another lifetime.'

Luci's eyes glowed a bright green and were fixed on Sebastian's, whose own eyes were now wide and filled with fear.

'It was you who took Zadkiel away from us. Because of you, I've been searching for my son for thousands of years. Your actions forced him to suffer an eternal cycle of pain lifetime after lifetime where he longed to, but couldn't, be reunited with this girl. His one true love. All,' she said, jabbing him in the chest, 'Because. Of. You!'

Sebastian winced and rubbed his chest.

'This is madness. Listen, you asked me to take you to Ella and I did. You promised I could do what I wanted with her afterwards. We had a deal.'

'I lied, you stupid fool. You made a pact with the Devil, Sebastian. The Devil always wins.'

Sebastian broke into a run, but Luci pointed at every door in the chapel, slamming them shut, each lock simultaneously clicking into place. They were trapped. Ella looked on in horror as Luci's voice got louder.

'You will listen to me. Turn around,' she cried out. She twirled her finger, and he spun on the spot until his startled eyes met hers. 'I rescued this girl once from you, and I will do it again. You think I'd let you touch another woman after the way you treated me in those Tuscan woods? Your soul is still as black now as it has always been. I kept you close this week because I've been hunting you down for two millennia. I'm going to hurt you as much as you hurt us.'

Sebastian's face drained of colour. He reached out for the pews on either side of him as his legs shook beneath him. Ella guessed he'd already seen what Luci was capable of. Three years ago, Ella had watched Zac use his powers on Sebastian after he'd attacked her, but something told her this was going to be a lot worse. Clearly, Sebastian was thinking the same.

'Please, Luci, don't get angry. I'm sorry. Whatever I did in the past, even the stuff I don't remember, I'm truly sorry. I've changed. Please, don't hurt me. I'll do anything you want.'

'Anything I want?'

'Yes. Anything.'

Luci appeared to be thinking.

'There's only one thing I want from you, Sebastian,' she whispered. 'I want you to die.'

Her arm shot out, and he screamed as her outstretched finger lifted his feet from the ground. Ella was paralysed by both fear and curiosity.

Was Zac's mother defending her? But wasn't she the Devil? And where the fuck was Zac? Ella jumped as Luci clicked her fingers, sending Sebastian flying into the wall where he fell back down with a thud.

'What do you think, Arabella?' she said, turning to her with a smile. 'That wasn't nearly bad enough, was it? Shall I try a bit harder?'

She didn't wait for a reply, immediately lifting him up again with a wave of her finger. His head flopped forward, and he groaned as he struggled to speak. Luci raised her hand higher and higher, turning him around until he was floating in front of the altar. Luci blinked, and his arms shot out to either side of him—a sacrificial Jesus.

'You said…I…couldn't…die.' Sebastian gasped, blood bubbling at his mouth.

'No,' Luci said, 'I said no one could kill you…except for me. The only reason I've kept you alive is so that no one could take this pleasure away from me. And the only reason I wanted *you* to take me to Ella was so she could watch me do this.' She raised her arms to the heavens, sending him so high that his head touched the chapel's tall ceiling. His face was an ashen mask streaked with red, his lips moving in protest but no words forming.

'Goodbye, Sebastian. May you never return because if you do, I will hunt you down for all of eternity. You will never be safe from me.'

With that, she dropped her arms to her sides and sent him falling through the air. Down he plummeted, faster and faster, his arms flailing and a strangled gurgle emanating from his lips. He dropped with such speed and force that as he approached the golden altar, his head collided with the huge, pointed crucifix, its tip piercing the back of his neck and exiting through his gaping mouth. His arms collapsed on either side of him, draped along the horizontal bars of the giant cross. His bulging eyes and skewered mouth gaped in perpetual fear. Blood poured down the ornate altar, snaking its way from the pulpit down the marble stairs until it formed a puddle at Ella's feet.

She looked up in horror at her murdered stepbrother and screamed and screamed and screamed—three years' worth of pain and anguish and anger flying out of her mouth like a swarm of plague-ridden flies.

Luci, as if she'd spent every last drop of energy slaying their shared foe, collapsed with a thud onto the marble steps, her head in her hands.

'Get out!' she shouted, her words fighting to be heard over Ella's cries. 'You can't give me back my son, so just go!'

Luci slumped forward, her shoulders shuddering as if she were crying, but Ella wasn't going to comfort her. She didn't want to go anywhere near the crazy woman after seeing the extent of her powers. Ella ran to the side door but it was locked, as were the double doors that led to the front of the building. She had to get out! Then she remembered the secret entrance to the library. She ran past Luci, who didn't look up. Avoiding the glassy-eyed stare of her stepbrother, who was hanging above her, she pushed a panel on the golden altar and climbed inside.

She could escape via the library. There was another door up there that would lead her to the back stairs and then outside. She would call the police, and then she'd check that her parents and Josh were OK. Had they really been sitting in their rooms all that time?

She ducked inside the secret entrance beneath the altar and, with one last glance at the sobbing woman, let the tiny golden door shut behind her.

33

ZAC COULDN'T SIT on the grass staring at Ella's hotel all day. Neither did he want to move.

He'd been sure Ella would come running to him once she'd seen the jewellery. She hadn't. She didn't want him after all this time; he had to accept that. Three years was nothing to him, but it was a long time for a human to be expected to wait. He'd loved her for two thousand years, but in reality they had only been together a couple weeks. He had to let her go.

But what was he meant to do with himself now?

He'd had every intention of escaping somewhere on his bike and getting his head around a life without Ella, until that crazy driver had nearly run him over and he'd had to swerve. He'd stopped to check the bike and now didn't want to get back on it. With the monastery still in view, he couldn't bring himself to leave.

Suddenly a scream rang out, a scream that wouldn't stop. It was such a piercing wail that goose bumps rose on his skin and his stomach fought its way up his throat. That sound was the last thing he'd heard before he died.

Ella was in trouble.

Forgetting his motorbike, he ran as fast as he could toward Ella's voice. Her cries filled every inch of the monastery grounds. They bounced off the tall trees and the curved archways as well as the stained glass windows of the tower and the cobbled stones beneath his pounding feet. He headed for the chapel, hoping he wasn't too late.

Her screaming had stopped by the time he reached the chapel doors. He leant against them, his chest rising and falling as he battled to catch his breath, but they were locked. Placing his palm against them, he waited for the telltale sound of the mechanisms moving inside. Tentatively, he pushed the door open, blinking until his eyes adjusted to the gloomy interior. The chapel was empty. Weren't Ella and Josh meant to be getting married right now?

He walked toward the altar, his eyes adjusting to the gloomy light, and squinted up at the large, life-size effigy of Christ hanging above the pulpit. Strange. This one was clothed and…no…it couldn't be. A dead man was impaled on the crucifix, his blank, soulless eyes staring out over an invisible congregation.

Zac's heart quickened. Where was Ella? Was that why she'd screamed? He ran to the front of the church and then stopped. A woman was sitting on the marble steps, her face in her hands, wearing a dress as bright red as the puddle of blood surrounding her.

Upon hearing his footsteps she sat up, pushed her dark hair away from her face, and stared at the man before her.

It was his mother.

'Zadkiel?' She stood up very carefully, wobbling on her high heels. She was shaking, her face streaked with black rivulets of mascara. 'Is that you, son?'

The woman looked and sounded like his mother…but it couldn't be. Could it?

'Zadkiel!'

She ran at him and threw her arms around his neck. He wrapped his own arms around her and breathed in the scent of her hair. The smell of his childhood. In an instant, he was back in their cottage in the Tuscan hills, playing in the stream, picking wildflowers and threading them in her long, thick hair. He tightened his hold around her.

'Mamá?'

She ran her fingers over the contours of his face and through his hair, checking that he was real. She turned his head this way and that, taking in every inch of him. It was as if she feared breaking contact with him in case he disappeared again.

'If it wasn't for your eyes, I would never have recognised you,' she said, stroking his hair.

'Mamá. You were the last person I expected to see today. What are you doing here?'

She stepped to the side and nodded at the murdered man hanging above their heads. The figure's face was dripping with blood, his broken features cracked by the enormous spike skewered through his mouth, but Zac still recognised him.

'Is that Sebastian Fantz? Did *you* do that?'

Luci's face twisted into a snarl.

'Of course. I've waited two thousand years to punish the man who murdered my son.'

'What? How…how do you know about that?'

'I was there.'

Zac thought back to that fateful day in Tuscany as if it were only yesterday. Arabella had mentioned a woman searching for her son in the woods. The soldier had shown up at the cottage, asking after a partially clothed woman who had escaped him. Had that woman been his own mother?

Zac knew Sebastian had once been Sabinus. He'd watched him over many lifetimes and had never seen his soul get any less dark, but he had no idea the monster had harmed his mother, too. Zac shuddered. Luci was studying him as he fit together all the pieces of their shared past.

'The woman in the woods—that was you?'

'Yes, son. Sabinus attacked me, he killed you, and then he became the reason Arabella slit her own throat. If it hadn't been for him, I would have found you in Fiesole, and you would have known what you were. You would have finally been aware of your greatness. I was moments away from seeing you when he drove his sword through your chest. I knew you weren't dead. You couldn't be. But Mikhael and his Choir got to you before I could. If it hadn't been for Sabinus—Sebastian—then you and Arabella would have stood a chance. We all would've. He ruined everything.'

He wrapped his arms around his mother again and, not for the first time, wondered why he hadn't murdered Sebastian himself three years ago. His mother was fearless, but Zac wasn't. He masked his fears and called them compassion. Perhaps it was time to start doing what *felt* right and not what he *thought* was right.

'My boy, my darling boy,' Luci whispered, holding him tight. 'I thought I'd never see you again. Ella told me you were dead.'

Zac's stomach lurched at the mention of her name. He stepped away from her embrace, noticing for the first time his mother wearing the amethyst jewellery. The jewellery Ella was meant to have received from him.

'Is she here? Is she hurt? I heard her scream.'

'She's fine,' Luci replied, looking up at Sebastian. 'She's safe now.'

Zac rubbed his face and murmured his thanks. It was too much to take in. His mother, Sebastian, Ella thinking he was dead. Was that why she was getting married? Would she still want him if she knew he was alive?

'When did you return?' Luci asked.

'I was gone for three years. I awoke seven days ago.'

'You returned quicker than I did.'

'Well, it still took me a week to find Ella.' He laid his hand on his mother's arm. 'Tell me, did she get married? Is she with Josh?'

'Not yet,' Luci replied, placing her own hand on his. 'I sort of crashed the wedding before it got started. Ella ran off, but her friends and family were sent to their rooms.' She laughed at the absurdity of the sentence. 'I mean, I ordered them out of harm's way. I'll make sure they don't remember any of this.'

'And what about him?' he said, looking up at the corpse. Sebastian's mouth was now a huge, gaping hole as his weight pulled on the cross's spike. His face was frozen in a Munch-like, silent scream as he slipped further down the cross. His mother really knew how to make a statement.

'I'll dispose of him. I have practice,' she said.

Zac nodded and kissed her on both cheeks.

'I'm so happy you are here, Mamá, but I need to see Ella now. I hope you understand. Where is she?'

Luci's face fell but she nodded. 'She's in the library. Push that panel over there and you'll reach it via a narrow staircase. I'll wait for you.'

Zac hugged her and ran to the panel in the wall.

'Son?'

His body was halfway through the doorway.

'Yes?'

'Come back to me.'

He grinned and squeezed himself into the tiny stairwell that led up to the watchtower and his girl.

34

THE KEY WAS so old it had broken inside the lock and it wouldn't turn. Ella had been trying for fifteen minutes, but her fingers were sore and it wouldn't budge. There was no way she could go back down to the chapel. What if that crazy murderer was still there? She had to get out the back door that led to the main road and call for help—but from whom? How exactly would she explain to the police that her stepbrother was impaled on a giant crucifix because the Devil, her angelic ex-boyfriend's mother, had been seeking retribution for what he did to her two thousand years ago?

Today was meant to be her wedding day, for fuck's sake!

She kicked at the back door, crying out in frustration. It was useless. She either had to wait until Luci left or spend the rest of the day looking out of the window in the vain hope someone saw her.

A dull, thumping noise sounded outside the library. Ella swung round and caught the sash of her wedding dress on the key sticking out of the lock, ripping a hole in the lace. *Shit!* She wasn't even married yet and she'd already ruined her dress. She stopped and listened again. Softly at first, and then gradually louder, footsteps echoed closer. Someone was climbing the stairs to the library.

Was Luci coming back for her? Did she want to kill her, too?

The footsteps grew louder and louder and then stopped. Whoever it was, they were outside the library door. She had bolted it shut, but if it *was* Luci then nothing would keep her out.

Ella looked around for something with which to defend herself but all she could see was cushions, dusty books, and a wooden stool. She picked up the stool and held it above her head. It probably wouldn't do much good against the Devil, but it may buy her enough time to push past her and get out of the tower.

She watched the bolt slide slowly across, and the door creaked open. A dark head appeared in the doorway and, without waiting any longer, Ella threw the stool as hard as she could at their face. There was a loud crack. She wasn't sure if it was the stool breaking or the person's jaw. She went to run past, but a hand shot out and stopped her.

'Nice to see you, too, Ella.'

It wasn't Luci.

She looked down at the hand blocking her way, her gaze moving over a male wrist, past an arm tattooed with feathers, and into the same blue eyes that had haunted her dreams since the first day she'd seen them.

The man shut the door behind him. The stool had left a deep cut on his forehead, but his eyes still sparkled like sapphires through the blood oozing down his face.

Life slowed down until it stopped with a clunk. Dust motes danced in the air between them, and the only sound was that of their shallow breaths. Ella's path, which had only just recently been straightened, was now twisting back on itself. Her world was tilting, and she didn't think she could hold on any longer. She didn't want to. She let go.

'Zac?'

'I told you I'd come back,' he said with a crooked smile.

His hair was short, and the tops of his arms were inked with beautifully painted feathers, each one unique and fluttering out from beneath his T-shirt. She traced her finger over them as if they were Braille and she was trying to read him better. A drop of blood fell onto his arm, and she wiped it away with her thumb. She felt him shiver beneath her fingertips.

'I hurt you,' she said.

He shrugged. 'I'm used to it. Loving you over the centuries has been nothing but pain, Ella. Sweet, exquisite pain.'

'I meant your eye. With the stool.'

'That will heal too, don't worry.'

Neither of them moved. Ella was afraid to speak, afraid that if she dared to breathe he'd be extinguished like a flame.

'Are you OK?' he asked.

'I thought you were dead, Zac. Where the hell have you been?'

She didn't wait for an answer; she couldn't wait another second for him. She wrapped her arms around him, his bloody cheek staining hers, and kissed his neck, his face, his injured forehead, and eventually found his lips.

'Ella.'

'Kiss me, Zac. Why aren't you kissing me?'

He pulled back and tucked a curl behind her ear. His finger stroked her cheek, and she nearly cried from the feel of his touch.

'Today's your wedding day,' he said, taking her wedding veil in his hands and watching it fall like water between his fingers.

Couldn't he feel her emotions right now? Yes, there were feelings of guilt and confusion, but they weren't as strong as the relief and love that coursed through every part of her.

She bit at the skin around her thumb and looked down at her feet, noticing there was blood on the hem of her skirt. It could have belonged to either Zac or Sebastian. Her stepbrother was dead, impaled on a cross downstairs, and her true love was back from the grave. Saliva pooled in the inside of her cheeks, and she swallowed down her nausea. What was she meant to do? She loved Zac. She loved Josh. She'd let them both down—one because she hadn't waited and the other because she should have.

'I don't want to marry him. Not now,' she heard herself say.

'Ella, you're on your rightful path. I'm too late.'

'No, you're not.'

'I heard you tell your friends you're happy. That I'm no longer important to you. I know you love Josh. That's OK.'

Ella's head snapped up, and she flinched at the pain she saw in his eyes.

'Don't tell me who to love, Zac, and don't tell me what I'm allowed to feel! If you heard what I said, then surely you could also feel my *real* emotions. Have you not sensed how confused and torn I've been today?'

He shook his head. 'I can no longer feel you. I have no idea what's in your heart.'

'Let me show you then.'

She leant forward and kissed his lips. His face was covered in blood, and now so were her hands. This time he kissed her back, his arms encircling her waist, and their embrace deepened. The blood from his head wound dripped into their mouths, and she swallowed it down hungrily. She didn't care. She wanted all of him. She wanted to feel his touch again, their breaths becoming one, his body against hers.

'Hey, wait a minute. Let me wipe my face.' He laughed.

He lifted her up and sat her on the high window seat where she used to read. It was as wide as a sofa, covered in dusty, old cushions, and overlooked the gardens. He took off his black T-shirt and used it to wipe his face clean. He went to dab her mouth, but she licked the blood from her lips before he could wipe it away.

'You look like a vampire,' he said, smiling.

'And you look like a different person, all tough and mysterious. What's with the new hair?'

He rubbed the back of his neck. 'It was matted and ruined when I re-awoke. It'll grow back.'

'Were you the courier Paloma mentioned? You brought the necklace back?'

He nodded, and a warm glow slid down her chest and settled in her stomach. He'd come back for her; he'd kept his word. She pulled him forward by the waistband of his jeans, gathering her dress up over her knees so she could put a leg on either side of him.

'Well, thank you for bringing it back, but you should have hung about a bit longer. Look at your face.' She ran her hand over his cheek, and he leant into her touch. 'I really did whack you hard. I'm sorry.'

'You know the day I fell in love with you, I had blood all over my face then, too. At least this time it's not goat's blood.' He laughed. 'Don't look at me like that; it's a lovely story. Maybe one day I'll tell you all about it.'

He cupped her face in his hands and stared deep into her eyes. When he did that, her whole world fell away, leaving them suspended in nothingness.

'You have no idea how many times I've watched you be born and watched you die, Ella. I can't do it again. This is it. I'm not going anywhere ever again.'

She placed her hand on his bare torso, above his heart, the feel of his hard chest beneath her fingertips taking her back to their first night together at her parents' house in Highgate. His eyes clouded over at the feel of her skin on his.

'I thought you weren't coming back, Zac.'

'As if I would ever let you down.' He stroked her cheek with his thumb. 'I meant it when I said I would love you forever. I've been saying it to you since the very beginning. I knew removing my wings would free me. After I saw the portrait of my mother and read the inscription on her jewellery, I knew it had to work. I had faith I would rise again.'

'I met your mother. She took the jewellery back off me.'

'I saw. I also saw what she did to Sebastian. Are you OK?'

'I will be once it's all sunk in. She's...Zac, your mother is Lucifer.'

'I know.' He placed his hands around her waist and pulled her closer to him, her chest now inches from his. 'I found out yesterday. She's not to be feared, though, Ella. She'd never harm you. She's saved you more than once in the past. It took me a week to find you, and I never imagined for one moment that I'd find my mother, too.'

'You've been searching for me for a week?'

'Yes, like I said before, I can no longer feel you. I would have got here faster if I could...especially had I known you were falling for another man.'

She rested her forehead against his chest and groaned.

'I'm sorry. I thought you were dead. Being with Josh felt...right.'

'Of course it did. It was fated, which is why it happened so fast. Do you love him?'

Ella hesitated. She didn't want to lie, but she didn't want to lose Zac again, either.

'Maybe. In a different way. But you, Zac. *You!* You're all I've ever wanted. I don't care about fate or destiny any longer; I want *you.* I've missed you so much.'

Zac leant down and kissed her. She could still taste the metal of his blood in her mouth, although his face had already healed. He was here, in her arms, his bare chest pressing against hers. She ran her hands up his back, her fingers feeling the two bumps between his shoulders where his wings had once been.

'Do you miss them?' she asked.

'I had them replaced.' He turned around and showed her a tattoo of a magnificent set of wings on his back.

She laughed. 'I think I could get used to this new bad-boy Zac.'

She was only half joking. He looked meaner now, stronger. She wrapped her legs around the back of his knees and pulled him closer.

'I want you.'

'What about Josh?'

Ella's hands hovered over his belt buckle. What about Josh? She loved him but couldn't marry him, not now that Zac was back. Zac was her soulmate—the only one who'd filled her dreams the last three years.

'I don't want to hurt him; he's a good man. If only there was a way to go back in time so he didn't fall in love with me…'

'There is,' Zac answered, kissing her lightly on the lips. 'I can make him forget you. If you're sure.'

Would it be the kinder thing to do? Or the cruellest?

She nodded. 'I'm sure. You and I belong together, Zac, and he deserves a better woman than I'm about to be.'

'OK. I'll make sure he only remembers you as a friend. A good friend, one that could never give herself to him as fully as he deserved. But you need to understand that I'm taking away his destiny, Ella. I don't feel good about it, and I don't want anyone to get hurt, either.'

'I don't know how you'll do it, but thank you.'

Zac nodded and glanced down at her hands resting on the waistband of his jeans. He looked back up at her slowly, his clear blue eyes burning with an icy intensity that shot through her like a laser beam. The last tendrils of her guilt and apprehension dissipated like smoke.

'Come here,' she said. 'Show me what I've been missing before I discover you're just a figment of my imagination.'

'Here?' he whispered.

'Here.'

'Right now?'

'Right now. I'm not having you disappear on me again.'

She reached back and unzipped her dress, but he stopped her. She reached for the buckle of his jeans, but he stopped her again.

'Don't you want me?' she asked.

'Oh, I do,' he said, 'but I want to watch you first. I want to see you leave and come back to me over and over again, as I have done for you.'

His hand travelled up her thigh. She took a sharp intake of breath as Zac's fingers slid beneath her lacy underwear. She reached for him, but he shook his head, his eyes now an indigo blue. She leant back against the window seat and let him tease her slowly, his stare fixed on hers, taking her to the brink and back. Finally, when she couldn't take any more, he let her go and all the empty darkness that she'd been harbouring inside of her since he'd left exploded into a light so bright she was blinded. She blinked until his beautiful face came into focus again.

'See? You returned to me, too,' he said, smiling.

She sat up and pulled his face down to hers, her lips speaking the words she was unable to say. She reached down for his belt buckle, and this time he let her.

Today was meant to be the first time she made love with Josh. But it was Zac's fingers unclipping her bra and his mouth kissing along her collarbone, his tongue gliding over her bare breasts. She arched her back against the window as he pulled her dress down further until it lay crumpled in a heap at their feet.

His smile disappeared, his eyes near black.

'I love you, Ella. Nobody could ever love you as I have, and no one could ever take your place. This is it. This is forever.'

She wrapped her legs around his waist, her hands grasping at his short hair, his lips never leaving hers. She no longer had to close her eyes to think of him. He was right there with her at last, and this time nothing would tear them apart.

35

'MY DRESS IS ruined,' she said as he zipped her back up again. 'Good job I have no intention of wearing it again.'

She sounded flippant, but he knew she was far from comfortable about breaking the news to her friends and family…let alone Josh. Zac shut out all voices of doubt in his mind. He'd promised himself he would follow his heart, not his head, and this was the right thing to do. It *was.*

'Want me to come with you when you tell him?' he asked, pulling his black T-shirt over his head. The blood had dried and was no longer visible.

'I don't know. Oh God, Zac, I'm going to break his heart.'

'Don't worry,' he said. 'I told you I can make him forget. Your parents, friends, none of them have to remember the last few days.'

Ella thought about it and shook her head.

'No. That's gutless and cruel. It would certainly be easier, but Josh deserves to know the truth—no matter how much it will make him hate me. We need to go downstairs right away. They're all probably still sitting in their room after your mother… Wait, what about Luci?'

Zac sighed. 'She'll be fine once you get to know her.'

'Does this mean I now have the original mother-in-law from hell?'

He laughed and kissed her. 'Don't worry, we're going to have a wonderful future together. I promise.'

'Don't make promises you can't keep, my friend,' a voice said from the doorway. 'Not interrupting, am I?'

'Gabriel!' Zac crossed the room and put his arm around his friend's neck, a big grin on his face. 'I found Ella, no thanks to you. I thought you were going to tell her I was coming?'

Would Ella recognise the archangel? Gabriel had been working behind the bar at Indigo the night they'd both been there, the night she was meant to have got together with Josh. He'd also been one of the angels who'd accompanied Mikhael when they'd come for Zac. Ella and Gabriel had stood side by side and watched the one they both loved die. By the look of horror on her face, she recognised him.

'I *was* going to tell her,' the archangel said. 'I came last night, but she was already with her fiancé. Now, where is that nice young man of yours, Ella? Because you looked ever so happy together the last time I saw you.'

Zac's jaw tensed, and Ella bit down on her lip.

'You should have told her I was coming, Gabriel.'

'Oh, come on! What could I do? You know I keep people on their path, Zadkiel, not lead them astray. I can still feel her, even if you no longer can.'

'So tell me what she's feeling now. Does she love him more than she loves me?'

Gabriel raised one eyebrow and smirked at the blush rising on Ella's cheeks.

'Oh, I think we can *both* see what she thinks of you right now. You don't need angelic magic to know that.'

Zac beckoned her over and kissed the top of her head. 'It all worked out in the end, right? Path or no path.'

'Please tell me you two didn't just…?'

'No!' Zac lied. 'I only just got here. You think I'd do that *here*, in an old library, while she wore her wedding dress and her fiancé waited downstairs?'

Gabriel raised his eyebrows again and looked at Ella, who turned her head away.

'Whatever. I need you to listen to me. You know I'm the archangel messenger, right? Well, I've come bearing crap news. Sit down.'

The door behind him opened, and Luci stepped in.

'Did someone say bad news? That's normally my cue.'

'Come in, why don't you!' Ella muttered. 'Join the fucking party.'

Luci ignored her. 'My two favourite boys in the same room!' She squeezed Zac's hand and then stroked Gabriel's cheek. 'My, my, you haven't changed a bit. Still as gorgeous as ever. I always said I chose the wrong archangel. So, have I missed anything interesting up in the clouds lately?'

Gabriel gave a loud and hollow laugh that reverberated off the stone walls of the library. 'Lucifer, you little minx. Look at you!' He gave her a big hug. 'You're still one goddamn sexy lady. Is that blood on you?'

'Yes. I impaled a man on a giant crucifix about an hour ago. He's gone now. What's this bad news you're bringing us?'

Us? Zac looked at Ella and tightened his hold on her. She, in turn, stepped closer into his embrace. He'd only been with her an hour and already they were surrounded by angels, the Devil, and impending bad news. He'd promised her all the drama would be over, and yet here it was.

'Mikhael knows Ella is getting married to her life path partner today,' Gabriel said. 'He's on his way to make sure it goes ahead as intended.'

'What?' Zac said. 'How does he know?'

'He's had a spy here, an angel who's been working with Ella. She rushed back to us a couple hours ago and told him.'

'That's not possible,' Ella cried, her eyes round and pleading with Zac. 'I think I'd know if I had an angel in my hotel. I haven't had anyone new working here lately…except…Paloma? Wait. She's an angel?'

'Was she really pretty and mysterious and unable to use a computer?' Gabriel asked.

'Yes?'

'Well there you go,' he said with exasperation. 'Big clue: if a person can't work electricity, they're not human. Anyway, Mikhael is on his way, so Ella has to marry Josh and you two fallen ones need to get the hell *out* of here.'

'No way!' Zac said, standing in front of Ella. 'No. I'm not going anywhere without her.'

Luci put her hand on Gabriel's arm and mouthed a 'thank you' to him.

'He's right, Zadkiel,' she said, still looking at the archangel. 'Mikhael can't sense us. He doesn't even know we returned, but he *can* find Ella whenever he wants. Let her marry Josh and walk away alive. Being with her is putting us all in danger.'

'Excuse me!' Ella cried. 'I am *here*, you know? And I don't *want* to marry Josh anymore. I want Zac. I love him. Mikhael can go fuck himself!'

Luci raised her eyebrows at Gabriel, and he laughed. 'Yep, I've met this feisty one before,' he said. 'She actually said that to Mikhael's face. The girl was seconds away from having his sword shoved right into her pretty skull, and she was mouthing off like that. I like her, Zadkiel, but you're not keeping her. Let's go.'

'Zac! Don't listen to them,' Ella said. 'We can deal with Mikhael. We've done it before.'

'No, we haven't,' he said. 'I killed myself to stop him from killing you. What am I meant to do now? Kill myself again? Gabriel and my mother are right—he's too powerful with that sword of his. We can't fight him, and I'm not going to let him murder you. Death at his hands means not coming back in another life. Not ever.'

'Well there must be something we can do!' she said, her voice shaking with anger.

He put his arm around her and placed a hand on his friend's shoulder. Ella was right; there had to be a way out of this mess.

'Gabriel. Please!'

'There's nothing you can do. We need to get out of here before dusk; that's when Mikhael and the Choir will arrive. Plus, someone needs to sort out those wall-staring zombies sitting in their bedrooms downstairs.'

'Oops, sorry about that,' Luci said, shrugging at Ella. 'I'll deal with it.'

'And kid, you need to do your magic voodoo on this girl as well. She needs to forget your sorry arse. I'm sick of this star-crossed-lovers nonsense. You're going to get your mother caught, and me too, and I'm not losing my sexy wings for any of this crap!'

'But Gabriel, this isn't just any woman—this is *Ella.* She's everything to me. Without her, I have nothing.'

'You have me now, son,' Luci said. 'You have me. You won't be alone. Do the right thing; let her live her life as she was always meant to. If you don't, then all of us will die. Including her.'

Ella looked like she was going to say something, but Luci started talking to her softly, their faces inches apart. Ella's eyes were locked on those of the fallen angel, and she began to nod in agreement at everything his mother was telling her.

Zac tried to pull her away, but Gabriel stood in his way.

'What are you doing, Mamá?' Zac shouted, trying to get past Gabriel. 'Leave her alone!'

'I will let you say your goodbyes, son,' she said. 'In the meantime, I'll go back to the hotel and release the others. I need to make sure I've wiped their minds from before the ceremony. I've told Ella that, in ten minutes, she'll forget we were here. She'll still think you're dead, she won't remember me killing Sebastian, and she'll have forgotten everything that happened after she got ready this morning—even the part where Paloma gave her the jewellery back. I'm keeping it. I doubt the angel spy will return to the hotel anyway.'

'Mamá! No! I can't have her think I never came back. What are you doing?'

'I'm saving all our lives, Zadkiel. Now say goodbye. You won't see her until she's born again in the next life.'

'But if she goes back to her path, she'll die. She only has eleven years left. If I'd taken her off her path, we could have avoided that. I could have helped her live longer. You've just killed her.'

'She'll die a lot quicker, and for eternity, if you stay with her.' Luci walked over to Ella, who was already in a stupefied state, and wiped a speck of blood off the side of her mouth. She frowned and then smiled a little. 'She'll be OK, son. You're doing the right thing.'

His mother left the room and Gabriel followed.

Zac stared at the closed door. How could this be happening? It had all been going so perfectly. How could he let Ella go after fighting so hard for her? Gabriel and his mother made everything sound so simple, but it wasn't. Ella was going to die now. Her and Josh would be dead within eleven years if he left now and by tomorrow if he stayed. He turned back to her, pushing down the ache in his throat.

'Ella, look at me.' He stroked her hair and blinked slowly. She mustn't see him cry. He stared into her eyes, her deep brown eyes that swallowed him whole. He was never going to gaze into that beautiful face again. He rubbed his own, wiping away his tears with the back of his hand. He knew she would return as someone else in the future, but for the first time ever, he wasn't prepared to accept it. He didn't want the next version of her; he wanted this one, the one who'd fallen in love with him.

Since their first life together, he'd never had his love reciprocated...until now. In this lifetime they'd made love, slept in the same bed, and enjoyed normal couple things—things like watching movies and talking about trivialities. He'd been back with her for just over an hour, after three years apart, and already he was being dragged away. Exactly as she'd feared.

A sob escaped his throat. Gabriel and his mother were right—it didn't matter how he felt about her, not if it was going to get them all killed.

Ella was in a deep trance now. Luci's magic had begun to take hold.

'You need to love me less, Ella,' he said, his hands trembling as they held her face.

'How?'

'By letting fate take the lead and returning to Josh. Will you do that for me?'

'Yes. I will do anything for you.' She was struggling to focus on him now; he could see the confusion on her face. 'Your eyes, Zac. They're fading. They're grey now. Why can't I see the blue anymore?'

'It's going to be fine,' he whispered. 'You're going to be so happy without me.'

'Zac! Where are you going? I can't see you properly.'

'I love you, Ella. *In aeternum te amabo.*'

He gave her one last kiss and stepped out of the library. Luci and Gabriel were waiting at the top of the stairs. He'd thought this time would be different, that in this lifetime he wouldn't be walking away. But history was good at repeating itself.

He hesitated in the doorway, but his mother shut the door behind him.

'Don't look back, son,' Luci said. 'Looking back hurts too much. The past is nothing but pain.'

'Terror made me cruel.'
~ Emily Bronte, *Wuthering Heights*

PART FOUR

LUCI THE HOUSE OF FIRE & WATER

ROERMOND, THE SPANISH NETHERLANDS 1613

I.

IT WAS NOT yet morning, and the sky was a smudge of lilac on a canvas of charcoal. Only one solitary starling greeted the day in song. Hailstones danced on the surface of the canal as Luci crossed the wooden bridge, lifting her hood against the sharp, relentless wind. The streets were empty save for a young girl running on the opposite bank, a thick blanket wrapped around her shoulders and her blonde hair flying in the wind. In the distance, Luci could just make out the huddled form of a man sitting in a doorway. She paid no attention to either as she gathered her hood tighter and silenced the howling weather.

Her whisperers had told her the house she was searching for had a curved roof and many windows. But in the end, it wasn't the architectural features that made it stand out from the others, it was the marks carved onto its door: perfect concentric circles created a pattern of flowers scratched onto its surface. They'd been painted over, but in the faint light of dawn, Luci still recognised the witches' marks protecting the town from the supposed evil that lay within. She was in the right place—she'd reached the House of Fire and Water.

Luci banged on the door and waited. It was early, and she didn't expect anyone to be awake yet. Drapes hung at the window, but all was quiet inside. Through a gap in the curtains, she could see a large hearth at the back of the room with a healthy fire burning. Inside, the entrance was laid out like a shop with a long counter, jugs and buckets sitting on the shelves. Every town had a shop like this, a place where one could purchase a flame or burning coals should they be careless enough to let their fires burn out. There was also a natural well in the back where fresh water could be found, for those not willing to use the water from the filthy canals. Fire and water—the two elements that sustained humanity. Except what really resided within that pretty house was much more sacred than earthly elements, and it was possibly more dangerous.

She knocked again, and a shadow passed by one of the windows upstairs. Perhaps a maid had been alerted and was scurrying to greet her.

The door creaked open and an aged face met hers, eyes narrow and brow furrowed.

Luci lowered her hood and smiled.

'I'm looking for Marisse.'

The woman peered at her through the crack in the door, refusing to open it any further.

'What do you want?'

'I'd like to come in. This weather is frightful.'

'The shop is not open yet. Try again in an hour.'

She went to shut the door, but Luci stopped it with her foot.

'I've been told that you are one of the strongest there are. You can't feel me, can you? That's why you won't let me in.'

The shopkeeper pushed Luci back and slammed the door shut, making the fallen angel laugh out loud. A key turned in the lock, as if that would keep her out. Luci had travelled from Germany to the Spanish Netherlands to meet this woman; she wasn't going to let a mere door stand in her way.

She laid a hand upon the lock, turning the key on the other side. *Let's see how the old lady reacts to* that *sight.* She pushed open the door, stepped into the room, and closed it behind her with a wave of her hand.

'I take it *you're* Marisse and that you weren't expecting me,' she said to the woman, who was now standing beside the hearth.

She was older than Luci had imagined. Her hair was coarse and greying, and no matter how much she attempted to tuck it beneath her bonnet, it kept springing out in wiry locks. Her dress was billowing and a drab brown, her eye colour completely nondescript. Not what Luci had expected at all. Her only redeeming feature was the rings covering her fingers. They were made of gold and inlaid with semiprecious stones interwoven with intricate designs of leaves and feathers. The jewellery sparkled in the weak winter light, which hardly illuminated the dim shop. Was this really the Marisse Luci had heard so much about?

The woman glared at her, still and silent.

'Confirm your name,' Luci said, making sure to look the shopkeeper in the eye.

'No.'

'Interesting. You won't do as I command.'

'I've never followed orders. Why would I start for you?' She squared her shoulders and stepped closer. 'Who are you, and how did you get in?'

'You know what I am,' Luci answered, 'or you wouldn't be so eager for me to leave.'

The old woman scowled in response and flicked her fingers, sending Luci flying backwards. She landed with a thud on the tiled floor in the corner of the shop.

'Tell me who you are and why I can't feel you,' the woman snarled through gritted teeth. 'And then we'll talk.'

Luci laughed even louder this time and shook the dust off her skirt as she stood.

'Oh, I like you, Marisse. So fierce. So fearless. It appears you are exactly what I hoped you would be: half of what I am—or at least half of what I used to be.'

'Used to be? I don't understand.'

'I'll explain everything in good time, but first we need to talk about your father.'

The old woman checked that the door was locked, pulled the curtains tighter together, and beckoned Luci to a barely visible small door behind the shop counter.

'Get in there.'

'You want to hide me in a cupboard?'

Marisse sighed. 'Get in. You've seen the markings on my door and what the villagers think of me. We can't talk out here.'

Narrow stone stairs led down into a dark, underground chamber. Candles were attached to the wall every few steps, which Marisse lit with a click of her fingers. Luci was impressed; this woman's gifts were beyond those she'd seen in others.

'Watch your head. It's a low ceiling,' the old woman said.

'What is this place?'

'A cellar. The house used to be a brewery. Through here.'

Marisse opened a second door, and they entered a room that looked like a library—but instead of books, there were jars upon jars of ointments and herbs labelled with clear, neat writing. Luci peered closer at the tiny, white labels.

'Where did you learn to write like this?' she asked.

'My father showed me.'

'You know what he was then? You met him?'

'Yes.' Marisse lit some more candles and an oil lamp that sat on the table. 'My father practically raised me after my mother died while pregnant. He was unable to save her, but he did save me. I lived with my grandmother in Germany, and he would visit some days, always in the early morning.'

'How did your mother die?'

'An accident with a horse. My father believed she was murdered and that I was the target.'

'And do you still see your father?'

It was a strange question to ask an old woman, but Luci knew what Marisse's father was.

'No, they killed him too. Azantiel was his name.'

Luci took a sharp intake of breath. She'd known the lesser angel—not within her own circle, he was one of the more vocal ones from the lower ranks. He'd been an obedient member of the Choir and one of Mikhael's favourites.

There was only one way to kill an angel, and Mikhael was the only one that could do it. Why was Azantiel dead?

'Azantiel was one of the good ones,' Luci said. 'Did Mikhael kill him?'

'Yes. You knew them both?'

'A long time ago, but I'm no longer aware of what their kind do.'

'Their kind? Are you not one of them?'

Luci shook her head.

Her whisperers had done well in leading her to Marisse. All over the globe, she had people lurking, listening, and reporting back to her. Her secret messengers were recruited for their ruthless talents. They lived between the shadows and only existed for her, no lives of their own and no idea of what they were doing or for whom. She didn't see it as a violation of their freedom; she'd rescued these men and women over the years prior to their being sentenced to death. As far as the real world knew, they were already dead—but Luci kept them around so that they could help her find Zadkiel.

That was all she cared about, that and killing his father.

Her whisperers had told her that a woman with strange powers had been shunned from her village in Germany. She'd escaped an arrest in Fulda in 1606 and then run away to Roermond in the south of the Netherlands.

'If you are not an angel, then what are you?' Marisse asked again. 'Why can't I feel you?'

'I'm Luci,' she replied, picking up one of the bottles on the shelf and smelling the contents before replacing the cork lid.

Looking around the room it was clear this woman had power and knowledge. A half-human, half-angel whose father had been murdered by the same being that tried to murder Luci. Was Mikhael after Marisse, too? How much did the old lady know? Would she be able to lead her to Zadkiel?

'My father never spoke of a woman called Luci.'

'I'm not a woman.'

She looked the old lady in the eye, but Marisse didn't once waver. Over the centuries, Luci had grown accustomed to reading people. Having lost her powers to feel emotion, she had learned the hard way whom to trust and whom to avoid, who was strong and who would betray her. Marisse was far from weak.

'I'm a fallen archangel,' Luci continued. 'Did your father never talk of someone named Lucifer? The mother of all creation who shaped your world, raised your people, and ruled alongside Mikhael until he murdered her for loving their son too much?'

Marisse clamped her hands over her mouth and then threw herself to the ground in a kneeling position. She rested her forehead on the cold stone floor and stretched her arms out on either side of her.

Luci laughed. 'Get up, get up. It's been a long time since anyone fell to their knees for me. Did Azantiel teach you that, too?'

'Yes, Your Highness. He said you were a queen among angels. A martyr for the cause. He was certain you'd return one day, that you were too powerful to be gone forever. How did you survive Archangel Mikhael's blade?'

Luci had met a few Nephilim in her time on Earth but never one like Marisse. Never one who knew so much about the realm.

'I rose again. Angels can't do that, but it appears archangels can. Nobody knows I'm alive.'

'Are you here to hurt me?' Marisse asked, standing with more strength and ease than the average woman her age.

'No, I'm here to get answers.'

Marisse nodded slowly. She leant against the wall, her head cocked to one side.

'How did you find me?'

Luci walked over to the old woman and held her face by her chin, turning it this way and that. The only light in the cellar came from a few candles, the oil lamp, and two high windows. People's feet could be seen walking along the cobbles above them. Outside, the day had finally started.

'I found you by chance,' Luci said. 'I have people that listen for me, that tell me things and send me messages. I've been hearing of your powers for some time. I was hoping to find a half-angel, and I did. You hide it well, Marisse. What is the matter with your eyes?'

The old woman pulled her face away from Luci's grasp and walked over to a table in the corner of the room where a jug and bowl stood. She poured some water into the palm of her hand, rubbed her face with it, and looked up. Her eyes shone in the gloom of the room like two glowing embers. They were the colour of flames, bright yellow cat's eyes.

Luci smiled. 'Aha, there it is. My goodness, you're good. What is that trick you do?'

'My father taught me everything I know, including what herbs to mix so I could bathe my eyes and change their colour.'

'What else did he tell you about being a Nephilim?'

'He explained my healing abilities, how I would be able to make things move, and how people would fear and hate me. That is why I remained unmarried and childless, and why I don't stay in one place for too long. I can't let people get close to me because I put them in danger. Mikhael killed my father and wants my kind dead. I hate him.'

'You're in good company. He tried to murder me too, and then he took away the son we had together.'

'Zadkiel?'

Luci grabbed her by the shoulders. 'You know my boy? Take me to him! Where is he? Does he know I'm alive?'

Marisse disentangled herself from the fallen angel's hold and shook her head.

'No, I have never seen an angel. The Choir think I died with my mother sixty-three years ago.'

'So how do you know about Zadkiel?'

'My father figured it out. He realised you'd given birth on Earth and that the child must have been special for Mikhael to have murdered you. When Zadkiel was brought Home, after he was supposedly killed in Italy, my father could tell straightaway that he belonged to Mikhael. It was the eyes, their extreme blueness. He was surprised that nobody else had guessed the truth.'

'Did he confront Mikhael about it?'

'Of course not. He was smarter than that. Instead, he got closer to the archangel. He became his closest friend and learned everything he needed to know. Over time, he discovered the warrior king's secrets, including how to destroy the sword. He then made sure he had a child on Earth; in fact, he had many so he could pass on the truth should anything happen to him. He told me everything.'

Luci folded her arms so the old lady couldn't see how much her hands were trembling. She'd known Mikhael for an eternity but had no knowledge of how he could be defeated. For years, she'd reasoned that even if she were able to get the sword off him and hack off his wings, he would still return just as she had. As long as that sword was in existence, Mikhael would rule their version of both heaven and Earth. Yet this woman knew something she didn't.

'You know how to take away his sword?'

'Yes.'

'And it will stop Mikhael's powers?'

'Yes.'

'Will you tell me how?'

'That depends.'

II.

Luci ran her finger along the jars on the shelves as Marisse fidgeted awkwardly beside her.

'Witch hunters?' she asked the old woman.

'Yes, I'm hoping you can help me. I escaped from them in Germany seven years ago, but I fear they've found me here.'

'What would they want with you?'

Marisse walked to the back of the cellar and returned with a book. She laid it on the table next to Luci and leafed through the thick pages, the writing inside faded in places.

'They want this. It's the book in which I wrote my father's teachings. They want to burn me and the Book of Light. Mikhael will stop at nothing to hunt down my kind, even if it means working alongside the church to rid the Nephilim of our gifts. My father was right when he said powerful men would see my abilities as an act against their make-believe God. Over the centuries, Mikhael has taught men to hate women who say no to them—because of you.'

Luci sighed and nodded. By defying Mikhael, she'd inadvertently killed many a powerful woman who had followed her.

'Do you think the witch hunters are yet another ploy by Mikhael to rid the world of Nephilim?'

'Absolutely, along with any other woman who makes a man's life difficult. Not long after my father was murdered, the hunters began to sweep through Europe, burning and drowning women and even the odd man and child—anyone who possessed a connection with the natural energy of the universe.'

Luci looked over the old woman's shoulder at the pages filled with notes and drawings, all annotated in the script of angels.

'You wrote all of this?'

'Yes. It's an angelic history—but one not written by the victors. It contains everything my father learned about his own kind and Mikhael. He told me that, after the warrior lord killed you and brought Zadkiel Home, he changed; he became angry and stopped the conception of Nephilim—creating the God fallacy as his cover. To begin with, my father couldn't understand the connection between your death and Mikhael not wanting women and angels to mix, but he worked it out. The Nephilim hold the key to Mikhael's destruction, so he stays safe by making sure none of us exist.'

Nephilim were the key? Luci turned the pages of the book and squinted at the writing. It had been a long time since she'd read angelic script. It made sense; everything this woman said made sense. She had no doubt Mikhael would have happily killed his own son had he been a Nephilim and not pure angel blood. Poor Zadkiel had no idea how powerful he really was. She had to find him.

'What do you have to do to be accused of witchcraft around these parts then?' Luci asked.

Marisse shrugged. 'Not a lot. From what I gather, a confident woman with a mind of her own is enough to make the hunters suspicious. We, the ones who don't worship a fake deity but listen to the earth and her energy instead, are the ones they fear. Many of us have angel blood running though our veins—the healers, the creators, the deep thinkers—but not all of us. I've helped women bring babies into this world peacefully and safely. I've laid my hands upon the scared and calmed them. I work with nature and her four elements—fire, water, air, and earth—and I feel what others feel. I do good. So, naturally, they blame me for the bad as well.'

'The bad?'

'Unexplained deaths, paralysed farm animals, people losing their jobs. I was accused of all sorts back in Germany, but I managed to escape. Surely you saw the marks upon my door? The hunters are now in the Netherlands, and if they find me here, they will burn me at the stake. They say us witches worship the Devil.'

This wasn't news. For sixteen hundred years, Luci had seen those who were different be persecuted for their free thinking. Jesus himself had done nothing but preach love and help the less fortunate, and he'd been killed for it. Neither was she surprised Mikhael was behind it all. Luci couldn't risk being caught up in this hysteria and revealing herself to the angels, yet she had to find out how to rid the realm of Mikhael and get her boy back. This woman was the only person she'd met in centuries who appeared to have the answers to all her questions.

'Devil worshipping?' Luci asked, laughing. 'That's ridiculous. I *am* the Devil, and I'm really not all that bad, I promise.' Noticing how Marisse's bright yellow eyes had begun to soften, Luci placed a hand on the woman's shoulder. Perhaps they could be friends after all. 'Tell me, Marisse, how can I help you?'

'Your powers. You said earlier that I didn't follow your commands; does that mean others do? Is that how you've survived this long?'

Luci nodded. 'I have power over the minds of humans, if that's what you mean. Plus, I've been known to kill a few men who have stood in my way. If you help me get my revenge on that bastard Mikhael, I promise to keep the hunters away from you. I'll destroy those who wish you harm.'

Marisse closed her eyes in thanks and smiled. 'Thank you, and please thank your whisperers for leading you to me.' She pointed at the book. 'Let me begin by showing you my notes. There's something in here about…' She looked up at the window above Luci's head where a pair of shoes was just visible through the narrow glass. 'I have to go. Someone has come to see me.'

Luci grabbed her arm as she headed to the door.

'I need to see the book, Marisse. Forget about customers.'

'I can't. This girl is in pain, a lot of pain. She came to me a few days ago. Can you not feel her turmoil?'

Luci shook her head. 'I lost that ability along with my wings. Can she not wait? I need you to show me the book.'

'Her name is Elien, and last week she lost a baby. She's practically a child herself. If I don't help her now, she may well die within the month. Her body is not healing well. You still think she should wait?'

Luci shook her head. She had no issue with human adults dying, as far as she was concerned most were dispensable—but not children and definitely not babies. Someone was knocking frantically at the door. Marisse ran up the stairs, the fallen angel following closely behind.

The urgent knocking had stopped by the time they had reached the top of the basement steps. Marisse yanked open the front door, but there was nobody there. She ran into the street.

'Stop!' she called out after the figure of a girl in the distance. 'Elien, stop! I can help you.'

Luci watched the interaction from inside the store, curious as to why anyone would go out of their way to help a stranger. Was the old woman in need of money that badly? Or was it more than that? Even back when Luci'd had the ability to feel the pain and emotions of others, she never remembered caring about them. The only people she'd ever helped were those who could better her own life.

Marisse finally returned to the house with the girl, locked the door behind them, and checked that the curtains were still closed. She paid no attention to Luci, who was now leaning against the wall and tapping her foot against the flagstone floor.

The girl was pale and nervous, but she was also pretty in a delicate way. Something about her was familiar—although over the last sixteen centuries Luci had seen so many people they were all beginning to look the same.

'Did anyone follow you here?' Marisse asked Elien, who she'd seated beside the fireplace. The girl was shaking, her eyes darting over the bare store. She looked at Luci and then quickly looked away again. The fallen angel sighed; she couldn't believe she was putting off getting information for this pathetic child.

'Nobody followed me,' she stuttered. 'Although I've noticed a man watching me lately, I don't think he means me ill. Will I get in trouble for coming here? It's just the other day, when I told you about my problems, you mentioned herbs. I have been scared to come back because people say that this house...what you do...is evil. But the bleeding won't stop. The pain is unbearable.'

Marisse rushed out to the cobbled patio at the back of the house and drew water from the well. She placed a clay cup of water on the counter and opened the small door in the wall.

'One moment, I won't be long,' she said before descending the stairs to the basement.

Luci eyed the girl. She had silky gold hair gathered up in a bonnet and a smattering of freckles on her pale face. Marisse was right; she was too young to be a mother. She was also utterly petrified.

'What's your name?' she asked.

The girl jumped.

'Elien. Are you a healer too?'

Luci shrugged. 'Of sorts. Why are you so scared?'

Before the girl had time to answer, Marisse came bustling back with two small jars in her hand. She sprinkled a pinch of herbs from each one into the water and handed the cup to Elien.

'Stay calm and drink this,' she said. 'I'm going to place my hand over your stomach, but you must keep still. It won't hurt. In fact, you will feel the pain wash away.'

'You haven't told me your fee,' Elien said. 'I may not have enough money to pay you.'

'Hush, child.'

'Marisse, listen to the child and take her money,' Luci called out. 'Why would you give away your powers for free?'

Marisse whipped her head around and scowled at the fallen angel. She then smiled at the girl and stroked her hair.

'Don't fret, my child. When I was not much older than you, I too lost a baby, and I vowed I would never let another woman suffer the same as I did.'

Luci had her answer—lost children. That was why the old woman hadn't turned the girl away. Her and the Nephilim had more in common than they realised.

Marisse laid her hands on Elien's lower stomach, barely touching the fabric of her skirt, and Luci watched as the tension in the young girl's face began to fade.

The old woman really was doing a great thing. For sixteen centuries, Luci had been searching for Zadkiel—but could she truly say she had ever been this selfless and giving? Not since Arabella in Tuscany had she sacrificed herself for the life of another, but then the girl *had* eventually led her to her son. Everything she did was to get to her son.

'Hold out your hand,' Marisse instructed Elien after ten minutes of healing. The girl looked dazed but calmer than when she'd first entered the building. She did as she was told.

Marisse laid a small piece of fabric onto Elien's open palm and shook out some light green herbs from the jar. 'Mix this with water before you sleep tonight and drink it,' the old woman said. She folded up the material into a square and closed Elien's hand over it. 'The bleeding will stop within an hour, along with the pain. Once you drink this potion, you will be able to carry a child again. You won't lose any more, I promise.'

Elien's eyes swam with tears and colour returned to her face once more.

'Is this witchcraft?' she whispered.

'Why do so many question an act of kindness?' Marisse said to the girl, her voice tinged with sorrow. 'Why do so many presume there is always darkness behind love and light? I have a gift, Elien, and today I decided to share it with you. Go home and rest and remember that all I sell is fire and water. The other two elements, the powers that come from the earth and the air, they are our secret. Do you understand?'

Elien nodded and tentatively went to stand before straightening up and smiling a large, beaming smile that lit up her young face.

'It no longer hurts! Thank you,' she said, hugging the old woman. 'You have no idea how you saved me today.'

'Yes, I do,' Marisse replied.

III.

'It's very kind of you to feed me,' Luci said, smiling at the old woman.

They were in a room above the shop, seated at a small table beside the window. Marisse poured out two glasses of beer and passed her a basket of bread.

'I wasn't sure if you were the same as us, if you needed to eat.'

'Well, I don't die if I don't eat, if that's what you mean,' she replied, biting into a carrot. 'I don't get thinner, I don't get fatter, and I don't get weaker. Sleep, food, and sex have no effect on my body except to pass the time. So, feel free to feed me.'

Marisse laughed and gave her another slice of smoked ham. A tabby cat that had been asleep on a chair in the corner of the room looked up, sniffed the air, and trotted over to Luci, who fed him some meat.

'It was very altruistic of you, doing what you did with that girl earlier.'

'Elien? She is very troubled, not just physically but also emotionally. I heard her arguing with a woman in the street earlier not long after she left us—the woman was accusing her of lying about losing her baby. I fear things will not end well for her.'

'Do you think she will report you to the witch hunters?'

'It's always a risk, but I don't think so. Before she left, I said she was free to return any time, night or day. I think she needs a friend more than anything.'

'Just be careful. There is such a thing as being *too* kind, you know.' The cat at Luci's feet began to wind around her ankles, and she dropped another piece of meat to the ground. 'I see you keep cats. You know what people say about old ladies and cats.'

'That we're lonely and take in stray animals for company?'

Luci smiled and stroked the animal. 'Don't worry about the gossips of this town. The hunters can't harm you while I'm around. I'll make sure of that.'

'Thank you.'

Marisse took a bite of her dinner, chewing slowly and looking at her new friend. She opened her mouth to speak and then closed it again. She took another mouthful, chewed, swallowed, and cleared her throat. 'Uhm…I hope you don't find me forward, but…I just wanted to ask. The magic you perform, the mind control, does it only work on people? I've been curious.'

'People? As opposed to…?'

'I mean, can you affect the minds of animals?'

Luci put down her fork, her eyes glinting in amusement.

'Yes, I can. Animals have been very useful at times. Some are harder than others to control, though. Dogs and horses can be told what to do as simply as obedient children can; they want to help. Other animals not so much.'

'Such as?'

'Well, rats never come when you call them, fish can't remember any commands, and cats don't like to be told what to do.'

Marisse laughed and looked down at her own pet, who was still staring up at their plate of ham.

'I'll show you,' Luci said. 'I will make the cat dance.'

Luci stared into the animal's eyes, but the cat did nothing but twitch its tail. It then walked in a circle, sat down, stood back up, shook its head, and glowered at the fallen angel.

'See, she won't be humiliated! That is why they are such great familiars. They are not easily swayed, although they do make wonderful accomplices.'

'Accomplices?'

'Oh yes, they don't take orders, but they are easily convinced to piss people off. I'll show you.'

At that moment, the cat jumped onto the table, took a mouthful of ham, and scampered out of the room. Marisse roared with laughter.

'You didn't even look in its eyes this time.'

'I don't need to with animals. Most are quite happy to annoy a human.'

Marisse reached over the table and rested her hand on Luci's. 'You do know how to have fun. Please say you will stay the night, if you don't have other plans.'

'Of course. You're the only reason I came to Roermond. I usually convince a rich man to let me stay with him when I need a bed for the night; it's less hassle than an inn. I accept the money they like to give me, too—although it has become so easy to control men lately that it has ceased to be entertaining.'

Marisse laughed again.

'Thank you. I feel safer with you around.'

'Well, I'm not doing it for free, my friend. You haven't yet told me what I need to know about your teachings, about ridding the realm of Mikhael. My fear of him is the only reason I've remained hidden and why my son doesn't know I'm alive. I want the bastard gone.'

Marisse's smile disappeared. She wiped her mouth on a napkin and left the room, returning moments later with the dusty, old book they had been looking at in the cellar. After Elien left that morning, Marisse and Luci had sat and talked for hours, sharing each other's life stories. Marisse seemed to have forgotten all about the magical book in the basement. Luci hadn't wanted to rush her—the old woman was clearly enjoying the company as well as having someone to confide in. In Luci she'd found someone she was able to completely open up with, and by the time they realised how hungry they were, lunchtime had passed and early evening had already begun to set in.

'It's all in here,' Marisse said, passing Luci the book. 'But I'm afraid there's no quick fix. The spell you would need to perform won't happen in my lifetime; in fact, I'll be surprised if you ever manage it. The things you need for the spell to work read like a shopping list of impossibilities.'

'Let me be the judge of that.' Luci opened the book and began thumbing through the pages. 'Where do I find all this information?'

'On the back page, spell six hundred and sixty-six. My father taught me many things while I was young; this was the final spell he shared before he was murdered.'

'Does Mikhael know about you and the book?'

'I don't think so, not its contents at least. The hunters destroy any book a witch has in her possession. In Germany, they ransacked my house and burned all my notes, my diaries, and my books before I got away—but this one remained hidden. It was the only one I managed to save.'

Luci turned to the last page and ran her finger over the strange markings.

'Does it make sense to you?' Marisse asked.

Luci wasn't listening; she was frowning at the pages.

'Nephilim are the key to his demise. It says here, "*The chosen Nephilim will complete the full spectrum of the soul.*" What does that mean?'

'I have no idea. My father said we'd know when the time was right—once we'd gathered them together,' Marisse replied with a shrug.

'It also says we need to work with six half-angels. Six? Is that right?'

'Yes, that's why Mikhael has been murdering us. I've always known my father was an angel, but I've never come across another. Perhaps many others who were accused of witchcraft were also my kind; I don't know.'

Luci continued to read, occasionally squinting at the markings and taking a bite of bread.

'From what I understand, in order to rid the realm of Mikhael and his murdering sword, we would need the help of six Nephilim, a feather from Mikhael's wings, and a feather from two other archangels who oppose him.'

'Yes. At the time, I asked my father to give me one of his feathers, but he explained the wings of a lesser angel don't count. They have to come from two archangels, two beings from the upper realm who hate Mikhael. I take it your wings didn't survive?'

Luci shook her head, but a small smile was forming on her lips.

'...and lastly we need the blood of three generations of archangels. Well, that's ridiculous; archangels don't bleed.'

'I know,' Marisse said. 'As I said, it's a list of the impossible, which I guess is the whole point and why no one has managed to overpower him.'

'It will be difficult, yes,' Luci said. 'But not impossible.'

She reached into the inside of her dress and pulled out a small leather pouch hanging by a string around her neck. She opened it up and took something out.

'What's that?' Marisse asked, taking the crumpled mass out of her hands.

'One of my feathers and one of Mikhael's. He fought with me in Italy over sixteen hundred years ago, and some of our feathers came loose. I imagine Zadkiel, who was only a child at the time, found them when he came looking for me. I discovered them years later inside an urn in our cottage and have carried them with me ever since as a reminder of what I once was. This is all that is left of them; will they do?'

Marisse grinned and nodded.

'This is amazing. You have two of the three, including Mikhael's, but they have practically turned to dust. We need to preserve them in such a way that they retain their power.'

Marisse gently placed them on the table and ran out of the room. When she returned, her hands were filled with jewellery that she also placed on the table.

'I make amulets, Luci. People pay me good money to mix my herbs with gold and create adornments that will keep them healthy. There is a plague spreading across Europe, but it rarely reaches the rich. That's because of me.'

Luci picked up a pendant and held it up to the candlelight. It was beautifully crafted and studded with brightly coloured gems.

'I saw the rings on your fingers when I arrived,' Luci said. 'I didn't realise you made them yourself.'

'Yes. Gold carries magic very well, as does silver and certain crystals.'

'How will that help me?'

'I can grind the feathers down, mix them with gold, and turn them into jewellery for you. They will last forever, and you can wear them until the time comes when you find the rest of the ingredients for the spell. Would you like that?'

Luci stood up and did something she hadn't done in a long time: she hugged the old woman and meant it.

'Yes, I would like that very much. Are there any crystals you can add that will help attract my son, too?'

'It depends on his frequency. My father explained that every archangel works on a different colour energy. You were black and Mikhael was white; the rest were the seven chakra colours. I know Gabriel is the messenger, so he's blue. Raphael heals, so he's green. I think I have them noted in here.' She flicked to the front of the book where a list of colours had been drawn, now faded to a dull rainbow. 'Of course. Zadkiel is the highest of them all, the Archangel of Mercy and Freedom. He's the colour indigo, so a lilac stone like amethyst should work. I will grind down the feathers, mix them with gold, and make you a necklace and a ring for each hand studded with amethyst. When the time comes that you find the other feather, perhaps even one belonging to your own son, you will be able to use it in the spell. Would you like me to inscribe the jewellery with something?'

'Yes.' Luci smiled. 'In angelic script, I want you to write "*The fallen shall rise again.*" Because that is exactly what I did—and I will do so again.'

For the first time in a long time, Luci felt closer to finding her son and ridding the world of Mikhael. She didn't have all the answers yet, but at least she had plenty of time.

IV.

Three days had passed since Marisse had helped Elien. Luci kept herself busy assisting the healer with herb drying, grinding, and bottling. During the day, Marisse would keep up the pretence of running the shop and supplying the townsfolk with fire or water, while Luci focused on keeping her friend's collection of little glass bottles filled with healing ointments. Marisse had made her the jewellery as promised, two rings and an amulet, which Luci wore with pride and relief.

A small, shiny reminder that there was hope—that one day she would find her boy and exact her revenge on Mikhael.

In the evenings, at dusk, the two would take long walks out to the forest where they would pick herbs and wild flowers. Marisse taught Luci which plants to pick at which time of day to enhance their potential to heal. Back at home, they would sit by the fire and talk into the night, the witch teaching Luci new spells, the cat on her lap and a pot of soup bubbling in the hearth. It was the closest to contentment that Luci had felt for a long time.

On the third evening, after they had eaten supper and settled down to pore over the book once more, there came a pounding at the door.

'Don't answer it,' Luci said. 'Nothing good ever arrives at a house this late at night.'

Marisse was already on her feet.

'It's the girl; she's upset. I won't be long.'

Luci put down the book and watched the shopkeeper answer the door, usher Elien into the shop, and talk to her in hushed tones. She couldn't hear what they were saying, but the girl's hair was no longer tied back into her bonnet and her eyes shone with a light that hadn't been there before. Marisse brought the girl into the back room and sat her beside Luci near the fire.

'…So, I didn't take the herbs as I had a big argument with my husband's cousin and threw them at her,' she said, continuing the conversation she'd started with Marisse at the door. 'I didn't mean to get so angry but she's a wicked, horrible woman, and I was so upset that she said I was useless for not giving her cousin an heir. I have been laying with my husband every night since you healed me, but I'm scared my misfortunes will befall me once more if I don't take the herbs. I have money to pay you this time, but I can't be long. He will beat me if he discovers that I snuck out of the house to see you.'

'Are the townsfolk still talking about this house?' Marisse asked the girl. 'Do they mean us harm?'

'Yes,' Elien whispered. 'They say you are both witches and that you dance with the Devil.'

Luci laughed and looked over at her friend, who was also smiling.

'No, we don't dance with the Devil,' Luci said to the girl, her voice slow and hypnotic. 'But it isn't the Devil you need to fear. It's those who fear the Devil that cause the biggest harm. Believe me, child, a little naughtiness can be a good thing sometimes.'

She winked at Marisse, who hid a laugh behind her hand.

'Don't worry, Elien. Luci is playing with you. My knowledge comes from angels. Nothing dark or evil lurks here, just love and light. That's what I used to heal you, love and light.'

Marisse patted the girl's hand and left for the basement to collect some bottles.

Elien glanced nervously at Luci and played with her fingers.

'My husband doesn't think any amount of naughtiness is a good thing. He says that over the last few days, I have become like a possessed woman.'

'Possessed?' Luci asked, leaning forward in her chair.

The girl's cheeks flushed a painful puce, although she no longer looked like the scared, innocent child she'd been three days ago.

'It's…it's nothing,' Elien stammered.

Perhaps with a little persuasion, she could have a decent conversation with the girl. What she was about to do wasn't entirely moral, but then neither was Luci. She looked Elien straight in the eyes and asked again.

'Why does your husband think you are possessed? Tell me your secrets, Elien.'

The girl blushed again and tucked her hair behind her ear, suddenly realising she was missing her bonnet. She chewed the skin around her thumb and stared at Luci as if an invisible thread bound them.

'After Marisse healed me I felt well—more than well. In fact, I had so much energy it was as if it was trying to escape me and I was going to burst at the seams. I was so happy that I was no longer in pain that as soon as Anke, that's my husband, returned from work I…' She blinked and Luci nodded. 'I, well, we lay together. Except this time, he didn't have to ask me; I wanted to. I did things to him that I didn't know a married couple could do. I felt so powerful. But I had my eyes closed because…'

'Go on,' Luci said, enjoying herself.

'Because I was thinking of another man.'

Luci laughed. Extracting dirty secrets was her favourite entertainment. Marisse was still in the basement. Luci could hear the clinking of bottles, so she had time to dig further.

'Who's this man you think of in your marital bed?' she asked the girl.

Elien's cheeks turned an even deeper shade of red.

'I don't know him; we have only spoken briefly. He watches me. I think he's a beggar; he's always sitting in a doorway or under a tree. The day I had an argument with my husband's cousin, I saw this boy in the woods. He told me his name, and he had eyes bluer than a summer sky. They shone so brightly I was both scared and excited. I felt like I knew him, like we had met before. He said he knew me from many other lifetimes.'

Luci was cleaning her nails, hardly listening to the girl. Her secrets were clearly not going to get more riveting than this. She wished that Marisse would hurry up so they could get back to discussing the angelic information in the book.

'So, you think of this man as you seduce your husband?' she asked.

'At first I didn't, but after the healing I did. His face swims before me, and I get a fluttering in my stomach every time I walk past him in the street. How can you long for someone you do not even know? Tonight, while Anke and I made love, I felt the magic curling tighter and tighter inside of me as I thought of this man and his blue eyes. Then something exploded within me. It felt like I was possessed by a spirit. My husband called my reaction ungodly.'

Luci laughed aloud and clapped her hands.

'Well, I'm yet to find a man who makes me lose myself in the moment. My experience with sex has been, somewhat, perfunctory to date. But I'm glad you found a way for it to bring you joy.'

'I have. Anke says it's unnatural for women to want to make love. He says it should be a duty for us to tolerate. He doesn't know about my lost babies and me coming to this house, let alone anything about the man that has been watching me—please don't tell him any of this. I just need the herbs. Then I will go back to Anke and try and control myself and stop thinking about Zadkiel. I want a family, a baby of my own, and then all will be well.'

Luci sat up.

'Say that again.'

'I want a baby with my husband,' she stammered.

Elien was no longer in a trance. Her fingers were red and raw from biting the skin around her nails. Now that she had come to her senses, she was clearly terrified about having disclosed her most private of secrets.

'No! Not the babies. You mentioned Zadkiel. This blue-eyed man you speak of, his name is Zadkiel?'

Luci looked at the girl properly and took a sharp intake of breath. Her eyes. Of course! She'd seen those eyes before, staring down at her from the leafy branches of a tree in Fiesole.

'The beggar?' the girl asked.

'Yes! This man who was watching you, what did he look like?'

Elien shook her head in tiny motions and looked down at her feet. Her arms were folded over her stomach and her eyes darted to the small door in the wall, no doubt hoping the old woman would return quickly and save her from the interrogation.

Luci sighed and stepped in front of the girl, crouching down until their eyes were level.

'Tell me what he looked like,' she said, trying to keep her voice steady. 'This is important.'

At that moment, Marisse stepped out of the door, two glass bottles in her hand.

'They were right at the back. I couldn't find them. Oh my dear, what is going on? Luci, sit down, you're scaring the child.'

'She knows where Zadkiel is,' the fallen angel cried, pointing at Elien, who now hunched on the stool.

'I don't know anything about this man, I promise you,' she pleaded with the two women.

'Just tell Luci who you saw,' Marisse said calmly, giving Luci a warning look and placing her hand on the girl's arm.

'He's a little older than me with dark, wavy hair that reaches his jawline. I think he is poor because he sits in the doorway opposite my house, just down the road from here. He always has his hood raised; sometimes all I can see are his bright blue eyes shining out from beneath it. His face is like something from a painting, a painting of a god or an angel.'

Luci was now holding the girl's face between her two hands, her own face inches from hers.

'Is he here? Tell me!'

'Luci, is this really necessary?' Marisse scolded. 'You're scaring her. How on earth would Elien know anything about your son?'

'It's her. I know her. This is Arabella, and all those that came after her…'

'But my name is Elien not…'

Luci lifted the girl up, stood her on a stool and pulled up her skirt to above her knees. Elien yelped in surprise.

'Look! The crescent birthmark on her thigh. That's the sign; every version of Arabella carries that mark.'

'Let go of her at once!' Marisse pulled Luci's hand away and the fabric dropped back down to the dusty floor.

Elien was crying silently now, but Luci didn't care. 'Marisse, this is the girl who will lead me to my son. He's out there; my boy is out there. I need to find him.'

She pushed past them both and ran out of the door, slamming it shut behind her. The bite of wind surprised her at first—she'd forgotten how cold it had turned over the last few days. Tiny flecks of snow swirled in the air like particles of dust in the sunlight. She considered returning to the house for her cloak, but she couldn't waste any more time. He had to be here somewhere! Her son had been on these very same streets watching that pathetic creature when he could have been with his own mother. Where was he?

She remembered seeing a man huddled in a doorway when she'd first arrived on Marisse's doorstep, but that could have been anyone. The town was full of beggars.

It was nearing the witching hour, and the streets were dark. The swollen moon was her only light, casting silvery shadows over the canal and making the snowflakes glitter. The streets were empty. The nearby church chimed its twelve dongs of midnight. Her son wasn't there.

Luci trudged her way back to the house, her arms wrapped tightly around herself and her feet shuffling along the icy cobbles.

Why did her failure to find her son continue to surprise her? This wasn't the first time she'd come close to seeing Zadkiel. How many more times must their paths cross before she got lucky and managed to reach him? All she wanted was to let him know she'd never left him, that every breath she'd taken over sixteen hundred years had been for him, to find him.

She crossed the small bridge back to Marisse's street and then stopped. A crowd had gathered outside the healer's door. There were raised voices, and Luci could hear Elien crying out. She broke into a run until she reached the edge of the crowd.

With a push and a shove she commanded her way through the throng of people, the crowd parting when she reached its centre. Three men dressed in black and wearing tall, dark hats were holding the top of Marisse and Elien's arms, the front door of the house still ajar behind them. Luci recognised the uniform—witch hunters.

'Luci! Help us!' her friend cried.

Nobody was looking at the fallen angel; instead, all eyes were on a portly, officious-looking man who had pushed his way to the front door and was now pointing at Elien.

'That's the girl! She works for me, and she's married to my wife's cousin, Anke. Her husband has been telling me about her wanton ways. Just half an hour ago, he ran to our home to report that his young wife, this girl right here, had run off in the dead of night. I knew she would be found at the home of witches. I've always suspected her wickedness, but after tonight, I know she has the Devil in her!'

Luci nodded her head and his legs collapsed from under him. She winked at the girl, but Elien had gone paler than the moon itself. She did nothing but stare back at Luci in horror.

'You see!' the man cried, struggling to stand but failing. 'They are evil. They just threw me to the ground with one of their wicked spells. Arrest them both immediately.'

'I haven't done anything wrong,' Elien stuttered. 'I don't understand why you accuse me of such things, Mr Visser.'

One of the men wrestled her arms behind her back and tied them with rope.

'Get off her!' Marisse cried, pulling at his sleeve. 'You have no right to come into my home and make wild accusations. She hasn't done anyone any harm.'

Mr Visser scrambled to his feet and pointed a finger in Elien's face. His eyes bulged, and his red cheeks trembled with indignation.

'This…this…demon-child is a murderer!'

There was an excited gasp from the crowd outside the House of Fire and Water. Neighbours, upon hearing the commotion, were leaving their houses and joining the throng. The mass of hysterical accusers was now five people deep.

'My wife gave birth to a dead child this morning,' Mr Visser continued. 'Less than three days ago, after leaving this very house, the wretched demon-girl you see before you cursed my wife with an evil spell. She threw herbs at her pregnant stomach and said she hoped she would feel the pain of losing a child. Black arts are performed in this house! These women fornicate with Satan and his demons!'

Tears streamed down Elien's cheeks. 'I had no idea Flore's baby died. I would never wish for anything so terrible to happen to any woman. I was just trying to explain to her that I had sought healing after miscarrying my own baby,' she said, sobbing, looking at the faces surrounding her.

Mr Visser pulled her out further into the street.

'Those tears she cries are tears of shame!' her boss shouted. 'She is guilty of witchcraft.'

'I did no such thing!'

'Oh, yes you did! I saw it with my own eyes!' One of Marisse's neighbours was standing at her front door, a large wooden cross in her hand. 'You wished that poor pregnant woman ill. You did!'

'She's right,' another man in the crowd said. 'I live on this street, and I've seen her come here three times just this week. Why else would two single women be taking in a young girl in the middle of the night? All of them are cavorting with the Devil himself.'

'Two women?' one of the men dressed in black said. 'Where's the other one?'

Luci looked on, ignoring Marisse and Elien's pleading stares. The old woman was strong enough to throw these men into the air by magic, but that would do her no good if she then had to escape Roermond.

She wouldn't make it out of the town alive if she proved herself to be more than human.

Luci could step up to the men, look them in the eye, explain it was one big misunderstanding, and stop this ridiculous charade right then and there. She could probably tell each person in the crowd, the entire town if she really wanted to, that they were all innocent and everyone would live in peace. Or she could do something else, something remarkable that may just get her son back. She could use Elien as bait—because where Arabella's troubled soul was, Zadkiel was never far behind.

Luci stepped forward and raised her hand.

'I believe you are looking for me.'

One of the men in black stopped tying Marisse's hands behind her back and grabbed Luci's arm. She let him tie her up as well—she would save her power for later.

'Witches. All of them. And I've just discovered their lair,' a third man shouted, running out of the house with his arms full of jars. 'There are satanic symbols drawn in chalk on the ground, candles, and all manner of things in bottles. They even have a couple of familiars down there; two cats hissed at me as I entered. Who knows what they have been doing in this house. I wouldn't be surprised if the powder in this bottle was the ground bones of babies!'

The crowd erupted with cries of 'murderers!' and 'Devil lovers!'

Luci laughed. 'And so it begins,' she said. 'Those with nothing to live for look for someone to blame for their misery, and those with the most to lose always fear a strong woman. I've seen this played out time and time again throughout history.'

'Only a truly evil person would laugh!' the neighbour shouted, brandishing her cross at Luci. 'This woman arrived the day the girl cursed poor Mr Visser's wife. Look at her with her tits practically falling out of her dress, sparkling jewels at her throat, and her dark hair flying in the wind. She's nothing but a wanton whore. She appeared out of thin air…on a broomstick, I'd wager.'

'Anke!'

Elien was shouting, her eyes frantically scanning the crowd. 'Where's my husband? Mr Visser, I've always worked hard for you. I have never done anything to hurt you or your family,' she pleaded. 'Fetch my husband.'

He spat in her face and poked a crooked finger at her chest.

'I took you on as a milkmaid just two months ago, Elien, but my milk hasn't been right since you started. One of my farmhands caught the plague last week, and now my wife has given birth to a dead child. Are you telling me this isn't your doing?'

'Yes, of course it isn't! Where's my husband? He will explain that I am not a bad person.'

'That isn't quite true either,' a deep voice at the back of the crowd said.

The people parted to let him through.

Luci surveyed the tall blond man before her. So, this was Elien's husband—the man that thought it acceptable to marry a girl so young, control her, and then judge her for taking any pleasure out of life.

'This isn't the woman I married,' he said quietly. 'She has been possessed. And she has killed our children.'

The crowd gasped. Elien was sobbing uncontrollably now, tears streaming down her face as she shook her head from side to side.

'Don't deny it, Elien. Flore has only just told me how you killed our children. That your body has been rejecting our babies, which is why you cast a spell on her and she lost hers. Is that what those bloody rags in the fire were? Did you *burn* our offspring as a sacrifice to the Devil that you now worship?'

Elien struggled to breathe through her tears.

'No. That's not how it was. I burnt the rags to hide my bleeding so I wouldn't anger you.'

'Our babies didn't die?'

'Yes, they did, but that wasn't my fault.'

'The Devil has taken you over, Elien!' Mr Visser shouted in her face. 'That is why disaster follows you. Everything you touch dies or is destroyed.'

'No!' she screamed, looking pleadingly at her husband. 'Anke, I'm a loving wife. Tell them.'

He turned away, unable to look at her.

'She isn't the same sweet girl I married,' he said, addressing the men in black. His voice was barely audible. 'Last Sunday, she didn't go to church with me; she stayed in bed.'

'I was unwell!' Elien screamed, but no one was listening.

'The last three nights, she has done things in the marital bed that no married woman should know about. She has renounced the Lord.' He turned to the crowd that had now gone quiet, waiting to hear what the witch's husband had to say. He held up his arms as if he were giving a sermon. 'She only cares for Satan now. I can see it in her eyes. As soon as the sun goes down, it isn't me she is thinking of.'

The men in black shook their heads gravely, their faces painted with revulsion and fear.

'When we make love, she shakes and writhes like a woman possessed. Her hunger for carnal pleasures is simply not becoming of a woman. Last night, she begged me to take her on all fours like a dog.'

The people in the crowd gasped and looked at one another in horror. Cries of 'whore' and 'demon-fucker' ran out across the sharp night air. An elderly lady at the front of the throng staggered backwards, clutching a Bible to her chest as if it would shield her from the words she was hearing.

'And did you?' one of the officials asked Anke. 'Did you succumb to her wild ways?'

'Of course I did. She had me under her spell. She urged me to do it faster and harder—and all the while she howled and shook like the Devil himself.'

Blood was boiling in Luci's veins. She could end this right now, set that vile man on fire and watch the crowd burn to ash. She could throw her captors and accusers into the canal beside them and hold them down until they were nothing but swollen, floating corpses. She could take Elien and Marisse far from here and show them places where women were revered, not hated. But she wanted her son back. Her son was watching Elien, and this was Elien's fate. Luci would have to remain calm and smart.

The young girl looked like she could no longer breathe and stood stock-still as if she were made of wood. Marisse was staring down at the ground, her eyes glassy with tears. They were both expecting Luci to save them. She would. But not yet.

Anke wouldn't look at Elien; instead, he was enjoying the attention of the crowd. He stepped forward and pointed at the three women.

'These women are conducting a Witches' Sabbath every night. They ride the Devil's cock and fill themselves up with the spawn of his evil before cursing us innocent folk. That is why my sons have died inside her rotten body, why the cows she touches produce curdled milk, and why the people she works with die or give birth to death.'

Jeers and shouts rose up from the throng.

'Leave her alone!' Marisse shouted. 'She is just a girl—a poor young girl who has lost her baby in the early stages. She isn't evil!'

'Shut up, you old hag!'

A rock flew out of the crowd and hit Marisse in the face, cutting her forehead.

'Luci, stop them! You said you would protect us!' Marisse shouted to her friend over the cries of her neighbours.

Luci, her arms pulled behind her back and her wrists tied with rope, simply smiled and shrugged. There was still time. If walking this earth for sixteen hundred years had taught her anything, it was that humans—especially men—were predictable. She had a plan, and so far they were playing straight into her hands.

'Search her for the Devil's mark!' a woman shouted out, throwing a rock at Elien.

'Don't touch me!' Elien screamed, but her voice was lost among the excited cheers of her audience as three men began pulling at her clothes. Removing a blade from his waist, one of the officials cut through the top of her dress and ripped it apart, revealing her breasts beneath. The crowd jeered louder.

Elien closed her eyes, her bottom lip bleeding from biting down on it so hard. Luci sighed, biding her time. Her stomach churned at the sight of the faces surrounding them, faces distorted in revulsion and sheer delight at the barbaric fate that awaited the pretty blonde girl. The men continued to rip her dress further, her breasts tightening as the cold air hit her bare skin. Bit by bit she was undressed, the heavy layers of fabric dropping to the ground, until she was completely naked except for the sleeves of her arms that now lay gathered around her bound wrists behind her back. She kept her eyes shut, shivering in fear and from the cold as the men poked a stick at her legs and back. They lifted her hair and looked at her neck, shoulders, and under her arms. They ran the stick down her back, making her tremble further.

'Look at her, she likes that. The Devil is certainly inside of her.'

'What are these lines across her stomach?' one of the hunters said.

Anke had walked away and her boss, Mr Visser, was looking at her naked, trembling body in disgust.

'They look like the Devil's claw marks,' he said with a sneer.

Marisse pulled against the restraints on her arms. 'This is ridiculous. She told you that she has carried and lost babies. All women get these marks on their bodies with pregnancy; it is the skin stretching. They mean nothing!'

'And this?' the hunter cried, jabbing the stick at Elien's knee. 'Look at the red welt upon her thigh, a crescent moon. The Devil has branded her! Her body serves as nothing but his plaything!'

'She is just a child,' Marisse shouted.

The man with the stick jabbed the old woman in the chest and pushed his face close to hers.

'She is a witch, and she will burn for her sins against God. The more of these tainted women we destroy, the less death and pestilence we will suffer in Roermond.'

The crowd cheered.

'What about the others?' a woman from the crowd shouted. She thrust her Bible into the hands of the man speaking. 'Make her read this. Witches can't read holy scriptures.'

He nodded and opened the book before Marisse.

'Read it.'

A look of panic passed across her face.

'My Dutch isn't very good. I was educated in Germany.'

'Lies!' the crowd shouted. 'Read the words of the Lord.'

Marisse took a deep breath and blinked back her tears. She squinted at the tiny words on the page before her.

'*Onze Vader,*' she whispered, her voice wavering on every word, '*die in de hemelen zijt, ge… gehei…geheili…*'

'She can't say the word holy,' the crowd jeered. 'Satan has her tongue. She can't do it!'

The book was taken away and returned to the woman, who hugged it to her chest again. All eyes were on Luci now, who hadn't said a word throughout the proceedings. Looking up at the three men she smiled.

'So, gentlemen. I presume it's my turn now?'

They were frowning at her, clearly confused as to why she was smiling and why she was so calm. She shrugged and turned to Elien. Nodding at the crumpled dress that laid at Elien's feet, Luci lifted her head and the dress rose slowly and draped itself over the girl's naked body. The crowd screamed, and a few of the women ran back into their houses, slamming their windows and doors closed. Luci laughed.

'Want to see more?'

A tabby cat appeared in the clearing before them. Marisse shooed it away, lightly tapping it with her foot, but the cat sat firmly beside Luci.

'The familiars!' a man cried.

Luci twitched her fingers behind her back and the cat was joined by a black cat and a scrawny tortoiseshell cat. Each one sat at the feet of one of the accused women. As the witch hunters stepped closer the cats hissed at them, backs arched and claws out, swiping out at the men in tall, black hats.

'Why are you doing this, Luci?' Marisse cried. 'You are innocent, too. You will make us all burn!'

'No, I won't,' she said, smiling. 'If they want witches, I'll give them witches. But you will go free. I always keep my promises.'

The men stared at one another in alarm. They didn't need any more evidence.

'Burn the cats, too!' a woman screamed. 'The Devil resides within the familiars. Burn the beasts before they eat our young!'

The men reached for the cats, who hissed and scratched them.

'Go,' Luci said, and the cats darted through the feet of the onlookers and disappeared into the crowd. 'You have your three witches now,' she said. 'Take us away, if you must.'

Elien looked at Marisse; both their eyes were wide with fear. They were silently questioning why Luci was leading them to the gallows or, worse, the burning pyres atop Galgeberg Hill.

The men in black pushed the women through the crowd of onlookers, holding tightly to the ropes around their wrists. Marisse and Elien kept their heads bent low and avoided the stares of their neighbours. The townspeople gathered behind the accused, their faces distorted in grim, gargoyle-like masks of anger and illuminated in dramatic relief by the lit torches they held. A bucket of fish guts and bones was thrown out of a window, the contents landing on Elien and causing her ripped dress to once again drop off her shoulders onto the muddy cobbles. Luci imagined that these people were known to her friend, decent folk who had once lent Marisse a cup of milk or an egg, and yet here they now stood on their doorsteps, shouting abuse at the witches being marched out of town.

Luci looked each and every one of them in the eye, smiling at the fear her stares instilled in them. She didn't want anyone to sleep easy tonight.

V.

'Get in there!' a young guard growled, pulling open a heavy iron door leading into a damp stone room.

Luci stumbled as Marisse was pushed into her, and Marisse fell headfirst into Elien's naked chest. It took a while for the old woman to get back on her feet. The man laughed at the other two women's feeble attempts to help Marisse while they still had their hands tied behind their back. Marisse wouldn't look at Luci; it was clear she thought the fallen angel had lied to her. But Luci's plan was working. The old woman would be free soon.

'You can't lock us up in here!' Elien cried. 'This is nothing more than a dungeon. We need water and blankets. We demand a fair trial!'

The man laughed again and stepped toward her. He twirled her golden hair around his finger and brought it up to his nose, inhaling deeply with his eyes closed.

'You're a pretty little thing. Shame you're nothing but a murdering Devil lover. You can't work your magic on me.'

'I'm no witch! This is unfair and barbaric. Marisse is old and Luci...she's innocent, too. I won't stay here and...'

Elien yelped as the guard slapped her face hard with the back of his hand. She fell back and hit her head on the stone wall, causing a thin trickle of blood to work its way down her forehead.

'Don't answer me back, murderer! You won't be here for long anyway—you'll be dead by the morning. See that?' He pointed at a small window above their heads. The hole in the wall had no glass, just two wrought iron bars running through the middle. 'That, through there, is Galgeberg Hill. They are building the pyres as we speak. This week alone, we've caught over sixty witches, and you'll all burn for the crimes you've committed against the Lord. The gallows are too good for you.'

Elien's face was now a mess of blood and tears that dripped down onto her shivering, naked body. Marisse pressed herself against the girl's side so she could wipe the blood on her shoulder. Grateful for her kindness, Elien leant into the woman's warmth.

Luci clenched her jaw as she looked at the pitiful sight of the two women. At the click of her fingers, she could snap the guard's head clean off, and by God she wanted to, but she had to bide her time.

The guard went to leave, but Luci stepped in front of him.

'You want me to beat you, too?' he said.

She stared into his eyes and spoke quietly.

'You will leave now, but before sunrise I want you to return with the following items: a horse, two blankets, clothes for Elien, water, and food. You will not tell a soul, and you will ensure you are not followed. Is that understood?'

The man nodded, repeated the list, and left the room. As soon as his footsteps receded into the distance, Luci yawned and then nodded at the wrists of the two women before her. Like two stiff snakes, the thick ropes began to unwind and slide to the ground.

'Untie me,' she said to Elien, who ran behind her and picked at the rope with swollen, numb fingers.

As soon as she was free, Marisse removed her apron and wrapped it around Elien, who immediately collapsed to the damp ground and rubbed her wrists.

'Why didn't you save us!' the old woman cried at Luci. 'Why did you let those animals capture us? You could have freed our hands at least!'

Luci smiled sadly and walked over to the two women, crouching beside them. She laid her hands on Elien's wrists, and immediately the red, blistered skin returned to normal.

'Firstly, I can only control that which I can see or point my hands at. I don't know why. I could have made someone untie me, but I couldn't have made the ropes move without looking at them. Anyway, there would have been no point at that stage. I had to play the game and let them think they were winning.'

'Why?' Elien whimpered, her teeth chattering.

Luci sat on the other side of her and draped her long skirt over her legs. Marisse did the same, the two women attempting to keep the young girl warm between them.

'Why? Because I have to see my boy, and you're going to help me. Every time you're close to death, he's there. He can't help himself. I've seen it before.' She cupped Elien's face in her hands and stroked away the red swelling the guard's slap had caused.

'Which boy? I've never been close to death before!'

'You don't know how special you are, Elien. You have lived many times before, and my son has loved you every time. I've been looking for him for centuries, and this time I won't fail. This time, Zadkiel will see me, too.'

Elien stared at her, silently mouthing Zadkiel's name over and over again.

'But won't we be escaping on the horse you just told the guard to bring us?' Marisse asked.

'*You* will, but just you. That horrid man will bring you the horse and us blankets and food, and he will accompany you home to collect your money and belongings. The Book of Light is still hidden beneath the flagstones in the basement; I doubt they will find it. Leave it there, and I will collect it at a later date.'

'But how will I escape Roermond?' Marisse said. 'I'm wanted for witchcraft!'

'With the guard. No one will question him. I will ensure he slits his own throat once you are safe. That will be my parting gift to you, my friend...his painful demise. I didn't like him.'

'What about me?' Elien said. 'Will I escape with Marisse?'

Luci took hold of Elien's chin and brought her face closer to hers. The girl was too sweet and pure for this dark world. Arabella had been the same. Why do the worst of men seek the best in women?

Elien had a path she had to follow, a date with destiny and death. Luci wasn't happy about doing what she had to do—but it was her only chance of finding Zadkiel.

'No. You won't leave with Marisse,' she answered.

'Why not?'

'Because, my lovely little honey trap, you are going to burn beside me.'

VI.

Luci stepped out of the dark cell and into the biting wind. She pushed her hair out of her face and stared at the crowd gathered on the hill. There were women and children jostling for space among angry men and priests, all attempting to get as close to the pyres as possible. Dozens of women were already tied to ladders and poles, dry sticks piled high around their ankles. Even though the tinder hadn't yet been lit, the pleas of the women were harrowing.

Elien had tied Luci's hands behind her back, and Luci had used her powers to do the same to her before the guards had returned to collect them. She looked back at the girl emerging from the dank room, her eyes wide as she noticed the hundreds of people that had gathered to watch her die. She turned full circle. A sob escaped her lips as her eyes settled on the side of the hill where the gallows stood, the carcasses of two decomposed men still swaying in the wind, purple tongues hanging out of their rotting mouths. Crows sat on their heads, pecking at their shrunken eyeballs and ripping at the decaying flesh like it was nothing more than yesterday's stale bread.

Marisse had successfully got away, and Luci had then explained to Elien the next stage of the plan. She was clearly confused and still feared Luci, but what choice did the girl have? Her fate was in the hands of a fallen angel.

When the guards had come for them that morning, Elien was no longer naked. The two of them had eaten and were warm beneath their blankets. Luci had ensured that the guard didn't question a thing—including where the third prisoner had gone.

The roar of the townspeople was deafening, growing louder as Elien came into their view. Cries of 'baby murderer' and 'Devil fornicators' hit her square in the face, and she flinched as if each word were a jagged rock.

'Where's the old hag?' one woman shouted as Luci and Elien were led to the three remaining stakes.

Luci stopped and turned to the crowd. A deathly hush descended as they waited for her to speak.

'Don't look her in the eye!' one man shouted out. 'That's how they do their magic. That's how the Devil works through them.'

Luci laughed, and they fell silent again. 'Marisse transformed herself into a crow and escaped out of the prison window.'

A ripple of excitement travelled through the crowd as they gazed up at the grey sky and the black specks circling them. A couple of people left the front of the crowd and sought shelter beneath a nearby tree. Luci laughed again. The guard pulled her away and pushed her in the direction of the unlit bonfires, where the other accused were tied and proclaiming their innocence.

'These are the last of them!' the guard shouted, pushing Luci again toward a post surrounded by bundles of kindling and branches. Two large men stood beside the pyres, their faces criss-crossed with scars. One man was missing an ear, and both were missing teeth.

Luci let them tie her up to the post and surround her with piles of branches and splintered wood. It didn't matter; she wouldn't be there long. Her son would be in the crowd soon, waiting to take Elien Home. As he always did. Except this time, Luci would be there, too, and he wouldn't be able to miss her. This time she would be burning beside his one true love, and he would see her. She planned to break free, rescue Elien, and give her boy what he'd always wanted—his two women back.

The guard with the missing ear leered at Luci, his remaining teeth rotten and brown.

'I've heard all about this one,' he said to the other man beside him as they tied her ankles to the post. 'Powerful little necromancer.'

She had hidden her necklace down her top, knowing full well that men like these would happily steal off a woman in her final hour. She still wore the rings, but they were concealed within her bunched-up fists. The men wrapped a rope around her neck and tied it tightly to the post. Luci didn't care; she was too busy scanning the crowd for Zadkiel. Where was he? She glanced at the empty pyre to her left. Elien wasn't there, either.

'Where are they taking the girl?' she shouted at the men beside her.

'Gallows. Her husband suddenly turned kind-hearted and decided to spare her the burn. He begged for quick and painless. Too good for a baby murderer, I say.'

No! This wouldn't work! The gallows were on the other side of the hill. Zadkiel would have his back to Luci if he was watching Elien die. He wouldn't know his mother was there.

'Don't take her!' Luci cried out as Elien was led away in the opposite direction.

The girl twisted around and stared at her, her eyes wide circles of fear.

'Shut your mouth, Satan-fucker. I've got special orders from on high for you, too,' the guard whispered in Luci's ear, his breath like a week-old bucket of rotting vegetables. 'They say you Devil women have dangerous eyes, so we won't be staring into them as you burn!'

He pulled a rough sack over Luci's head and tied it with string. She struggled to break free, but her cries were muffled beneath the hood. *Shit!* In sixteen hundred years, this had never happened. Without the use of her eyes or hands, she couldn't control anything. She wouldn't die, of course. If she were to burn, she would still rise again from the ashes—she had done it before—but she'd never been unable to free herself like right now.

The cries of the crowd were reaching a deafening pitch. The burning had begun. Luci could hear every branch around her catch alight, crackling and popping. Beside her, women whimpered and screamed. The air sang with despair. She coughed as a thick smoke began to fill the bag over her head. She couldn't breathe, and she couldn't see her boy.

Was Zadkiel out there? Was Elien still alive?

She felt the heat before she heard the kindling at her feet catch alight. Her pyre had been lit. She couldn't afford to wait for the fire to burn through her ropes until she was freed.

Death or no death, the pain was still going to happen. Despite her ability to heal, she preferred not to burn in the first place.

She ran her thumb over the rings on her fingers—the rings that she hoped would one day bring forth the demise of Mikhael—and smiled as she thought of her friend Marisse. Had Marisse got away? Was the book still safely hidden?

She'd never forget the look on the faces of the crowd after she'd told them Marisse had turned into a crow. Fear allowed the stupid to believe anything they were told. It was always easier to blame the unknown, the powerful, and the things they didn't understand than to search inside themselves and take responsibility for the wrong in their lives.

Then it came to her. There *was* a way out of her predicament, and it would also get her boy's attention. It was time to make history... again.

Luci couldn't control the minds of people without talking and looking at them, and she couldn't control inanimate objects without pointing at them, but if she could move her fingers just a little and really concentrate, then she should be able to control the minds of animals. It wasn't only Luci who was famed for strength, cunning, and jet-black feathers.

Her fingers were swollen and numb from the tight rope around her wrists, but she was still able to move them a little. She closed her eyes and focused on the images of the crows at the gallows and the flock of black birds circling the hill, waiting for the dead to stop twitching. She made a beckoning motion with her middle finger and immediately heard the cry of a crow coming closer.

It was working!

She felt it land on her wrists and start to peck at the rope tying her hands together. She beckoned with her finger again and another landed on her shoulder, pulling at the rope around her neck and loosening the hold of the sack over her face. She had to see if Zadkiel was there. She had to free herself before Elien was hanged, or Zadkiel would be gone before she reached him. She felt a thump at her feet as another bale of hay was thrown at the base of the pyre and set alight. Fire crackled at her ankles, the heat rising beneath her long skirt. It wouldn't be long before her clothing burst into flames and her body quickly followed.

With one last tug from the bird's beak, her hands were finally free. She pulled off her hood and looked around her. The screams of the burning women had quickly become one with the roar of the fires. It was hard to make out the crowd through the dense smoke billowing around her. Some of the onlookers had turned their backs on the witches and were now watching the gallows where three women already hung, their limp bodies swaying like broken rag dolls. The guards were cutting them down and looping new rope over the frames. Elien was next, which meant one of the many hooded men in the crowd was Luci's son. She didn't have a moment to lose.

She raised her arms up high, as if praising the god she knew had never existed, and looked up at the sky. The swirling grey clouds began to turn black as dozens, then hundreds, and then thousands of crows gathered above the jeering crowd. The townspeople, upon seeing the skies suddenly darken and the witch free herself from her restraints, began to point and scream. Luci threw her arms down and commanded the birds to attack.

People scattered in all directions as the crows tore into their flesh and ripped at their clothes. Hats and caps were trampled underfoot. Birds clawed and scratched at people's faces, their talons tangled in people's hair, their beaks pecking at wide, frightened eyes. The accused were still burning, some of them now slumped on top of the flames, nothing more than charred masses of blistered skin—but there was no one left to watch them. The onlookers were now running from the hill toward the town, the roar of the fires drowned out by the deafening flurry of thousands of wings.

Luci reached down her top and took out her necklace, using the clasp to fasten it around her neck. She needed all the help she could get. Untying the rope around her waist and feet, she walked down the burning pyre. As she did so, her long skirt set alight. Those cowering from the birds screamed anew at the vision of the burning witch walking toward them.

But she didn't want them; she was searching for her son.

At the gallows, the crowd had also thinned out. Most people were curled on the ground in tight balls, birds pulling at their hair and clothes, or they were running for their lives. All except for the giant guard who had kept his post, unconcerned by the crows swarming around him, determined to finish the job he'd started. Elien was the last person left to hang.

'Zadkiel! Where are you?' Luci cried, running to the other side of the hill, her eyes scanning the faces of the villagers.

She tripped over a pile of flesh and blood. Dead crows and people lay scattered on the ground, black feathers falling like ash over the bloody bodies of the fallen victims. Luci was still too far away from the gallows to be heard, but she could see Elien and the noose hanging around her neck. The guard was fighting off two crows that were pecking at his neck and hands as the girl, now standing on the edge of the wooden platform, looked around her in panic. She was also examining the faces of the few people left standing. Was she searching for Luci to save her? Or was she too looking for Zadkiel?

The birds knew not to attack Elien and they tried to help her, but no matter how much they tore at the fibres, they could do nothing about the thick rope hanging around Elien's neck.

Everybody in the crowd was now either screaming and running or crouched on the ground with their arms over their heads—all except for one solitary figure. A hooded man, his back to Luci, was the only still soul among the chaos. Luci ran faster toward him, shouting out her boy's name, her skirt still ablaze and singeing the grass over which she ran. She could no longer feel the flames licking at her ankles and thighs. All she cared about was Zadkiel.

Elien had now seen her and was shouting out Luci's name, her voice lost among the commotion. But as Luci got closer, she realised it wasn't her name the girl was calling out. It was Zadkiel's. It was Luci's son Elien had seen, and Elien was calling out for his help. Zadkiel didn't move though. He never did. He wasn't there to save her; he was there to take her Home.

Luci threw her arms up, intent on knocking over the gallows, but instead she tripped over a dead body covered in hungry crows. She sent more of the birds to swarm at the giant guard, but he grabbed them around the neck one by one, twisted their heads in his large hands, and threw them to the ground. Luci stumbled to her feet, flames now licking around her waist, as the guard turned his attention back to the young girl. Elien was already waiting in position on the gallows' platform.

'No!' Luci screamed.

With one last glance at the burning woman running toward him, the guard pushed the girl off the edge and sent her to her death.

'Elien!' Luci screamed as the guard walked away, still hitting the birds swooping down at him.

She was nearly at the gallows now, trying to use her powers to raise her son's true love through the air and take the strain off her neck, but she was too late. Elien was dead. Zadkiel was already beside the swinging girl, his back to his mother. Luci watched him pull Elien back up to the platform, cut her loose, and gather her onto his lap. She saw his head dip as he bowed down to kiss her, and then he was gone. Again.

Luci dropped to the ground, the flames on her clothes slowly turning to thick smoke from the wet mud in which she sat. She looked around her at the carnage she'd created. Bodies lay strewn upon the hillside, clusters of hungry birds pecking at their mangled faces and empty eye sockets. Women and children sobbed uncontrollably in the doorways of the surrounding houses, the fire of the raging pyres reflected in the glass of their windows.

The accused were all now dead, burned alive or hanged. They'd been innocent women whose only crime was being defiant and strong.

Luci had failed and in her wake had left nothing but death. The only survivor had been her—the witch that wouldn't burn.

She clasped the necklace around her neck and screamed up at the sky as black feathers rained down upon her.

36

ZAC RAISED HIS glass and nodded at his mother. She was probably expecting a smile from him but, after being forced to abandon Ella, he couldn't imagine ever smiling again.

'This is weird,' he said.

'What is?'

'Sitting by the sea with you, drinking...what is this?'

'Sex on the Beach.'

'How inappropriate.'

He took a sip and screwed up his nose. It tasted of boiled sweets. The little sandy bay was empty and so was the beach bar. Luci had ordered everyone to leave and then had helped herself to the contents of the bar. His mother made a mean cocktail, although nothing she did surprised him anymore.

Four hours had passed since Zac had said goodbye to Ella, and it was taking every ounce of his resolve not to turn around and run back to her. He'd watched her die countless times in the past, which had never been easy, but this time was different. This time he'd set out to stay with her forever, and yet he'd still been forced to walk away against his own will. He knew Gabriel and Luci had been right about leaving Ella behind, but it still hurt. And it still felt wrong.

As soon as they'd left the library and ensured everyone's memories had been wiped clean, the archangel had vanished and Luci had ordered Zac to get on the back of the motorbike. She hadn't even given her son time to hold on before riding far too fast away from the old monastery and his soulmate. They'd travelled along the Costa de la Luz coastline until they found a pretty hotel by the sea, and here they were, acting like normal people on a weekend away.

'Tell me you have a plan,' he said.

Luci had changed out of her ridiculous ballgown and was wearing a pair of jean shorts and a T-shirt. Zac recognised them—they were Ella's. Could his mother be any crasser? She peered at him over the top of her sunglasses and leant back on the sun lounger.

'A plan?' she echoed. 'Of course not. It's finally time to relax and enjoy ourselves. I have my wonderful son back. You have no idea how happy I am right now.'

He turned away from her beaming smile and stared out to sea. The fact that his mother was alive, and right there beside him, hadn't sunk in yet. Since he'd killed himself and returned, all he'd focused on was Ella and what he would do when he saw her. He hadn't imagined he'd find Luci at the same time.

Over the centuries, he'd thought back to the sweet mother of his childhood, a kind and gentle woman who'd looked after him and made the pain go away. He'd been told by Mikhael that his mother had been a normal woman, someone he'd never see again. Yet here she was, not human at all, instead a reckless, dangerous fallen angel who didn't care how he was feeling. Couldn't she see how broken he was? Luci claimed to love him and want him but wanting someone wasn't the same as wishing the best for them.

He sighed. Maybe that was his problem. He'd always wanted every version of Arabella, but the original girl he'd fallen in love with was gone forever. Wanting Ella had never been the best thing for *her*—it was what *he* wanted. Being together had always led to pain for both of them.

'Do you realise how many times I missed you throughout history?' Luci said.

Zac turned to his mother, who was now kneeling beside his sun lounger.

'What?'

'I came really close to finding you so many times. I watched you get murdered by the soldier back in Fiesole, I visited The Angel Inn in London after you and Gabriel were spotted there, I've seen you in every city and on every street—even in places you've never been. In Roermond, I burned at the stake so you would notice me, but you still didn't.'

Roermond? She'd been one of the burning witches? All he remembered about that time was sweet Elien. The way her hair had shone as if made of spun gold, even on a dull day, and the sweet smattering of freckles on her nose. He'd only known her briefly and had spoken to her just a handful of times, but he'd been watching her, drinking her in, hoping that she was happy. She'd been too young and too good to have died such a terrible death.

He thought back to the gallows on that bitterly cold day. How had his mother been there? He remembered the burning women, the screams, the freezing cold mud splashing up his legs as he'd raced to be beside a dying Elien, and...the crows. Of course! That was the day birds attacked the crowd. It hadn't occurred to him that magic had been behind the onslaught.

'You did that? You summoned crows to get my attention?'

'Yes,' Luci said. 'I was trying to save Elien, too. I called out to you, but as usual you only had eyes for her.'

Zac took a large gulp of his cocktail and waited for it to numb his mind. All this time, he'd thought his mother was dead but she'd been doing everything in her power to find him. How many other times had their paths crossed? How long had he been oblivious to his mother's attempts to find him while he worked for Mikhael, convinced he was an orphaned Nephilim, focusing all his energy on his lost love? Was this going to be his destiny, too? Forever roaming the world in search of Arabella and the women she became in each lifetime?

Luci reached out and squeezed his hand.

'I wish I'd known you were there,' he said, meaning it.

'Everything worked out in the end, son. We're the fallen few now, the only two of our kind. Can't you see? Now that you have joined me, we have the power to do whatever we want!'

He shook his head slowly.

'But I don't care about power, Mamá. I returned for you and Ella. That's all I ever wanted—the two most important women in my life. Just tell me how I can get her back.'

Luci sighed and laid a hand on his.

'You can't. Not in this lifetime.'

'But…'

'Son, you heard what Gabriel said.' Luci fished the lemon out of her drink, sucked on it, and narrowed her eyes at Zac. 'Ah, Gabriel. I'd forgotten how attractive that archangel is. I mean, it's been two millennia since I last saw him, but my goodness, he really did look handsome this afternoon. It's those cheekbones and the way he…'

'Mamá!'

'Sorry, you're right, not appropriate. What was I saying? Oh yes. You can't get back with Ella during this lifetime. It would be suicidal, Zadkiel. If Mikhael is watching her, then you have to keep away. Now that she's back on her path, he'll be extra vigilant, so make sure you're not in the shadows. His sword is what makes him great and, no matter how strong you and I are, as long as he has that weapon, he can end her life forever.'

Zac thought back to the day he'd hacked off his own wings with that very same sword. How the tip of Mikhael's blade had been poised over the crown of Ella's head, seconds away from ending every one of her future lives. Zac should have sliced Mikhael's wings off, too, but then his father would have simply returned as Zac himself had done. Mikhael couldn't die, just as he and Luci couldn't.

'How will I find Ella in her next lifetime?' he asked.

'Luck, my darling boy. It's not easy. I spent over two thousand years searching for that piece-of-shit Sebastian. I vowed I'd repay him for what he did to us all, and only last week did I find his rotten soul in his current incarnation. What makes you think you'll even find her the next time? And more to the point, how do you know she'd want you in the next life as much as she wanted you in this one?'

Zac hadn't thought about it like that. When he'd ended his life, all he'd imagined was returning to Earth and being with Ella forever. He hadn't thought about the life they'd live, whether their children would have been safe, or what he'd do when she eventually died and he remained earthbound, the same age he'd been for thousands of years. He could never give her the life she deserved. His battle to return had been for nothing.

'I don't know what it is to not have her in my life, Mamá. She's married by now, and all this time she's been thinking I didn't come back for her. That I broke my promise. When she dies, I won't be by her side like I've always been. I'll never take her Home again.'

Luci sighed and looked up to the sky.

'Get a grip, son. You're boring me. We are going to be walking this planet for many years to come, and time is the only thing we have on our side. Just wait a few years, ten or twenty, and when Mikhael is confident you're not coming back...then explain it all to her.'

Zac shook his head again and rubbed his eyes.

'I can't do that! I told you, in eleven years Ella and Josh will be dead. Ella drowns alongside her husband at age thirty-four; that's their fate. It's meant to be. She's back on track now, which means her destiny is set and she won't return for many years after her death. If I don't see her soon, I never will again. Not as Ella, anyway.'

Luci pulled his head into her chest and stroked his short hair.

'I'm sorry things turned out like this, son. I truly am. But this moping about stops today. You no longer have any link with her. She's gone. It's over.'

'I can't…I can't live without her.'

'You think, after all these years, I have not loved and lost as well? There have been men in my life, gods among men, who…' Luci looked away.

He looked up at his mother. Was she upset? About a man?

She looked down at him, her watery eyes shining like bright green sea glass. 'You have no idea what my heart has suffered, Zadkiel. You can't imagine the things I've been through or the extent of my loss. Two thousand years is a long time; it hasn't all been fun and games. But you and I, we live forever, and we keep going. You know what you do when you reach the very bottom, son? You kick off the ground and push yourself up to the surface again. Of course you can live without her—we can all survive without the things we want and the people we need.' She held him tighter to her. 'You'll never be alone again, my boy. I'm not going anywhere.'

Zac closed his eyes and breathed in the scent of his mother; it was the smell of his childhood, a time when everything was OK.

'What am I going to do, Mamá?'

'You are going to live, Zadkiel. You're finally free; no one controls you. We're untouchable, invincible, and unstoppable. I've waited two millennia to have a partner in crime. Let's go crazy and see the world in style.'

Zac was more powerful than he had ever imagined. Luci and Gabriel had both said so, but he felt far from strong. Could he ever be as brave as his mother?

'I don't know how you can be so positive about this state of in-between that we're in.'

'Because I get what I want and do what I want!'

'But I don't want to go through life brainwashing everyone to get my own way.'

'Brainwashing?' Luci snorted. 'They are only *people*, Zadkiel. Humans come and go so much, it gets tedious. Who cares about them? Anyway, I don't like the term "brainwashing." I call it "dazzle." It sounds much more glamorous that we are dazzling our way through life.'

'Dazzle? That's a crap word. I'm not using it.'

'Well, up until a few weeks ago, I was the only one that could do it so I could call it whatever I wanted. Fine, call it brainwashing if it eases your conscience. But you can't deny it's very useful.'

She was right. It *was* useful, but it still made him uncomfortable.

'I don't want to steal and lie for all of eternity.'

'Oh, for fuck's sake, Zadkiel. Don't then! Get a fake ID and a proper job. Pay your taxes, moan about the weather, and go to IKEA on the weekend like every other unimaginative idiot on this planet. I couldn't care less how you live your life, but you'd be a fool to settle for a boring human existence when you can have it all.'

Luci picked up their empty cocktail glasses and returned to the beach bar. He could hear the sound of bottles clinking and ice being shaken in two metal cups.

She was right. He could do anything now. It was time to get his head around a life without Ella. The original plan had never been to have a relationship with her. He'd done what he'd intended to do ever since their first meeting three-and-a-half years ago—he'd got her back on her path. She was with Josh, and she was happy. Plus, Luci had killed Sebastian, so she was also safer now. Perhaps Ella didn't love Josh the same way she'd loved him, but she *did* love him. At least she'd lead a content life in ignorant bliss until it was time for her life to end. It was better that way. It had to be.

He rubbed his face. So why did her happiness feel as sharp and painful as the sword Sabinus had driven through his heart?

'Here, drink this,' Luci said, handing him a bright blue drink.

He downed it in one gulp and wiped his mouth on the back of his arm. Fine, he would listen to his mother and try to live a little.

'You're right, Mamá. We survived Mikhael, and he doesn't know we exist. We should make the most of it.'

'Survived? Nothing good ever comes from just surviving, Zadkiel. We rose again! We soared! We won! Surviving implies that we were once victims. I'm no victim.'

Zac smiled. Life was certainly going to be interesting with his mother by his side.

'It still feels like Mikhael won, though,' he said. 'Gabriel told me the Choir turned against him when I died. He's losing control, and it's making him angry. You know he was going to kill Ella? Death Eternal. Forever!'

'He's a cruel bastard, Zadkiel, and he's capable of much worse than that.'

'And we're powerless to do anything!'

'Actually, we're not.' Luci unclipped the necklace from around her neck and passed it to Zac. She then took off the two matching rings and handed them to him, too. 'What do you see, son?'

Zac turned the jewellery over in his hand, rubbing his finger over the angelic inscriptions on the back, thinking back to the day he'd done the same thing in Leo's Spanish cottage.

'I see amethyst stones, gold, and angelic script.'

'Yes, but there's more to it than that. I was shocked and relieved to see this chain around Ella's neck today; I thought I had lost it forever during the Spanish Civil War. Long story. Anyway, this jewellery was made for me in 1613 by a Dutch witch named Marisse. She was a dear friend and a powerful Nephilim, fathered by the lesser angel Azantiel—do you remember him?'

'Of course. He fathered quite a few secret Nephilim and was caught in the end. I was at his Judgement when Mikhael took his wings. He must have died, though, surely? Only we archangels survive having our wings removed.'

'Yes, he's dead. But he was killed not because he'd disobeyed Mikhael, as you all thought, but because he hated Mikhael and had discovered how to destroy Mikhael's sword and render him powerless. Azantiel knew his end was near, so he told his daughter how Mikhael could be finished, and she in turn told me. In fact, it was all written down in a very old book. I lost the Book of Light years later to pirates…' She looked down, swallowed, and then sniffed. 'But I remember everything that was written inside it; we don't need the book to perform the magic.'

Zac's eyes widened. If there was a way of taking the power away from his father, then Zac would be free to be with Ella and neither of them would be persecuted again. He could take her off her path, and she wouldn't die as planned. They could live a normal life together until she died of old age years from now.

'What did this Nephilim tell you? What was in the book?'

'Well, it's complicated. Practically impossible, actually. It involves three spells and six Nephilim. Spell number 666. Have you heard of it before?'

'666? As in the number of the…?'

Luci took a sharp intake of breath. 'Don't say it. Honestly, that fucking father of yours and his Devil lies. No, it's not an evil number. In fact, 666 is the most powerful spell there is.'

• • • • •

Afternoon turned to early evening. Zac and Luci had drunk more cocktails and convinced a passing local to bring them some tapas from the hotel restaurant. While they ate, Luci explained everything there was to know about the power of the necklace and what they needed to do to end Mikhael's reign.

'So that's why my father's been killing Nephilim since the birth of Jesus—because they lead to his destruction?'

'Exactly. If I hadn't discovered his feather and mine hidden in our cottage in Fiesole all those years ago, the spell would be impossible. But we stand a chance now; everything has fallen perfectly into place.'

It hurt to think of how close he'd once been to living a normal life in Tuscany with his precious Arabella. Thinking of that time pained him, but he'd never forgotten discovering those magnificent feathers the day his mother had disappeared.

'They were yours and Mikhael's? I never made the connection. I found them caught up in the jasmine plant the day you disappeared.'

'You have no idea how hard I fought that monster when he came to take me away. I was so scared he'd find and kill you, too, son. Our fight was an ugly one and he won, taking my precious wings and throwing me half naked into the woods—leaving me for dead. Thank goodness some plumes were left behind.'

'So they are inside the jewellery that was made to destroy him?'

'Yes. I thought I'd lost the amulet and rings sixty years ago; I was convinced I was back at square one. Luckily fate is on our side and we have the feathers back. Now we just need one of yours.'

Zac thought back to the glass frame beneath Ella's bed and the large, fluffy white plume within it. Was he ready to start an angelic war?

No, he wasn't.

'I don't have a feather,' he said.

Luci smiled and held her son's face in her hands. 'But Ella did. I found it in her room when I took some of her clothes. Look.'

She rummaged inside a large cloth bag she'd been carrying and produced a giant white feather that fluttered in the light breeze. His feather.

'You stole from her?'

'Oh, lighten up, will you! We have one part of the spell covered. We're nearly there.'

'But it was hers. She has nothing left of me now.'

Luci waved her hands up and down as if his words were smoke.

'You need to focus on us, son. You and me, that's all that matters now. Move on.'

Zac turned away from her. Is this what two thousand years alone did to a person? It turned them callous and insensitive? Or had she always been so cruel?

'You had no right to take away her memory of me!'

'No, I didn't, but I'm playing the long game. If we win and get rid of that bastard father of yours, you will get her back anyway. If we manage it before her premature demise, that is.'

He got it now. Luci saw life as one big game; it was shining in her eyes. A ruthless game where having Zac all to herself, and getting her revenge on Mikhael, were the only prizes. Was she laughing at him? Did she find him ridiculous and weak?

'What happens now that we have the feathers? What about the rest of the spell? The blood and Nephilim part is impossible.'

'Nothing is impossible, Zadkiel. We just need to be patient. Let me see… We need the blood of three generations of archangels. Well, you and I bleed now that we are fallen, so if you were to have a child, we would have our third generation.'

'Mamá, the only child I am ever prepared to father will be with Ella. Yet it won't be in this lifetime, not while Mikhael is still on a Nephilim killing spree.'

'You're telling me you didn't have sex with Ella in the library?'

'No! Of course not!' he cried, his face prickling with the shame of lying. 'Anyway, why can't *you* do it? Have another child and then wait for grandchildren.'

Her face clouded over. She looked down at the glass in her hand.

'You think I haven't tried?' she said quietly. 'You think I haven't lain with men, even those I despised, anyone that I thought could help replace the boy I once lost? I came close a few times…'

'I didn't realise,' Zac mumbled.

'Of course you didn't because you only think of yourself. The only being that can get me pregnant on Earth is another archangel,' she said. 'Which is difficult to do when none of them know I'm still alive, and other than Gabriel they probably all still hate me. Even a Nephilim doesn't hold the power to create an offspring that will survive.' She swallowed and shook her head as if clearing away images from long ago. Then she smiled. 'Mind you, after seeing how handsome Gabriel looked today, perhaps…'

'Mamá!'

Luci waved her hands up and down again, her face stony with concentration.

'Fine, fine, whatever. You may change your mind about having a child one day. We can still do this. Since I learned about the spell nearly four hundred years ago, I have been plotting, taking notes, and studying the teachings of witches and angel experts so I could finally exact our revenge on your father. We have the feathers and most of the blood, but it's the last part that concerns me. I just don't know where we can find six Nephilim, seeing as you're not prepared to make me some.'

'Mamá, stop it! I won't bring children into this world just so they can be your foot soldiers. Mikhael would kill them anyway.'

'Well then, we wait until—by some kind of miracle—six Nephilim are conceived in one lifetime and we somehow find out about it.'

It was Zac's turn to smile. This could actually work. If he could help his mother find the Nephilim within eleven years, he could rid the world of Mikhael and his sword and save Ella. It was worth a shot.

'Actually, there might be another way,' he said, grinning at his mother. 'Gabriel mentioned the Choir went crazy the year I died. They came to Earth and mixed with many women, although he wasn't as delicate about describing it that way. Over the last two years, Mikhael has murdered most of the Nephilim born to these women, masking the deaths as natural or accidents. But I don't think he knew about them all. Gabriel said many angels mixed the modern way, consensually and freely at music festivals, college campuses, and nightclubs. I believe it's no longer frowned upon like it was when poor Mary had to escape to Bethlehem.'

'What are you telling me, Zadkiel?'

'What if Mikhael missed a few? What if there are little Nephilim toddlers running around right now?' he said, thinking of Raphael's children, but not daring to let his mother know everything. Not yet.

Luci closed her eyes and smiled.

'When you cut off your own wings, Zadkiel, you set in motion the beginning of the end for Mikhael—and you didn't even know it! This is it, the reckoning we've been waiting for. Although, for the spell to work, we'll have to wait until these children of shadows are at least teenagers. Until their eyes get bright.'

'What? We haven't got time to wait! We have to find them all within eleven years, before Ella dies.'

'No!' Luci shouted. 'I will not steal a child away from its mother!'

Zac leant forward and put his head in his hands. He was tired. Loving Ella was relentless and exhausting, and it would never be over. When would he ever get to the end of this perpetual chase? All he'd ever wanted was to be how they had once been on that one day by the stream in Fiesole, happy and relaxed and in love. If he could have gone back in time, he would've made that day beneath the fig tree last forever.

'I have to be with her, Mamá. I need to change her path and stop her from dying. I can't do that while Mikhael retains his power.'

Luci looked at him with a strange expression on her face. Part puzzled, part amused.

'Zadkiel, when I saw you with Ella, she had blood around her mouth. Was that her own blood?'

'What does that have to do with anything?'

'Just answer me.'

'No. The blood was mine. I was injured, and when she kissed me some must have got in her mouth. Why is it important?'

Luci smiled and walked back to the bar. She mixed more ice while humming a tune he recognised from his childhood.

'My darling boy, I wouldn't worry too much about having a deadline. I think we have more time than you could ever imagine.'

'What do you mean?'

'I mean we finally have the answer to your question.'

'What question?'

'You asked whether I had a plan. Well, this is it: we're going to destroy the King of Angels and get Ella back.'

She handed him an elaborate cocktail complete with a paper umbrella and a cherry on a stick. She popped the cherry into her mouth and winked at him.

'That bastard father of yours is going to wish he'd killed himself instead of us. It's time for the fallen to rise again.'

37

SIX WEEKS LATER

FOUR HOURS INTO her flight to LAX, Ella's mind had wandered back to her wedding day. She couldn't help it; it was like a scab she couldn't help picking. There was something not quite right about that day, but she couldn't put her finger on it. She daren't mention it to Josh again. She'd pondered over her feelings of unease so many times during their last few weeks together that he was beginning to think she was regretting their hasty wedding.

But why couldn't she shake off the feeling?

For a start, there had been a rip in the lace sash of her wedding dress—one that had definitely not been there when she'd got ready that morning. As Ella had walked down the aisle toward her father, her mother beside her and gripping Ella's arm proudly, she'd also noticed a red stain on the hem of her gown. It looked like blood, but how was that possible?

The ceremony had been perfect, but she'd struggled to concentrate on her father's beautiful words. Her head had been pounding, and she'd been distracted by a dark red mark running vertically down the golden crucifix behind him. She'd put her jitters down to wedding nerves and hadn't mentioned her headache or any of her concerns to Josh, her friends, or her parents all day. It wasn't until she'd heard Mai Li ask Felicity if there were any headache tablets at the hotel and then heard Leo mention during dinner that he'd been struggling with a migraine all day that she wondered whether perhaps they'd all eaten something bad at the restaurant the night before. Was it food poisoning that had made her feel so poorly?

And what about the dark silhouettes on the balcony of the chapel? She could have sworn there were people in the shadows watching them. Had she been so ill she'd hallucinated? She asked her father and he said he hadn't seen anybody, but Ella was sure someone had been up there. What if it had been Mikhael and his archangels searching for Zac? Or what if one of them had been Zac himself?

Her stomach lurched at the thought of the angel. She'd waited for him throughout her entire wedding day. As she'd been getting ready, she'd expected to see his reflection in the mirror. As she'd stood in front of the altar, imagining him crashing through the heavy wooden doors to proclaim his undying love, her back had prickled with anticipation.

Had she really wanted him to stop her?

She loved Josh, but she knew deep down that getting married to him had been the ultimate test. Just like the night she'd thrown herself off the roof of the hotel and Zac had flown to her rescue, she was daring her soulmate to intervene. But this time he hadn't. He couldn't.

As soon as Ella had said 'I do,' she knew she'd said goodbye to Zac forever. Whatever it was he'd attempted to do to save her life on that fateful night three years previous hadn't worked. Mistakes *did* happen in Zac's world. There were no miracles.

'I can't believe I'm moving to Hollywood,' she said to Josh beside her.

He grinned her favourite smile that showed the dimple on his cheek.

'Are you worried? You know, we can always move back to Spain if you don't like LA.'

Ella shook her head. 'No, I'm excited. We've talked about this; it's easier for me to leave the hotel with my parents than it is for you to walk away from all those films you're contracted to shoot. Oh my God, I'm married to a Hollywood actor. So surreal.'

'You think this is surreal?' He kissed her lightly. 'Just wait until I tell the world you're my wife. You'll have to shut down your Twitter account because there's going to be such a massive teen backlash.'

He winked, and she laughed. She didn't have Twitter or Facebook or any of that stuff anymore, and she couldn't care less what the media said. There was nothing anyone could say or do anymore that would make her change her mind about Josh. The love they had for one another was fated; nobody could argue with that.

Ella and Josh were the only ones seated in first class. An air hostess offered them a glass of champagne, but Ella shook her head. It was the first time she'd ever said no to free champagne; she was turning over a new leaf in more ways than one.

'Go on, it's free,' Josh whispered to her, but she shook her head again and mumbled something about a headache while pulling her coat up higher around her neck. Why were aeroplanes always so cold?

'Could my wife and I have some blankets, please?' he asked the air hostess.

Wife! Her stomach flipped every time he called her that, and he did it at every opportunity. They'd been husband and wife for over a month now, but it still sounded strange to her. It felt like she was in one of his movies and they were fooling around, playing make-believe.

Instead of a honeymoon abroad, Ella and Josh had spent a few days after the wedding with her friends and parents and then set off on a Spanish road trip. Virtually unknown in the south of Spain, Josh had enjoyed his anonymity as they'd explored the Moorish ruins of Cádiz, Seville, and Córdoba. They'd even driven to the picturesque town of Ronda to visit her grandmother. Ella loved her father's mother, someone she'd only got to know over the last three years. Her Abuela Imaculada had cooed over the handsome *niño* and mockingly scolded them for not having invited her to their wedding, only backing down when she learned that at least it had been held in a Catholic chapel and that the priest had been her very own son.

'Bah,' she'd cried, waving a wrinkly finger at them both. 'Your father should never have entered the priesthood. Has he still not got together with your mother? He speaks of no one else, you know! As if God wouldn't forgive a man for putting love before his faith. Look at you both; you've recognised the importance of love. When you meet "the one," you hold on to them and you never let go. If only your father had the same courage to follow his heart.'

Ella had hugged her grandmother tightly and told her they were heading to London and then on to Los Angeles since Josh's parents hadn't been told the news yet. When she also told her grandmother that her father was leaving the priesthood and had decided to stay in Tarifa with her mother to run the hotel, the old lady had cried tears of joy.

'Aha, perhaps your *Mamá y Papa* will finally give in to love!' her grandmother had exclaimed, wiggling her eyebrows.

'Who knows, *Abuela?* But I promise, as soon as I hear anything, I will tell you. In the meantime, we will send you flight tickets for our big showbiz wedding once we're settled in America.'

'And I will be in all those celebrity magazines, too?' she asked, her dark eyes twinkling. 'Oh, *mi niña*, that would be very exciting.'

Ella twisted her engagement ring and the simple white gold band beside it around, thinking about how much had changed in the last few months. *This is for life*, she told herself. Mrs de Silva forever.

As always, Zac had been right. Her whole life had slotted into place as soon as she'd followed her path. Moving to Hollywood was a big leap of faith, but at least there would be no angels in Los Angeles. She laughed aloud at her own joke and looked over at Josh. He was resting his head against the plane window, headphones in and eyes closed. The sight of him still gave her butterflies.

Their first night together, the day of their wedding, had been exactly as she'd hoped it would be, gentle but passionate, their lovemaking taking on a natural rhythm. It felt right. There was that word again. Right. Easy. Making love to him wasn't a connection of souls as it had always been with Zac. Yet neither had it felt like her one-night stands had—as if she were feeding an empty monster that could never be sated.

Being with Josh was beautiful, natural, and perfect. She loved loving him. It felt wonderful to finally be at peace.

She leant over and kissed his cheek. His eyes flickered open and focused on hers as he mouthed the words 'I love you.'

What was he going to say when she told him her news and ruined everything?

She flinched as another shooting pain coursed through her abdomen. She'd felt ill for a couple of weeks now but hadn't wanted to worry anyone. Instead, she'd searched online and discovered that it was normal and that it was to be expected during the early stages. She was scared. She'd made so many plans with Josh. He had films to shoot, and she was going to go back to uni to study photography. But now, everything was going to be cut short. She laid a hand on her stomach and took a deep breath.

'Josh?'

He looked up at her and took off his headphones.

'I need to tell you something,' she said.

She'd followed her path just as she'd been told to do, and it had led to this. Was it her destiny? Surely Josh would understand they couldn't fight fate, that things would work out and that they'd get through whatever life threw at them.

Josh frowned at his new wife, his face mirroring the concern on hers. 'What's the matter?'

She chewed at the red skin around her thumb. Was this really the right time to break the news?

'Ella, say something. You're making me nervous.'

She thought back to all the forks in the road that had led her to this moment. It didn't make sense—Ella had been so careful; they both had. She'd been with no one but Josh for two months, yet…Fate wasn't something you could stop. Zac had been the only being who'd ever had the power to do that, but he was no longer in her life.

'I'm pregnant,' she said. 'Six weeks pregnant.'

Josh was silent at first, and then he gathered her up in his arms so tightly Ella didn't think he'd ever let go. She could feel his body shaking against hers. Was he crying? She wrapped her arms around him and pressed her face into the crook of his neck, breathing in the scent of him. Her husband.

In that moment, she made a promise to herself. No more talk of angels. No more thoughts of magic or past lives. Zac hadn't returned for her. Her soulmate was dead, and she would never see him again. The sooner she came to terms with that, the easier her new life was going to be. She was with the right man now, the only one she was meant to love.

She held her husband's hand against her stomach, and he smiled down at her.

'Our destiny,' he whispered.

A tear rolled down her cheek, and she smiled back at him. Her fate was sealed. Who was she to fight it?

Author's Note

This book is more than a story, it's a tribute to women; the hunted and hurt, the misunderstood and misrepresented, and the ones who love so fiercely they lose themselves along the way. When I created Luci, I had no idea that I would be watching a character unfurl and become someone much larger than intended—someone that tapped into a lot of my own feelings about motherhood, relationships and the struggles women face day-to-day. Luci does a lot of bad things; she's not a nice person. Although her history is an understandably good reason for her selfish and cruel actions, it's no excuse—yet you can't help warming to her. Why? Perhaps we're all sick of being expected to be 'nice.' I very much intended for readers to question that and ask themselves whether, if we had her powers, we'd ever take such extreme action against a millennia of injustice.

Although The Indigo Chronicles is a fictitious series of books, the past life aspects were heavily influenced by my own metaphysical experiences. Through meditation and regression therapy, I have re-lived my own drowning at the hands of witch hunters and been a lonely girl in Fiesole during the Roman occupation (amongst many other lives). I only saw a few glimpses of these existences, but I used them as inspiration to weave Ella's past lives together and make them part of her larger story. Some people believe past life 'memories' are literal, others see them as metaphorical representations of our fears or self- beliefs. I don't think it matters what these visions truly are, as long as they help you understand yourself better. If you're interested in past life regression there are a lot of great online meditations you can listen to, but please be careful if seeking a psychic to assist you. Do your research, not all are reputable.

I moved from Spain to the Netherlands halfway through writing *Son of Secrets*. It's always been important for me to play homage to the places I know and love in my stories, and for the first eighteen months in the country I actually lived in the original *House of Fire and Water*. My impressive (but creepy) 16th century canal house home in Delft of the same name became a huge source of inspiration. It was no stretch to imagine witches living there once-upon-a-time, and yes…I was very happy to move to a more modern house eventually.

For those of you interested in history, quite a lot has been written about the witch hunts of Roermond. The site of the Netherland's biggest witch hunt, it resulted in sixty-four people being burned to death following an outbreak of the plague blamed on 'suspicious women.' Sadly, strong 'nasty' women are still being vilified by power-hungry, old, white men. I'd like to think we all have enough of Luci inside of us to stop history repeating itself. Don't wait for someone to rescue you, because none of us are princesses—we're queens. Act like one.

I hope you enjoyed the second part of Zac's and Ella's story. In the third and final book, *Children of Shadows*, we jump forward in time and meet the Nephilim who hold the power to bring down Mikhael and the angelic realm. Expect new characters, more historical flashbacks and plenty of shocks and twists along the way!

Acknowledgments

I have no idea how this book was finished; in fact I have little recollection of writing it. A lot of tough things happened at the time and the story seemed to unfold miraculously all by itself in a bewildering haze of darkness and new beginnings.

My first thanks, as always, goes to my readers. Your support for *The Path Keeper* has been incredible and I would never have got this far without you. To all the bloggers, reviewers, social media followers, booksellers, librarians, schools, event planners and dedicated #ZellaForever fans—I see every single one of you.

As always Joni, Vern and Rebecca at BHC Press, thank you for all your hard work. And *grazie* to my foreign rights agent Cristina Galimberti for giving The Indigo Chronicles wings to fly around the world with.

This book is a no-nonsense feminist tribute to the women who taught me that anything is possible if you have the balls to go for it. This is for you, Simmo Girls—my courageous and selfless mum and the wonderful Jemma Harding, Anastasia Brand, Emily Bowers, Angela Denton and Wendy Hohenberg. Don't ever stop shining.

Thank you to my dad, Desi Juste, who's creativity sparked a lifetime of imagination. Hope you're up for reading yet another one! And to Bob Dew, your beautiful words at the beginning of all three books deserve a book of their own.

It's not easy being friends with a writer and dealing with their extreme emotions. So, Renée Veldman-Tentori, Manuela Damant and Steffi Thomas—thank you. Your strength, support, wisdom and kindness has been a sturdy raft in some very choppy Dutch waters. You'll always be in my Queendom. And thank you to my bestie Elaine Kayes for not only being a fantastic friend for twenty (!!) years, but also for reading *Son of Secrets* at the very beginning and pointing out that it's going to ruffle a lot of feathers. Ha, as if you expected anything less!

To my Team, you're amazing, please don't ever let go of my hand. I will need you, like, forever. And a very special thank you to my eight most hardcore readers and Zac fans—in alphabetical order, because I have no favourites! Claire Knight (The Captain), Ellie Stone (The Artist), Kristen Dawn (The Poet), Liss Wheeler (The Witch), Melanie Keeler (The Director), Phoenix Tier (The Overthinker), Simone Birkholtz (The Basketcase) and Tegan Gislason (The Procrastinator)—I couldn't have done this without you all, my own 24/7 support network of fangirling drama and straight-talking honesty. You're awesome, can't wait to see what amazing things you all do in the future!

A big shout out to the Loomies (always) and to my fellow writers at Novel19s, The Fiction Café, The Glass House Girls and The Savvies. Especially Anna Day, Emma Cooper, Holly Seddon, Isabella May, Jaqueline Silvester, Kristin Anderson, Sarah Norris and Teuta Metra for your feedback and friendship. Thanks for letting me go on, and on, and on about this crazy writing world of ours. There's no one I'd prefer to be trapped in a perpetual loop of turmoil and elation with.

And lastly, thank you to the three people to whom this book is dedicated. Pete, Isabelle and Olivia, I love you. You are my world. Every word I write, I write for you.

ABOUT THE AUTHOR

N.J. Simmonds began her career in glossy magazines and marketing, before becoming a freelance writer and consultant. She now fills her days writing books about fearless women, magic and adventure. Originally from North London, with Spanish parentage, N.J. Simmonds currently lives in the Netherlands with her husband and two daughters.

Follow her writing adventures on:
Twitter (@NJSimmondsTPK)
and at njsimmonds.com

Lightning Source UK Ltd.
Milton Keynes UK
UKHW010734020222
398089UK00001B/191